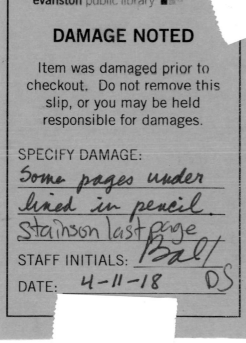

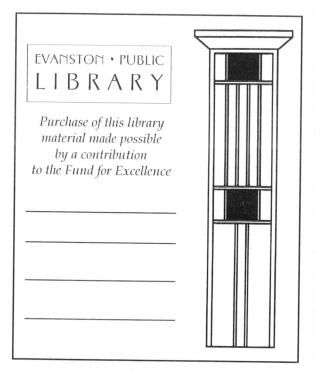

MADAME BOVARY

GUSTAVE FLAUBERT

MADAME BOVARY

Provincial Ways

Translated with an Introduction and Notes by

LYDIA DAVIS

VIKING

VIKING
Published by the Penguin Group
Penguin Group (USA) Inc., 375 Hudson Street, New York, New York 10014, U.S.A. • Penguin Group
(Canada), 90 Eglinton Avenue East, Suite 700, Toronto, Ontario, Canada M4P 2Y3 (a division of Pearson
Penguin Canada Inc.) • Penguin Books Ltd, 80 Strand, London WC2R 0RL, England • Penguin Ireland,
25 St. Stephen's Green, Dublin 2, Ireland (a division of Penguin Books Ltd) • Penguin Books Australia
Ltd, 250 Camberwell Road, Camberwell, Victoria 3124, Australia (a division of Pearson Australia Group
Pty Ltd) • Penguin Books India Pvt Ltd, 11 Community Centre, Panchsheel Park, New Delhi–110 017,
India • Penguin Group (NZ), 67 Apollo Drive, Rosedale, North Shore 0632, New Zealand (a division of
Pearson New Zealand Ltd) • Penguin Books (South Africa) (Pty) Ltd, 24 Sturdee Avenue, Rosebank, Johan-
nesburg 2196, South Africa

Penguin Books Ltd, Registered Offices: 80 Strand, London WC2R 0RL, England

This translation first published in 2010 by Viking Penguin, a member of Penguin Group (USA) Inc.

10 9 8 7 6 5 4 3 2 1

LIBRARY OF CONGRESS CATALOGING-IN-PUBLICATION DATA
Flaubert, Gustave, 1821–1880.
  [Madame Bovary. English]
  Madame Bovary / Gustave Flaubert ; translated with an introduction and notes by
Lydia Davis.
    p. cm.
  Includes bibliographical references.
  ISBN 978-0-670-02207-6
  1. Physicians' spouses—Fiction.   2. Married women—Fiction.   3. Adultery—Fiction.
4. Middle class—France—Fiction.   I. Davis, Lydia, 1947– II. Title.
  PQ2246.M2E5 2010
  843'.8—dc22   2010010328

Printed in the United States of America
Designed by Carla Bolte • Set in Adobe Garamond

CONTENTS

MADAME BOVARY

PART I

PART II

PART III

INTRODUCTION

Readers who do not want to know the details or the denouement of the plot should read this introduction only after they have read the novel.

"Yesterday evening, I started my novel. Now I begin to see stylistic difficulties that horrify me. To be simple is no small matter." This is what Flaubert wrote to his friend, lover, and fellow writer Louise Colet on the evening of September 20, 1851, and the novel he was referring to was *Madame Bovary*. He was just under thirty years old.

Picture a large man, handsome though fleshy and prematurely balding, with clear blue-green eyes and a voice that could be loud and gruff (he was known to "bellow," both while trying out his sentences and while having dinner with his friends), bent over his desk, working by lamplight with a goose-quill pen (he abhorred a metal nib). He writes very slowly and painfully, drafting—and revising—much more material than he will keep in the end. His concentration is deep, intense, and enduring; he stays with his work for many hours at a time. His mother will sometimes leave the house all afternoon to do an errand in town and find him, on her return, in exactly the same position as when she left.

Generally he starts work in the early afternoon and works until the early hours of the morning, breaking only for dinner. His study is a spacious room on the second floor that looks out past a tulip tree over a towpath to the river. Despite the many hours of meticulous work, he often then, at one or two in the morning, writes a long letter to Colet, perhaps as a form of release. It is thanks to these letters, which continued until their breakup two and a half years later, that we can follow so closely the progress of his work on the novel.

Because he discards a good deal of material, and prunes back severely the material he keeps, he produces very few finished pages—he variously reports one page per week, one every four days, thirteen pages in three months, thirty pages in three months, ninety pages in a year. (This in contrast with the ease of his first version of *The Temptation of Saint Anthony,* drafted earlier—five hundred pages in eighteen months, he said.) Yet he makes steady progress. His closest friend, the poet Louis Bouilhet, comes almost without fail every Sunday, when Flaubert reads aloud to him what he has done that week. Bouilhet responds, often severely: he likes it very much, or Flaubert should cut further, or there are too many metaphors.

Flaubert spent about four and a half years writing the novel, staying closeted with his work for months at a time, only periodically taking the train to Paris for some days of city life and sociability with friends, though he did not always stop working when he was there.

He finished it sometime in March of 1856; it was then accepted for publication by his longtime friend Maxime Du Camp, one of the editors of *La Revue de Paris,* and was published serially in that journal in six installments from October 1 to December 15. Henry James describes coming upon it in this form "when a very young person in Paris" and picking it up "from the parental table." "The cover . . . was yellow, if I mistake not." He recalls "taking it in with so surprised an interest," as he read it "standing there before the fire, my back against the low beplushed and begarnished French chimney piece."

Although certain scenes had been cut from this version as a precaution—which perhaps had the opposite effect, of arousing suspicions—the government brought charges against it for being a danger to morality and religion. The trial took place on January 29, 1857, and lasted one day; Flaubert and the magazine were acquitted a week later. When the book appeared as a single volume that April, it bore a second dedication, to Marie-Antoine-Jules Sénard, the forceful and eloquent Rouen lawyer who had defended him.

The very approach that made the novel vulnerable to prosecution by the Second Empire government was what made it so radical for fiction of its day—it depicted the lives of its characters objectively, without idealizing, without romanticizing, and without intent to instruct or to draw a moral lesson. The novel, soon to be labeled "realist" by his contemporaries, though Flaubert resisted the label, as he resisted belonging to any literary "school," is now viewed as the first masterpiece of realist fiction. Yet its radical nature is paradoxically difficult for us to see: its approach is familiar to us for the very reason that *Madame Bovary* permanently changed the way novels were written thereafter.

Flaubert was born on December 12, 1821, in his family's apartment in a wing of the hospital of which his father was chief surgeon, in the port city of Rouen. He showed an interest in writing from a very early age and published his first work at sixteen but was persuaded by his father to attend law school. Suffering his first epileptic attack at age twenty-three, he was forced (though without reluctance) to give up his law studies and from then on devoted himself almost exclusively to writing. By that time he had already begun the first version of his novel *A Sentimental Education.*

The family had acquired a large, comfortable house overlooking the Seine in the hamlet of Croisset, a few miles from Rouen, and it was here that he settled. After the death of both his father and his sister in 1846, the household was to consist, for many years, of Flaubert, his mother, and his little niece Caroline, whom he helped to raise, as well as the servants who looked after them. Aside from some traveling, some vacations by the seaside at Trouville, and some intervals of living in Paris, he spent most of the rest of his life at Croisset.

Drawn to the exotic, he wrote a draft of another novel, *The Temptation of Saint Anthony,* but suspended work on it in 1849 when Bouilhet and Du Camp so disliked it, after a marathon four-day reading, that they suggested he throw it in the fire. He did not abandon either of his early novels, however: he was to finish *A Sentimental Education* in 1869 and *The Temptation of Saint Anthony* in 1872.

He had, therefore, written a great deal, though to the literary world he was unknown, before he began what was to be his first published novel.

To counter Flaubert's tendency to wax lyrical and effusive in response to exotic materials, Bouilhet suggested he take as subject for his next novel something quite mundane. The story of Madame Bovary is based, in fact, on two local dramas: the adultery and subsequent suicide of one Delphine Delamare, the wife of a local public health officer, and the disastrous spending habits and ultimate financial ruin of Louise Pradier, the wife of a sculptor Flaubert knew personally. A third influence on the novel was the regional fiction of Balzac, whom Flaubert greatly admired. The book would be about not only a woman whose character fatally determined the course of her life but also the place in which she lived and its confining effect on her. After first considering Flanders as a setting, Flaubert settled on his native Normandy, so familiar to him.

The main action of the novel unfolds squarely within the July Monarchy of Louis-Philippe (1830–48), an interval of relative calm in French history and, for Flaubert, the years that had embraced his adolescence and early adulthood. Unlike *A Sentimental Education,* the novel contains little hint of political unrest: here the drama is domestic and local, and the larger outside world hardly intrudes.

It was during the reign of Louis-Philippe, who was known as the *roi bourgeois,* or "Citizen King," because of his bourgeois manner and dress, that the middle class was most explicitly defining itself as distinct from the working class and the nobility. And one of Flaubert's motivating forces in his approach to the material of the novel was his scorn for the bourgeoisie, though he readily included himself among them. What he despised, really, was a certain type of bourgeois attitude—later codified in his *Dictionary of Accepted Ideas.* It included certain traits such as intellectual and spiritual superficiality, raw ambition, shallow culture, a love of material things, greed, and above all a mindless parroting of sentiments and beliefs. He delighted in attacking this kind of thinking wherever he witnessed it: his letters are full of jabs and gibes, whether against a pompous cousin visiting Croisset for the day or a fellow writer in Paris who prided himself on being invited to dine with a government minister.

The novel is full of markers of the culture of Flaubert's time that we in our time may not recognize as such: La Chaumière dance hall in Paris; Pompadour clocks and statuettes; the poet Béranger; the novelist Sir Walter Scott; fireworks; tourist attractions in Italy; a plethora of English importations, including horse racing and the casual use of English words and expressions. Flaubert is holding up a mirror to the middle- and lower-middle-class world of his day, with all its little habits, fashions, fads. French readers who belonged to that world would recognize themselves (or their parents) and either blush or laugh complicitly: they, or their parents, might play whist in the evening (as did the king himself), or have a similar piece of coral on the mantelpiece or the same print on the parlor wall; perhaps it was their aunt who, like Emma, coveted a tilbury—that fashionable English carriage—or a mouth-rinsing bowl on the dinner table; or perhaps a self-important uncle, like Homais, hoped to be awarded the cross.

It isn't as clear to us, reading the novel in the twenty-first century, that these were not necessarily thoughtful individual choices but rather symptoms of a blind adherence to conventional—and often questionable—taste. But what Flaubert called stupidity was not limited to the bourgeoisie. Or rather, if he had a lifelong habit of watching for stupidity and relishing examples of it, he found it in "all of humanity"; all of humanity was bourgeois. He could not shave, for instance, without laughing at the stupidity of it.

In a letter written to Colet as he was composing the first meeting of Emma and Léon, he explains that what interests him is the grotesqueness of a supposedly lofty conversation between two sensitive, poetic individuals that is, in fact, wholly made up of clichéd ideas. He realizes early on that he has set himself a formidable task: to take this grotesqueness as his subject, to write a novel about shallow, unsympathetic people in a dreary setting, some of whom make bad choices and come to a horrific end. There will be no romanticizing the subject—in fact, the whole project is opposed to the romantic. The heroine, infatuated with romanticism, comes to grief because of it—because of her craving for impossible dreams, her refusal to accept the ordinariness of her life and its limited possibilities for happiness.

Nor is there any moralizing on the part of the author—one reason the novel was so vulnerable to attack by the government. The story contains no sermon to point out its moral; it has no "good" moral exemplar to offer in contrast to the "bad" woman that Emma is. The author does not condemn her behavior but, rather, may even have some sympathy for her; nor does he pass judgment on any of the other characters. The story is uncompromising: the heroine commits adultery and then suicide; her good husband dies, too; her innocent child is fated to have a hard life; the evil moneylender who has been the instrument of Emma's downfall prospers; the conniving, hypocritical, and disloyal "friend," Homais, is rewarded with a coveted medal.

Flaubert chose to create characters who are less than admirable and to treat them with ironic objectivity—he remarks in another letter, as he works on the scene between Emma and Léon, "This will be the first time, I think, that one will see a book that makes fun of its young leading lady and its young leading man." Yet he goes on to say that "irony takes nothing away from pathos." Which is echoed by Vladimir Nabokov in his lecture on the novel: "The ironic and the pathetic are beautifully intertwined."

Flaubert wants his readers to be moved by the characters. He states explicitly, for instance, in the case of Charles's grief, "I hope to cause tears to flow with the tears of this one man." Again, in another letter: "In my third part, which will be full of comical things, I want people to cry."

And although there is hardly a sympathetic character among them—some readers may feel that possible exceptions to this are Emma's father; or the pharmacist's assistant, Justin; or Charles himself—we do feel at least glimmers of sympathy or liking, at moments. It may be true that every one of Homais's statements is a completely conventional "accepted idea," yet it is hard not to enjoy his cunning, his enterprise, his intellectual explorations, and even to agree with him sometimes. One cannot help feeling some respect for Emma's bravery at the end, her moment of true affection for Charles, her interest in her own dying: "She was observing herself curiously, to see if she was in pain. But no! Nothing yet. . . . 'Ah! It's a small thing, really—death!' she thought; 'I'll fall asleep, and everything will be over!'" We are indeed moved, though perhaps not to the extent Flaubert may have hoped—the prevailing irony may distance us too much from the story, even as it enhances its dramatic horror.

Nor is he himself unaffected by the characters. "I am in their skin," he says—though he later qualifies that skin as "antipathetic." We know that he sometimes found himself weeping as he wrote and that he so identified with Emma during her last days that he was physically ill.

———

Flaubert's aim was to write the novel "objectively," leaving the author out of it. Although *Madame Bovary* is filled with political and social detail reflecting Flaubert's very strong views (his friend Émile Zola describes how Flaubert could not tolerate being contradicted in an argument), his technique is to present the material without comment, though occasionally a comment does slip in. To report the facts objectively, to give a painstaking objective description—of a ridiculous object, for instance—should be comment enough. Flaubert remarks in another letter to Colet, of the scene in which Emma goes to the curé for help, "The episode is to have at most six or seven pages without a single reflection or explanation coming from the author (all in direct dialogue)."

In place of the author's comment, then, the details of the scenes and the acute psychological portraits must convey everything—and, for Flaubert, direct dialogue, too, functioned to portray the characters more than to move the plot forward. Detailed description would bring the reader into the presence of the material. To be effective, the details must be closely observed, carefully chosen, precise, and vivid, as in the description of Emma's bridal bouquet after she has thrown it into the fire: "The little cardboard berries burst open, the binding wire twisted, the braid melted; and the shriveled paper petals, hovering along the fireback like black butterflies, at last flew away up the chimney."

If the novel is to move or interest a reader, Flaubert will have to transform what he sees as a sordid world, wholly through the power of his style, into a work of formal and stylistic beauty—all the while writing it in a manner against his own natural inclinations. He says outright many times that he is afraid he won't pull it off: everything must depend on the style.

In keeping with his plain, almost clinical approach to the material, he schooled himself to be very sparing with his metaphors. Often enough, in his intensive revising, the version he cut out was more lyrical than the one he let stand. Marcel Proust, for one, writing more than sixty years after the publication of the novel, regretted the absence of metaphor, since he believed, as he said, that "only metaphor can give a sort of eternity to style." But he admitted that there was more to style than metaphor alone.

Proust goes on to say that in all of Flaubert there is not a single beautiful metaphor. Yet here is another lovely comparison to a butterfly: after she has given herself to Léon for the first time, in the closed carriage that careens through Rouen, Emma tears up the note of rejection she had uselessly written him, and "a bare hand passed under the little blinds of yellow canvas and threw out some torn scraps of paper, which scattered in the wind and alighted, at a distance, like white butterflies, on a field of red clover all in bloom."

If objective description was Flaubert's literary method, that objectivity was always imbued with irony. To see and judge a thing with a cool eye was to judge it with the irony that had been a part of his nature since he was a child. His irony pervades the book, coloring each detail, each situation, each event, each character, the fate of each character, and the overarching story.

It is present in his choice of names: the old rattletrap of a coach called "Swallow"; the many character names, such as Bovary itself, that are variations of the French for "ox"; the evil moneylender Lheureux ("happy one").

It is present in the words and phrases in the novel to which he gives special emphasis—in the manuscript he would have underlined them, of course, as he does similar language in his correspondence; in print they are italicized. They appear throughout the novel, starting on the first page with *new boy*. With this emphasis he is drawing attention to language that was commonly, and unthinkingly, used to express shared ideas that were also unquestioned. Some, such as *new boy,* are relatively innocuous; others may reveal a malevolent prejudice, such as the comment made by Madame Tuvache, the mayor's wife, to her maid (reported as indirect speech), when she learns that Emma has taken a walk alone with Léon: "*Madame Bovary was compromising herself.*"

Flaubert's irony is present in the eloquent juxtapositions he creates between the "poetic" and the brutally commonplace, with an effect that is sometimes humorous, sometimes shocking, but that always draws us up short, breaks the "mood." An exquisite passage—often a description of nature—will be undercut, as though here Flaubert is also undercutting his own lyrical impulse, by what immediately follows it, a banal, mundane comparison or action. There are numerous examples.

Emma, for instance, is lying on the ground in the woods, still tremulous from her first lovemaking with Rodolphe, in tune with the surrounding natural landscape, which is fully and sensuously described; the passage ends with the flat statement that Rodolphe, a cigar between his teeth, is mending a bridle. Much later in the story, in a boat with Léon, Emma feels a chill at the thought of Rodolphe with other women; the boatman, who has unknowingly upset her, spits into his palm and takes up his oars. Crushingly, pathetically, after Emma's death, as she is being laid out, one of the women working over her admires her beauty in rather glib terms—how alive she still looks; as if in rebuke, when the woman lifts Emma's head to put on her wreath, black liquid runs out of her mouth. Flaubert the obdurate antiromantic could not be more clearly in evidence than at this moment.

As in the above examples, it is the incisive specificity of the poetic details and then the abruptness with which Flaubert "cuts" to the equally specific but disturbing or brutal details that jolts us so.

Some of these ironic juxtapositions produce not horror, or pathos, but humor.

For instance, during the scene at the agricultural fair, the poetic and romantic exchanges between Rodolphe and Emma, observing from above in the town hall, are punctuated (without authorial comment) by the sober announcements of awards for agricultural advancements in such areas as "manure" and "use of oilseed cakes." Or the humor arises from a juxtaposition of disproportionate elements, as, for instance, in the case of the writings of Homais, who is a journalist as well as an apothecary: sometimes it is the grandiosity of his style that is out of keeping with the banality of his subject (cider); or, as he reports the festivities, it is the glorious colors in which he paints them in his article that have little relation to what we know of them in all their paltriness and insufficiency.

Or it is not in Homais's writing but in his manner that the disproportion lies—between his pomposity, in a moment of embarrassment with the grieving Charles, and the obviousness of his statement: "Homais thought it appropriate to talk a little horticulture; plants needed humidity."

Yet complicating our reactions to these moments is, in one instance, during the awards ceremony at the agricultural fair, some modicum of respect for the concerns of the proponents of advances in agriculture, and, in another, as Homais waters Charles's plants after his tactless question about the funeral, some sympathetic understanding of the pharmacist in his moment of embarrassment. Our emotional responses to the incidents of the novel are never entirely unmixed, which is of course one of the sources of its power.

Because Homais is something of a writer, and a character obviously much enjoyed by Flaubert (who refers to him affectionately in his letters as "my pharmacist" and occasionally likes to use an expression Homais might have used), it is hard not to think that he must represent a comment on the role or the practice of the writer, or one aspect of it. In fact, late in the novel, Flaubert the great reviser insinuates a moment of self-parody that would be comical if it weren't subsumed by the drama of Emma's final hours. As Emma lies gravely ill, Homais must send word by messenger to the two doctors who might be able to save her. He goes home and bends to his task, but although speed is of the essence, he is so agitated (and so particular about his prose style) that he requires no less than fifteen drafts to find the right wording.

Twice, at least, we are allowed to experience an event and then to read Homais's written version of it. Homais's material (like Flaubert's) is mundane and subject to lapses into mediocrity—the fireworks at the conclusion of the agricultural fair are damp and they fizzle, a complete failure. But he transforms this material, inflates it, gives it importance and success, by a grandiloquent style that Flaubert, tongue in cheek, describes in a letter as "philosophic, poetic, and progressive"—and by his outright lies. A piece of writing, Flaubert seems to be demonstrating, may always be false: the writer has the power to transform reality as he wishes. Words, particularly in print, have the perfidious power to misrepresent and betray. And eloquence is especially dangerous: the better one can write, the more persuasively one can lie.

Though Homais is the only "professional" writer in the book, other styles of writing appear in the course of it: Emma's father's letters, the speeches of the officials, Rodolphe's farewell note to Emma, Charles's instructions for the coffining. Flaubert, entering fully, always, into his characters' points of view, shifts gears convincingly as he moves in and out of these other styles, no less alien to him, perhaps, than the style of narration of the book as a whole. His own natural style, after all, he says in one letter, is that of *Saint Anthony:* what he wishes he could be writing are "grand turns of phrase, broad, full periods rolling along like rivers, a multiplicity of metaphors, great bursts of style."

What he is trying to achieve in this book, instead, is a style that is clear and direct, economical and precise, and at the same time rhythmic, sonorous, musical, and "as smooth as marble" on the surface, with varied sentence structures and with imperceptible transitions from scene to scene and from psychological analysis to action.

Though he did not write poetry himself, Flaubert complains in a letter to Colet, "What a bitch of a thing prose is! It's never finished; there's always something to redo. Yet I think one can give it the consistency of verse. A good sentence in prose should be like a good line in poetry, *unchangeable,* as rhythmic, as sonorous."

Yet Proust, in the course of his vehement response, in 1920, to a negative article about Flaubert, commented (admiringly) on what he called Flaubert's "grammatical singularities," which, he said, expressed "a new vision"; our way of seeing external reality was radically changed by Flaubert's "entirely new and personal use" of the past definite, the past indefinite, the present participle, certain pronouns, and certain prepositions. He went on to talk about other singularities: Flaubert's unprecedented manner of using indirect discourse, his unconventional handling of the word "and"—omitting it where one would expect it and inserting it where one would normally not look for it—his emphatically "flat" use of verbs, and his deliberately heavy placement of adverbs. But it was Flaubert's innovative use of the imperfect tense that most impressed Proust: "This [use of the] imperfect, so new in literature," he said, "completely changes the aspect of things and people."

The *imparfait,* or imperfect, tense in French is the form of the past tense that expresses an ongoing or prevailing condition, or a repeated action. It is most usually conveyed in English by "would" or "used to." Expressing a continuing state or action, and thereby signaling the continuity of time itself, it perfectly creates the effect Flaubert was seeking—what Nabokov describes as "the sense of repetition, of dreariness in Emma's life." Thus, early in her marriage, Charles's (tiresomely predictable) habits are described using a string of verbs in the imperfect: "He would return home late. . . . Then he would ask for something to eat. . . . He would take off his frock coat. . . . He would tell her one by one all the people he had met . . . he would eat the remains of the beef hash with onions . . . then go off to bed, sleep on his back, and snore."

While the imperfect, as agent of "background" description and habitual activity, was traditionally, before Flaubert, subordinated to the simple past tense, used to narrate finite action, with Flaubert, the habitual and the ongoing are foregrounded, and the division between description and action is blurred, as is the division between past and present, creating a sustained immediacy in the story. Even the speeches of the characters are often reported indirectly in the imperfect (as, for instance, in the mayor's wife's comment quoted above: "*Madame Bovary was compromising herself*"), allowing Flaubert to slip seamlessly into a character's point of view without abandoning the detachment of the third-person narration. The narration remains dynamic despite the fact that a large proportion of the book, in Flaubert's view at least, is exposition or preparation for action.

In a letter to Colet of January 15, 1853—sixteen months into the book— Flaubert worries about the amount of "action" so far: "I have now lined up five chapters of my second part in which nothing happens." An exaggeration, of course—but he felt there was going to be a great quantity of exposition, or prologue, and then very little unfolding action, before the conclusion. This, too, had not been done before—to tell a story with so little action. He believed that those proportions were true to life: "A blow lasts a minute but is anticipated for months—our passions are like volcanoes: always rumbling but only intermittently erupting." Yet he worried that the demands of aesthetics required something different.

If Proust calls *A Sentimental Education* "a long report" in which the characters do not really take part in the action, Flaubert calls *Madame Bovary* a "biography," one that takes the form of an extended analysis of one woman's psychology. But he believed that it could, even so, have the pace of action: "It also seems to me not impossible to give psychological analysis the rapidity, clarity, passion of a purely dramatic narration. This has never been tried and would be beautiful." It would seem, in fact, that this was just the sort of action that really interested Flaubert: the subtle shifts of feeling created in a reader by description and by psychological analysis. "I maintain that images are action," he says. "It is harder to sustain a book's interest by this means, but if one fails, it is the fault of style."

———

Many of Flaubert's transitions are indeed imperceptible, while others are abrupt; at still other points in the novel, the narration suddenly makes a rapid advance, covering months or years in a paragraph or two. But there is a tight unity to the novel as a whole, arising not only from its extreme economy—in which every element serves more than one function— but also from its recurring words, phrases, images, and actions. A small sampling would be: butterflies (actual and metaphorical, as in the passages quoted above); constructions in layers (Charles's schoolboy cap, the wedding cake, Emma's nesting coffins); Emma's intermittent attraction to religious faith; Homais's quoted writings; Charles "suffocating" with emotion twice near the end of the book; the same phrase—*bloquer les interstices*—used first literally, to describe "filling the gaps" between Emma's body and the sides of the coffin, and then figuratively, during the awkward last conversation between Rodolphe and Charles.

Particularly prevalent are recurring images involving water, the sea, and boats. These include the "skiffs by moonlight" in Emma's convent reading, the gondola in her daydream of a future life with Rodolphe, the actual "skiff by moonlight" in which Léon and she go to the island each evening of their three-day "honeymoon," and the gondola-shaped bed in the hotel room where she and Léon thereafter meet every week.

Most striking, however, is the repeated image of a sealed vessel (twice a carriage, once a coffin) in the tossing waves of a troubled sea. It appears first in a pompous speech by the official who takes the podium at the opening of the agricultural fair, as he pays homage to the "king . . . who . . . guides the Chariot of State amid the unceasing perils of a stormy sea." Then, in the famous consummation scene in Part III of the novel, in which Emma gives herself to Léon during the prolonged ride through the city, the king is replaced by the driver of the hackney cab, steering (rather carelessly) "a carriage with drawn blinds that kept appearing and reappearing, sealed tighter than a tomb and tossed about like a ship at sea." Here Flaubert has taken the speechifier's mixed metaphor and added the simile of the sealed tomb. He then brings back the comparison at the end of the novel, as Emma's nesting coffins, hammered and soldered, are borne to the cemetery: "the bier moved forward in little jolts, like a boat pitching with every wave."

Such is the tight construction of the novel, and the utter conviction of the detailed descriptions and psychological portraits throughout, that we compliantly ignore, most of the time, any passing questions we may have either about inconsistencies in the plot or about implausibility in plot elements, the most conspicuous being that Charles never suspects any of Emma's betrayals, never notices the sound of the sand striking the shutters as he and she sit reading, never receives an anonymous letter from a busybody. (And how does he, deeply in debt by now, pay for Emma's three coffins?) If space and time as handled in the novel are both "elastic," as has been said by some critics, so is plausibility. And yet this is not a distraction as we read—it is barely noticeable. The requirements of psychology take precedence over plausibility and consistency in time and space, and the psychology is entirely convincing.

The Earlier Drafts

Flaubert worked from successive plans, following them, revising them. He wrote numerous drafts of every passage, often rewriting and perfecting it before cutting it out altogether—at one point he estimated that he had 120 finished pages but to achieve them had written 500. (He revised by cutting, whereas Proust revised by expanding.) In rewriting he would watch out for poor assonances, bad repetitions of sounds and of words (especially *qui* and *que,* which he occasionally underlined and apologized for even in his letters)—Zola remarks that "often a single letter exasperated him."

He did not burn these early drafts but left them for us to pore over—approximately 4,500 pages in all, residing in the Municipal Library in Rouen. They are available to us in clearly legible form—even online (at http://www.bovary.fr)—because they have been transcribed by volunteers, under the direction of Yvan Leclerc, at the Centre Flaubert de l'université de Rouen, who have reproduced every rejected scene, every false start, every cross-out. The drafts are an invaluable resource to scholars and, of course, to translators.

Flaubert's intensive cutting meant that occasionally a sentence or phrase was omitted that left a passage slightly ambiguous or puzzling, or simply left room for a (mistaken) assumption. What was in the little bottles held by the ladies at the La Vaubyessard ball in their gloved hands? Not perfume, we see from an earlier draft, but vinegar—which is much more interesting, though of course if we are conscientious, we can't insert that information into the text.

Elsewhere, other puzzles are solved: Why was Charles, when a student, stamping his foot on the wall of his room while he ate lunch? The answer is in an earlier draft: to warm himself. Why was the church hung with straw mats? To protect the parishioners from the cold. Again, we won't insert more information into the text than is there in the original, but now we won't jump to mistaken conclusions either.

A more extended example of how Flaubert rethought one moment of a scene may demonstrate the fascination of watching him at work, and that is Charles at Emma's graveside. From a careful reading of the final, printed version of the French, we may suspect that Charles did not in fact take the aspergillum that was held out to him by Homais, even if it is easy to assume he did. And if we test our suspicion by looking at the early drafts, we see these progressive changes in the transaction, as Flaubert envisaged it: (1) Lheureux (not Homais) passes the aspergillum to Charles, he drops it; (2) Lheureux offers it to him, he refuses it; (3) Homais holds it out to him, he "does not want it." In the final draft, Flaubert cuts out any reaction to the aspergillum on Charles's part: Homais simply holds it out to him, and Charles does not explicitly refuse it, nor does he explicitly take it, instead falling to his knees in the earth and throwing the earth into the grave by the handfuls. If we simply trust the words of the original and translate them as "held out to him" rather than "passed to him," we will get it right, but it would be easy to get it wrong.

A Note on the Translation

"A good sentence in prose," says Flaubert, "should be like a good line in poetry, *unchangeable,* as rhythmic, as sonorous." To achieve a translation that matches this high standard is difficult, perhaps impossible. Of course, a translation even of a less exacting stylist requires millions of tiny, detailed decisions; many reconsiderations; the testing of one word or phrase against another multiple times. In the case of *Madame Bovary,* there are unusually many previous translations—I count at least nineteen into English—and it is intriguing to observe how differently previous translators have made these decisions.

In the second draft of my translation, I looked at ten others, eventually an eleventh, the most recent. As I made extensive comparisons, trying to arrive at good solutions in meaning, vocabulary, and construction, I came to know five or six of them quite well. The great variety among the translations depends, of course, on two factors: how each translator handles expressive English and how liberally or narrowly each defines the task of the translator.

Curiously, in the case of a writer as famously fixated on his style as Flaubert was, many of the translations do not try to reproduce that style, but simply to tell this engrossing story in their own preferred manner. And so the reader in search of *Madame Bovary* has a wide choice: Gerald Hopkins's 1948 version, with added material in almost every sentence; Francis Steegmuller's nicely written, engaging version, smoother than Flaubert's, with regular restructuring of the sentences and judicious omissions and additions (1957); the stolidly literal, sometimes inaccurate version by the very first, Eleanor Marx Aveling (1886), which caused Nabokov much indignation in his marginal notations but to which he resorted in teaching the novel; that version as revised (not always happily) by Paul de Man (or, rumor has it, by his unacknowledged wife), who chose to omit the italics, for example. There is *Madame Bovary* with fewer of those pesky semicolons, with serial "and"s supplied, with additional metaphors. There is a version in which Charles is made to sob on the last page, another in which he is made to say "Poor thing!" when his first wife dies. There is even Flaubert complete with the involuntary repetitions that he so disliked.

Perhaps Flaubert was mistaken when he believed that the success of the book would depend entirely on its style—since various of his translators over the years have composed deeply affecting versions that do not reproduce it. Yet he would not listen, but was infuriated, when Zola remarked that there was more to the book, after all, than its style.

It should be noted that painstaking as Flaubert was about certain features of the prose, he was quite casual when it came to others, particularly pronoun reference and capitalization. Where ambiguous pronoun references are not utterly confusing, they have been retained as he wrote them. As for his inconsistency in capitalization (as in the frequent variation of "Square" and "square"), I have also chosen to retain it. This inconsistency was apparently not the result of an editorial oversight, since the original French text went through numerous editions by different hands in which it remained, surviving even into the most definitive 1971 Gothot-Mersch edition. Evidently, either Flaubert did not care, as Proust believed he simply did not care about certain pronoun references, or, perhaps more likely, he capitalized instinctively, unthinkingly. In any case, since it is part of the experience of the French reader, I have let it stand.

Flaubert also regularly wrote sentences containing what is called the comma splice, in which clauses are strung together in a series, separated only by a comma and without a conjunction. The clearest example of this is one of the shortest sentences, near the end of the novel: "Night was falling, rooks were flying overhead." One effect of this construction is to give each clause equal weight and value. Another effect is sometimes to speed the action forward, speed our thoughts as readers forward through time or material, so that even the full stop at the end of the sentence seems a momentary pause. Then again, sometimes the construction counterbalances lyrical or dramatic material by the subtlest hint of a certain matter-of-factness. It is a habit of Flaubert's that I have chosen to retain.

One last note: there is a sentence near the beginning of the novel that perhaps cries out to be "improved" by having a fully parallel structure: "He was a boy of even temperament, who played at recess, worked in study hall, listening in class, sleeping well in the dormitory, eating well in the dining hall." Again, the imbalance has been left as it is in French.

A Note on the Endnotes

The notes at the back of the present volume attempt to be as detailed and extensive as is reasonably possible. They go beyond explaining mysterious references that would be difficult to research, such as "Pulvermacher hydroelectric belts" and Homais's remedies, and clarifying historical references, as to King Henri IV, "the Béarnais." Erring on the side of inclusiveness, they define such domestic items as fabrics and types of carriages, medical practices such as bloodletting, distinctive social signals such as the yellow gloves worn by dandies, and so forth. Most of these latter sorts of notes are meant to identify the multitude of things deeply embedded in the customs and culture of the time in which the novel is set, things that would have been self-evident to its readers at the time of its publication. Flaubert, after all, deliberated long and hard about what should be included and what should be left out of this assiduously pruned novel, so we must assume he had strong reason to specify cambric, barege, and twill, or landau, berlin, and tilbury, and even took pleasure in specifying them; we should therefore, perhaps, make some attempt to understand what they are. Similarly, pastimes such as whist and *trente et un* or common sights in the street, such as the stone *bornes*—sometimes guard stones, sometimes milestones or boundary markers—should at least be not entirely opaque to the twenty-first-century reader. That reader is therefore asked to forgive instances where more explanation is given than is needed: if you were raised Catholic, you will know perfectly well what genuflection is; if not, then perhaps not.

The notes are provided "blind"—that is, without marks on the pages of the text—so that they will not intrude between the reader and the experience of the novel. It should be possible to enjoy the book uninterrupted, but if more background information is wanted, it is available.

SUGGESTIONS FOR FURTHER READING

Barnes, Julian. *Flaubert's Parrot*. New York: Alfred A. Knopf, 1985.

Brombert, Victor. *The Novels of Flaubert: A Study of Themes and Techniques*. Princeton: Princeton University Press, 1966.

Brown, Frederick. *Flaubert: A Biography*. New York: Little, Brown, 2006.

Flaubert, Gustave. *Bouvard and Pécuchet*, tr. Mark Polizotti. Includes *Dictionary of Accepted Ideas*. Champaign, Ill.: Dalkey Archive Press, 2005.

———. *Correspondance II (juillet 1851–décembre 1858)*, ed. Jean Bruneau. Paris: Éditions Gallimard (Éditions de la Pléiade), 1980.

———. *The Letters of Gustave Flaubert 1830–1857*, selected, edited, and translated by Francis Steegmuller. Cambridge, Mass.: Harvard University Press, 1979, 1980.

———. *Madame Bovary: moeurs de province*. Paris: Éditions Garnier Frères, 1971. Edited by Claudine Gothot-Mersch. Some of the material in the present introduction was developed in response to the rich and extensive discussion of the novel in Madame Gothot-Mersch's introduction, which itself draws on previous critical work.

———. *A Sentimental Education*, tr. Robert Baldick. New York: Penguin Books, 1964. Other English translations also available.

Goncourt, Edmond de, and Jules de Goncourt. *Pages from the Goncourt Journals*, tr. Robert Baldick. New York: New York Review of Books, 2007.

James, Henry. "Gustave Flaubert" in *Notes on Novelists, with Some Other Notes*. New York: Charles Scribner's Sons, 1914.

Lottman, Herbert. *Flaubert: A Biography*. Boston: Little, Brown, 1989.

Maraini, Dacia. *Searching for Emma: Gustave Flaubert and Madame Bovary*, tr. Vincent J. Bertolini. Chicago: University of Chicago Press, 1998.

Nabokov, Vladimir. *Lectures on Literature*, ed. Fredson Bowers. New York: Harcourt Brace Jovanovich, 1980.

Proust, Marcel. "Marcel Proust évoque Flaubert," in *La Nouvelle Revue Française*, January 1, 1920.

Steegmuller, Francis. *Flaubert and Madame Bovary: A Double Portrait*. New York: Farrar, Straus & Giroux, 1939, 1966.

Thirlwell, Adam. *Miss Herbert*. London: Jonathan Cape, 2007.

Vargas Llosa, Mario. *The Perpetual Orgy: Flaubert and Madame Bovary,* tr. Helen
    Lane. New York: Farrar, Straus & Giroux, 1986.
Wood, James. *How Fiction Works.* New York: Farrar, Straus & Giroux, 2008.
Zola, Émile. "Gustave Flaubert," in *Les Romanciers naturalistes* (1881). In *Oeuvres
    complètes.* Paris: F. Bernouard, 1928.

CHRONOLOGY

1821 December 12: Gustave Flaubert born at the Hôtel-Dieu, in Rouen; his father is head ("chief surgeon") of the hospital. His brother, Achille, is eight years old.

1824 Birth of Caroline Flaubert, his sister, who was to become his close friend.

1825 Coronation of Charles X, an unpopular, reactionary, repressive monarch.

1830 The July Revolution, marking the end of the Restoration; accession of Louis-Philippe to the throne of France, supported by the discontented upper bourgeoisie and the liberal journalists. His reign, the "July Monarchy," will last until 1848; Algeria is conquered toward the end of it. After the February Revolution of 1848, he will abdicate, fleeing to England and later dying there. He is known as the "Citizen King" because of his bourgeois manner and dress.
       Flaubert is eight years old.

1831 Flaubert writes precociously impressive pieces such as his *Éloge de Corneille* (In Praise of Corneille), as well as numerous theater pieces performed at home.

1832 Flaubert enters the Collège Royal, soon to be a boarder. Reads and admires *Don Quixote*.

1834 His friendship with Louis Bouilhet begins.

1836 Writes several stories. In Trouville, meets the woman he will love for most of his life, though this love is probably never consummated: Elisa Foucault, ten years older and soon to marry Maurice Schlésinger. She is very likely the model for the heroine of *L'Éducation sentimentale* (A Sentimental Education).

1837 More writings, including "Passion et Vertu" (Passion and Virtue), one source of *Madame Bovary*. First publication.

1838   Writes "Mémoires d'un fou" (Memoirs of a Madman), an autobiographical narrative.

1840   Receives his baccalaureate degree. Takes a trip to the Pyrenees, Marseille, and Corsica with family friend Dr. Cloquet.

1841   Registers as law student in Paris, while continuing to live at home.

1842   Writes *Novembre* (November), his second autobiographical narrative. Moves to Paris. Passes his first bar exam in December.

1843   Becomes friends with Maxime Du Camp. Fails his second bar exam. Begins writing first version of *L'Éducation sentimentale*. Frequents the salon of Louise Pradier, wife of a sculptor; some aspects of her life will inspire material in *Madame Bovary*.

1844   Falls from a carriage during a seizure, exhibiting the first symptoms of a disease that is most likely a form of epilepsy. Gives up his law studies for good. Family acquires house in Croisset and moves there.

1845   Completes first version of *L'Éducation sentimentale*. He and his family accompany his sister, Caroline, on her honeymoon trip to Italy. In Genoa, he sees and is struck by the painting *The Temptation of Saint Anthony* by Pieter Brueghel the Younger.

1846   Death of his father, then of his sister. Settles at Croisset with his mother and his niece Caroline, whom he will help to raise. During a trip to Paris, meets Louise Colet, who becomes his mistress.

1847   Trip to Brittany with Du Camp, an account of which he writes entitled *Par les champs et par les grèves* (By Fields and Shores).

1848   February Revolution; end of July Monarchy, abdication of Louis-Philippe. Flaubert witnesses the "February days" with Louis Bouilhet and Maxime Du Camp. Memories of these scenes will provide material for a later version of *L'Éducation sentimentale*. First quarrel with Louise Colet. Begins *La Tentation de Saint Antoine* (The Temptation of Saint Anthony).

1849   Reads *Saint Antoine* aloud to Bouilhet and Du Camp, who do not like it. Departure for the Orient with Du Camp.

1850   Travels in Egypt, Beirut, Jerusalem, Constantinople, Greece.

1851   Travels in Greece and Italy. Returns to Croisset and begins writing *Madame Bovary* on September 19.

1854   Last friendly correspondence with Louise Colet. Relationship ends.

1856   Finishes writing *Madame Bovary* in March. Publication of the novel in *La Revue de Paris* in six installments October 1–December 15. Resumes work on *Saint Antoine*.

1857 One-day trial of Flaubert and the editors of the *Revue,* on charges of offenses against public morality and religion. Acquittal delivered one week later. Publication of *Madame Bovary* in book form by Michel Lévy in April. Begins his exotic historical romance, *Salammbô.*

1858 Visits Carthage and Tunisia, researching *Salammbô.*

1859–62 Writes *Salammbô.* Frequent visits to Paris. *Salammbô* appears in November 1862.

1863 Begins correspondence with George Sand; meets Ivan Turgenev.

1864–69 Works on *L'Éducation sentimentale.* Social life includes Princesse Mathilde, Prince Napoléon, the Goncourt brothers, George Sand, Ivan Turgenev.

1866 Named Chevalier of the Legion of Honor.

1869 Death of Bouilhet. Publication of *L'Éducation sentimentale.*

1870 Embarks on the third version of *Saint Antoine.* Franco-Prussian War begins. Becomes lieutenant in the Garde Nationale. Prussians stay at Croisset in November.

1871 Insurrection in Paris. Sees, socially, Victor Hugo, Théophile Gautier, Alphonse Daudet, Guy de Maupassant, Émile Zola.

1872 Death of Flaubert's mother. Completion of *La Tentation de Saint Antoine* (third version).

1873 Growing friendship with de Maupassant.

1874 Publication of *La Tentation de Saint Antoine.* Flaubert prepares to begin writing *Bouvard et Pécuchet.*

1875 In order to help his niece Caroline and her husband out of a desperate financial situation, Flaubert ruins himself: he will be hard up for the rest of his life. He begins writing the story "La Légende de Saint Julien Hospitalier" (The Legend of Saint Julian the Hospitaler).

1876 Completes "Saint Julien," writes "Un Coeur Simple" (A Simple Heart), and begins "Hérodias." Death of Louise Colet. Death of George Sand.

1877 Publication of *Trois contes* (*Three Tales*). Flaubert goes back to work on *Bouvard et Pécuchet,* which will remain unfinished at his death.

1879 Awarded an honorary position paying three thousand francs per year, which allows him to survive.

1880 May 8, Flaubert dies of a cerebral hemorrhage at age fifty-eight.

1881 Publication of the unfinished *Bouvard et Pécuchet,* along with the *Dictionnaire des idées reçues* (Dictionary of Accepted Ideas).

To

MARIE-ANTOINE-JULES SÉNARD

Member of the Paris Bar
Ex-President of the National Assembly
and Former Minister of the Interior

My dear and illustrious friend,

Allow me to inscribe your name at the very beginning of this book, even before its dedication; for it is to you, above all, that I owe its publication. By its inclusion in your magnificent presentation of my case, this work of mine has acquired for me an unforeseen authority. Accept here, therefore, the homage of my gratitude, which, however great it may be, will never reach the height of your eloquence and your devotion.

Paris, April 12, 1857   Gustave Flaubert

TO LOUIS BOUILHET

MADAME BOVARY

PART I

We were in Study Hall, when the Headmaster entered, followed by a *new boy* dressed in regular clothes and a school servant carrying a large desk. Those who were sleeping woke up, and everyone rose as though taken by surprise while at work.

The Headmaster motioned us to sit down again; then, turning to the study hall teacher:

"Monsieur Roger," he said to him in a low voice, "here is a pupil I am entrusting to your care; he is entering the fifth. If his work and his conduct are deserving, he will be moved up to *the seniors,* as befits his age."

Still standing in the corner, behind the door, so that one could hardly see him, the *new boy* was a fellow from the country, about fifteen years old, and taller than any of us. His hair was cut straight across the forehead, like a village choirboy's, his manner sensible and very ill at ease. Although he was not broad in the shoulders, his suit jacket of green cloth with black buttons must have pinched him around the armholes, and it showed, through the vents of its cuffs, red wrists accustomed to being bare. His legs, in blue stockings, emerged from a pair of yellowish pants pulled tight by his suspenders. He wore stout shoes, badly shined, studded with nails.

We began reciting our lessons. He listened to them, all ears, as attentive as though to a sermon, not daring even to cross his legs or to lean on his elbow, and at two o'clock, when the bell rang, the teacher was obliged to alert him, so that he would get in line with us.

We were in the habit, when we entered the classroom, of throwing our caps on the floor, so that our hands would be free; from the doorsill, we had to hurl them under the bench, in such a way that they struck the wall, making a lot of dust; it was the *thing to do.*

But either because he had not noticed this maneuver or because he had not dared go along with it, after the prayer was over, the *new boy* was still holding his cap on his knees. It was one of those head coverings of a composite order, in which one can recognize components of a busby, a lancer's cap, a bowler, an otter-skin cap, and a cotton nightcap, one of those sorry objects, indeed, whose mute ugliness has depths of expression, like the face of an imbecile. Ovoid and stiffened with whalebones, it began with three circular sausages; then followed alternately, separated by a red band, lozenges of velvet and rabbit fur; next came a kind of bag terminating in a cardboard-lined polygon, covered with an embroidery in complicated braid, from which hung, at the end of a long, excessively slender cord, a little crosspiece of gold threads, by way of a tassel. It was new; the visor shone.

"Stand up," said the teacher.

He stood up; his cap fell. The whole class began to laugh.

He bent over to pick it up. A boy beside him knocked it down again with a nudge of his elbow; he retrieved it again.

"Get rid of that helmet of yours," said the teacher, who was a wit.

There was a burst of laughter from the class that disconcerted the poor boy, so that he did not know whether he should keep his cap in his hand, leave it on the floor, or put it on his head. He sat down again and laid it on his knees.

"Stand up," said the teacher, "and tell me your name."

Stammering, the *new boy* articulated an unintelligible name.

"Again!"

The same mumble of syllables was heard, muffled by the hooting of the class.

"Louder!" shouted the teacher. "Louder!"

The *new boy*, summoning an extreme resolve, then opened an inordinately large mouth and bawled at the top of his lungs, as though shouting to someone, the word *Charbovari*.

Now an uproar exploded all at once, rose in a *crescendo*, with outbursts of shrill voices (they howled, they barked, they stamped, they repeated: *Charbovari! Charbovari!*), then continued in isolated notes, quieting with great difficulty and sometimes resuming suddenly along the line of a bench from which a stifled laugh would start up again here and there, like a half-spent firecracker.

However, under a rain of penalties, order was gradually restored in the classroom, and the teacher, having managed to grasp the name of Charles Bovary, having had it dictated to him, spelled out, and read back, at once commanded the poor fellow to go sit on the dunce's bench, at the foot of the platform. He began to move but, before going, hesitated.

"What are you looking for?" asked the teacher.

"My c . . . ," said the *new boy* timidly, casting uneasy glances around him.

"Five hundred lines for the entire class!" The furious exclamation put an end, like the *Quos ego,* to a fresh squall. "Now, keep quiet!" continued the indignant teacher, wiping his forehead with the handkerchief he had just taken from inside his toque. "As for you, *new boy,* you will copy out the verb *ridiculus sum* for me twenty times."

Then, more gently:

"Come now! You'll find your cap; it hasn't been stolen!"

All was calm again. Heads bent over satchels, and for two hours the *new boy's* behavior continued to be exemplary, even though, from time to time, a pellet of paper fired from the nib of a pen came and splattered on his face. But he would wipe himself off with his hand and remain motionless, his eyes lowered.

That evening, in Study Hall, he drew his cuff guards from his desk, put his little things in order, carefully ruled his paper. We saw him working conscientiously, looking up all the words in the dictionary and taking great pains. Thanks, no doubt, to this willingness he displayed, he did not have to go down into the lower class; for while he knew his rules passably well, he had almost no elegance in his constructions. It was the curé of his village who had started him on Latin, his parents, for reasons of economy, having delayed as long as possible sending him to school.

His father, Monsieur Charles-Denis-Bartholomé Bovary, a former assistant army surgeon, compromised, in about 1812, in some business involving conscription and forced, at about that time, to leave the service, had then profited from his personal attributes to pick up a dowry of sixty thousand francs, presented in the form of a hosier's daughter, who had fallen in love with his fine appearance. A handsome, boastful man, jingling his spurs loudly, sporting side-whiskers that merged with his mustache, his fingers always garnished with rings, and dressed in gaudy colors, he had the appearance of a valiant soldier, along with the easy enthusiasm of a traveling salesman. Once married, he lived for two or three years off his wife's fortune, dining well, rising late, smoking great porcelain pipes, coming home at night only after the theater, and haunting cafés. The father-in-law died and left little; he was indignant at this, *went into manufacturing,* lost some money at it, then retired to the country, where he intended to *cultivate the land*. But since he hardly understood farming any better than he did chintz, since he rode his horses instead of putting them to the plow, drank his cider by the bottle instead of selling it by the barrel, ate the best poultry in his yard and greased his hunting shoes with the fat of his pigs, he soon realized that it would be better to abandon all financial enterprises.

For a rent of two hundred francs a year, therefore, he found, in a village on the borders of the Caux region and Picardy, a dwelling of a sort that was half farm, half gentleman's residence; and there, morose, gnawed by regrets, railing at heaven, envying all the world, he shut himself away at the age of forty-five, disgusted with men, he said, and determined to live in peace.

His wife had been madly in love with him at one time; she had doted on him with countless slavish attentions that had estranged him from her even further. Once lively, expansive, and wholeheartedly affectionate, she had become, as she aged (like stale wine turning to vinegar), difficult in temper, shrill, nervous. She had suffered so much, without complaining at first, when she saw him running after every slut in the village and when a score of low-life places would send him back to her at night surfeited and stinking drunk! Then her pride had rebelled. She fell silent, swallowing her rage in a mute stoicism, which she maintained until her death. She was constantly out on errands, on business. She would go see the lawyers, the presiding judge, remember the due dates of the notes, obtain extensions; and, at home, she would iron, sew, wash, look after the workers, settle the accounts, while Monsieur, troubling himself about nothing, eternally sunk in a sullen torpor from which he roused himself only to say unpleasant things to her, sat smoking by the fire, spitting in the ashes.

When she had a child, he had to be put out to nurse. Back in their house, the little boy was spoiled like a prince. His mother fed him on jams; his father let him run around without shoes, and, imagining himself an enlightened thinker, even said that he could go quite naked, like the young of animals. In opposition to the mother's inclinations, he had in mind a certain manly ideal of childhood, according to which he tried to mold his son, wanting him to be brought up ruggedly, in a spartan manner, to give him a good constitution. He sent him to bed without a fire, taught him to drink great drafts of rum and to jeer at church processions. But, peaceable by nature, the boy responded poorly to his efforts. His mother kept him always trailing after her; she would cut out cardboard figures for him, tell him stories, converse with him in endless monologues, full of melancholy whimsy and beguiling chatter. In the isolation of her life, she transferred into that childish head all her sparse, shattered illusions. She dreamed of high positions, she saw him already grown, handsome, witty, established, in bridges and roads or the magistracy. She taught him to read and even, on an old piano she had, to sing two or three little ballads. But to all this, Monsieur Bovary, little concerned with literature, said it *was not worth the trouble!* Would they ever have enough to keep him in a state school, to buy him a practice or set him up in business? Besides, *with a little nerve, a man can always succeed in the world.* Madame Bovary would bite her lips, and the child would roam at will through the village.

He would follow the plowmen and drive away the crows, throwing clods of earth at them till they flew up. He would eat blackberries along the ditches, tend the turkeys with a long stick, toss the hay at harvest time, run through the woods, play hopscotch on the porch of the church on rainy days, and, on the most important holy days, beg the sexton to let him ring the bells so that he could hang with all his weight on the great rope and feel himself borne up by it in its flight.

And so he grew like an oak. He acquired strong hands, good color.

When he turned twelve, his mother saw to it that his studies were begun. The curé was entrusted with this. But the lessons were so brief and so poorly understood that they could not be of much use. They were given at idle moments, in the sacristy, standing up, in haste, between a baptism and a burial; or the curé would send for his pupil after the Angelus, when he did not have to go out. They would go up to his room, they would settle in; the gnats and moths would circle around the candle. It was warm, the child would fall asleep; and the good man, dozing off with his hands on his belly, would soon be snoring, his mouth open. At other times, when Monsieur le curé, on his way back from carrying the last sacrament to some ill person in the environs, spied Charles wandering the countryside, he would call out to him, sermonize him for a quarter of an hour, and profit from the occasion to make him conjugate a verb at the base of a tree. The rain would come and interrupt them, or an acquaintance passing by. Moreover, he was always pleased with him, even said that the *young man* had a good memory.

This could not be as far as Charles went. Madame was emphatic. Ashamed, or, rather, tired out, Monsieur gave in without a struggle, and they waited one more year until the boy had made his first communion.

Another six months went by; and, the following year, Charles was finally enrolled in the school in Rouen, taken there by his father himself, toward the end of October, at the time of the Saint-Romain fair.

It would be impossible by now for any of us to recall a thing about him. He was a boy of even temperament, who played at recess, worked in study hall, listening in class, sleeping well in the dormitory, eating well in the dining hall. He had as local guardian a wholesale hardware dealer in the rue Ganterie, who would take him out once a month, on a Sunday, after his shop was closed, send him off to walk along the harbor looking at the boats, then return him to the school by seven o'clock, before supper. In the evening, every Thursday, he would write a long letter to his mother, with red ink and three pats of sealing wax; then he would review his history notebooks or read an old volume of *Anacharsis* that was lying around in the study hall. Out walking, he would talk to the servant, who, like him, was from the country.

By dint of applying himself, he stayed somewhere in the middle of the class; once he even earned a first honorable mention in natural history. But at the end of his third year, his parents withdrew him from the school in order to have him study medicine, convinced that he would be able to go on alone to the baccalaureate.

His mother chose a room for him, on the fifth floor, overlooking the Eau de Robec, in the home of a dyer she knew. She concluded the arrangements for his room and board, procured some furniture, a table and two chairs, sent home for an old cherrywood bed, and bought, as well, a little cast-iron stove, with the supply of wood that was to warm her poor child. Then she departed at the end of the week, after a thousand injunctions to behave himself, now that he was going to be abandoned to his own care.

The curriculum, which he read on the notice board, made his head swim: a course in anatomy, a course in pathology, a course in physiology, a course in pharmacy, a course in chemistry, and one in botany, and one in clinical practice and one in therapeutics, not to mention hygiene and materia medica, names with unfamiliar etymologies that were like so many doors to sanctuaries filled with solemn shadows.

He understood none of it; though he listened, he did not grasp it. He worked nonetheless, he possessed bound notebooks, he attended all the lectures, he never missed a hospital round. He accomplished his little daily task like a mill horse, which walks in circles with its eyes covered, not knowing what it is grinding.

To spare him expense, his mother would send him each week, by the carrier, a piece of roast veal, on which he would lunch in the morning when he returned from the hospital, stamping his feet against the wall. Then he would have to hurry to his classes, in the amphitheater, in the hospital, and return home along all those streets. In the evening, after the meager dinner provided by his landlord, he would go back up to his room and back to work, his damp clothes steaming on his body, in front of the red-hot stove.

On fine summer evenings, at the hour when the warm streets are empty, when servant girls play at shuttlecock in front of their doors, he would open his window and lean on his elbows. The stream, which makes this part of Rouen into a kind of sordid little Venice, flowed past below him, yellow, violet, or blue, between its bridges and its railings. Workmen, squatting on the bank, washed their arms in the water. On poles projecting from the tops of attics, hanks of cotton dried in the air. Across from him, beyond the rooftops, extended the great, pure sky, with the red sun going down. How good it must be out there! How cool under the beech trees! And he would open his nostrils wide to breathe in the good smells of the country, which did not reach him.

He grew thinner, his body lengthened, and his face took on a sort of plaintive expression that made it almost interesting.

Quite naturally, out of indifference, in time he released himself from all the resolutions he had made. Once he missed the hospital rounds, the next day his class, and, savoring this idleness, gradually he did not return.

He acquired the habit of going to taverns, along with a passion for dominoes. To shut himself up every night in a grimy public room, in order to tap on a marble table with little mutton bones marked with black dots, seemed to him a precious assertion of his freedom, which raised him in his own esteem. It was like an initiation into the world, an access to forbidden pleasures; and as he went in, he would put his hand on the doorknob with a joy that was almost sensual. Then many things that had been repressed in him opened up; he learned songs by heart and sang them to his lady friends, he developed an enthusiasm for Béranger, knew how to make punch, and at last experienced love.

Owing to this preparatory work, he completely failed his public health officer's examination. They were waiting for him at home that very evening to celebrate his success!

He set off on foot and stopped at the entrance to the village, where he sent someone to get his mother, told her everything. She made excuses for him, shifting the blame for his failure to the unfairness of the examiners, and steadied him a little, taking it upon herself to sort things out. Only five years later did Monsieur Bovary know the truth; it was old by then, he accepted it, incapable, moreover, of supposing that any man descended from him could be a fool.

Charles therefore set to work again and prepared, unremittingly, the subjects for his examination, for which he learned all the questions by heart in advance. He passed with a fairly good grade. What a great day for his mother! They put on a grand dinner.

Where would he go to practice? To Tostes. There was only one elderly doctor there. For a long time, Madame Bovary had been waiting for him to die, and the old gentleman had not yet breathed his last when Charles was installed across the road, as his successor.

But it was not enough to have raised her son, seen to it that he got his medical training, and discovered Tostes for his practice: he needed a wife. She found him one: a bailiff's widow from Dieppe, who was forty-five years old with an income of twelve hundred livres.

Although she was ugly, thin as a lath, as thick with pimples as the spring is with buds, Madame Dubuc certainly had no lack of suitors to choose from. To achieve her ends, Mère Bovary was obliged to supplant them all, and she very skillfully foiled even the intrigues of a pork butcher favored by the clergy.

Charles had foreseen in marriage the advent of a better situation, imagining that he would have more freedom and would be able to do as he liked with himself and his money. But his wife was the one in charge; in company he had to say this, not say that, eat no meat on Fridays, dress as she expected, pester at her command those clients who had not paid. She would open his letters, spy on his movements, and listen to him, through the wall, when he saw patients in his office, if they were women.

She had to have her hot chocolate every morning, she wanted endless attention. She complained incessantly about her nerves, about her chest, about her spirits. The sound of footsteps was painful to her; if people left her, the solitude would become loathsome to her; if they came back, it was to see her die, no doubt. In the evening, when Charles returned home, she would take her long, thin arms out from under her sheets, put them around his neck, and, having made him sit down on the edge of the bed, begin telling him about her troubles: he was forgetting her, he loved someone else! They had told her she would be unhappy; and she would end by asking him to give her some tonic for her health and a little more love.

[2]

One night, at about eleven o'clock, they were awoken by the sound of a horse stopping just in front of the door. The maid opened the attic window and conferred for some time with a man who had remained below, in the street. He had come to fetch the doctor; he had a letter. *Nastasie* went down the stairs, shivering, and undid the lock and the bolts one by one. The man left his horse and, following the maid, entered immediately behind her. He drew from inside his gray-tufted wool cap a letter wrapped in a scrap of cloth and presented it delicately to Charles, who leaned his elbow on the pillow to read it. Nastasie, next to the bed, was holding the light. Madame, out of modesty, remained turned toward the space between the bed and the wall, showing her back.

This letter, sealed with a little seal of blue wax, begged Monsieur Bovary to go immediately to the farm called Les Bertaux to set a broken leg. Now, from Tostes to Les Bertaux it is a good six leagues cross-country, going by way of Longueville and Saint-Victor. The night was dark. Madame Bovary the younger was afraid her husband would have an accident. So it was decided that the stableboy would go on ahead. Charles would leave three hours later, when the moon rose. They would send a boy to meet him, to show him the road to the farm and open the gates in front of him.

At about four o'clock in the morning, Charles, well wrapped in his cloak, set off for Les Bertaux. Still drowsy from the warmth of his sleep, he swayed to the peaceful trot of his mare. Whenever she stopped of her own accord in front of one of those holes edged with brambles that farmers dig alongside their furrows, Charles, waking with a start, would quickly recall the broken leg and try to summon up what he remembered of all the fractures he knew. The rain was no longer falling; day was beginning to dawn, and on the branches of the leafless apple trees, birds were perched motionless, ruffling their little feathers in the cold morning wind. The flat country spread out as far as the eye could see, and the clumps of trees around the farms formed patches of dark violet at distant intervals on that vast gray surface, which vanished, at the horizon, into the bleak tones of the sky. Charles, from time to time, would open his eyes; then, his mind tiring and sleep returning of itself, he would soon enter a sort of somnolence in which, his recent sensations becoming confused with his memories, he would see himself double, at once student and married man, lying in his bed as he had been just now, crossing a surgical ward as in the past. The warm smell of the poultices would mingle in his head with the tart smell of the dew; he would hear the iron rings of the bed curtains running on their rods and his wife sleeping . . . As he was passing through Vassonville, he saw, by the side of a ditch, a young boy sitting on the grass.

"Are you the doctor?" asked the child.

And at Charles's answer, he took his wooden shoes in his hands and began to run in front of him.

The officer of health, as he went along, learned from what his guide said that Monsieur Rouault must be an extremely well-to-do farmer. He had broken his leg the evening before, as he was returning from *celebrating Twelfth Night* at the home of a neighbor. His wife had been dead for two years. He had only his *young lady* living with him; she helped him run the house.

The ruts became deeper. They were approaching Les Bertaux. The little boy, gliding through a hole in a hedge, disappeared, then reappeared at the far end of a farmyard to open the gate. The horse was slipping on the wet grass; Charles bent low to pass under the branches. The watchdogs in the kennel were barking and pulling on their chains. When he entered Les Bertaux, his horse took fright and shied violently.

It was a prosperous-looking farm. In the stables, one could see, through the open upper halves of the doors, great workhorses feeding tranquilly from new racks. Along the sides of the buildings extended a large dung

heap, steam was rising from it, and, among the hens and turkey
or six peacocks were scratching about on top of it, a luxury in a
poultry yard. The sheepfold was long, the barn was lofty, with walls as
smooth as a hand. In the shed were two large carts and four plows, with
their whips, their collars, their full harnesses, whose blue wool fleeces
were dirtied by the fine dust that fell from the lofts. The yard sloped away
upward, planted with symmetrically spaced trees, and the cheerful din
of a flock of geese resounded near the pond.

A young woman in a blue merino dress embellished with three flounces
came to the door of the house to receive Monsieur Bovary, whom she
showed into the kitchen, where a large fire was blazing. The farmhands'
breakfast was bubbling all around it, in little pots of unequal sizes. Damp
clothes were drying inside the hearth. The fire shovel, the tongs, and the
nose of the bellows, all of colossal proportions, shone like polished steel,
while along the walls extended an abundant array of kitchen utensils, on
which glimmered unevenly the bright flame of the hearth, joined by the
first gleams of sunlight coming in through the windowpanes.

Charles went up to the second floor to see the patient. He found him
in his bed, sweating under the covers, having hurled his cotton nightcap
far away from him. He was a stout little man of fifty, with white skin and
blue eyes, bald in front, and wearing earrings. He had by his side, on a
chair, a large carafe of eau-de-vie from which he would help himself from
time to time to keep up his courage; but as soon as he saw the doctor, his
excitement subsided, and instead of swearing as he had been doing for
the past twelve hours, he began to groan feebly.

The fracture was simple, without complications of any kind. Charles
could not have dared to hope for an easier one. And so, recalling his
teachers' manners at the bedsides of the injured, he comforted the patient
with all sorts of lively remarks—a surgeon's caresses that are like the oil
with which he greases his scalpel. For splints, they went off to fetch, from
the cart shed, a bundle of laths. Charles chose one, cut it into pieces, and
polished it with a shard of window glass, while the maidservant tore up
some sheets to make bandages, and Mademoiselle Emma worked at sewing some pads. She was a long time finding her needle case, and her father
grew impatient; she said nothing in response; but, as she sewed, she kept
pricking her fingers, which she then raised to her mouth to suck.

Charles was surprised by the whiteness of her fingernails. They were glossy, delicate at the tips, more carefully cleaned than Dieppe ivories, and filed into almond shapes. Yet her hand was not beautiful, not pale enough, perhaps, and a little dry at the knuckles; it was also too long and without soft inflections in its contours. What was beautiful about her was her eyes: although they were brown, they seemed black because of the lashes, and her gaze fell upon you openly, with a bold candor.

Once the bandaging was done, the doctor was invited by Monsieur Rouault himself to *have a bite* before leaving.

Charles went down into the parlor, on the ground floor. Two places, with silver mugs, were laid there on a little table, at the foot of a large canopied bed hung in calico printed with figures representing Turks. One caught a scent of orrisroot and damp sheets escaping from the tall oak cupboard that faced the window. On the floor, in the corners, stowed upright, were sacks of wheat. This was the overflow from the nearby granary, which one reached by three stone steps. As decoration for the room, there hung from a nail, in the middle of the wall whose green paint was flaking off under the saltpeter, a head of Minerva in black pencil, framed in gilt and bearing on the bottom, written in Gothic letters: "To my dear Papa."

They talked first about the patient, then about the weather they were having, about the severe cold spells, about the wolves that roamed the fields at night. Mademoiselle Rouault did not enjoy herself much at all in the country, especially now that she was almost solely responsible for the care of the farm. Because the room was chilly, she shivered as she ate, revealing her full lips, which she had a habit of biting in her moments of silence.

Her neck rose out of a white, turned-down collar. Her hair, whose two black bands were so smooth they seemed each to be of a single piece, was divided down the middle of her head by a thin part that dipped slightly following the curve of her skull; and just barely revealing the lobes of her ears, it went on to merge in the back in an abundant chignon, with a wavy movement near the temples that the country doctor noticed for the first time in his life. Her cheeks were pink. She wore, like a man, tucked between two buttons of her bodice, a tortoiseshell lorgnette.

When Charles, after going up to say goodbye to Père Rouault, came back into the parlor before leaving, he found her standing, her forehead against the window, gazing out into the garden, where the beanpoles had been blown down by the wind. She turned around.

"Are you looking for something?" she asked.

"My riding crop, please," he answered.

And he began hunting around on the bed, behind the doors, under the chairs; it had fallen to the floor, between the sacks and the wall. Mademoiselle Emma saw it; she leaned over the sacks of wheat. Charles, gallantly, hurried over, and as he, too, stretched out his arm in the same gesture, he felt his chest brush against the girl's back, stooping beneath him. She straightened up quite red in the face and looked at him over her shoulder, holding out his whip.

Instead of returning to Les Bertaux three days later, as he had promised, he went back the very next day, then twice a week regularly, not counting the unexpected visits he made from time to time, as though by chance.

Everything, moreover, went well; healing progressed according to the book, and when, after forty-six days, Père Rouault was seen trying to walk alone in his farmyard, people began to consider Monsieur Bovary a man of great ability. Père Rouault said that he would not have been better treated by the foremost doctors of Yvetot or even Rouen.

As for Charles, he did not try to ask himself why he took such pleasure in going to Les Bertaux. Had he thought about it, he would no doubt have attributed his zeal to the gravity of the case, or perhaps to the profit he hoped to make from it. Still, was this why his visits to the farm formed, among all the drab occupations of his life, such a charming exception? On these days he would rise early, set off at a gallop, urge on his animal; then he would dismount to wipe his feet on the grass, and put on his black gloves before going in. He liked to find himself arriving at the farmyard, to feel the gate against his shoulder as it turned, and the rooster crowing on the wall, the boys coming to meet him. He liked the barn and the stables; he liked Père Rouault, who would clap him in the palm of the hand, calling him his savior; he liked Mademoiselle Emma's small clogs on the washed flagstones of the kitchen; her raised heels made her a little taller, and when she walked in front of him, the wooden soles, lifting quickly, would clack with a dry sound against the leather of her ankle boots.

She would always see him out as far as the foot of the front steps. When his horse had not yet been brought around, she would stay there. They had said goodbye, they did not go on talking; the fresh air surrounded her, lifting in disarray the stray wisps of hair on the nape of her neck or tossing her apron strings so that they snaked like banners about her hips. Once, during a thaw, the bark of the trees was oozing in the yard, the snow on the tops of the buildings was melting. She was on the doorsill; she went to get her parasol, she opened it. The parasol, of dove-gray iridescent silk, with the sun shining through it, cast moving glimmers of light over the white skin of her face. She was smiling beneath it in the mild warmth; and they could hear the drops of water, one by one, falling on the taut moiré.

During the early days of Charles's visits to Les Bertaux, Madame Bovary the younger never failed to ask after the patient, and she had even, in the double-columned book she kept, chosen for Monsieur Rouault a nice blank page. But when she found out that he had a daughter, she made inquiries; and she learned that Mademoiselle Rouault, raised in a convent, among the Ursulines, had received, as they say, *a fine education,* that she knew, consequently, dancing, geography, drawing, how to do tapestry work and play the piano. That was the limit!

"So," she said to herself, "that's why he has such a smile on his face when he goes to see her, and why he wears his new waistcoat, even though it might get ruined by the rain? Oh, that woman, that woman! . . ."

And she detested her instinctively. At first she relieved her feelings by making allusions that Charles did not understand; then with parenthetical remarks that he allowed to pass for fear of a storm; finally with point-blank reproaches that he did not know how to answer. —How was it that he kept going back to Les Bertaux, seeing as Monsieur Rouault was healed and those people hadn't paid yet? Ah! Because there was *a certain person* there, someone who knew how to make small talk, who did embroidery, who had a fine mind. That was what he liked: he wanted young ladies! And she went on:

"Old Rouault's daughter, a young lady! Come now! The grandfather was a shepherd, and they have a cousin who was nearly taken to court for striking a man viciously during a quarrel. She needn't bother to put on such airs, nor show herself at church on Sunday in silk, like a countess. Poor old fellow, anyway—without last year's rapeseed, he'd have had a hard enough time paying his arrears!"

Out of lassitude, Charles stopped going back to Les Bertaux. Héloïse, after much sobbing and many kisses, in a great explosion of love, had made him swear, his hand on his prayer book, that he would not go there anymore. He therefore obeyed; but the boldness of his desire protested against the servility of his behavior, and, with a sort of naïve hypocrisy, he felt that this prohibition against seeing her gave him, in some way, the right to love her. Also, the widow was thin; she had long teeth; in every season she wore a little black shawl whose point hung down between her shoulder blades; her hard body was wrapped in dresses like sheaths that were too short for her and showed her ankles, with the ribbons of her wide shoes crisscrossing over her gray stockings.

Charles's mother would come see them from time to time; but after a few days, it would seem that the daughter-in-law had sharpened her mother-in-law against her own hard edge; and then, like two knives, they would set about scarifying him with their remarks and their observations. He was wrong to eat so much! Why offer a drink to everyone who stopped in? How stubborn not to wear flannel!

It happened that early in the spring, a notary in Ingouville, custodian of the Widow Dubuc's capital, sailed off on a favorable tide, taking away with him all the money in his keeping. Héloïse, it is true, also possessed, besides a share in a ship valued at six thousand francs, her house in the rue Saint-François; and yet, of all that fortune that had been so loudly vaunted, nothing, except a few pieces of furniture and some rags of clothing, had ever appeared in the household. The thing had to be cleared up. The house in Dieppe was found to be riddled with mortgages down to its pilings; what she had placed with the notary, God only knew, and her share in the ship did not amount to more than a thousand ecus. So she had lied, the fine lady! In his anger, the elder Monsieur Bovary, breaking a chair on the flagstones, accused his wife of having brought calamity down upon their son by hitching him to an old nag whose harness wasn't worth her skin. They came to Tostes. They had it out. There were scenes. Héloïse, in tears, throwing herself into her husband's arms, begged him to defend her from his parents. Charles tried to speak up for her. His parents became furious, and they left.

But *the blow had struck home.* A week later, as she was hanging the wash in her yard, she began spitting blood, and the next day, while Charles, his back turned, was at the window closing the curtain, she said: "Oh, my God!," sighed, and lost consciousness. She was dead! How astonishing it was!

When everything was over at the cemetery, Charles went back to his house. He found no one downstairs; he went up to the second floor, into the bedroom, saw her dress still hanging at the foot of the alcove; then, leaning on the writing desk, he remained there till evening, lost in a sorrowful reverie. She had loved him, after all.

[3]

One morning, Père Rouault came to bring Charles the payment for setting his leg: seventy-five francs in forty-sou coins, and a turkey. He had heard about his misfortune and consoled him as best he could.

"I know how it is!" he said, clapping him on the shoulder; "I was like you, too! When I lost my poor dear late wife, I would go off into the fields to be all alone; I would fling myself down under a tree, I would cry, I would call out to the good Lord, I would tell him all kinds of nonsense; I wanted to be like the moles, I saw them up there in the branches, they had worms wriggling around in their insides, dead, you know. And when I thought that other men were with their good little wives at that very moment, holding them in their arms, I would beat the ground with my stick; I was half crazy, couldn't eat; the idea of going to the café made me sick, you can't imagine. Well, very quietly, as one day nosed along on the heels of the next, spring coming on top of winter and fall after summer, it passed, bit by bit, drop by drop; it went away, it disappeared, it died down, I mean, because you're always left with something on the bottom, a sort of a . . . weight, here, on your chest! But since that's our fate, all of us, you mustn't let yourself waste away, you mustn't want to die yourself, just because someone else has died. You must shake it off, Monsieur Bovary; it'll pass! Come see us; my daughter thinks of you from time to time, you know, and she says you're forgetting her. Here we are, it's nearly spring; we'll have you come out and shoot a rabbit in the warren, to divert you a little."

Charles followed his advice. He returned to Les Bertaux. He found everything the same as the day before—that is, as five months before. The pear trees were already in bloom, and old Rouault was on his feet now, coming and going, which made the farm livelier.

Believing that it was his duty to lavish on the doctor as many polite attentions as possible, because of his painful situation, he begged him not to take his hat off, spoke to him softly, as though he were ill, and even pretended to lose his temper because they had not prepared him something a bit more delicate than all the rest, such as little custards or poached pears. He told stories. Charles caught himself laughing; but the memory of his wife, returning to him suddenly, sobered him. They brought in the coffee; he stopped thinking about her.

He thought about her less, as he became used to living alone. The novel pleasure of independence soon made solitude more tolerable. He could now change the hours of his meals, come home or go out without giving reasons, and, when he was very tired, stretch his arms and legs out to the sides, in his bed. And so he coddled himself, pampered himself, and accepted the consolations offered him. On the other hand, his wife's death had been rather useful to him professionally, because for a month people had said over and over: "That poor young man! What a misfortune!" His name had gotten around, his practice had increased; and in addition he could go to Les Bertaux as he liked. He had an aimless sort of hope; a vague happiness; he thought his face better looking as he brushed his whiskers in front of the mirror.

He arrived one day at about three o'clock; everyone was in the fields; he entered the kitchen but at first did not notice Emma; the shutters were closed. Through the slits in the wood, the sun cast over the flagstones long, narrow stripes that broke at the angles of the furniture and trembled on the ceiling. On the table, flies were walking up the used glasses and buzzing as they drowned at the bottom, in the dregs of cider. The daylight that came down the chimney, turning the soot on the fireback to velvet, touched with blue the cold cinders. Between the window and the hearth, Emma was sewing; she was not wearing a scarf, and one could see, on her bare shoulders, little drops of sweat.

As was the fashion in the country, she offered him something to drink. He refused, she insisted, and finally invited him, laughing, to have a glass of liqueur with her. So she went to get a bottle of curaçao from the cupboard, took down two small glasses, filled one to the rim, poured almost nothing in the other, and, after having touched it to his, raised it to her mouth. As it was almost empty, she leaned back to drink; and with her head back, her lips thrust out, her neck tense, she laughed at feeling nothing, while the tip of her tongue, passing between her delicate teeth, licked with little stabs at the bottom of the glass.

She sat down and took up her work again, a white cotton stocking to which she was making repairs; she sewed with her forehead lowered; she did not speak, nor did Charles. A draft of air, passing under the door, pushed a little dust over the stone floor; he watched it drift and heard only the pulse beating inside his head, and the cry of a hen, in the distance, laying an egg in the yard. Emma, from time to time, would cool her cheeks by pressing against them the palms of her hands, which she would then chill on the iron knobs of the great firedogs.

She complained of having suffered, since the beginning of the season, from dizzy spells; she asked if sea bathing would be useful; she began to talk about the convent, Charles about his school, words came to them. They went up to her room. She showed him her old music notebooks, the small books she had been given as prizes, and the wreaths made of oak leaves, left in the bottom of a cupboard. She talked to him, too, about her mother, about the cemetery, and even showed him, in the garden, the bed from which she gathered flowers, on the first Friday of each month, to put on her grave. But their gardener understood nothing; their servants were so bad! She would have liked very much, if only during the winter at least, to live in town, although the long, fine days made the country perhaps even more tiresome during the summer; —and depending on what she was saying, her voice was clear, high-pitched, or suddenly languorous, trailing off in modulations that sank almost to a murmur, when she was talking to herself, —sometimes joyful, her eyes wide and innocent, and sometimes half closing her lids, her gaze drowned in boredom, her thoughts wandering.

That evening, as he was returning home, Charles took up again one by one the words she had used, trying to recall them, to complete their meaning, in order to re-create for himself the portion of her life that she had lived during the time when he did not yet know her. But he could never see her, in his mind, differently from the way he had seen her the first time, or the way he had just left her. Then he wondered what would become of her, whether she would marry, and whom. Alas! Père Rouault was very rich, and she! . . . so lovely! But Emma's face kept returning to linger before his eyes, and something monotonous like the drone of a top kept buzzing in his ears: "But what if you were to get married! What if you were to get married!" That night, he could not sleep, his throat was tight, he was thirsty; he got up to drink from his water jug, and he opened the window; the sky was covered with stars, a warm wind was passing, in the distance, dogs were barking. He turned his face toward Les Bertaux.

Thinking that after all he had nothing to lose, Charles resolved to put the question when the opportunity arose; but each time it did arise, his fear of not finding the proper words sealed his lips.

Père Rouault would not have been sorry to have someone relieve him of his daughter, who was hardly any use to him in his house. Inwardly he excused her, believing she had too much spirit for farming, a vocation accursed by heaven, since one never saw a millionaire involved in it. Far from having made a fortune, the poor fellow was losing money every year: for though he excelled in the marketplace, where he took pleasure in the stratagems of the job, farming itself, with the interior management of the farm, suited him less than anyone. He never willingly took his hands out of his pockets, and spared no expense for anything to do with his life, wanting good food, a good fire, and a good bed. He liked hard cider, a rare leg of lamb, *glorias* well beaten. He took his meals in the kitchen, alone, facing the fire, at a little table they brought to him already set, as in the theater.

And so when he noticed that Charles's cheeks turned red in the presence of his daughter, which meant that one of these days Charles would ask for her hand in marriage, he pondered the whole matter in advance. He certainly found him a little *puny,* and this wasn't the sort of son-in-law he would have wished for; but he was said to be sober in his habits, thrifty, well educated, and he would probably not haggle too much over the dowry. Therefore, since Père Rouault was going to be forced to sell twenty-two acres of *his property,* since he owed a good deal to the mason, a good deal to the harness maker, since the shaft of the press needed to be repaired:

"If he asks me for her," he said to himself, "I'll give her to him."

Around Michaelmas, Charles had come to spend three days at Les Bertaux. The last had slipped away like the ones before, receding from one quarter hour to the next quarter hour. Père Rouault was seeing him on his way; they were walking in a sunken lane, they were about to take leave of each other; this was the moment. Charles gave himself as far as the corner of the hedge, and at last, when they had passed it:

"Maître Rouault," he murmured, "I have something I would like to say to you."

They stopped. Charles was silent.

"Well, tell me what's on your mind! Don't I know all about it already?" said Père Rouault, laughing gently.

"Père Rouault . . . Père Rouault," stammered Charles.

"For my part I couldn't ask anything better," continued the farmer. "My little girl probably feels the same, but still, we must put it to her and see. You be on your way, then; I'm going back to the house. If it's yes, understand, you won't have to come back, because of the other folks, and besides, it would be too much for her. But so you don't sweat blood, I'll push the shutter wide open against the wall: you'll be able to see it back there, if you lean over the hedge."

And he went off.

Charles tied his horse to a tree. He hurried to stand in the path; he waited. Half an hour passed, then he counted nineteen minutes on his watch. Suddenly there was a noise against the wall; the shutter had been folded back, the latch was still quivering.

The next day, at nine o'clock, he was at the farm. Emma blushed when he went in, while trying to laugh a little, to maintain her composure. Père Rouault embraced his future son-in-law. They put off talking about the financial arrangements; they had, after all, some time ahead of them, since the marriage could not decently take place before the end of Charles's mourning, that is, toward the spring of the following year.

The winter was spent in expectation of this. Mademoiselle Rouault busied herself with her trousseau. Part of it was ordered in Rouen, and she made some chemises and nightcaps for herself from fashion patterns that she borrowed. During the visits that Charles paid to the farm, they would talk about the preparations for the wedding; they would wonder which room the dinner should be given in; they would muse over the number of courses that would be needed and what the entrées would be.

Emma, however, would have liked to be married at midnight, by torch-light; but Père Rouault found the idea incomprehensible. So there was a wedding celebration to which forty-three people came, during which they remained at table for sixteen hours, which started up again the next day and carried over a little into the days that followed.

[4]

The guests arrived early in carriages, one-horse jaunting-cars, two-wheeled charabancs, old gigs without tops, spring-carts with leather curtains, and the young people from the nearest villages in wagons in which they stood in lines, resting their hands on the rails to keep from falling, going at a trot and badly shaken about. Some came from ten leagues away, from Goderville, from Normanville, and from Cany. All the relatives of both families had been invited, quarrels with friends had been mended, letters had been sent to acquaintances long lost from sight.

From time to time, a whip would be heard cracking behind the hedge; soon the gate would open: it was a cariole entering. Galloping to the bottom of the front steps, it would stop short and discharge its passengers, who would emerge from all sides rubbing their knees and stretching their arms. The ladies, in bonnets, wore dresses in the fashion of the town, gold watch chains, tippets with the ends crossed under their belts, or small colored fichus attached in the back with a pin, showing the napes of their necks. The little boys, dressed the same as their papas, seemed uncomfortable in their new suits (indeed, many of them were wearing a pair of boots that day for the first time in their lives), and one would see next to them, breathing not a word in the white dress from her first communion, lengthened for the event, some tall girl of fourteen or sixteen, probably a cousin or older sister, red in the face, gaping, her hair greased with rose pomade, very much afraid of soiling her gloves. Since there were not nearly enough stableboys to unhitch all the carriages, the gentlemen turned up their sleeves and went to it themselves. According to their different social positions, they wore tailcoats, frock coats, long jackets, cutaways—good tailcoats, embraced by a family's highest esteem and taken from the cupboard only on solemn occasions; frock coats with great skirts that floated in the wind, cylindrical collars, pockets as ample as bags; jackets of coarse cloth, ordinarily worn with some sort of cap circled with brass at its visor; very short cutaways, with two buttons in the back set close together like a pair of eyes and panels that seemed to have been cut from a single block of wood by a carpenter's ax. A few others still (but these, of course, would be dining at the foot of the table) were wearing dress smocks, that is, with collars folded down on the shoulders, backs gathered in small pleats, and waists fastened very low with a stitched belt.

And the shirts bulged from the chests like breastplates! Every man was freshly shorn, ears stuck out from heads, cheeks were close-shaven; some, indeed, who had risen before dawn, not having been able to see clearly as they shaved, had diagonal gashes under their noses or, along their jaws, patches of peeled skin as broad as three-franc ecus, which, inflamed by the cold air during the ride, marbled with pink patches all those great beaming white faces.

Since the town hall was half a league from the farm, they went there on foot and came back in the same manner, after the ceremony had been performed at the church. The procession, at first united like a single colorful scarf, undulating over the countryside, along the narrow path winding between the green wheat fields, soon lengthened out and broke up into different groups that loitered to talk. The fiddler walked in front, his violin trimmed with ribbons at its scroll; then came the married couple, the relatives, the friends in no particular order; and the children lagged behind, amusing themselves tearing the bell-shaped flowers off the oat stems or playing among themselves, out of sight. Emma's dress, too long, trailed a little at the hem; from time to time, she would stop to lift it up, and then, delicately, with her gloved fingers, she would remove the coarse grass and small spikes of thistle, while Charles, his hands empty, waited until she had finished. Père Rouault, a new silk hat on his head and the cuffs of his black coat covering his hands down to the nails, gave his arm to the elder Madame Bovary. As for the elder Monsieur Bovary, who, really despising all these people, had come simply in a frock coat of military cut with one row of buttons, he was delivering barroom compliments to a blond young peasant woman. She bowed her head, blushed, not knowing what to answer. The others in the wedding party talked business or played tricks behind one another's backs, rousing their spirits in advance; and if one listened, one could always hear the scraping of the fiddler, who went on playing across the fields. When he noticed that the others were far behind him, he would stop to catch his breath, rub his bow with rosin for a long time so that the strings would squeak all the more loudly, and then begin walking again, lowering and raising the neck of his violin by turns, to mark the beat firmly for himself. The noise of the instrument frightened away the little birds for a long distance around him.

It was in the cart shed that the table had been set up. On it there were four roasts of beef, six fricassées of chicken, stewed veal, three legs of mutton, and, in the middle, a nice roast suckling pig, flanked by four andouille sausages flavored with sorrel. At the corners stood the eau-de-vie, in carafes. Sweet cider in bottles pushed its thick foam up around the corks, and every glass had been filled to the brim, beforehand, with wine. Large plates of yellow custard that quivered at the slightest knock to the table displayed, on their smooth surfaces, the initials of the newlyweds drawn in arabesques of nonpareils. They had gone to Yvetot to find a pastry cook for the tarts and the nougats. Since he was just starting up in the area, he had done things carefully; and he himself carried in, at dessert time, a masterpiece of confection that caused people to cry out. At the base, first, there was a square of blue cardboard representing a temple with porticoes, colonnades, and statuettes of stucco all around, in niches spangled with gold paper stars; then on the second tier was a castle keep made of sponge cake, surrounded by tiny fortifications of angelica, almonds, raisins, and orange sections; and lastly, on the topmost layer, which was a green meadow with rocks and with lakes made of jam and boats of nutshells, a little Cupid was swinging on a chocolate swing whose two poles ended in two real rosebuds, for knobs, at the top.

They ate until nightfall. When they were tired of sitting down, they would go for a walk in the farmyards or play a game of cork-penny in the barn; then they would come back to the table. A few of them, toward the end, fell asleep there and snored. But at coffee time, everything came to life again; they broke into song, they had contests of strength, they lifted weights, they played "under my thumb," they tried to raise the carts onto their shoulders, they said off-color things, they kissed the ladies. At night, when it was time to leave, the horses, gorged to the nostrils with oats, could hardly get into the shafts; they kicked, they reared, they broke their harnesses, their masters swore or laughed; and all night long, in the moonlight, along the country roads, there were runaway carriages racing at full gallop, bounding into ditches, leaping over stretches of gravel, catching on embankments, with women leaning out the door to seize the reins.

Those who stayed at Les Bertaux spent the night drinking in the kitchen. The children had fallen asleep under the benches.

The bride had begged her father that she be spared the customary

pranks. Nevertheless, one of their cousins, a fishmonger (who had actually brought, as a wedding present, a couple of soles), was about to squirt
water with his mouth through the keyhole, when Père Rouault came
along just in time to stop him, explaining that the importance of his
son-in-law's position did not permit of such improprieties. The cousin,
however, yielded only with difficulty to these arguments. Inwardly, he
accused Père Rouault of being proud, and he went off into a corner to join
four or five other guests who, having by chance been served the cheapest
cuts of meat several times in succession at table, also felt they had been
poorly treated and were whispering against their host, quietly hoping he
would ruin himself.

The elder Madame Bovary had not opened her mouth all day. No
one had consulted her about either her daughter-in-law's toilette or the
arrangements for the banquet; she went to bed early. Her husband, instead
of following her, sent to Saint-Victor for some cigars and smoked until
dawn, drinking grogs made with kirsch, a mixture unknown to the company, which inspired still greater respect for him.

Charles was not a wit by nature, he had not been brilliant during the
wedding festivities. He had responded feebly to the quips, puns, double
entendres, compliments, and off-color remarks people felt duty bound
to level at him from the moment the soup was served.

The next day, however, he seemed another man. It was he whom one
would have taken for the virgin of the day before, while the bride revealed
nothing from which one could have guessed anything. Even the shrewd-
est did not know what to say, and they contemplated her, when she came
near them, with inordinately keen attention. But Charles hid nothing.
He called her "my wife," addressed her as *tu,* asked everyone where she
was, looked for her everywhere, and would often draw her out into the
grounds, where he could be seen from a distance, among the trees, putting his arm around her waist and continuing to walk half bent over her,
his head rumpling the lace in the opening of her bodice.

Two days after the wedding, the bride and groom left: Charles, because
of his patients, could not stay away longer. Père Rouault had them driven
back in his carriage and went with them himself as far as Vassonville.
There, he kissed his daughter one last time, got down, and set out for
home again. When he had walked about a hundred yards, he stopped, and
as he saw the carriage moving away into the distance, its wheels turning

in the dust, he gave a deep sigh. Then he recalled his own wedding, his own earlier days, his wife's first pregnancy; he, too, had been very happy, the day he took her away from her father's house to his own, when he had carried her behind him on the horse trotting over the snow; for it was close to Christmas, and the fields were all white; she was holding him with one arm, her basket hooked over the other; the wind was whipping the long lace streamers of her Cauchois headdress, so that at times they blew across his mouth, and when he turned his head, he would see close to him, against his shoulder, her rosy little face smiling silently under the gold ornament on her bonnet. From time to time, she would warm her fingers by putting them inside his coat. How long ago it all was! By now, their son would have been thirty! Then he looked back; he saw nothing on the road. He felt as sad as an empty house; and, affectionate memories mingling with black thoughts in his brain, which was fogged by the vapors of the feast, for a moment he thought of taking a walk in the direction of the church. As he was afraid, however, that the sight of it would make him even sadder, he went straight back home.

Monsieur and Madame Charles arrived in Toste at about six o'clock. The neighbors came to the windows to see their doctor's new wife.

The old servant presented herself, curtsied to her, apologized because dinner was not ready, and urged Madame, while waiting, to become acquainted with her house.

[5]

The brick housefront was exactly flush with the street, or rather the high road. Behind the door hung a cloak with a short cape, a bridle, a black leather cap, and, in the corner, on the floor, stood a pair of leggings still covered with dried mud. To the right was the parlor, that is, the room they used for eating and for sitting. A canary yellow wallpaper, set off at the top by swags of pale flowers, trembled perpetually over its whole extent on its poorly stretched canvas; curtains of white calico, edged with red braid, crisscrossed the length of the windows, and on the narrow mantelpiece sat resplendent a pendulum clock with a head of Hippocrates, between two silverplated candlesticks under oval globes. On the other side of the hallway was Charles's office, a small room about six paces wide, with a table, three chairs, and an office armchair. The volumes of the *Dictionary of Medical Science,* whose pages were uncut but whose bindings had suffered from all the successive sales through which they had passed, by themselves almost entirely filled the six shelves of a pine bookcase. The smell of sauces cooking penetrated through the wall during consultations, just as from the kitchen one could hear the patients coughing in the consulting room and recounting in detail their entire histories. Next, opening directly onto the yard, with its stables, was a large derelict room containing an oven and now serving as woodshed, cellar, and storeroom, full of old pieces of iron, empty barrels, disused garden implements, along with a quantity of other dusty things whose function it was impossible to imagine.

The garden, longer than it was wide, ran back between two clay walls covered with espaliered apricots, to a thorn hedge that separated it from the fields. In the middle was a slate sundial, on a masonry pedestal; four flower beds filled with spindly wild roses surrounded symmetrically the more useful square of serious plantings. At the far end, under the spruce trees, a plaster curé stood reading his breviary.

Emma went up into the bedrooms. The first was not furnished at all; but the second, which was the conjugal bedroom, contained a mahogany bed in an alcove hung with red drapes. A box made of seashells adorned the chest of drawers; and on the writing desk, by the window, there stood, in a carafe, a bouquet of orange flowers, tied with white satin ribbons. It was a bridal bouquet, the other woman's bouquet! She looked at it. Charles noticed, picked it up, and carried it off to the attic, while, sitting in an armchair (they were placing her things around her), Emma thought about her own wedding bouquet, which was packed away in a cardboard box, and wondered, dreamily, what would be done with it if by chance she were to die.

She occupied herself, during the first days, with planning changes in her house. She took the globes off the candlesticks, had new wallpaper hung, the stairwell painted, and seats made for the garden, around the sundial; she even asked how she could acquire a pool with a fountain and fish. And her husband, knowing that she liked to go for drives, found a secondhand *boc,* which, once it had new lamps and mudguards of padded leather, looked almost like a tilbury.

So he was happy, without a care in the world. A meal alone with her, a walk in the evening on the big road, the gesture of her hand touching the bands of her hair, the sight of her straw hat hanging from the hasp of a window, and many other things that Charles had never suspected would be a source of pleasure now formed the continuous flow of his happiness. In bed, in the morning, and side by side on the pillow, he would watch the sunlight passing through the down on her blond cheeks, half covered by the scalloped tabs of her nightcap. Seen from so close, her eyes appeared larger to him, especially when she opened her eyelids several times in succession as she awoke; black when in shadow and dark blue in broad daylight, they seemed to hold layer upon layer of colors, denser deep down and lighter and lighter toward the enameled surface. His own eyes would lose themselves in those depths, and he would see himself in miniature down to his shoulders, with the silk scarf he wore around his head and the top of his half-open nightshirt. He would get up. She would go to the window to watch him leave; and she would remain there with her elbows on the sill, between two pots of geraniums, her dressing gown loose around her. Charles, in the street, would be buckling his spurs, his foot up on the guard stone; and she would go on talking to him from above, tearing off with her teeth and blowing down to him some bit of flower or leaf, which would flutter, float, make half circles in the air like a bird, and catch, before falling, in the ill-combed mane of the old white mare, motionless at the door. Charles, on horseback, would send her a kiss; she would answer with a wave, she would close the window, he would leave. And then, on the highway stretching out before him in an endless ribbon of dust, along sunken lanes over which the trees bent like an arbor, in paths where the wheat rose as high as his knees, with the sun on his shoulders and the morning air in his nostrils, his heart full of the joys of the night, his spirit at peace, his flesh content, he would ride along ruminating on his happiness, like a man continuing to chew, after dinner, the taste of the truffles he is digesting.

Up to now, what had there been in his life that was good? Was it his time in school, where he remained shut in between those high walls, alone among schoolmates wealthier or better than he at their studies, who laughed at his accent, who made fun of his clothes, and whose mothers came to the visiting room with pastries in their muffs? Was it later, when he was studying medicine, his purse never fat enough to pay for a contra dance with some little working girl who might have become his mistress? After that, he had lived for fourteen months with the widow, whose feet, in bed, were as cold as blocks of ice. But now he possessed, for always, this pretty woman whom he so loved. The universe, for him, did not extend beyond the silky contour of her underskirt; and he would reproach himself for not loving her more, he would want to see her again; he would return home quickly, climb the stairs, his heart pounding. Emma, in her room, would be dressing; he would come in on silent feet, he would kiss her on the back, she would cry out.

He could not refrain from constantly touching her comb, her rings, her scarf; sometimes he would give her great full-lipped kisses on her cheeks, or a string of little kisses up her bare arm, from the tips of her fingers to her shoulder; and she would push him away, with a weary half smile, as one does a clinging child.

Before her marriage, she had believed that what she was experiencing was love; but since the happiness that should have resulted from that love had not come, she thought she must have been mistaken. And Emma tried to find out just what was meant, in life, by the words "bliss," "passion," and "intoxication," which had seemed so beautiful to her in books.

[6]

She had read *Paul and Virginia,* and she had dreamed of the little bamboo house, the Negro Domingo, the dog Faithful, but most of all of the sweet friendship of a good little brother who goes off to fetch red fruit for you from great trees taller than church steeples, or runs barefoot over the sand, bringing you a bird's nest.

When she was thirteen years old, her father himself took her to the city, to place her in the convent. They stayed at an inn in the Saint-Gervais quarter, where they were served supper on painted plates depicting the story of Mademoiselle de La Vallière. The explanatory legends, crossed here and there by knife scratches, all glorified religion, refined sentiments, and the splendors of the Court.

Far from being unhappy at the convent in her early days there, she liked the company of the good sisters, who, to amuse her, would take her to the chapel, down a long corridor from the refectory. She played very little during recreation time, understood her catechism very well, and it was always she who answered Monsieur le vicaire when he asked the hard questions. Living thus, without ever leaving the temperate atmosphere of the classrooms, and among these white-faced women with their rosaries and copper crucifixes, she sank gently down into the mystical languor exhaled by the perfumes of the altar, the coolness of the fonts, and the glow of the candles. Instead of following the Mass, she would gaze in her book at the holy pictures with their azure edges, and she loved the sick ewe, the Sacred Heart pierced with sharp arrows, or poor Jesus falling, as he walked, under his cross. She tried, as mortification, to go a whole day without eating. She searched her mind for some vow she could fulfill.

When she went to confession, she would invent little sins in order to stay there longer, on her knees in the darkness, her hands together, her face at the grille beneath the whisperings of the priest. The metaphors of betrothed, spouse, heavenly lover, and marriage everlasting that recur in sermons stirred unexpectedly sweet sensations in the depths of her soul.

In the evenings, before prayers, a pious work was read aloud to them in the study hall. During the week, it was some digest of Biblical history or Abbé Frayssinous's *Lectures,* and, on Sunday, for a change, passages from *The Genius of Christianity.* How she listened, the first few times, to those sonorous lamentations of romantic melancholy, reechoing through the earth and eternity! If her childhood had been spent in a room behind some shop in a commercial district, then perhaps she would have been open to those lyrical invasions of nature, which ordinarily come to us only as expressed by writers. But she knew the country too well; she knew the bleating flocks, the milking, the plows. Accustomed to the calm aspects of things, she turned, instead, toward the more tumultuous. She loved the sea only for its storms, and greenery only when it grew up here and there among ruins. She needed to derive from things a sort of personal gain; and she rejected as useless everything that did not contribute to the immediate gratification of her heart, —being by temperament more sentimental than artistic, in search of emotions and not landscapes.

At the convent there was a spinster who came every month, for a week, to work in the linen room. Under the protection of the archdiocese because she belonged to an old family of gentry ruined during the Revolution, she would eat in the refectory at the good sisters' table and, after the meal, stay for a brief chat with them before going back up to her needlework. Often the boarders would slip out of study hall to go see her. She knew by heart the love songs of the century before and would sing them softly as she plied her needle. She would tell stories, give you news, do errands for you in town, and lend the older girls, secretly, one of the novels that she always had in her apron pocket, and from which the good old maid herself would devour long chapters in the intervals of her task. They were always and only about love, lovers, paramours, persecuted ladies fainting in lonely pavilions, postilions killed at every stage, horses ridden to death on every page, gloomy forests, troubled hearts, oaths, sobs, tears, and kisses, skiffs by moonlight, nightingales in groves, *gentlemen* brave as lions, gentle as lambs, virtuous as no one ever is, always well dressed, and weeping like tombstone urns. And so for six months, at the age of fifteen, Emma soiled her hands with the greasy dust of those old lending libraries. With Walter Scott, later, she became enamored of things historical, dreamed of studded leather chests, guardrooms, and troubadors. She would have liked to live in some old manor, like one of those long-bodiced chatelaines who, under the trefoiled ogives, would spend her days, elbow on stone sill and chin in hand, watching a white-plumed horseman come galloping from the depths of the countryside on a black horse. At that time she worshipped Mary Stuart and felt an ardent veneration for illustrious or ill-fated women. Joan of Arc, Héloïse, Agnès Sorel, La Belle Ferronnière, and Clémence Isaure, for her, stood out like comets against the shadowy immensity of history, in which there still appeared here and there, but less visible in the darkness and without any relation among them, Saint Louis and his oak, Bayard dying, certain of Louis XI's ferocities, a little of Saint Bartholomew, the Béarnais's plume, and always the memory of the painted plates on which Louis XIV was extolled.

In music class, in the ballads she sang, the only subjects were little angels with wings of gold, madonnas, lagoons, gondoliers—peaceable compositions that allowed her to glimpse, through the silliness of the style and the indiscretions of the notes, the enticing phantasmagoria of real feelings. Some of her schoolmates would bring to the convent the keepsake albums they had received as New Year's gifts. They had to hide them, it was quite a business; they would read them in the dormitory. Delicately handling their beautiful satin bindings, Emma would stare, dazzled, at the names of the unknown authors who had signed, most often counts and viscounts, under their compositions.

She would shiver, her breath lifting the tissue paper off the engravings; it would rise up half folded and fall back gently against the page. There was a young man in a short cloak behind a balcony railing, clasping in his arms a young girl in a white dress wearing a mesh bag at her belt; or anonymous portraits of English *ladies* with blond curls who gazed out at you with their wide light-colored eyes from under their round straw hats. Some were shown lying back in carriages, gliding through parks, where a greyhound would bound ahead of a team driven at a trot by two little postilions in white knee breeches. Others, dreaming on sofas beside an unsealed letter, would gaze at the moon through a half-open window half draped in a black curtain. Innocents with a tear on their cheek would kiss the beak of a turtledove through the bars of a Gothic birdcage or, smiling, their head nearly touching their shoulder, would pick the leaves off a daisy with tapering fingers that curved up at the tips like Turkish slippers. And you were there, too, you sultans with long pipes, swooning under arbors, in the arms of dancing girls, you Giaours, Turkish sabers, fezzes, and you especially, wan landscapes of dithyrambic countries, which often show us both palm trees and pines, tigers to the right, a lion to the left, Tartar minarets on the horizon, in the foreground Roman ruins, then crouching camels; — the whole framed in a very tidy virgin forest, with a great perpendicular ray of sunshine quivering on the water, where, standing out as white scratches against the steely gray background, widely spaced swans are swimming.

And the shade of the Argand lamp, attached to the wall above Emma's head, shone on all these pictures of the world, which passed before her one after another, in the silence of the dormitory, to the distant sound of some late hackney cab still rolling along the boulevards.

When her mother died, she wept a great deal in the first few days. She had a memorial picture made for herself with the dead woman's hair, and in a letter she sent to Les Bertaux, full of sorrowful reflections on life, she asked to be buried in the same grave, later. The good man thought she was ill and came to see her. Emma was inwardly satisfied to feel that she had, at her first attempt, reached that rare ideal of pallid lives, which mediocre hearts will never attain. And so she allowed herself to slip into Lamartinean meanderings, listened to harps on lakes, to the song of every dying swan, to the falling of every leaf, to pure virgins rising to heaven, and to the voice of the Eternal speaking in the valleys. She became bored with this, did not want to admit it, continued out of habit, then out of vanity, and was at last surprised to find that she was at peace, and that there was no more sadness in her heart than there were wrinkles on her forehead.

The good nuns, who had been so confident of her vocation, perceived with great surprise that Mademoiselle Rouault seemed to be slipping out of their control. They had, indeed, lavished upon her so many masses, retreats, novenas, and sermons, so thoroughly preached the respect owed to the saints and martyrs, and given so much good advice concerning the modesty of the body and the salvation of her soul, that she did what horses do when pulled by the reins: she stopped short and the bit slipped from her teeth. That spirit of hers, practical in the midst of its enthusiasms, loving the church for its flowers, music for the words of its songs, and literature for its power to stir the passions, rebelled before the mysteries of faith, just as she grew ever more irritated by its discipline, which was antipathetic to her nature. When her father withdrew her from school, no one was sorry to see her go. The Mother Superior even thought she had become, lately, rather irreverent toward the community.

Back at home, Emma at first enjoyed ordering the servants about, then grew sick of the country and missed her convent. By the time Charles came to Les Bertaux for the first time, she considered herself to be thoroughly disillusioned, with nothing more to learn, nothing more to feel.

But her impatience for change, or perhaps the nervous excitation caused by the presence of this man, had been enough to make her believe she at last possessed the marvelous passion that until then had remained like a great rosy-feathered bird hovering in the splendor of a poetical sky; —and now she could not convince herself that the calm life she was living was the happiness of which she had dreamed.

[7]

She sometimes imagined that these were, nevertheless, the most beautiful days of her life—the honeymoon, as it was called. To savor its sweetness, she would doubtless have had to go off to one of those lands with melodious names where the days following a wedding have a softer indolence! In a post chaise, under curtains of blue silk, you climb the steep roads at a walk, listening to the postilion's song as it echoes through the mountains, mingling with the bells of the goats and the muffled sound of a waterfall. As the sun goes down, you stand together on the shore of some bay, inhaling the fragrance of the lemon trees; then, at night, alone on the terrace of a villa, your fingers intertwined, you gaze at the stars and make plans. It seemed to her that certain places on earth must produce happiness, like a plant that was peculiar to that soil and grew poorly in any other spot. If only she could have leaned her elbows on the balcony of a Swiss chalet or locked away her sadness in a cottage in Scotland, with a husband dressed in a long-skirted black velvet coat, soft boots, a pointed hat, and ruffles at his wrist!

Perhaps she would have liked to confide in someone about all these things. But how does one express an uneasiness so intangible, one that changes shape like a cloud, that changes direction like the wind? She lacked the words, the occasion, the courage.

If Charles had wished it, however, if he had suspected it, if his gaze, just once, had read her thoughts, it seemed to her that her heart would have been relieved of its fullness as quickly as the ripe fruit falls from an espaliered tree at the touch of a hand. But while the intimacy of their life grew ever closer, an inner detachment formed, which loosened her ties to him.

Charles's conversation was as flat as a sidewalk, and everyone's ideas walked along it in their ordinary clothes, without inspiring emotion, or laughter, or reverie. He had never been interested, he said, when he lived in Rouen, in going to the theater to see the actors from Paris. He did not know how to swim, or fence, or fire a pistol, and he was not able to explain to her, one day, a riding term she had encountered in a novel.

But shouldn't a man know everything, excel at a host of different activities, initiate you into the intensities of passion, the refinements of life, all its mysteries? Yet this man taught her nothing, knew nothing, wished for nothing. He thought she was happy; and she resented him for that settled calm, that ponderous serenity, that very happiness which she herself brought him.

She would draw, sometimes; and Charles found it most entertaining to stand there and watch her bending over her pad, half closing her eyes to see her work better, or forming pellets of bread crumbs on her thumb. As for the piano, the faster her fingers raced, the more he marveled. She would strike the keys with assurance and run down the entire keyboard from top to bottom without stopping. When it was thus assaulted by her, the old instrument, with its buzzing strings, could be heard as far as the edge of the village if the window was open, and often the bailiff's clerk, who was passing on the main road, bareheaded and in slippers, would stop to listen, holding his piece of paper in his hand.

Moreover, Emma knew how to manage her household. She would send the patients the statements for their consultations in well-phrased letters that did not sound like invoices. When, on a Sunday, they had some neighbor to dinner, she would contrive to present a stylish dish, understood how to build a pyramid of greengages on some vine leaves, would serve little pots of preserves turned out on plates, and she even talked about buying mouth-rinsing bowls for the dessert course. All of this reflected a good deal of credit on Bovary.

Charles came to respect himself more because he possessed such a wife. In the parlor, he would proudly show off two small sketches of hers, done in graphite, which he had had framed in very wide frames and hung against the wallpaper with long green cords. Coming out of Mass, one would see him standing on his doorstep wearing a fine pair of carpet slippers.

He would return home late, at ten o'clock, sometimes midnight. Then he would ask for something to eat, and since the maid had gone to bed, it was Emma who would serve him. He would take off his frock coat in order to dine more comfortably. He would tell her one by one all the people he had met, the villages where he had been, the prescriptions he had written, and, satisfied with himself, he would eat the remains of the beef hash with onions, cut the rind off his cheese, munch an apple, empty his carafe, then go off to bed, sleep on his back, and snore.

Since he had long been used to wearing a nightcap, his scarf would not stay on his ears; thus his hair, in the morning, lay tousled over his face and whitened by the down from his pillow, whose strings would come undone during the night. He always wore stout boots, which had at the instep two thick creases slanting up toward the ankles, while the rest of the upper continued in a straight line, stretched as though by a foot made out of wood. He would say *they were plenty good enough for the country.*

His mother approved of this thriftiness—for she would come to see him as she had in the past, whenever there had been some particularly violent squall in her own household; and yet the elder Madame Bovary seemed prejudiced against her daughter-in-law. She felt that her *style was too lofty for their station in life;* wood, sugar, and candles *vanished as fast as in a grand house,* and the amount of charcoal consumed in the kitchen was enough to do the cooking for twenty-five! She tidied her linen in the cupboards and taught her to watch the butcher when he brought the meat. Emma accepted these lessons; Madame Bovary lavished them; and the words "my daughter" and "my mother" were exchanged all day long, accompanied by a little quiver of the lips, each woman uttering gentle speeches in a voice trembling with rage.

In Madame Dubuc's day, the old woman had felt that she was still the favorite; but now Charles's love for Emma seemed to her a desertion of her own affection, an encroachment on what belonged to her; and she observed her son's happiness in sad silence, like a ruined man gazing in through a window at people sitting around the dinner table in a house that had once been his own. In the guise of remembering times past, she would remind him of her struggles and sacrifices and, comparing them to Emma's negligence, would conclude that it was not reasonable to adore her so exclusively.

Charles did not know what to answer; he respected his mother, and he loved his wife infinitely; he considered the judgment of the one to be infallible, and yet he found the other irreproachable. When Madame Bovary had gone, he would try to venture timidly, and in the same terms, one or two of the mildest observations he had heard his mama make; Emma, proving to him with one word that he was mistaken, would send him back to his patients.

Meanwhile, acting upon theories that she believed to be sound, she kept trying to experience love. By moonlight, in the garden, she would recite all the passionate rhymes she knew by heart and would sing melancholy songs to him, with a sigh; but she would find that she was as calm afterward as she had been before, and Charles seemed neither more loving nor more deeply moved.

When in this way she had made some attempt to strike the tinder against her heart without causing a single spark to fly from it, incapable, in any case, of understanding something she was not experiencing herself, just as she was incapable of believing in anything that did not manifest itself in a conventional form, she easily persuaded herself that Charles's passion was no longer extraordinary. His effusions by now followed a pattern; he would embrace her at set times. This was a habit among his other habits, like a dessert course foreseen in advance, after the monotony of dinner.

A gamekeeper, cured by Monsieur of a congestion of the lungs, had given Madame a little Italian greyhound; she would take it on her walks, for she did sometimes go out so as to be alone for a little while and not have to look at the eternal garden and the dusty road.

She would go as far as the beech grove at Banneville, near the abandoned pavilion that forms one corner of the wall next to the fields. In the broad barrier ditch there, among the grasses, grow tall reeds with sharp-edged blades.

She would begin by looking all around to see if anything had changed since the last time she had come. She would rediscover, in the same places, the foxgloves and the wallflowers, the clumps of nettles surrounding the large rocks, and the patches of lichen along the three windows, whose shutters, always closed, were crumbling with rot on their rusty iron bars. Her thoughts, at first aimless, would wander at random, like her greyhound, who would circle through the fields yipping after the yellow butterflies, chasing the shrews, or nibbling the red poppies at the edge of a stand of wheat. Then her ideas would gradually settle, and, sitting on the grassy turf, digging into it with little thrusts of the tip of her parasol, Emma would ask herself again and again:

"Oh, dear God! Why did I ever marry?"

She would wonder whether there hadn't been some way, through other chance combinations, of meeting a different man; and she would try to imagine those events that had not taken place, that different life, that husband whom she did not know. All of them, in fact, were unlike this one. He could have been handsome, witty, distinguished, attractive, as were those, no doubt, whom her old schoolmates from the convent had married. What were they doing now? In the city, amid the din of the streets, the buzz of the theaters, and the lights of the ballrooms, they were leading lives in which the heart expands, the senses blossom. But her own life was as cold as an attic with a north-facing window, and boredom, that silent spider, was spinning its web in the darkness in every corner of her heart. She would remember the days when the prizes were given out, when she would step up onto the stage to go collect her little wreaths. With her hair in a braid, her white dress and her prunella-cloth shoes showing beneath, she looked charming, and as she returned to her seat, gentlemen would lean over to pay her compliments; the courtyard was filled with barouches, people were saying goodbye to her from the carriage doors, the music teacher bowed to her as he walked past with his violin case. How far away it all was! How far away!

She would call Djali, take her between her knees, run her fingers over her long, delicate head, and say to her:

"Come, give your mistress a kiss; you, at least, have no troubles."

Then, contemplating the melancholy expression of the slender animal as it yawned slowly, she would be moved and, comparing her to herself, would talk to her aloud as though comforting some afflicted soul.

Sometimes, sudden squalls would blow up, winds that rolled in from the sea over the entire plateau of the Caux region, carrying a salty freshness far into the fields. The rushes would whistle close to the ground, and the leaves of the beeches would rustle, shivering rapidly, while the tops of the trees, still swaying, continued their loud murmur. Emma would pull her shawl tight around her shoulders and stand up.

In the avenue, a green light dimmed by the leaves shone on the smooth moss that crackled softly under her feet. The sun was setting; the sky was red between the branches, and the trunks of the trees, all the same, planted in a straight line, looked like a brown colonnade standing out against a background of gold; a sudden fear would come over her, she would call Djali, hurry back to Tostes by the main road, sink down into an armchair, and all evening long she would remain silent.

But toward the end of September, something extraordinary occurred in her life: she was invited to La Vaubyessard, the home of the Marquis d'Andervilliers.

Secretary of State during the Restoration, the Marquis, seeking to reenter political life, had long been preparing for his candidacy for the Chamber of Deputies. In winter, he would make generous distributions of firewood, and, at departmental council meetings, he was always eloquent in demanding better roads for his district. He had had, during the very hot weather, an abscess in his mouth, of which Charles had relieved him as though miraculously, by giving it just the right nick of his lancet. The steward, sent to Tostes to pay for the operation, reported, that evening, that he had seen some superb cherries in the doctor's little garden. Now, the cherry trees at La Vaubyessard were not doing well, Monsieur the Marquis asked Bovary for some cuttings, took it upon himself to thank him for them in person, noticed Emma, thought that she had a pretty figure and that she did not greet him like a peasant; and so at the château they did not believe they were going beyond the bounds of condescension nor, on the other hand, making a blunder, by inviting the young couple.

One Wednesday, at three o'clock, Monsieur and Madame Bovary, seated in their *boc*, left for La Vaubyessard, with a large trunk fastened on behind and a hatbox positioned in front of the apron. Charles had, in addition, a cardboard box between his legs.

They arrived at nightfall, as the lamps in the park were being lit to guide the carriages.

[8]

The château, modern in its construction, Italian in style, with two projecting wings and three flights of steps in front, stretched across the far end of an immense lawn on which a few cows were grazing among widely spaced clumps of tall trees, while little rounded bouquets of shrubs, rhododendrons, mock oranges, and snowballs lifted their tufts of green at unequal heights along the curved line of the sandy drive. A stream ran under a bridge; through the mist one could make out buildings with thatched roofs scattered over the meadow, which was bordered by two gently sloping wooded hillsides, and, in the back, in two parallel lines among the groves of trees, stood the coach houses and stables, remains of the old château that had been pulled down.

Charles's *boc* stopped in front of the center flight of steps; servants appeared; the Marquis came forward and, offering his arm to the doctor's wife, led her into the entrance hall.

It was very lofty, paved with marble flagstones, and the sounds of footsteps and voices echoed through it as in a church. Opposite rose a straight staircase, and to the left a gallery that looked out on the garden led to the billiards room, from which one could hear, at the door, the caroming of the ivory balls. As she was passing through it on her way to the drawing room, Emma saw men with serious faces standing around the game, their chins resting on their high cravats, all of them decorated, smiling silently as they made their shots. Against the dark woodwork of the wainscoting, large gilded frames bore, along their lower edges, names written in black letters. She read: "Jean-Antoine d'Andervilliers d'Yverbonville, Comte de La Vaubyessard and Baron de La Fresnaye, killed at the Battle of Coutras, October 20, 1587." And on another: "Jean-Antoine-Henry-Guy d'Andervilliers de La Vaubyessard, Admiral of France and Knight of the Order of Saint Michael, wounded in combat at La Hougue-Saint-Vaast, May 29, 1692, died at La Vaubyessard, January 23, 1693." Then one could barely make out those that came after, because the light from the lamps, directed down onto the green cloth of the billiards table, left the room floating in shadow. Burnishing the horizontal canvases, it broke over them in fine crests, following the cracks in the varnish; and from all those great black squares bordered in gold there would emerge, here and there, some lighter part of the paint, a pale forehead, a pair of eyes looking at you, wigs uncoiling over the powdery shoulders of red coats, or the buckle of a garter high up on a plump calf.

The Marquis opened the door of the drawing room; one of the ladies stood up (the Marquise herself), came forward to meet Emma, and asked her to sit down next to her, on a love seat, where she began talking to her in a friendly way, as if she had known her for a long time. She was a woman of about forty, with lovely shoulders, an aquiline nose, a drawling voice, who was wearing, that evening, on her chestnut hair, a simple lace fichu that hung down behind in a triangle. A fair-haired young person was sitting beside her, in a tall-backed chair; and some gentlemen, each of whom had a little flower in his jacket buttonhole, were chatting with the ladies all around the fireplace.

At seven o'clock, dinner was served. The men, who were more numerous, sat at the first table, in the entrance hall, and the ladies at the second, in the dining room, with the Marquis and the Marquise.

As she went in, Emma felt enveloped in warm air, a mingling of the scents of the flowers and fine linen, the savor of the meats and the smell of the truffles. The candles in the candelabras cast long flames over the silver dish covers; the facets of the crystal glasses, covered in a dull mist, reflected a pale glimmer from one to the other; clusters of flowers stood in a line down the whole length of the table; and on the broad-rimmed plates, napkins folded in the shape of bishops' mitres each held, in the opening between its two folds, a small oval roll. The red claws of the lobsters overhung the edges of the platters; large fruits were piled on moss in openwork baskets; the quails wore their feathers; coils of steam rose into the air; and, grave as a judge in his silk stockings, knee breeches, white tie, and jabot, the butler conveyed the platters, already carved, between the shoulders of the guests and with a flick of his spoon would cause the piece one had chosen to leap forth. On the tall porcelain stove with its copper bands, a statue of a woman draped to the chin stared motionless at the room full of people.

Madame Bovary noticed that several of the ladies had not put their gloves in their glasses.

Meanwhile, at the head of the table, alone among all these women, bent over his full plate, his napkin knotted behind him like a child, an old man sat eating, drops of sauce falling from his mouth. His eyes were rimmed with red, and he wore his hair in a short pigtail wound in black ribbon. This was the Marquis's father-in-law, the old Duc de Laverdière, once a favorite of the Comte d'Artois, in the days of the hunting parties at Le Vaudreuil, home of the Marquis de Conflans, and he had been, they said, the lover of Queen Marie Antoinette, between Monsieur de Coigny and Monsieur de Lauzun. He had led a riotous life of debauchery, filled with duels, wagers, abductions of women, he had devoured his fortune and alarmed all his family. A servant, behind his chair, named loudly in his ear the dishes he pointed at with his finger, stammering; and Emma's eyes returned again and again of their own accord to this old man with his pendulous lips, as to something extraordinary and august. He had lived at Court and slept in the beds of queens!

Iced Champagne was poured. Emma shivered over every inch of her skin as she felt that cold in her mouth. She had never seen pomegranates or eaten pineapple. Even the powdered sugar seemed to her whiter and finer than elsewhere.

Afterward the ladies went up to their rooms to get ready for the ball.

Emma prepared herself with the meticulous care of an actress at her debut. She arranged her hair as the hairdresser had advised, and slipped into her barege gown, laid out on the bed. Charles's pants were tight around his stomach.

"My foot straps are going to bother me when I dance."

"Dance?" repeated Emma.

"Yes!"

"You're out of your mind! They'd make fun of you. Stay in your seat. Besides, it's more suitable for a doctor," she added.

Charles said nothing more. He was walking back and forth, waiting for Emma to finish dressing.

He saw her from behind in the mirror, between two candles. Her dark eyes seemed darker. Her bands of hair, gently swelling out over her ears, shone with a blue luster; a rose in her chignon trembled on its pliant stem, with artificial drops of water at the tips of its leaves. Her dress was pale saffron, set off by three sprays of pompon roses mingled with greenery.

Charles came to kiss her on the shoulder.

"Leave me alone!" she said. "You're rumpling me."

One could hear a violin ritornello and the sounds of a horn. She went down the stairs, resisting an impulse to run.

The quadrilles had begun. People were arriving. They were pushing one another. She positioned herself near the door, on a bench.

When the contra dance was over, the floor was left free for the men who stood around chatting in groups and the liveried servants carrying large trays. Along the line of seated women, painted fans were fluttering, bouquets half concealed smiling faces, and little gold-stoppered bottles twirled in half-open hands whose white gloves showed the outlines of their nails and hugged their flesh at the wrist. Lace trimmings, diamond brooches, medallion bracelets trembled on bodices, sparkled on chests, clinked on bare arms. Hair well pressed down over the forehead and twisted at the nape bore garlands, bunches, or sprays of myosotis, jasmine, pomegranate blossoms, wheatears, or cornflowers. Red-turbaned mothers scowled serenely in their seats.

Emma's heart beat a little faster when, her partner holding her by the tips of her fingers, she took her place in line and waited for the stroke of the bow to start them off. But her anxiety soon vanished and swaying to the rhythm of the orchestra, she glided forward with gentle motions of her neck. A smile would rise to her lips at certain subtleties from the violin, which sometimes played alone when the other instruments were silent; one could hear the bright sound of gold louis being flung down on the cloth surfaces of the tables in the next room; then everything would start up again at the same time, the cornet would send forth a resonant note, feet would tread rhythmically again, skirts balloon out and brush the floor, hands join together, part; and the same eyes that had lowered before you one moment would come back to stare into your own.

A few of the men (perhaps fifteen) between the ages of twenty-five and forty, scattered among the dancers or chatting in doorways, were distinguished from the rest of the crowd by a family resemblance, despite their differences in age, dress, or feature.

Their coats, better cut, seemed made of suppler cloth, and their hair, brought forward in curls at their temples, glazed by finer pomades. They had the complexion of wealth, that white skin which is set off by the pallor of porcelain, the shimmer of satin, the finish of handsome furniture, and which is maintained in its health by a prudent regimen of exquisite foods. Their necks turned comfortably in low cravats; their long side-whiskers rested upon downturned collars; they wiped their lips on handkerchiefs embroidered with large monograms and redolent of a pleasing scent. Those who were beginning to age had a youthful look, while a touch of maturity overlay the faces of the younger. In their indifferent gazes floated the tranquillity of passions daily gratified; and beneath their gentle manners was visible that particular brutality imparted by domination in rather easy things, in which one's strength is exerted and one's vanity tickled, the handling of thoroughbred horses and the company of fallen women.

A few steps from Emma, a gentleman in a blue coat was deep into Italy with a pale young woman in pearls. They were marveling over the size of the pillars in Saint Peter's, over Tivoli, Vesuvius, Castellammare, and the Cascine, the roses of Genoa, the Colosseum by moonlight. Emma was listening with her other ear to a conversation full of words she did not understand. People were gathered around a very young man who, the week before, had beaten Miss Arabella and Romulus and won two thousand louis by jumping a ditch in England. One man was complaining about his racers getting fat; another, that printing mistakes had garbled the name of his horse.

The air in the ballroom was heavy; the lamps were growing dim. People were drifting back into the billiards room. A servant climbing up onto a chair broke two windowpanes; at the noise of the shattered glass, Madame Bovary turned her head and noticed in the garden, against the window, the faces of countrypeople looking in. Then the memory of Les Bertaux returned to her. She saw the farm again, the muddy pond, her father in a smock under the apple trees, and she saw herself as she used to be, skimming cream with her finger from the pans of milk in the milk house. But under the dazzling splendors of the present hour, her past life, so distinct until now, was vanishing altogether, and she almost doubted that she had ever lived it. She was here; and then, surrounding the ball, there was nothing left but darkness, spread out over all the rest. She was at that moment eating a maraschino ice, holding it with her left hand in a silver-gilt shell and half closing her eyes, the spoon between her teeth.

Near her, a lady dropped her fan. A dancer was passing.

"I wonder if you would be so kind, sir," said the lady, "as to pick up my fan for me. It's here behind the couch!"

The gentleman bowed, and as he was extending his arm, Emma saw the hand of the young lady toss something white, folded in a triangle, into his hat. The gentleman, retrieving the fan, gave it to the lady respectfully; she inclined her head in thanks and inhaled her bouquet.

After supper, at which there were many Spanish wines and Rhine wines, soups made of shellfish and soups made of almond milk, Trafalgar puddings and all sorts of cold meats with jellies around them that quivered in the platters, the carriages, one after another, began to leave. By drawing aside a corner of the muslin curtain, one could see the glow of their lamps slipping away into the darkness. The benches cleared; a few card players still remained; the musicians cooled the tips of their fingers on their tongues; Charles was half asleep, his back resting against a door.

At three o'clock in the morning, the cotillion began. Emma did not know how to waltz. Everyone was waltzing, even Mademoiselle d'Andervilliers, and the marquise; no one was left but the guests of the château, a dozen people or so.

Nevertheless, one of the waltzers, whom they familiarly called *vicomte* and whose very low-cut vest seemed molded to his chest, came up to Madame Bovary and for the second time invited her to dance, assuring her that he would guide her and that she would manage perfectly well.

They began slowly, then went faster. They were turning: everything was turning around them, the lamps, the furniture, the paneled walls, the parquet floor, like a disk on a spindle. As they passed close to the doors, the hem of Emma's dress would catch against his pants; their legs would slip in between one another; he lowered his gaze to her, she raised hers to him; a numbness came over her, she stopped. They set off again; and with a quicker motion, the vicomte, drawing her along, disappeared with her to the far end of the gallery, where, breathing hard, she nearly fell and, for a moment, leaned her head on his chest. And then, still whirling, but more gently, he returned her to her seat; she leaned back against the wall and put her hand over her eyes.

When she opened them, a lady was sitting on a stool in the middle of the drawing room with three waltzers on their knees in front of her. She chose the vicomte, and the violin began again.

People were looking at them. They would pass by and then return, she holding her body motionless and her chin lowered, and he in the same posture as before, his back arched, his elbow rounded, his mouth forward. That woman certainly could waltz! They went on for a long time and wore out everyone else.

People chatted for another few minutes, and after the goodbyes, or rather the good-mornings, the guests of the château went to bed.

Charles was dragging himself up by the banister, his knees *were giving way under him.* He had spent five straight hours standing by the tables, watching them play whist without understanding anything about it. And so he gave a great sigh of contentment after pulling off his boots.

Emma put a shawl over her shoulders, opened the window, and leaned on her elbows.

The night was dark. A few drops of rain were falling. She breathed in the damp wind, which cooled her eyelids. The music of the dance was still humming in her ears, and she made an effort to stay awake in order to prolong the illusion of this luxurious life that she would soon have to leave behind.

The first light of dawn appeared. She looked at the windows of the château for a long time, trying to guess which were the rooms of all those people she had observed the night before. She would have liked to know what their lives were like, to enter into them, to become part of them.

But she was shaking with cold. She undressed and curled up between the sheets against Charles, who was asleep.

There were many people at breakfast. The meal lasted ten minutes; no liquor was served, which surprised the doctor. Then Mademoiselle d'Andervilliers collected some pieces of brioche in a little basket, to carry to the swans on the ornamental pond, and they went off to stroll through the greenhouse, where strange plants bristling with hairs rose in pyramidal tiers under hanging vases, which, like overcrowded nests of serpents, let fall from their rims long interlaced ropes of green. The orangery, which lay at the far end, led, under cover, to the outbuildings of the château. The Marquis, to entertain the young woman, took her to see the stables. Above the basket-shaped racks, porcelain plaques bore in black the names of the horses. Each animal moved restlessly in its stall when they passed near it clucking their tongues. The floor of the saddle room gleamed to the eye like a drawing-room parquet. The carriage harness rose in the middle on two revolving posts, and the bits, whips, stirrups, curb chains were arranged in a line all the way down the wall.

Charles, meanwhile, went to ask a servant to harness his *boc*. It was brought out in front of the steps, and after all the bundles had been stowed away in it, the Bovary couple said their thank-yous to the Marquis and Marquise and started back to Tostes.

Emma, silent, was watching the wheels turn. Charles, poised on the very edge of the seat, was driving with his arms apart, and the little horse was going along at an ambling trot between the shafts, which were too wide for it. The slack reins slapped against its rump, soaking up the foam, and the box tied on behind struck the body of the carriage with loud, regular thumps.

They were on the heights of Thibourville when before them, suddenly, several horsemen rode past laughing, cigars in their mouths. Emma thought she recognized the vicomte: she turned around and saw on the horizon only the motion of their heads dipping and rising, with the unequal cadence of the trot or gallop.

A quarter of a league farther on, they had to stop and mend the breeching, which had broken, with some rope.

But Charles, giving the harness one last glance, saw something on the ground, between the legs of his horse; and he picked up a cigar case with a green silk border all around it and a coat of arms in its center like a carriage door.

"There are even two cigars in it," he said; "that'll be for tonight after dinner."

"So you smoke?" she asked.

"Sometimes, when I get the chance."

He put his find in his pocket and whipped up the pony.

When they reached home, dinner was far from ready. Madame flew into a rage. Nastasie answered rudely.

"Get out!" said Emma. "What impertinence. I'm discharging you."

For dinner there was onion soup, and a piece of veal with sorrel. Charles, sitting opposite Emma, said, rubbing his hands together happily:

"How nice it is to be back home!"

They could hear Nastasie weeping. He was rather fond of the poor girl. She had kept him company on many an idle evening, in earlier days, when he was a widower. She was his first patient, his oldest acquaintance in the area.

"Have you really let her go?" he said at last.

"Yes. What's to stop me?" she answered.

Then they warmed themselves in the kitchen while their bedroom was being prepared. Charles began smoking. He smoked with his lips thrust forward, spitting constantly, recoiling at each puff.

"You'll make yourself ill," she said scornfully.

He put down his cigar and ran to the pump to swallow a glass of cold water. Emma, seizing the cigar case, flung it quickly to the back of the cupboard.

How long the next day was! She walked in her little garden, going and coming along the same paths, stopping in front of the flower beds, the espaliered tree, the plaster curé, contemplating with amazement all these things from the past that she knew so well. How distant the ball already seemed to her! What was it that put such a distance between the morning of the day before yesterday and the evening of this day? Her trip to La Vaubyessard had made a hole in her life, like those great chasms that a storm, in a single night, will sometimes open in the mountains. Yet she resigned herself: reverently she put away in the chest of drawers her beautiful dress and even her satin shoes, whose soles had been yellowed by the slippery wax of the dance floor. Her heart was like them: contact with wealth had laid something over it that would not be wiped away.

And so remembering that ball became an occupation for Emma. Each time Wednesday returned, she would say to herself as she woke: "Ah! A week ago . . . two weeks ago . . . three weeks ago, I was there!" And little by little, the faces became confused in her memory, she forgot the tunes of the contra dances, she no longer saw the liveries and the rooms as distinctly; some of the details vanished, but her longing remained.

[9]

Often, when Charles was out, she would go to the cupboard and take the green silk cigar case from between the folds of the linen, where she had left it.

She would look at it, open it, and even sniff the fragrance of its lining, a mingling of verbena and tobacco. Who did it belong to? . . . The vicomte. Perhaps it was a gift from his mistress. It had been embroidered on some rosewood frame, a dainty little implement kept hidden from all other eyes, the occupation of many hours, and over it had hung the soft curls of the pensive worker. A breath of love had passed among the stitches of the canvas; each stroke of the needle had fastened into it a hope or a memory, and all those interlaced threads of silk were merely an extension of the same silent passion. And then, one morning, the *vicomte* had taken it away with him. What had people talked about, as it lay on one of those broad mantelpieces, between the vases of flowers and the Pompadour clocks? She was at Tostes. And he—he was in Paris, now; out there! What was it like—Paris? The name itself was so vast! She would repeat it to herself softly, to give herself pleasure; it would resound in her ears like the great bell of a cathedral; it would blaze before her eyes even on the labels of her jars of pomade.

At night, when the fishmongers, in their carts, passed under her windows singing the "Marjolaine," she would wake up; and as she listened to the noise of the iron-rimmed wheels, which, when they reached the edge of town, would quickly be deadened by the earth:

"They'll be there tomorrow!" she would say to herself.

And she would follow them in her thoughts as they climbed and descended the hills, passed through the villages, filed along the highway by the light of the stars. After an indeterminate distance, there was always a confused place where her dream died away.

She bought herself a map of Paris, and, with the tip of her finger on the map, she would take walks in the capital. She would go along the boulevards, stopping at each corner, between the lines of the streets, in front of the white squares that represented the houses. Her eyes tired at last, she would close her lids, and in the darkness she would see gas jets twisting in the wind, and carriage steps unfolding with a clatter before the theater colonnades.

She took out a subscription to *Corbeille,* a women's magazine, and to *Le Sylphe des Salons.* Skipping nothing, she would devour all the reports of first nights, horse races, and soirées, would take an interest in a singer's debut, the opening of a shop. She knew the latest fashions, the addresses of the good tailors, the days for going to the Bois and the Opéra. In Eugène

Sue, she studied descriptions of furnishings; she read Balzac and George Sand, seeking in them the imagined satisfaction of her own desires. She would bring her book with her even to the table, and she would turn the pages while Charles ate and talked to her. The memory of the Vicomte would always return to her as she read. She would find similarities between him and the invented characters. But the circle of which he was the center gradually grew larger around him, and the halo he wore, separating from his face, spread farther out, illuminating other dreams.

And so Paris, vaster than the Ocean, glimmered before Emma's eyes in a rosy haze. But the teeming life of that tumultuous place was divided into separate parts, sorted into distinct tableaux. Emma saw only two or three, which concealed the rest from her and themselves alone represented all of humanity. The world of ambassadors walked over gleaming parquet floors, through drawing rooms lined with mirrors, around oval tables covered with velvet cloths fringed with gold. Here were trailing gowns, high mysteries, anguish concealed behind a smile. Next came the society of duchesses: here, one was pale; one rose at four o'clock; the women, poor angels! wore Brussels lace at the hems of their petticoats, and the men, their abilities unappreciated beneath their frivolous exteriors, rode their horses to death for the enjoyment of it, went to spend the summer season at Baden, and eventually, at about forty years of age, married heiresses. In the private rooms of restaurants, where one has supper after midnight, the motley crowd of literary folk and actresses would laugh by candlelight. They were as prodigal as kings, full of idealistic ambitions and delirious fantasies. Theirs was a life elevated above others, between heaven and earth, among the storm clouds, something sublime. As for the rest of the world, it was lost, without any exact place, as though it did not exist. The closer things were to her, anyway, the more her thoughts shrank from them. Everything that immediately surrounded her—the tiresome countryside, the idiotic petits bourgeois, the mediocrity of life—seemed to her an exception in the world, a particular happenstance in which she was caught, while beyond, as far as the eye could see, extended the immense land of felicity and passion. In her desire, she confused the sensual pleasures of luxury with the joys of the heart, elegance of manner with delicacy of feeling. Didn't love, like a plant from India, require a prepared soil, a particular temperature? Sighs in the moonlight, long embraces, tears flowing over hands yielded to a lover, all the fevers of the flesh and the languors of tenderness thus could not be separated from the balconies of great châteaux filled with idle amusements, a boudoir with silk blinds, a good thick carpet, full pots of flowers, and a bed raised on a dais, nor from the sparkle of precious stones and shoulder knots on servants' livery.

The boy from the relay post, who came to groom the mare each morning, would cross the hallway in his thick sabots; his smock had holes in it; his feet, in his slippers, were bare. This was the groom in knee breeches with whom she had to be content! When his task was finished, he would not return that day; for Charles, when he came home, would lead his horse into the stable himself, take off the saddle, and put on the halter, while the maid would bring a truss of straw and heave it, as best she could, into the manger.

To replace Nastasie (who finally left Tostes, shedding streams of tears), Emma took into her service a girl of fourteen, an orphan with a sweet face. She forbade her to wear cotton caps, taught her she must address one in the third person, bring a glass of water on a plate, knock on doors before entering, and showed her how to iron, starch, dress her, attempting to turn her into her own lady's maid. The new servant obeyed without a murmur so as not to be dismissed; and since Madame usually left the key in the sideboard, every evening Félicité would help herself to a small supply of sugar and eat it alone, in bed, after saying her prayers.

In the afternoon, sometimes, she would cross the street to go talk to the postilions. Madame would stay upstairs in her room.

She would wear a wide-open dressing gown that revealed, between the shawl collars of the bodice, a pleated shift with three gold buttons. Her belt was a cord with heavy tassels, and her little garnet-colored slippers bore a cluster of broad ribbons that fell over the instep. She had bought herself a blotter, stationery, a pen holder, and envelopes, although she had no one to write to; she would dust her shelves, look at herself in the mirror, pick up a book, then, dreaming between the lines, let it fall on her knees. She longed to travel or to return to her convent. She wanted both to die and to live in Paris.

Charles would ride his horse through snow, through rain, along the little byways. He ate omelets at farmhouse tables, thrust his arm into damp beds, received the warm spurts of blood from bloodlettings in his face, listened to death rattles, examined basins, folded back plenty of dirty underclothes; but every evening, he would return to a blazing fire, a set table, a soft chair, and a woman dressed with elegance, charming, and smelling so fresh that one did not even know where the fragrance came from, or if it was not her skin perfuming her shift.

She would delight him with countless niceties; it was sometimes a new way of fashioning paper sconces for the candles, a flounce she would change on her dress, or the extraordinary name for a perfectly simple dish that the servant had spoiled, but every last bit of which Charles would swallow with pleasure. In Rouen she saw some ladies wearing clusters of charms on their watches; she bought some watch charms. She wanted two large vases of blue glass on her mantelpiece and, sometime after, an ivory sewing box, with a silver-gilt thimble. The less Charles understood these refinements, the more captivating he found them. They added something to the pleasure of his senses and to the sweetness of his home. They were like gold dust sprinkled all along the little path of his life.

He was healthy, he looked well; his reputation was firmly established. The countrypeople loved him dearly because he was not proud. He patted the children, never went into taverns, and, on top of that, inspired confidence by his morality. He was particularly successful with catarrhs and ailments of the chest. Very fearful of killing his patients, Charles, in fact, scarcely prescribed anything but sedative potions, from time to time an emetic, a footbath, or leeches. Not that surgery frightened him; he would bleed people heavily, like horses, and when it came to extracting teeth, he had a *fist of iron.*

Finally, *in order to keep up to date,* he took out a subscription to *La Ruche Médicale,* a new journal whose prospectus he had received. He would read a little of it after dinner, but the warmth of the room, in combination with his digestion, would put him to sleep after five minutes; and he would stay there, his chin on his hands and his hair spread out like a mane as far as the base of the lamp. Emma would look at him and shrug her shoulders. What if, at least, her husband had been one of those ardent and taciturn men who work at night over their books, and at last, at sixty, when rheumatism sets in, wear a row of decorations on their black, ill-made coats? She would have liked the name Bovary, which was hers, to be famous, she would have liked to see it displayed in bookstores, repeated in newspapers, known to all of France. But Charles had no ambition! A doctor from Yvetot, with whom he had recently found himself in consultation, had humiliated him at the very bedside of the patient, in front of the assembled relatives. When Charles told her the story, that evening, Emma flew into a rage against his colleague. Charles was moved. He kissed her on the forehead with a tear. But she was fuming with shame; she wanted to strike him, she went into the hallway to open the window, and breathed in the cool air to calm herself.

"What a pathetic man! What a pathetic man!" she said softly, biting her lips.

She was feeling more irritated by him anyway. With age, he was developing coarse habits; at dessert, he would cut up the corks of the empty bottles; after eating, he would run his tongue over his teeth; when swallowing his soup, he would make a gurgling sound with each mouthful; and because he was beginning to grow stout, his eyes, already small, seemed to have been pushed up toward his temples by the swelling of his cheeks.

Emma would sometimes tuck the red edge of his sweater back inside his vest, straighten his cravat, or toss aside the faded gloves he was preparing to put on; and this was not, as he thought, for his sake; it was for herself, in an expansion of egotism, a nervous vexation. Sometimes, too, she would talk to him about the things she had read, such as a passage from a novel, a new play, or the *high society* anecdote being recounted in the paper; for, after all, Charles was someone, always an open ear, always a ready approbation. She confided many secrets to her greyhound! She would have done the same to the logs in the fireplace and the pendulum of the clock.

Deep in her soul, however, she was waiting for something to happen. Like a sailor in distress, she would gaze out over the solitude of her life with desperate eyes, seeking some white sail in the mists of the far-off horizon. She did not know what this chance event would be, what wind would drive it to her, what shore it would carry her to, whether it was a longboat or a three-decked vessel, loaded with anguish or filled with happiness up to the portholes. But each morning, when she awoke, she hoped it would arrive that day, and she would listen to every sound, spring to her feet, feel surprised that it did not come; then, at sunset, always more sorrowful, she would wish the next day were already there.

Spring returned. She had fits of breathlessness with the arrival of the first warm days, when the pear trees flowered.

From early in July, she began to count on her fingers how many weeks remained to her before October, thinking the Marquis d'Andervilliers would perhaps give another ball at La Vaubyessard. But all of September went by without letters or visitors.

After the weariness of this disappointment, her heart remained empty, and then the succession of identical days began again.

So now they were going to continue one after another like this, always the same, innumerable, bringing nothing! Other people's lives, however dull they were, had at least the possibility that something would happen. A chance occurrence would sometimes lead to an infinite number of sudden shifts, and the setting would change. But for her, nothing happened, God had willed it! The future was a dark corridor, with the door at its end firmly closed.

She gave up music. Why play? Who would hear her? Since she would never be able to play in a concert, in a short-sleeved velvet dress, on an Érard piano, striking the ivory keys with her light fingers and feeling a murmur of ecstasy circulate around her like a breeze, it was not worth the trouble of boring herself with studying. She left her drawing portfolios and her tapestry work in the cupboard. What was the use? What was the use? Sewing irritated her.

"I've read everything," she would say to herself.

And she would hold the tongs in the fire till they turned red, or watch the rain fall.

How sad she was, on Sundays, when they rang vespers! She would listen, with dazed attention, as the cracked chimes of the bell sounded one by one. A cat on the rooftops, walking slowly, would arch its back to the pale rays of the sun. The wind, on the big road, would blow trails of dust. In the distance, now and then, a dog would howl; and the bell, at equal intervals, would continue its monotonous tolling, which vanished into the countryside.

Meanwhile, they were coming out of church. The women in waxed clogs, the farmers in new smocks, the little children skipping about bareheaded in front of them—they would all return home. And until nightfall, five or six men, always the same ones, would stay behind playing cork-penny in front of the main door to the inn.

The winter was cold. The panes, every morning, were thick with frost, and the light, falling dull white through them as if through ground glass, sometimes did not vary all day long. At four o'clock in the afternoon, the lamp had to be lit.

On days when it was nice out, she would go down into the garden. The dew had left a silvery lace on the cabbages, with long bright threads stretching from one to the next. No birds could be heard, everything seemed to be sleeping, the espalier covered with straw and the vine like a great ailing serpent under the coping of the wall, on which, as one went up close, one could see wood lice creeping about on their many legs. Among the spruces, near the hedge, the curé in the three-cornered hat reading his breviary had lost his right foot, and the plaster, flaking off in the frost, had left white scabs on his face.

Then she would go back up, close the door, spread apart the coals, and, faint from the heat of the fire, feel the heavier weight of the boredom that was descending on her again. She would have gone down to chat with the maid, but a certain reticence held her back.

Every day, at the same hour, the schoolmaster, in a black silk cap, would open the shutters of his house, and the village policeman would pass, wearing his sword over his smock. Evenings and mornings, the post-horses, three by three, would cross the street to go drink from the pond. Now and then, the door of a tavern would set its bell tinkling; and when the wind was blowing, one could hear creaking on their two rods the hairdresser's little copper basins, which served as the sign for his shop. For decoration it had an old fashion-plate glued to a windowpane and a wax bust of a woman with yellow hair. The hairdresser, too, lamented the vocation that had never come to pass, his ruined future, and, dreaming of a shop in a large city, such as Rouen, for example, on the harbor, near the theater, he would spend all day walking back and forth from the village hall to the church, gloomily waiting for customers. When Madame Bovary raised her eyes, she would see him always there, like a sentinel on guard duty, in his worsted cloth jacket with his fez over one ear.

In the afternoon, sometimes, a man's head would appear outside the parlor windows, a sunburned head with black side-whiskers, slowly smiling a broad, gentle, white-toothed smile. A waltz would immediately begin, and in a little salon on top of the organ, dancers as tall as one's finger—women in pink turbans, Tyrolean men in cutaways, monkeys in black suits, gentlemen in knee breeches—would circle round and round among the armchairs, sofas, console tables, replicated in fragments of mirror whose corners were joined together by a net of gold paper. The man would turn his crank, looking to the right, to the left, and toward the windows. Now and then, at the same time that he shot a long stream of brown saliva against the guard stone, he would lift the instrument with his knee, for its hard strap tired his shoulder; and the music, sometimes plaintive and droning, sometimes joyful and headlong, would issue from the box buzzing through a curtain of pink taffeta, from behind a grid of brass arabesque. They were tunes that people played elsewhere in theaters, that people sang in salons, that people danced to at night under illuminated chandeliers, echoes of the world coming all the way to Emma. Endless sarabandes unfurled in her head, and, like a dancing girl on a flowered carpet, her thoughts would leap with the notes, sway from dream to dream, from sadness to sadness. When the man had received the alms in his cap, he would pull down an old blue wool cover, shift his organ onto his back, and move off with a heavy step. She would watch him go.

But it was most of all at mealtimes that she could not bear it any longer, in that little room on the ground floor, with the stove that smoked, the door that squeaked, the walls that seeped, the damp flagstones; all the bitterness of life seemed to be served up on her plate, and, with the steam from the boiled meat, there rose from the depths of her soul other gusts of revulsion. Charles took a long time eating; she would nibble a few nuts, or, leaning on her elbow, amuse herself drawing lines on the oilcloth with the tip of her knife.

Now she let everything in the house go, and the elder Madame Bovary, when she came to spend part of Lent at Tostes, was very surprised at the change. Indeed, she, once so neat and refined, would now go whole days without dressing, wear stockings of gray cotton, and use a candle for light. She would repeat that they had to economize, since they were not rich, adding that she was very content, very happy, that she liked Tostes very much, and other novel remarks that closed the mother-in-law's mouth. Moreover, Emma no longer seemed inclined to follow her advice; once, even, when Madame Bovary took it upon herself to maintain that employers ought to oversee their servants' religious life, she had answered her with an eye so angry and a smile so cold that the good woman did not meddle again.

Emma was becoming difficult, capricious. She would order dishes for herself and not touch them, would one day drink only pure milk and, the next, cups of tea by the dozen. Often she would stubbornly refuse to go out, then she would feel stifled, open the windows, put on a thin dress. After she had browbeaten her maid, she would present her with gifts or send her for a stroll to visit the neighbors, just as she would sometimes throw the poor all the silver coins in her purse, though she was scarcely tenderhearted or easily touched by another's emotion, like most people born of countryfolk, whose souls always retain something of the hardness of their fathers' hands.

Toward the end of February, Père Rouault, in memory of his recovery, came in person with a superb turkey for his son-in-law, and he stayed at Tostes for three days. Since Charles was seeing patients, Emma kept him company. He smoked in the bedroom, spat on the andirons, chatted about crops, calves, cows, chickens, and the town council; so that she closed the door behind him, when he left, with a feeling of relief that surprised even her. What was more, she no longer hid her scorn for anything, or anyone; and she would sometimes express singular opinions, condemning what was generally approved, and commending perverse or immoral things: which made her husband stare at her wide-eyed.

Would this misery last forever? Would she never find a way out of it? And yet she was certainly just as good as all those women who lived happy lives! She had seen duchesses at La Vaubyessard with heavier figures and more vulgar manners, and she cursed God's injustice; she would lean her head against the walls and cry; she would think with envy of tumultuous lives, nights at masked balls, outrageous pleasures, and all the wild emotions, unknown to her, that they must inspire.

She grew pale and had palpitations of the heart. Charles administered valerian and camphor baths. Everything he tried seemed to irritate her further.

On certain days, she would chatter with feverish abandon; these states of excitement would be followed suddenly by periods of torpor in which she would stop speaking, stop moving. What would revive her at these times was for her to douse her arms with a bottle of eau de Cologne.

Because she complained constantly about Tostes, Charles imagined that the cause of her illness undoubtedly lay in some local influence, and, fixing on that idea, he thought seriously of setting up his practice elsewhere.

At that, she began drinking vinegar to lose weight, contracted a dry little cough, and completely lost her appetite.

It cost Charles to leave Tostes after four years and at a time *when he was beginning to establish himself.* Still, if it had to be . . . ! He drove her to Rouen to see his old teacher. It was a nervous disease: she should have a change of air.

After looking here and there, Charles learned that in the region of Neufchâtel, there was a sizable market town called Yonville-l'Abbaye, whose doctor, a Polish refugee, had just decamped the week before. And so he wrote to the local pharmacist to find out the size of the population, how far away his closest colleague would be, how much per year his predecessor had earned, and so forth; and, the replies being satisfactory, he resolved to move in the spring, if Emma's health did not improve.

One day while tidying a drawer in anticipation of her departure, she pricked her fingers on something. It was a piece of wire in her wedding bouquet. The orange-blossom buds were yellow with dust, and the satin ribbons, with their silver piping, were fraying at the edges. She threw it into the fire. It flared up more quickly than dry straw. Then it lay like a red bush on the embers, slowly being consumed. She watched it burn. The little cardboard berries burst open, the binding wire twisted, the braid melted; and the shriveled paper petals, hovering along the fireback like black butterflies, at last flew away up the chimney.

When they left Tostes, in March, Madame Bovary was pregnant.

PART II

Yonville-l'Abbaye (so named for an old abbey of Capuchin friars of which even the ruins no longer exist) is a market town eight leagues from Rouen, between the Abbeville and the Beauvais roads, in the bottom of a valley watered by the Rieule, a small river that flows into the Andelle after working three mills near its mouth, and in which there are a few trout that boys like to fish with lines on Sundays.

You leave the highway at La Boissière and continue level as far as the top of Les Leux hill, from which you first discern the valley. The stream that runs through it creates two regions distinct in physiognomy: everything on the left is in pasture, everything on the right is tillage. The grassland extends under a fold of low hills to join at the far end the pastures of the Bray country, while to the east, the plain, rising gently, broadens out and extends its blond wheat fields as far as the eye can see. The water that runs along the edge of the grass divides with its line of white the color of the meadows from the color of the furrows, so that the countryside resembles a great mantle, unfolded, its green velvet collar edged with silver braid.

On the horizon before you, when you arrive, you have the oaks of the Argueil forest and the escarpments of the Saint-Jean hill, streaked from top to bottom by long, irregular trails of red; these are the marks left by the rains, and their brick-red tones, standing out so clearly in slender threads against the gray of the mountain, come from the abundance of ferruginous springs that flow beyond, in the surrounding countryside.

Here you are on the borders of Normandy, Picardy, and Île-de-France, a mongrel region where the language is without expressive emphasis, just as the landscape is without character. It is here that they make the worst Neufchâtel cheeses in the whole district, while farming is costly, because a good deal of manure is needed to enrich this crumbly soil full of sand and stones.

Until 1835, there was no passable road for reaching Yonville; but at about that time they established a *major local route* that connects the Abbeville road to that of Amiens and is sometimes used by carters going from Rouen into Flanders. Nevertheless, Yonville-l'Abbaye has stood still, despite its *new outlets*. Instead of improving the cultivated lands, the people here persist in maintaining the pastures, however depreciated they may be, and the lazy town, moving away from the plain, has continued naturally to grow toward the river. You can see it from far off, stretched out along the bank, like a cowherd taking his nap at the water's edge.

At the foot of the hill, after the bridge, and planted with young aspens, begins a roadway leading you in a straight line to the first houses of the area. They are enclosed within hedges, in the middle of yards full of scattered outbuildings, presses, cart sheds, and distilleries standing here and there under dense trees bearing ladders, poles, or scythes hooked over their branches. The thatched roofs cover the top third or so of the low windows, like fur caps pulled down over eyes, and the thick, bulging panes are garnished with a nub in the middle, like the base of a bottle. Against the plaster wall, which is traversed diagonally by black timbers, there sometimes clings a thin pear tree, and the ground floors have at their door a little swing gate to guard them against the chicks, who come to the doorsill to peck at the crumbs of brown bread soaked in cider. Meanwhile, the yards become narrower, the habitations draw closer together, the hedges disappear; a bundle of ferns dangles below a window at the end of a broom handle; there is a farrier's forge and then a cartwright with two or three new carts outside, jutting into the road. Then through the railings appears a white house beyond a circle of lawn decorated with a Cupid, its finger on its mouth; two cast-iron urns stand at either end of the flight of front steps; brass plates gleam at the door; it is the notary's house, and the handsomest in the region.

The church is on the other side of the street, twenty paces farther on, at the entrance to the square. The little cemetery that surrounds it, enclosed by an elbow-high wall, is so filled with graves that the old stones, flush with the ground, form a continuous pavement on which the grass has drawn regular green rectangles. The church was rebuilt new in the last years of the reign of Charles X. The wooden vault is beginning to rot at the top and has cavities of black, here and there, in its blue. Above the door, where the organ would be, is a gallery for the men, with a spiral staircase that echoes under their wooden shoes.

The daylight, coming in through the plain glass windows, falls obliquely on the pews set at right angles to the wall, on which is nailed here and there a piece of straw matting with these words below it in large letters: "Pew of Monsieur So-and-So." Farther on, at the point where the nave narrows, the confessional stands opposite a small statue of the Virgin wearing a satin gown, coiffed in a tulle veil spangled with silver stars, and colored crimson on the cheeks like an idol from the Sandwich Islands; lastly, a copy of *The Holy Family, presented by the Minister of the Interior,* hanging over the main altar between four candlesticks, closes the perspective at the far end. The choir stalls, of pine, have remained unpainted.

The market, that is, a tile roof supported by about twenty posts, takes up about half of the large Yonville square. The town hall, built *from designs by a Paris architect,* is a sort of Greek temple that forms the corner, next door to the pharmacist's house. It has on the ground floor three Ionic columns and, on the second floor, a semicircular gallery, while the tympanum at its top is occupied by a Gallic cock, resting one foot on the Charter and holding in the other the scales of justice.

But what chiefly strikes the eye, across from the Lion d'Or inn, is the pharmacy belonging to Monsieur Homais! In the evening, particularly, when his lamp is lit and the red and green jars that embellish his shop window cast the glow of their two colors far out over the ground; then, through them, as if through Bengal lights, the shadow of the pharmacist can be seen leaning his elbows on his desk. His house, from top to bottom, is placarded with inscriptions in running script, in round hand, in block capitals: "Vichy, Seltzer, and Barèges Waters, Depurative Syrups, Raspail's Medicine, Arabian Racahout, Darcet's Pastilles, Regnault's Ointment, Bandages, Baths, Medicinal Chocolates, etc." And the shop sign, which occupies the entire width of the shop, bears the gold letters: *Homais, Pharmacist.* Then, at the back of the shop, behind the large scales fastened to the counter, the word *Laboratory* unfurls above a glass door that repeats yet one more time, halfway up, the word *Homais* in gold letters on a black background.

After that, there is nothing more to see in Yonville. The street (the only one), the length of a rifle shot and lined by a few shops, ends abruptly where the road bends. If you leave it on your right and follow the base of Saint-Jean hill, you soon reach the cemetery.

At the time of the cholera outbreak, in order to enlarge it, they knocked down a section of wall and bought three acres of land next to it; but that whole new portion is almost uninhabited, the graves, as before, continuing to pile up near the gate. The caretaker, who is at the same time gravedigger and beadle in the church (thus deriving from the parish corpses a twofold profit), has taken advantage of the empty piece of ground to plant potatoes in it. Year by year, however, his little field shrinks, and when an epidemic occurs, he does not know whether he ought to rejoice at the deaths or lament the graves.

"You're feeding off the dead, Lestiboudois!" the curé said to him at last, one day.

This grim remark made him think; it stopped him for a time; but even today he continues to cultivate his tubers, and even maintains coolly that they come up by themselves.

Since the events that are about to be recounted here, nothing, indeed, has changed in Yonville. The tin tricolored flag still turns on top of the church steeple; the dry-goods shop still waves its two calico streamers in the wind; the pharmacist's fetuses, like bundles of white punk, decay more and more in their cloudy alcohol; and above the main door of the inn, the aged gold lion, faded by the rains, still displays to the passersby its poodle ringlets.

The evening the Bovarys were to arrive in Yonville, the widow Madame Lefrançois, mistress of the inn, was so very busy that she was sweating large drops as she stirred her pots. The following day was market day in the town. The meats had to be cut up in advance, the chickens gutted, soup and coffee prepared. In addition, she had the meal to get for her boarders and for the doctor, his wife, and their maid; the billiards room was echoing with bursts of laughter; three millers, in the small parlor, were calling for eau-de-vie; the wood was blazing, the charcoal was crackling, and on the long kitchen table, among the quarters of raw mutton, stood stacks of plates trembling to the jolts of the block where the spinach was being chopped. From the poultry yard, one could hear the squawking of the chickens as the servant girl chased them down in order to cut their throats.

A man in green leather slippers, his skin slightly pitted by smallpox, wearing a velvet cap with a gold tassel, was warming his back at the fireplace. His face expressed nothing but self-satisfaction, and he seemed as much at peace with life as the goldfinch suspended above his head in a wicker cage: this was the pharmacist.

"Artémise!" shouted the mistress of the inn, "cut some kindling, fill the carafes, and bring some eau-de-vie! And hurry up! If only I knew what dessert to give these people you're waiting for! Lord! The moving men are starting up that racket in the billiards room again! And their cart is still planted right in front of the gate! The *Hirondelle* is quite liable to smash into it when it comes! Call Polyte and tell him to put it in the shed! . . . To think that since this morning, Monsieur Homais, they've played perhaps fifteen games and drunk eight pots of cider! . . . Oh, they're going to tear my cloth," she went on, watching them from a distance, her skimmer in her hand.

"No great harm in that," answered Monsieur Homais; "you'd buy another!"

"Another billiards table!" exclaimed the widow.

"That one is falling to pieces, Madame Lefrançois; I tell you again, you're hurting yourself! You're only hurting yourself! And besides, nowadays players want narrow pockets and heavy cues. They don't play billiards anymore; everything has changed! You've got to keep up with the times! Look at Tellier, now . . ."

The innkeeper turned red with vexation. The pharmacist added:

"Whatever you may say, his billiards table is nicer than yours; and supposing they organized a patriotic tournament for Poland, for example, or the flood victims of Lyon . . ."

"Beggars like him don't scare us!" interrupted the innkeeper, shrugging her fat shoulders. "Look here, Monsieur Homais! As long as the Lion d'Or exists, people will come. Don't worry, we've got hay in our boots! And one of these mornings you'll see the Café Français closed, and a nice big notice stuck up on the shutters! . . . Change my billiards table," she continued, talking to herself, "when this one's so handy for folding my wash, and it's slept six travelers at once in hunting season! . . . Now, what's keeping that slowpoke Hivert!"

"Are you going to wait for him before you give your gentlemen their dinner?" asked the pharmacist.

"Wait for him? What about Monsieur Binet! You'll see him come in on the stroke of six, because there's no one on this earth as punctual as he is. He always has to sit in his own place in the little dining room! He'd rather you kill him than make him eat his dinner anywhere else! And how finicky he is! And how fussy about his cider! He's not like Monsieur Léon; now, that one comes in sometimes at seven o'clock, seven-thirty; he doesn't even look at what he's eating. What a good young man! Never one word louder than the last."

"That's because there's a good deal of difference, you see, between someone who's had an education and an old cavalryman turned tax collector."

The clock struck six. Binet came in.

He was dressed in a blue frock coat that hung straight down all around his thin body, and a leather cap with ear flaps tied up on top of his head by strings, revealing, under the raised visor, a bald forehead flattened by the long presence of a helmet. He wore a black wool vest, a horsehair collar, gray trousers, and, in all seasons, highly polished boots with two parallel bulges caused by the upward pressure of his toes. Not a hair passed beyond the line of his blond chin whisker, which, outlining his jaw, framed, like the edging of a flower bed, his long, gloomy face with its small eyes and hooked nose. He was skilled at all card games and a good hunter, he wrote in a beautiful hand, and in his home he had a lathe on which he spent his time fashioning napkin rings with which he cluttered his house, with the jealousy of an artist and the egotism of a bourgeois.

He headed for the small dining room; but first the three millers had to be gotten out of there; and during the whole of the time his place was being set, Binet remained silently in his seat next to the stove; then he closed the door and took off his cap as usual.

"If he wears out his tongue, it won't be from making polite conversation!" said the pharmacist, as soon as he was alone with the innkeeper.

"He never talks any more than that," she answered; "last week I had two cloth salesmen here, lively fellows, and they told such funny stories that night I laughed till I cried; well, he just sat there like a dead fish, and didn't say a word."

"Yes," said the pharmacist, "he has no imagination, no wit, none of those qualities that make a man good company!"

"And yet they say he has abilities," the innkeeper objected.

"Abilities!" replied Monsieur Homais. "He! Abilities? In his own line of work, perhaps," he added more calmly.

And he went on:

"Ah! That a businessman with considerable connections, or a lawyer, a doctor, a pharmacist, should be so engrossed that they become odd or even surly—I can understand that; history is full of such examples! But at least they're thinking about something. Take me, for instance—how many times have I searched my desk looking for my pen so as to write a label, and found, at last, that I have put it behind my ear!"

Meanwhile, Madame Lefrançois had gone to the door to see if the *Hirondelle* was coming. She gave a start. A man dressed in black suddenly entered the kitchen. One could make out, in the last gleams of twilight, his florid face and athletic body.

"What may I offer you, Monsieur le curé?" asked the mistress of the inn, reaching to the mantelpiece for one of the brass candlesticks lined up there, with their candles, in a colonnade. "Will you have something to drink? A drop of cassis, a glass of wine?"

The clergyman refused very civilly. He had come to pick up his umbrella, which he had forgotten the other day at the Erncmont convent; and after asking Madame Lefrançois if she would be so kind as to send it around to him at the presbytery that evening, he left for the church, where the Angelus was tolling.

When the pharmacist could no longer hear the sound of his shoes on the square, he pronounced the curé's behavior of a moment before to have been quite unsuitable. This refusal to accept any refreshment seemed to him the most odious sort of hypocrisy; all the priests tippled where no one could see them, and they were trying to bring back the days of the tithe.

The innkeeper came to her curé's defense:

"Anyway, he could take four like you and bend them over his knee. Last year, he helped our people get in the straw; he could carry as many as six bundles at once—he's that strong!"

"Bravo!" said the pharmacist. "Then go ahead and send your girls to confession to strapping fellows with temperaments like his! Personally, if I were the government, I'd want the priests to be bled once a month. Yes, Madame Lefrançois, every month an ample phlebotomy, in the interests of law and order and morality!"

"Quiet, Monsieur Homais! You're ungodly! You have no religion!"

The pharmacist answered:

"I do have a religion, my own religion; in fact, I have even more than any of them, with their masquerades and their hocus-pocus! Unlike them, I worship God! I believe in the Supreme Being, in a Creator, whoever he may be, I don't really care, who has put us here on earth to perform our duties as citizens and family men; but I don't need to go into a church and kiss a silver platter and reach into my pocket to fatten a pack of humbugs who eat better than we do! Because one can honor him just as well in a forest, in a field, or even by gazing up at the ethereal vault, like the ancients. My own God is the God of Socrates, Franklin, Voltaire, and Béranger! I favor *The Profession of Faith of a Savoyard Vicar* and the immortal principles of '89! I cannot, therefore, accept the sort of jolly old God who strolls about his flower beds cane in hand, lodges his friends in the bellies of whales, dies uttering a groan and comes back to life after three days: things absurd in themselves and completely opposed, what is more, to all physical laws; which simply goes to show, by the way, that the priests have always wallowed in a shameful ignorance in which they endeavor to engulf the peoples of the world along with them."

He fell silent, looking around for an audience, for in his excitement the pharmacist had for a moment believed he was in the middle of a town-council meeting. But the innkeeper was no longer listening to him; she was straining her ears toward a distant sound of wheels. The noise of a carriage could be heard mingled with the clatter of loose horseshoes striking the ground, and at last the *Hirondelle* stopped in front of the door.

It was a yellow box carried by two great wheels that came up as high as the canopy, blocking the travelers' view of the road and spattering their shoulders. The little panes of its narrow hatch windows trembled in their frames when the carriage was closed, and retained patches of mud, here and there, on their ancient coating of dust, which even the rainstorms did not entirely wash away. It was hitched to three horses, the first alone in front, and when they went down a hill, it would bump against the ground.

Several of Yonville's citizens appeared in the square; they were all talking at once, asking for news, for explanations, for their hampers; Hivert did not know which of them to answer first. It was he who ran errands in town for the country people. He would go into the shops, bring back rolls of leather for the shoemaker, scrap iron for the farrier, a barrel of herrings for his employer, bonnets from the milliner, toupees from the hairdresser; and all along the road, on the way back, he would distribute his packages, hurling them over the farmyard walls, standing up on his seat and shouting at the top of his voice, while his horses went along by themselves.

An accident had delayed him: Madame Bovary's greyhound had run off across the fields. They had whistled for it a good quarter of an hour. Hivert had even gone half a league back, expecting to see it at any minute; but he had had to continue on his way. Emma had wept, lost her temper; she had blamed Charles for this misfortune. Monsieur Lheureux, a dry-goods merchant, who happened to be with her in the carriage, had tried to console her with numerous examples of lost dogs recognizing their masters after many long years. He had heard of one, he said, that had come back to Paris from Constantinople. Another went fifty leagues in a straight line and swam across four rivers; and his own father had had a poodle that, after twelve years' absence, had suddenly jumped up on his back, one evening, in the street, as he was on his way to dine in town.

[2]

Emma got out first, then Félicité, Monsieur Lheureux, and a wet nurse, and they had to wake Charles in his corner, where he had dropped off into a deep sleep as soon as night fell.

Homais introduced himself; he offered his compliments to Madame, his respects to Monsieur, said he was enchanted to be of service to them, and added cordially that he had taken the liberty of inviting himself to join them for dinner, his wife, as it happened, being absent.

In the kitchen, Madame Bovary went over to the fireplace. With the tips of two fingers, she grasped her dress at knee height, and, having raised it as far as her ankles, held her foot, shod in its little black boot, out to the flame above the leg of mutton that was turning on its spit. The fire shone on her fully, penetrating with a raw light the weave of her dress, the regular pores of her white skin, and even her eyelids, which she closed from time to time. A bright red glow passed over her each time a gust of wind came through the half-open door.

From the other side of the fireplace, a young man with fair hair was watching her in silence.

Because he was very bored in Yonville, where he worked as a clerk for the lawyer Guillaumin, Monsieur Léon Dupuis (for this was he, the other regular guest at the Lion d'Or) would delay his mealtime, hoping some traveler would come to the inn with whom he could converse during the evening. On days when his work was finished, he had no choice, not knowing what else to do, but to arrive at the exact hour and endure from soup to cheese the unrelieved company of Binet. So it was with pleasure that he accepted the innkeeper's proposal that he dine with the new arrivals, and they went into the large room, where Madame Lefrançois, with a sense of occasion, had had the four places laid.

Homais asked permission to keep his fez on, for fear of contracting a coryza.

Then, turning to his neighbor:

"Madame is a little tired, no doubt? One is so dreadfully shaken about in our *Hirondelle!*"

"That's quite true," answered Emma; "but I always find disruption interesting; I like a change of scene."

"It's such a dismal thing," sighed the clerk, "always to be stuck in the same place!"

"If you were like me," said Charles, "constantly obliged to be in the saddle . . ."

"But there's nothing more charming, it seems to me," Léon went on, addressing Madame Bovary. "When one can do it," he added.

"As a matter of fact," said the apothecary, "the practice of medicine is not very arduous in our area; for the condition of our roads permits the use of a carriage, and generally one is quite well paid, the farmers being prosperous. Medically speaking, apart from ordinary cases of enteritis, bronchitis, bilious attacks, and so forth, now and then we have some intermittent fevers at harvest time, but on the whole, very little that's serious, nothing especially noteworthy, except a good deal of scrofula, due, no doubt, to the deplorable hygienic conditions of our peasants' homes. Ah, yes, you'll find yourself struggling against a good many prejudices, Monsieur Bovary, a good deal of pigheaded adherence to tradition, which all your scientific efforts will run up against every day; for people still resort to novenas, relics, the curé, instead of doing the natural thing and going to the doctor or the pharmacist. Still, the climate is not, in truth, bad, and we can even number a few nonagenarians in the community. The thermometer (I have made the observations myself) descends in the winter as low as four degrees and in the warm season reaches twenty-five, thirty centigrade at the very most, which gives us twenty-four Réaumur maximum or, to put it another way, fifty-four Fahrenheit (English measure), and no more!—and, in fact, we're sheltered from the north winds by the Argueil forest on the one hand, from the west winds by the Saint-Jean hill on the other; and yet this warmth, which, because of the water vapor given off by the stream and the considerable presence of cattle in the meadows, exhaling, as you know, a good deal of ammonia, that is to say nitrogen, hydrogen, and oxygen (no, just nitrogen and hydrogen), and which, sucking the moisture from the earth's humus, mingling all these different emanations, bringing them together in a bundle, so to speak, and itself combining with the electricity diffused in the atmosphere, when there is any, could eventually, as in the tropical countries, engender unhealthy miasmas; —this warmth, I say, is tempered precisely in the quarter from which it comes, or rather from which it would come, that is, in the south, by the southeast winds, which, having cooled as they passed over the Seine, sometimes swoop down upon us, like breezes from Russia!"

"Do you at least have some nice walks in the area?" asked Madame Bovary, speaking to the young man.

"Oh, very few!" he answered. "There's a place they call the Pasture, at the top of the hill, by the edge of the forest. I go there sometimes on Sundays, and stay there with a book, watching the sunset."

"I think nothing is as wonderful as a sunset," she said, "especially at the seaside."

"Oh, I love the sea!" said Monsieur Léon.

"And doesn't it seem to you," replied Madame Bovary, "that one's spirit roams more freely over that limitless expanse, and that contemplating it elevates the soul and gives one glimpses of the infinite, and the ideal?"

"It's the same with mountain scenery," Léon said. "A cousin of mine traveled in Switzerland last year, and he told me you can't imagine the poetry of the lakes, the charm of the waterfalls, the enormous effect of the glaciers. You see incredibly tall pine trees across the torrents, cabins hanging from precipices, and, when the clouds part, entire valleys a thousand feet below you. Such spectacles must inspire one, move one to prayer, to ecstasy! I'm no longer surprised at that famous musician who excited his imagination by playing his piano in front of some imposing scene."

"Are you a musician?" she asked.

"No, but I'm very fond of music," he answered.

"Ah, don't listen to him, Madame Bovary," interrupted Homais, leaning over his plate. "That's sheer modesty. —How can you say that, my boy! Eh! The other day, in your room, you were singing 'L'Ange Gardien' so charmingly. I could hear you from the laboratory; you were rendering it like an actor."

Léon, indeed, lived at the pharmacist's, where he had a little room on the third floor looking out on the square. He blushed at this compliment from his landlord, who had already turned to the doctor and was enumerating to him one after another the principal inhabitants of Yonville. He was telling anecdotes, offering facts; no one knew exactly how large the notary's fortune was, *and there was the Tuvache family,* who put on such airs.

Emma went on:

"And what sort of music do you prefer?"

"Oh! German music, the kind that makes you dream."

"Are you familiar with the Italians?"

"Not yet; but I'll hear them next year, when I go to live in Paris, to finish my law studies."

"As I've had the honor of explaining to your husband," said the pharmacist, "speaking of poor Yanoda, who has run off—thanks to his extravagance, you'll find yourselves enjoying one of the most comfortable houses in Yonville. Its main convenience, for a doctor, is that it has a door opening on *the Alley,* so that people can enter and leave without being seen. Besides that, it's furnished with everything pleasant to have in a home: laundry room, kitchen and pantry, living room for the family, apple loft, and so on. He was a go-ahead sort who didn't worry about costs! He had an arbor built at the bottom of the garden, by the water, just for drinking beer in the summer, and if Madame likes to garden, she'll be able to . . ."

"My wife doesn't take much interest in that," said Charles. "Even though she has been told she ought to exercise, she'd rather stay in her room all the time and read."

"Like me," replied Léon; "what could be better, really, than to sit by the fire in the evening with a book, while the wind beats against the windowpanes, and the lamp burns? . . ."

"Oh, yes," she said, her great, dark, wide-open eyes fixed on him.

"You forget everything," he went on, "and hours go by. Without moving, you walk through lands you imagine you can see, and your thoughts, weaving in and out of the story, delight in the details or follow the outlines of the adventures. You merge with the character; you think you're the one whose heart is beating so hard within the clothes he's wearing."

"It's so true! It's so true!"

"Have you ever had the experience," Léon went on, "while reading a book, of coming upon some vague idea that you've had yourself, some obscure image that comes back to you from far away and seems to express absolutely your most subtle feelings?"

"I have felt that," she answered.

"That's why I'm especially fond of the poets," he said. "I think verses are more tender than prose, and more apt to make you cry."

"Yet they're tiresome in the end," Emma said; "these days, what I really adore are stories that can be read all in one go, and that frighten you. I detest common heroes and moderate feelings, the sort that exist in real life."

"Yes," observed the clerk, "those works that don't touch the heart, it seems to me, miss the true aim of Art. It is so pleasant, amid all the disenchantments of life, to be able to let one's mind dwell on noble characters, pure affections, and pictures of happiness. For me, living here, far away from the world, it's my only distraction; Yonville has so little to offer!"

"Like Tostes, I suppose," Emma continued; "that's why I always belonged to a lending library."

"If Madame would do me the honor of using it," said the pharmacist, who had heard these last words, "I myself have at her disposal a library composed of the best authors: Voltaire, Rousseau, Delille, Walter Scott, *L'Écho des Feuilletons,* among others, and in addition, I receive different periodicals every day, including *Le Fanal de Rouen,* since I have the advantage of being its correspondent for the districts of Buchy, Forges, Neufchâtel, Yonville, and vicinity."

For two and a half hours now, they had been at the table; for the servant Artémise, indolently dragging her worn-out old list slippers over the flagstones, would bring the plates out one at a time, forget everything, pay attention to nothing, and constantly leave the billiards-room door ajar, so that the tip of its latch kept knocking against the wall.

Without noticing, while he was talking, Léon had rested his foot on one of the rungs of the chair in which Madame Bovary was sitting. She was wearing a little blue silk tie that held her collar of fluted cambric as straight as a ruff, and depending on how she moved her head, the lower part of her face would sink into the linen or gently emerge from it. In this way, sitting side by side, while Charles and the pharmacist talked on, they entered upon one of those aimless conversations in which any remark made at random brings you back to the unvarying core of a shared feeling. Plays in Paris, titles of novels, new quadrilles, the world they did not know, Tostes, where she had lived, Yonville, where they now were—they explored everything, talked about everything, until dinner was over.

When the coffee was served, Félicité went off to prepare the bedroom in the new house, and soon the guests got up from the table. Madame Lefrançois was sleeping by the embers, while the stableboy, a lantern in his hand, was waiting for Monsieur and Madame Bovary, to lead them to their house. There were wisps of straw mingled in his red hair, and he limped on his left leg. When he had taken the curé's umbrella in his other hand, they set out.

The town was asleep. The posts in the marketplace cast long shadows. The earth was gray, as on a summer night.

But because the doctor's house was fifty steps from the inn, they had to say good night almost immediately, and the company dispersed.

As soon as she entered the front hall, Emma felt the chill from the plaster descend on her shoulders like a damp cloth. The walls were new, and the wooden steps creaked. In the bedroom, on the second floor, a pale light came through the curtainless windows. One could glimpse the tops of trees, and beyond them the meadows, half drowned in the mist that smoked in the moonlight along the course of the stream. In the middle of the room, heaped together, were dresser drawers, bottles, curtain rods, gilded poles, with mattresses over the chairs and basins on the floor, —the two men who had brought the furniture having left everything there, carelessly.

It was the fourth time she had gone to bed in an unfamiliar place. The first was the day she entered the convent, the second that of her arrival in Tostes, the third at La Vaubyessard, the fourth this one; and each had turned out to be in some sense the inauguration of a new phase of her life. She did not believe that things could seem the same in different places, and since the portion of her experience thus far had been bad, what remained to be consumed would surely be better.

[3]

The next day, when she awoke, she saw the clerk in the square. She was in her dressing gown. He lifted his head and greeted her. She gave a quick nod and closed the window.

Léon waited all day for six o'clock to come; but when he entered the inn, he found only Monsieur Binet, already at the table.

The dinner the previous evening had been a notable event for him; never before had he talked for two hours in succession with a *lady*. How, then, had he been able to tell her, and in such language, so many things that he would not have been able to express so well before? He was usually shy and maintained the sort of reserve that partakes at once of modesty and dissimulation. People in Yonville felt that his manners were very *correct*. He would listen to the arguments of his elders and did not seem at all hotheaded in politics, a remarkable thing in a young man. And he possessed talents, he painted with watercolors, knew how to read the treble clef, and was quite likely to occupy himself with literature after dinner, when he was not playing cards. Monsieur Homais esteemed him for his learning; Madame Homais was fond of him because of his amiability, for he would often go out into the garden with the Homais children, dirty little urchins, very badly brought up and somewhat lymphatic, like their mother. To look after them, they had, besides the maid, the pharmacy student Justin, a distant cousin of Monsieur Homais's who had been taken into the house out of charity, and who also acted as servant.

The apothecary proved to be the best of neighbors. He advised Madame Bovary about the tradesmen, had his cider merchant come specially, tasted the drink himself, and watched, down in the cellar, to see that the cask was properly placed; he also told her how to acquire a provision of butter at a low price, and concluded an arrangement with Lestiboudois, the sacristan, who, in addition to his ecclesiastical and funerary functions, looked after the principal gardens in Yonville by the hour or by the year, according to the preference of the owners.

The need to occupy himself with another person was not the only motive impelling the pharmacist to such obsequious cordiality; there was a plan behind it.

He had broken the law of 19 Ventôse, Year XI, Article 1, which forbids any individual not possessing a diploma to practice medicine; with the consequence that, on the basis of mysterious denunciations, Homais had been summoned to appear in Rouen, before the king's prosecutor, in his private chambers. The magistrate had received him standing, in his robe, ermine on his shoulders and toque on his head. It was morning, before the convening of the court. One could hear the stout boots of the policemen passing in the corridor, and the distant sound of heavy locks turning. The pharmacist's ears rang so loudly that he thought he was about to have a stroke; he foresaw the deepest of dungeons, his family in tears, the pharmacy sold, all the glass jars dispersed; and he had to go into a café and drink a glass of rum with Seltzer water in order to restore his spirits.

Little by little, the memory of this admonition faded, and he continued, as before, to give innocuous consultations in his back room. But the mayor bore a grudge against him, some of his colleagues were jealous, he had to be on his guard against everything; by forming an attachment to Monsieur Bovary through these courtesies, he would win his gratitude and prevent him from speaking out later if he noticed something. So every morning Homais would bring him *the paper,* and often, in the afternoon, he would leave the pharmacy for a moment to drop in on the officer of health for a little conversation.

Charles was gloomy: he had no patients. He would remain sitting for hours on end, without speaking; he would go nap in his consulting room or watch his wife sew. For distraction, he did odd jobs around the house, and he even attempted to paint the attic with a remnant of color left by the painters. But money matters preoccupied him. He had spent so much on the repairs at Tostes, on Madame's clothes, and on the move that the entire dowry, more than three thousand ecus, had melted away in two years. And then, how many things had been damaged or lost on the way from Tostes to Yonville, quite aside from the plaster curé, which, knocked from the cart by a particularly hard jolt, had shattered into a thousand pieces on the pavement of Quincampoix!

A more agreeable concern came to distract him, namely, his wife's pregnancy. As her term drew near, she became all the more dear to him. Another bond of the flesh was being established between them, and something like a pervasive sense of a more complex union. When, from a distance, he watched her indolent steps and her waist turning gently above her uncorseted hips, when, across from her, he contemplated her at his ease, as she sat tired in her armchair, his happiness could no longer be contained; he would stand up, he would kiss her, run his hands over her face, call her "little mama," try to get her to dance, and, half laughing, half crying, babble all sorts of fond pleasantries that came into his head. The idea of having engendered a child delighted him. Nothing was lacking to him now. He knew the entire scope of human existence, and he sat down to it serenely with both elbows on the table.

Emma felt great surprise at first, then wanted to be delivered, so as to know what it was like to be a mother. But since she could not spend the money that she would have liked, to have a boat-shaped cradle with pink silk curtains and embroidered baby bonnets, she gave up on the layette in a fit of bitterness and ordered the whole of it from a seamstress in the village, without choosing or discussing anything. And so she did not enjoy those preparations that stimulate a mother's tenderness, and her affection, from the beginning, was perhaps somewhat attenuated by this.

However, since at every meal Charles talked about the little one, she soon began to give the thought of it more constant attention.

She wanted a son; he would be strong and dark, she would call him Georges; and this idea of having a male child was a sort of hoped-for compensation for all her past helplessness. A man, at least, is free; he can explore every passion, every land, overcome obstacles, taste the most distant pleasures. But a woman is continually thwarted. Inert and pliant at the same time, she must struggle against both the softness of her flesh and subjection to the law. Her will, like the veil tied to her hat by a string, flutters with every breeze; there is always some desire luring her on, some convention holding her back.

She gave birth one Sunday, at about six o'clock, as the sun was rising.

"It's a girl!" said Charles.

She turned her head away and fainted.

Almost immediately, Madame Homais rushed in and kissed her, as did Mère Lefrançois, of the Lion d'Or. The pharmacist, being a man of discretion, merely offered her some provisional congratulations, through the half-open door. He asked to see the child and deemed it well formed.

During her convalescence, she spent a good deal of time thinking of a name for her daughter. First, she reviewed all those with Italian endings, such as Clara, Louisa, Amanda, Atala; she quite liked Galsuinde, and better still Yseult or Léocadie. Charles wanted the child named after his mother; Emma was opposed. They went through the calendar from end to end, and they consulted people outside the family.

"Monsieur Léon," said the pharmacist, "with whom I was talking about this the other day, is surprised that you haven't chosen Madeleine, which is so exceedingly fashionable these days."

But the elder Madame Bovary protested loudly against this sinner's name. As for Monsieur Homais, his predilection was for all those names that recalled a great man, an illustrious deed, or a noble idea, and it was according to this system that he had baptized his four children. Thus, Napoléon represented glory, and Franklin freedom; Irma, perhaps, was a concession to romanticism; but Athalie, a tribute to the most immortal masterpiece of the French stage. For his philosophical convictions did not impede his artistic enthusiasms; the thinker in him did not in the least stifle the man of feeling; he was able to make distinctions, differentiate imagination from fanaticism. In the tragedy in question, for example, he found fault with the ideas but admired the style; he condemned the conception but applauded all the details; and he was incensed by the characters, though he raved about their speeches. When he read the great passages, he was transported; but when he thought how the pulpiteers were profiting from it to sell their goods, he was grieved, and in this confusion of feelings in which he found himself entangled, he would have liked simultaneously to set the laurel wreath on Racine's head with his own two hands and to argue with him for a good quarter of an hour.

At last, Emma remembered that at the La Vaubyessard château she had heard the marquise address a young woman as Berthe; from that moment, the name was decided, and since Père Rouault could not come, they asked Monsieur Homais to be godfather. The gifts he gave were all products of his establishment, namely, six boxes of jujubes, a whole jar of racahout, three pans of marshmallow paste, and, in addition, six sticks of sugar candy that he had found in a cupboard. The evening of the ceremony, there was a large dinner; the curé was there; the company became excited. Over the liqueurs, Monsieur Homais intoned "The God of Good Folks." Monsieur Léon sang a barcarolle, and the elder Madame Bovary, who was godmother, a romantic ballad from the time of the Empire; finally the elder Monsieur Bovary demanded that the child be brought downstairs, and he proceeded to baptize her with a glass of Champagne, pouring it over her head from above. This mockery of the first sacrament filled the Abbé Bournisien with indignation; Père Bovary responded with a quotation from "The War of the Gods," and the curé tried to leave; the ladies pleaded; Homais intervened; and they succeeded in getting the clergyman to return to his seat, where he tranquilly picked up from his saucer his half-drunk demitasse of coffee.

The elder Monsieur Bovary stayed on for another month at Yonville, dazzling its inhabitants with a superb silver-braided policeman's cap that he wore in the mornings when he smoked his pipe in the square. Being also in the habit of drinking a good deal of eau-de-vie, he would often send the maid to the Lion d'Or to buy him a bottle, which would be written down on his son's account; and to perfume his foulards, he used up his daughter-in-law's entire supply of eau de Cologne.

She was not in the least displeased with his company. He had been around the world: he would talk about Berlin, Vienna, Strasbourg, his time as an officer, the mistresses he had had, the grand luncheons he had enjoyed; then, too, he was charming toward her and would even, sometimes, in the stairway or the garden, seize her around the waist, exclaiming:

"Look out, Charles!"

Then the elder Madame Bovary became alarmed for her son's happiness, and, fearing that her husband would in the long run exert an immoral influence on the young woman's ideas, she hastened to advance their departure. Perhaps she had graver fears. Monsieur Bovary was a man to whom nothing was sacred.

One day, Emma felt a sudden need to see her little daughter, who had been put out to nurse with the carpenter's wife; and without looking at the almanac to see if the six weeks of the Virgin had elapsed, she set off toward Rolet's house, which lay at the far end of the village, at the bottom of the hill, between the main road and the meadows.

It was noon; the shutters of the houses were closed, and the slate roofs, gleaming under the raw light of the blue sky, seemed to give off glittering sparks at the crests of their gables. A sultry wind was blowing. Emma felt weak as she walked; the stones of the sidewalk hurt her; she wondered if she should not return home, or go inside somewhere and sit down.

At that moment, Monsieur Léon appeared from a nearby door with a bundle of papers under his arm. He came up to greet her and stood in the shade in front of Lheureux's shop, under the gray awning that projected from it.

Madame Bovary said that she was going to see her child, but that she was beginning to feel tired.

"If . . . ," said Léon, not daring to continue.

"Do you have business somewhere?" she asked.

And when the clerk answered, she asked him to go with her. By evening, it was known throughout Yonville, and Madame Tuvache, the mayor's wife, declared in her maid's presence that *Madame Bovary was compromising herself.*

To reach the wet nurse's house, one had to turn left, after leaving the street, as though going to the cemetery, and follow a little path, between cottages and yards, bordered by privets. These were in flower, and the speedwell, too, the hawthorns, the nettles, and the slender wild blackberries that arced up out of the thickets. Through holes in the hedges, one could see, in the farmyards, a hog on a dunghill, or cows in their wooden collars, rubbing their horns against the trunks of the trees. The two of them walked slowly, side by side, she leaning on him and he slowing his step to match hers; in front of them flitted a swarm of flies, buzzing in the warm air.

They recognized the house by an old walnut tree that shaded it. It was low and roofed in brown tiles, and outside, beneath its attic dormer, hung a string of onions. Bundles of brushwood, leaning against the thorn hedge, surrounded a bed of lettuces, a few stalks of lavender, and some sweet peas tied up on sticks. Dirty water trickled out over the grass, and all around were odds and ends of tattered old garments, knitted stockings, a red calico wrapper, and a large, coarse linen sheet spread lengthwise on the hedge. At the sound of the gate, the wet nurse appeared, holding on her arm a nursing child. With her other hand, she was pulling along behind her a poor, sickly little boy whose face was covered with scrofulous sores, the son of a Rouen knit-goods dealer, left here in the country by his parents, who were too occupied with their business.

"Come in," she said. "Your little one is over there sleeping."

The bedroom, on the ground floor, the only one in the house, had a wide curtainless bed at its back wall, while the kneading trough occupied the side containing the window, one pane of which had been patched with a round of blue paper. In the corner, behind the door, a row of boots with gleaming hobnails stood under the slab of the washbasin, next to a bottle full of oil which bore a feather at its neck; a copy of *Mathieu Laensberg* was flung on the dusty mantelpiece among gunflints, candle stubs, and pieces of tinder. Lastly, the final superfluous touch to this room was a picture of Fame blowing her trumpets, cut out, no doubt, from some perfume company's prospectus and nailed to the wall with six shoe tacks.

Emma's child was sleeping on the floor, in a wicker cradle. She picked her up along with the blanket that was wrapped around her and began to sing softly as she swayed back and forth.

Léon walked about in the room; it seemed strange to him to see this lovely lady in her nankeen dress in the midst of all this wretchedness. Madame Bovary blushed; he turned away, thinking that perhaps his eyes had expressed some impertinence. Then she laid the child back down; it had just spit up on her collar. The wet nurse immediately came over to wipe it off, assuring her that it would not show.

"Over and over again, she does this to me," she said, "and I'm forever cleaning her off! Might you be so kind as to leave an order with Camus the grocer, that he would let me take a little soap when I need it? 'Twould be still more of a convenience to you, that I wouldn't be bothering you."

"Very well, very well!" said Emma. "Goodbye, Mère Rolet!"

And she went out, wiping her feet on the doorsill.

The good woman went with her as far as the end of the yard, all the while talking about the trouble she had getting up during the night.

"It wears me out so, sometimes I fall asleep in my chair; so you might also at least let me have just a pound of ground coffee, that would do me for a month? I would have it in the morning with some milk."

After having submitted to her thanks, Madame Bovary went off; and she was a little way down the path when, at the sound of sabots, she turned her head: it was the wet nurse!

"What is it?"

Then the countrywoman, drawing her aside, behind an elm tree, began talking to her about her husband, who, with his job and the six francs a year that the captain . . .

"Get on with it," said Emma.

"Well," the wet nurse resumed, heaving a sigh after every word, "I'm afraid he'll be vexed to see me drinking coffee on my own—you know, men . . ."

"But you will have some," repeated Emma. "I will give you some! . . . You are bothering me!"

"Alas! My poor dear lady, it's just that, on account of his wounds, he has terrible cramps in the chest. He even says that cider makes him feel weak."

"Now, do hurry up, Mère Rolet!"

"Well, then," the wet nurse resumed, with a curtsy, "if it wasn't too much to ask of you"—she curtsied again—"if you would"—and her eyes were pleading—"a little jug of eau-de-vie," she said at last, "and I'll rub your little one's feet with it, for they're as tender as my tongue."

Having got rid of the wet nurse, Emma took Monsieur Léon's arm again. She walked quickly for some time; then she slowed down, and her glance, which had been roaming about before her, rested on the shoulder of the young man, who was wearing a frock coat with a black velvet collar. His chestnut hair fell over it, straight and neatly combed. She noticed his fingernails, which were longer than was customary in Yonville. It was one of the clerk's great occupations, to care for them; and he kept, for that purpose, a special penknife in his writing desk.

They returned to Yonville along the water's edge. In the warm season, the wider banks revealed the garden walls down to their bases, with short flights of steps descending to the stream. It flowed noiselessly, swift and cold to the eye; tall, slender grasses bent over together, pushed by the current and, like loosened green manes of hair, spread through its limpid waters. Now and then, a thin-legged insect walked or settled on the tip of a reed or the blade of a water lily. The sun pierced with a ray the little blue droplets of the waves that came collapsing one after another; old lopped willows mirrored their gray bark in the water; beyond, all around, the meadows seemed empty. It was dinnertime on the farms, and the young woman and her companion heard nothing as they walked but the cadence of their steps on the earth of the path, the words they said to each other, and the brushing of Emma's dress as it rustled around her.

The garden walls, their copings stuck with pieces of bottle, were as warm as the panes of a greenhouse. In among the bricks, wallflowers had grown up; and with the edge of her open parasol, Madame Bovary, as she passed, crumbled a few of their faded flowers into yellow dust, or a branch of the honeysuckle and the clematis that hung outside would trail for a moment over the silk and catch on the fringe.

They were talking about a troupe of Spanish dancers who were expected soon at the theater in Rouen.

"Will you be going?" she asked.

"If I can," he answered.

Had they nothing else to say to each other? Yet their eyes were full of a more serious conversation; and while they forced themselves to find commonplace remarks, they felt the same languor invading them both; it was like a murmur of the soul, deep, continuous, louder than the murmur of their voices. Surprised by a sweetness new to them, they did not think of describing the sensation to each other or of discovering its cause. Future joys, like tropical shores, project over the immensity that lies before them their native softness, a fragrant breeze, and one grows drowsy in that intoxication without even worrying about the horizon one cannot see.

In one spot, the ground had been churned up by the trampling of the cattle; they had to walk on large green stones, spaced at intervals in the mud. Often she would stop for a minute to look where to place her little boot, —and, tottering on the unsteady rock, her elbows in the air, her body bent, her eye irresolute, she would laugh, afraid of falling into the puddles.

When they reached her garden, Madame Bovary pushed open the small gate, ran up the steps, and disappeared.

Léon went back into his office. The boss was not there; he glanced at the files, then trimmed a quill pen for himself, and at last picked up his hat and left.

He went out into the Pasture, at the top of the Argueil hill, at the edge of the forest; he lay down on the ground under the firs and looked at the sky through his fingers.

"How bored I am!" he said to himself; "how bored I am!"

He felt he was to be pitied for living in this village, with Homais for a friend and Monsieur Guillaumin for a master. The latter, entirely occupied with business, wearing gold-rimmed glasses and red side-whiskers against his white cravat, understood nothing about the finer subtleties of the intellect, although he affected a stiff English manner that had dazzled the clerk at first. As for the pharmacist's wife, she was the best wife in Normandy, as gentle as a sheep, cherishing her children, her father, her mother, her cousins, weeping over the misfortunes of others, letting everything go in her household, and detesting corsets; —but she was so slow to move, so boring to listen to, so common in her looks and so limited in her conversation that he had never dreamed, even though she was thirty years old, he was twenty, they slept in neighboring rooms, and he talked to her every day, that she could be a woman for someone, or that she possessed any attributes of her sex except the dress she wore.

And who else was there? Binet, a few merchants, two or three tavern keepers, the curé, and lastly Monsieur Tuvache, the mayor, with his two sons, wealthy, loutish, dim-witted men who worked their own lands, feasted by themselves at home, were pious besides, and altogether intolerable company.

But against the shared background of all these human faces, Emma's stood out, isolated and yet more distant; for he sensed between her and him something like a formless chasm.

In the beginning, he had gone to her house several times in the company of the pharmacist. Charles had not seemed extremely interested in receiving him; and Léon did not know what course to take, between his fear of being indiscreet and his desire for an intimacy that he believed was almost impossible.

[4]

With the coming of the first cold weather, Emma left her bedroom and moved into the parlor, a long, low-ceilinged room with a piece of coral on the mantel spreading its many branches before the mirror. Sitting in her armchair, beside the window, she could watch the villagers go past on the sidewalk.

Twice a day, Léon went from his study to the Lion d'Or. Emma, from a distance, would hear him coming; she would lean forward, listening; and the young man would glide past behind the curtain, always dressed the same, without turning his head. But at dusk, when, her chin in her left hand, she had abandoned in her lap the tapestry work she had begun, she would often start at the appearance of that shadow suddenly slipping past. She would stand up and order the table to be set.

Monsieur Homais would arrive during dinner. His fez in hand, he would enter with silent steps so as not to disturb anyone and would always repeat the same phrase: "Good evening, all!" Then, when he had settled in his place, close to the table, between husband and wife, he would ask the doctor for news of his patients, and the doctor would consult him on the likelihood of his being paid. Then they would talk about what was *in the newspaper.* Homais, by that time of day, knew it almost by heart; and he would relay it in its entirety, including the editorials and the stories of each and every catastrophe that had occurred in France or abroad. But, the subject being exhausted, he would soon venture some observations on the dishes he saw before him. Sometimes, half rising, he would even delicately point out to Madame the tenderest morsel or, turning to the servant, give her some advice about the manipulation of stews or the hygiene of seasonings; his manner of talking about aroma, osmazome, juices, and gelatin was dazzling. As his head was in fact more crowded with recipes than his pharmacy with jars, Homais excelled at making any number of jams, vinegars, and sweet liqueurs, and he was also familiar with the latest inventions in economical calefactors, along with the art of preserving cheeses and healing sick wines.

At eight o'clock, Justin would come get him so that he could close the pharmacy. Monsieur would look at him with a cunning eye, especially if Félicité happened to be present, because he had noticed that his pupil was fond of the doctor's house.

"My young lad," he would say, "is beginning to get ideas, and I believe, devil take me, that he's in love with your maid!"

But a more serious fault, and one with which he reproached him, was that he persisted in listening to their conversations. On Sundays, for instance, they could not get him to leave the parlor, where Madame Homais had summoned him to take the children away, for they were falling asleep in the armchairs, their backs dragging down the loose calico slipcovers.

Not many people came to the pharmacist's soirées, since his scandal-mongering and political opinions had alienated one after another a variety of respectable people. The clerk was unfailingly present. As soon as he heard the bell ring, he would hurry to Madame Bovary, take her shawl, and put to one side, under the pharmacist's desk, the capacious list slippers she wore over her shoes in snowy weather.

First they would have a few rounds of trente et un; then Monsieur Homais would play *écarté* with Emma; Léon, behind her, would give advice. Standing with his hands on the back of her chair, he would gaze at the teeth of her comb biting into her chignon. With each movement she made laying down her cards, her dress would lift on the right side. From her pinned-up hair, a brownish shadow descended her back and, paling by degrees, gradually lost itself in the darker shadows. Her skirt lay draped over the chair on both sides, ballooning out in ample folds, and spread down to the floor. When sometimes Léon felt the sole of his boot resting on it, he would draw back, as though he had stepped on someone.

When the card game was finished, the apothecary and the doctor would play dominoes, and Emma would move to another chair, lean her elbows on the table, and leaf through *L'Illustration*. She had brought along her fashion magazine. Léon would sit down next to her; they would look at the pictures together and wait for each other at the bottoms of the pages. Often she would ask him to read some poems to her; Léon would declaim them in a languid voice, which he would carefully let die away at the love passages. But the noise of the dominoes interfered; Monsieur Homais was good at the game, he would beat Charles by a full double six. Then, having reached three hundred, the two of them would stretch out in front of the fireplace and soon fall asleep. The fire was dying down in the embers; the teapot was empty; Léon was still reading. Emma would listen to him, absently turning the lampshade, its gauze painted with Pierrots in carriages and tightrope dancers with their balancing poles. Léon would stop, indicating with a gesture his sleeping audience; then they would talk to each other in low voices, and the conversation they had would seem the sweeter to them because it was not overheard.

And so a kind of partnership was established between them, a continuing commerce in books and love songs; Monsieur Bovary, little given to jealousy, was not surprised by this.

For his name day, he received a fine phrenological head, all marked out with numbers down to the thorax and painted blue. This thoughtful attention came from the clerk. He paid him many others, even doing his errands for him in Rouen; and when a certain novelist's latest book inspired a fashionable craze for succulent plants, Léon bought some for Madame and brought them back in the *Hirondelle,* holding them on his knees and pricking his fingers on their hard spines.

She had a small raised shelf installed against her casement window to hold her little pots. The clerk, too, had his small hanging garden; they would see each other tending their flowers at their windows.

Of the windows in the village, there was one even more frequently occupied; for on Sundays, from morning till night, and every afternoon, if the weather was bright, one could see at an attic dormer the lean profile of Monsieur Binet bending over his lathe, whose monotonous whirring was audible as far as the Lion d'Or.

One evening, when he returned home, Léon found in his room a coverlet of velvet and wool with foliage designs on a pale background. He called Madame Homais, Monsieur Homais, Justin, the children, the cook, he spoke of it to his employer; everyone wanted to see the coverlet; why was the doctor's wife being so *generous* to the clerk? It seemed odd, and they formed the definite opinion that she must be *his sweetheart*.

He implied as much, since he would talk to you incessantly about her loveliness and her wit, so much so that Binet answered him once quite savagely:

"What does it matter to me, since I don't belong to her circle!"

He tormented himself searching for some means of *making his declaration* to her; and, always torn between a fear of displeasing her and the shame of being such a coward, he would cry with discouragement and desire. Then he would act with energy and decision; he would write letters, which he would tear up, give himself deadlines, which he would then extend. Often he would set off with the intention of risking everything; but that resolution would quickly desert him in Emma's presence, and when Charles, arriving unexpectedly, invited him to climb into the *boc* and go along with him on a visit to some patient in the environs, he would immediately accept, bid Madame goodbye, and leave. Wasn't her husband, after all, a part of her?

As for Emma, she never questioned herself to find out if she loved him. Love, she believed, must come suddenly, with great thunderclaps and bolts of lightning, —a hurricane from heaven that drops down on your life, overturns it, tears away your will like a leaf, and carries your whole heart off with it into the abyss. She did not know that the rain forms lakes on the terraces of houses when the drainpipes are blocked, and thus she would have lived on feeling quite safe, had she not suddenly discovered a crack in the wall.

[5]

It was a Sunday afternoon in February, when the snow was falling.

They had all gone off, Monsieur and Madame Bovary, Homais and Monsieur Léon, to see a flax mill that was being built in the valley, half a league from Yonville. The apothecary had taken along Napoléon and Athalie, to give them some exercise, and Justin was with them, carrying some umbrellas over his shoulder.

Nothing, however, could have been less interesting than this point of interest. A great expanse of empty land, on which lay, here and there, among the heaps of sand and stones, a few already rusty cogwheels, surrounded a long rectangular building pierced with numbers of little windows. It was not yet finished, and the sky could be seen through the joists of the roofing. Attached to the beam of the gable end, a bouquet of straw mingled with ears of wheat was snapping its red, white, and blue ribbons in the wind.

Homais was talking. He was explaining to *the party* how important this establishment would be in the future, computing the strength of the floors, the thickness of the walls, and regretting keenly that he did not have a measuring stick, such as Monsieur Binet possessed for his personal use.

Emma, who had given him her arm, was leaning lightly against his shoulder, and she was watching the far-off disk of the sun suffusing the mist with its dazzling pallor; but then she turned her head: there was Charles. He had his cap pulled down over his eyebrows, and his thick lips were quivering, which gave a stupid look to his face; even his back, his placid back, was irritating to look at, and she found displayed there, on his coat, all the man's dullness.

As she was contemplating him, deriving a sort of depraved sensual pleasure from her irritation, Léon took a step closer. The cold that was turning him pale seemed to add something softer and more languorous to his face; between his cravat and his neck, the loose collar of his shirt revealed his skin; an earlobe showed below a lock of hair, and his large blue eyes, lifted toward the clouds, seemed to Emma more limpid and lovely than mountain lakes mirroring the sky.

"Naughty boy!" the apothecary shouted suddenly.

And he ran over to his son, who had just plunged into a heap of lime to coat his shoes with white. At the scoldings that rained down on him, Napoléon began to howl, while Justin wiped off his feet with a twist of straw. But a knife was needed; Charles offered his.

"Ah!" she said to herself; "he carries a knife in his pocket, like a peasant!"

The frost was descending, and they turned back toward Yonville.

That evening, Madame Bovary did not go to her neighbors' house, and when Charles had gone, when she was alone, the comparison returned with the sharpness of an almost immediate sensation and with the lengthening of perspective that memory gives to objects. Gazing from her bed at the bright fire that was burning, she once again saw Léon standing, as she had seen him out there, flexing his cane with one hand and with the other holding Athalie, who was sucking peacefully on a bit of ice. She found him charming; she could not stop thinking about him; she recalled other things he had done on other days, words he had spoken, the sound of his voice, his whole person; and she said again, thrusting her lips out as though for a kiss:

"Yes. Charming! Charming! . . . Is he in love?" she asked herself. "Who is he in love with? . . . Why . . . it's me!"

All the evidence arose before her at once, her heart leaped. The flame in the fireplace cast a joyful, tremulous light on the ceiling; she turned onto her back, stretching her arms.

Then began the eternal lament: "Oh, if only heaven had willed it! Why can't it be? What kept it from happening? . . ."

When Charles returned home at midnight, she appeared to wake up, and when he made some noise getting undressed, she complained of a migraine; then asked casually what had happened during the evening.

"Monsieur Léon," he said, "went upstairs early."

She could not help smiling, and she fell asleep with her soul full of a new enchantment.

The next day, at nightfall, she had a visit from Monsieur Lheureux, the dry-goods merchant. He was a clever man, this shopkeeper.

Born a Gascon, but now a Norman, he combined his southern volubility with a Cauchois cunning. His soft, fat, beardless face looked as though it had been dyed with a decoction of clear licorice, and his white hair intensified the harsh brilliance of his little black eyes. No one knew what he had been before: peddler, said some; banker at Routot, according to others. What is certain is that he could do complicated calculations in his head that dismayed even Binet. Polite to the point of obsequiousness, he stood with his back always half inclined, in the position of someone making a bow or extending an invitation.

After leaving his hat with its band of crepe by the door, he placed a green box on the table and began by complaining to Madame, with a profusion of compliments, that he had failed to gain her confidence before now. A poor shop like his was not destined to attract so *elegant* a lady; he stressed the word. However, she had only to place an order, and he would take it upon himself to provide her with whatever she might want, whether in the way of haberdashery, linens, knitwear, or fancy goods; for he went to the city four times a month, regularly. He dealt with the best houses. She could mention his name at the Trois Frères, the Barbe d'Or, or the Grand Sauvage; all the gentlemen there knew him as well as their own brothers! Today, he had come to show Madame, as he was passing by, a few articles he happened to have, thanks to a very rare opportunity. And he withdrew from the box half a dozen embroidered collars.

Madame Bovary examined them.

"I don't need anything," she said.

Then Monsieur Lheureux delicately exhibited three Algerian scarves, several packets of English needles, a pair of straw slippers, and, lastly, four eggcups made of coconut shell with openwork carving done by convicts. Then, both hands on the table, his neck outstretched, his upper body leaning forward, his mouth open, he followed Emma's gaze as it roamed indecisively over these goods. From time to time, as if to remove some dust, he would give a flick of a fingernail to the silk of the scarves, which were unfolded at full length; and they would ripple with a soft sound, the gold spangles in their fabric sparkling like little stars in the greenish light of the dusk.

"How much are they?"

"A trifle," he answered, "a mere trifle; but there's no hurry; whenever you like; we're not Jews!"

She thought for a few moments, and ended by again thanking Monsieur Lheureux, who replied without emotion:

"Very well, we'll come to an understanding later on; I've always gotten along with the ladies—except in the case of my own wife, that is!"

Emma smiled.

"What I wanted to tell you," he went on with a simple, good-natured air, after his joke, "was that I'm not worried about the money . . . I could give you some, if need be."

She made a gesture of surprise.

"Ah!" he said quickly, in a low voice; "I wouldn't have to go far to find it for you; you can count on that!"

And he began asking after Père Tellier, the proprietor of the Café Français, whom Monsieur Bovary was treating at the time.

"What's the matter with him, anyway, old Père Tellier? . . . He coughs hard enough to shake the whole house, and I'm afraid he'll soon be needing a wooden overcoat more than a flannel undershirt. He was such a wild one when he was young! The sort, madame, that doesn't have the least self-discipline! He burned himself to a crisp with eau-de-vie! But all the same, it's distressing to see an old acquaintance go."

And while he was buckling up his box, he talked on in this way about the doctor's patients.

"It's the weather, no doubt," he said, looking at the windowpanes with a glum expression, "that's causing all this illness! I myself don't feel altogether up to the mark; in fact, one of these days I should come and consult Monsieur about a pain I have in my back. Well, goodbye, Madame Bovary; at your disposal; your very humble servant!"

And he closed the door gently behind him.

Emma had dinner brought to her in her bedroom, by the fireside, on a tray; she took a long time eating; everything seemed good to her.

"How sensible I was!" she said to herself, thinking about the scarves.

She heard footsteps on the stairs: it was Léon. She rose, and, from the top of the chest of drawers, took the uppermost dishcloth from a pile to be hemmed. She appeared very busy when he came in.

The conversation languished, Madame Bovary abandoning it every minute, while he himself remained quite ill at ease. Sitting in a low chair, next to the fire, he was turning the ivory needle case in his fingers; she was plying her needle, or, from time to time, gathering the folds of the cloth with her nail. She did not speak; he said nothing, captivated by her silence, as he would have been by her words.

"Poor boy!" she was thinking.

"What doesn't she like about me?" he was wondering.

At last, however, Léon said that one of these days he would have to go to Rouen, on business connected with his practice.

"Your music subscription has run out—should I renew it?"

"No," she answered.

"Why?"

"Because . . ."

And, pursing her lips, she slowly drew out a long needleful of gray thread.

This work irritated Léon. It seemed to be roughening the tips of Emma's fingers; a compliment occurred to him, but he did not risk it.

"Then you're giving it up?" he went on.

"What?" she said quickly. "Music? Oh, heavens, yes! Haven't I my house to look after, my husband to care for, a thousand things, really, so many duties that are more important!"

She looked at the clock. Charles was late. Then she pretended to be worried. Two or three times she even repeated:

"He's so good!"

The clerk was fond of Monsieur Bovary. But this affection of hers surprised him unpleasantly; nevertheless, he joined in praising him, as he had heard everyone else do, he said, especially the pharmacist.

"Ah! He's a fine man," said Emma.

"Indeed he is," said the clerk.

And he began to talk about Madame Homais, whose very slovenly appearance usually inclined them to laugh.

"What does that matter?" Emma interrupted. "A good wife and mother doesn't worry about how she looks."

Then she fell silent again.

It was the same on the following days; her talk, her manner, everything changed. She was seen to take her housekeeping to heart, return to church regularly, and manage her servant more strictly.

She took Berthe back from the wet nurse. Félicité would bring her in when visitors came, and Madame Bovary would undress her to show off her arms and legs. She would declare that she adored children; they were her consolation, her joy, her folly, and she would accompany her caresses with lyrical effusions that, to anyone not from Yonville, would have recalled La Sachette in *Notre-Dame de Paris*.

When Charles came home, he would find his slippers placed next to the embers to warm. Now his vests no longer lacked a lining, nor his shirts buttons, and it was even a pleasure to look into the cupboard and contemplate all the cotton caps arranged in equal piles. She no longer sulked, as she once had, at taking a walk in the garden; whatever he proposed was always agreed to, even though she might not understand the wishes to which she submitted without a murmur; —and when Léon saw him by the fireside, after dinner, his hands on his stomach, his feet on the firedogs, his cheek flushed as he digested his food, his eyes moist from happiness, the child crawling over the carpet, and this woman with her slender figure leaning over the back of his chair to kiss him on the forehead:

"What madness!" he would say to himself. "And how can I reach her?"

Thus, she seemed to him so virtuous and inaccessible that all hope, even the faintest, abandoned him.

But by renouncing her in this way, he was placing her in an extraordinary situation. She was divested, in his eyes, of the fleshly attributes from which he had nothing to hope for; and in his heart, she rose higher and higher, withdrawing further from him in a magnificent, soaring apotheosis. His was one of those pure sentiments that do not impede the pursuit of one's life, that one cultivates because they are so rare, and the loss of which would afflict one more than their possession delights.

Emma grew thinner, her cheeks paler, her face longer. With her black bands of hair, her large eyes, her straight nose, her birdlike step, always remaining silent now, did she not seem to pass through life scarcely touching it and to bear on her forehead the faint imprint of some sublime predestination? She was so sad and so calm, at once so gentle and so reserved, that in her presence one felt captivated by an icy charm, the way one shivers in a church amid the fragrance of flowers mingling with the cold of the marble. Nor did others escape this seduction. The pharmacist liked to say:

"She's a woman of great capacity. She would not be out of place as the wife of a subprefect."

The village housewives admired her thrift, the patients her courtesy, the poor her charity.

But she was filled with desires, with rage, with hatred. That dress with its straight folds concealed a heart in turmoil, and those reticent lips said nothing about its torment. She was in love with Léon, and she wanted to be alone so as to delight more comfortably in his image. The sight of him in person disturbed the sensual pleasure of this meditation. Emma trembled at the sound of his footsteps; then, in his presence, her emotions subsided, leaving only an immense astonishment that ended in sadness.

Léon did not know, when he left her house in despair, that she would rise immediately after he went, in order to watch him in the street. She would concern herself with his comings and goings; she would study his face; she would invent an elaborate story to have a pretext for visiting his room. The pharmacist's wife seemed to her very fortunate to sleep under the same roof; and her thoughts were continually settling on that house, like the pigeons of the Lion d'Or coming to dip their pink feet and white wings in the channels of its eaves. But the more conscious Emma was of her love, the more she suppressed it, to keep it from being visible and to diminish it. She would have liked Léon to suspect it; and she imagined chance events, catastrophes, that would have made that possible. What held her back was probably laziness or fear, and discretion, as well. She would think that she had kept him at too great a distance, that time had run out, that everything was lost. Then the pride, the joy of saying to herself, "I am virtuous," and of adopting an air of resignation as she looked at herself in the mirror, would console her a little for the sacrifice she thought she was making.

Then her physical desires, her cravings for money, and the fits of melancholy born of her passion, all merged in a single torment; —and instead of putting it out of her mind, she clung to it more, provoking herself to the point of pain and seeking every opportunity to do so. She was irritated by a dish badly served or a door half open, lamented the velvet she did not have, the happiness that eluded her, her too-lofty dreams, her too-narrow house.

What exasperated her was that Charles seemed unaware of her suffering. His conviction that he was making her happy seemed an idiotic insult, and his certainty of this, ingratitude. For whom, then, was she being so good? Wasn't he himself the obstacle to all happiness, the cause of all misery, and, as it were, the sharp-pointed prong of that complex belt that bound her on all sides?

And so she directed at him alone the manifold hatred born of her troubles, and every attempt she made to diminish that hatred only increased it; for her useless effort gave her yet another reason for despair and contributed even more to her estrangement from him. Her own gentleness goaded her to rebel. The mediocrity of her domestic life provoked her to sensual fantasies, matrimonial affection to adulterous desires. She wished Charles would beat her, so that she could more justly detest him, avenge herself. She was sometimes surprised at the shocking conjectures that entered her mind; and yet she had to keep smiling, hear herself say again and again that she was happy, pretend to be happy, let everyone believe it!

There were times, however, when she was disgusted by this hypocrisy. She would be seized by the temptation to run off with Léon, somewhere far away, to try out a new destiny; but immediately a formless chasm, full of darkness, would open in her soul.

"Besides, he doesn't love me anymore," she would think. "What will become of me? What help can I hope for, what consolation, what relief?"

She was left shattered, breathless, unmoving, quietly sobbing, tears running down her face.

"Why don't you tell Monsieur?" the maid would ask, when she came in during one of these fits.

"It's nerves," Emma would answer. "Don't say anything to him; it would upset him."

"Oh, yes!" Félicité would say. "You're just like the Guérin girl, Père Guérin's girl, he was a fisherman from Le Pollet, I knew them at Dieppe before I came to you. She was so sad, so very sad, that when you saw her standing in the doorway of her house, you would think you saw a funeral pall hanging in front of the door. What ailed her, it seemed, was a kind of fog she had in her head, and the doctors couldn't do anything, nor the curé either. When it took her too hard, she would go off all alone to the seaside, such that the customs officer, when he made his rounds, would often enough find her lying flat on her face on the pebbles, in tears. Then, after she married, it left her, so they say."

"But with me," Emma would reply, "it was after I married that it began."

[6]

One evening when the window was open and, sitting on the sill, she had just been watching Lestiboudois, the beadle, trimming the boxwood hedge, she suddenly heard the chiming of the Angelus.

It was the beginning of April, when the primroses are in bloom; a warm wind tumbles over the newly spaded flower beds, and the gardens, like women, seem to be grooming themselves for the festivities of summer. Through the slats of the arbor and all around, beyond, one could see the stream flowing through the meadows, tracing its sinuous, vagabond course over the grass. The evening mist was passing among the leafless poplars, softening their outlines with a tinge of violet, paler and more transparent than fine gauze caught in their branches. In the distance, cattle were walking; neither their steps nor their lowing could be heard; and the bell rang on and on, continuing in the air its peaceful lamentation.

With this steady chiming, the young woman's thoughts strayed among old memories of her youth and boarding school. She recalled the great candelabras, which rose, on the altar, higher than the flower-filled vases and the tabernacle with its little columns. She wished that once again, as in the old days, she could be part of the long line of white veils marked here and there with black by the stiff cowls of the good sisters bending over their prie-dieux; on Sundays, at Mass, when she lifted her head, she would see the sweet face of the Virgin among the bluish eddies of rising incense. And now she was filled with tenderness; she felt soft and utterly abandoned, like the downy feather of a bird turning in a storm; and it was without conscious awareness that she made her way toward the church, inclined to any devotion, so long as her soul might be absorbed in it and all of life disappear into it.

On the square, she met Lestiboudois, who was returning; for rather than cut his day short, he preferred to interrupt his chore and then take it up again, with the result that he rang the Angelus at his own convenience. Besides, the ringing, when done earlier, alerted the children that it was time for catechism.

Already, a few who happened to have arrived were playing marbles on the slabs in the cemetery. Others, straddling the wall, were swinging their legs, their sabots felling the tall nettles that had grown up between the little enclosing wall and the nearest gravestones. This was the only green area; all the rest was stones, and always covered in fine dust, despite the vestry broom.

Children in slippers were running about there, as though on a parquet floor made just for them. Their shrill voices could be heard over the booming of the bell, which diminished with the oscillations of the thick rope that hung down from the top of the bell tower and trailed on the ground. Swallows flew past uttering little cries, cutting the air with the blades of their flights, and went swiftly back into their yellow nests under the tiles of the gutter overhang. At the far end of the church, a lamp was burning, or rather, the wick of a night-light in a hanging glass. Its glow, from far away, seemed like a whitish spot trembling on the oil. A long ray of sunlight crossed the whole of the nave and deepened the darkness of the side aisles and corners.

"Where is the curé?" Madame Bovary asked a young boy who was amusing himself by shaking the turnstile on its slack pivot.

"He's coming," he answered.

And indeed, the door of the presbytery creaked; Abbé Bournisien appeared; the children fled headlong into the church.

"Those scamps!" murmured the clergyman. "Always the same!"

And, picking up a tattered catechism that he had stumbled over:

"They've no respect!"

But as soon as he saw Madame Bovary:

"Excuse me," he said, "I didn't recognize you."

He thrust the catechism into his pocket and stopped, continuing to swing between two fingers the heavy key to the sacristy.

The gleam of the setting sun struck him full in the face and lightened the color of his woolen cassock, shiny at the elbows, frayed at the hem. Spots of grease and snuff followed the line of little buttons over his broad chest and grew more numerous the farther they were from his neckband, on which rested the abundant folds of his red chin; his skin was scattered with yellow blotches that disappeared among the coarse hairs of his graying beard. He had just dined and was breathing noisily.

"How are you faring?" he added.

"Not well," answered Emma; "I'm in pain."

"Why, so am I," replied the clergyman. "These first warm days weaken one terribly, don't they? Well, there's nothing to be done! We're born to

suffer, as Saint Paul says. But, now, what does Monsieur Bovary think
about this?"

"Oh, him!" she said with a gesture of disdain.

"What!" replied the simple man, quite surprised; "hasn't he prescribed
something for you?"

"Ah!" said Emma; "it isn't earthly remedies I need."

But the curé kept looking away, into the church, where the children,
on their knees, were shoving one another with their shoulders and top-
pling over like a row of ninepins.

"I would like to know . . . ," she went on.

"Just you wait, Riboudet," shouted the clergyman angrily, "I'll box
your ears for you, you miserable scalawag!"

Then, turning to Emma:

"That's young Boudet, the carpenter's son; his parents are very well
off and let him do as he likes. And yet he'd be a quick learner if he chose
to; he's very bright. Sometimes, as a joke, I call him Riboudet (like the
hill on the way to Maromme); sometimes I even say 'mon Riboudet.' Ha,
ha! Mont-Riboudet! The other day, I reported my little witticism to His
Grace, and he laughed . . . he was kind enough to laugh at it. —And
Monsieur Bovary, how is he?"

She did not seem to hear him. He went on:

"Always has his hands full, no doubt? Because he and I are certainly
the two busiest people in the parish. But he treats the body," he added
with a heavy laugh, "while I treat the soul!"

Emma fixed her supplicating eyes on the priest.

"Yes . . . ," she said, "you offer comfort for every sort of misery."

"Ah! Don't talk to me about that, Madame Bovary! Just this morning,
I had to go to Bas-Diauville for a cow that had the *bloat;* they thought it
was bewitched. Every one of their cows, for some reason or other . . . Oh,
I beg your pardon! Longuemarre and Boudet! Blast you! Stop that!"

And with one bound, he plunged into the church.

The boys, by now, were crowding around the high lectern, climbing
onto the cantor's stool, opening the missal; some, moving stealthily, were
about to venture into the confessional. But the curé descended on them
suddenly, raining down a shower of slaps right and left. Seizing them
by their jacket collars, he lifted them off the ground and set them back

down on their knees on the choir pavement, hard, as if he were trying to plant them there.

"Well, now," he said when he returned to Emma, opening his large calico handkerchief and putting a corner of it between his teeth, "the farmers certainly deserve our sympathy!"

"Others do, too," she answered.

"Assuredly! The working folk in the towns, for instance."

"I didn't mean them . . ."

"I beg your pardon! But I've known poor mothers of families, virtuous women I assure you, veritable saints, who hadn't even a crust of bread."

"But what about those women," Emma replied (and the corners of her mouth twisted as she spoke), "those women, Monsieur le curé, who have bread, but have no . . ."

"Fire in winter," said the priest.

"Oh! What does it matter?"

"What! What does it matter? It seems to me, don't you know, that when one is warm, and well fed . . . because, really . . ."

"My God! My God!" she sighed.

"Are you feeling unwell?" he asked, coming closer with a worried look; "it's probably something you ate, isn't it? You should go back home, Madame Bovary, and have a little tea; that'll pick you up; or perhaps a glass of cool water with some brown sugar."

"Why?"

And she looked like someone waking from a dream.

"You were putting your hand to your forehead. I thought you were feeling faint."

Then, recollecting:

"But you were asking me something, weren't you? What was it? I can't remember."

"I? Oh, nothing . . . nothing . . . ," Emma repeated.

And her gaze, which was wandering around, slowly came to rest on the old man in his cassock. They contemplated each other, face-to-face, without speaking.

"Well, Madame Bovary," he said at last, "please excuse me, but duty before everything, you know; I must see to my little scapegraces. First Communion looms already. We'll still be caught unprepared, I'm afraid!

Which is why, from Ascension on, I keep them every Wednesday *precisely* one hour longer. Poor things! It's never too early to guide them in the way of the Lord, as, in fact, He himself advised, through the mouth of His divine Son . . . Good health, madame; my respects to Monsieur, your husband!"

And he went into the church, genuflecting at the door.

Emma saw him disappear between the double rows of pews, walking with heavy steps, his head a little tipped toward one shoulder, his hands half open hanging by his sides.

Then she turned on her heels, in a single motion like a statue on a pivot, and set off for home. But the curé's stern voice, the clear voices of the children, still reached her ears and continued sounding behind her:

"Are you a Christian?"

"Yes, I am a Christian."

"What is a Christian?"

"A Christian is one who, being baptized . . . baptized . . . baptized . . ."

She climbed her stairs holding on to the railing, and when she reached her bedroom, she let herself fall back into an armchair.

The wan light from the windows was fading in gentle undulations. The pieces of furniture, each in its place, seemed to have grown stiller and to be sinking into an ocean of shadow. The fire was out, the clock ticked on, and Emma vaguely marveled that these things should be so calm while within herself she felt such turmoil. But between the window and the sewing table, there was little Berthe, tottering in her knitted booties, trying to reach her mother, to catch hold of the ends of her apron strings.

"Leave me alone!" said Emma, pushing her away with her hand.

The little girl soon came back, even closer to her knees; and, leaning on them with her arms, she looked up at her with her big blue eyes, while a thread of clear saliva dropped from her lip onto the silk of the apron.

"Leave me alone!" the young woman said again, very irritated.

Her face terrified the child, who began screaming.

"Oh, leave me alone, won't you!" she said, thrusting her off with her elbow.

Berthe fell at the foot of the chest of drawers, against the brass fittings; she cut her cheek; the blood ran. Madame Bovary rushed to pick her up, broke the bellpull, called the servant at the top of her voice; and she was about to begin cursing herself when Charles appeared. It was dinnertime, he had come home.

"Look, my dear," Emma said to him calmly, "the baby was playing and has just fallen and hurt herself."

Charles reassured her that it was not at all serious, and he went off to find some diachylon.

Madame Bovary did not go down to the dining room; she insisted on remaining alone to look after her child. Then, as she watched her sleeping, the worry that she still felt dissipated gradually, and she appeared in her own eyes quite foolish and quite good to have allowed herself to be upset over so unimportant a thing. Berthe, indeed, was no longer sobbing. Her breathing, now, was barely perceptible as it lifted the cotton coverlet. A few large teardrops had gathered in the corners of her half-closed eyelids, through whose lashes one could glimpse two pale, sunken pupils; the adhesive plaster, stuck to her cheek, pulled the stretched skin to one side.

"How strange," thought Emma. "The child is so ugly!"

When at eleven o'clock Charles came back from the pharmacy (where he had gone after dinner to return what was left of the diachylon), he found his wife standing by the cradle.

"I tell you it'll be all right," he said, kissing her on the forehead. "Don't torment yourself, my poor dear, you'll make yourself ill!"

He had stayed at the apothecary's for a long time. Even though he had not seemed very upset, Monsieur Homais had nonetheless attempted to cheer him up, to *raise his spirits.* They had talked about the various dangers with which childhood was threatened, and the thoughtlessness of servants. Madame Homais knew something about this, since she still bore on her chest the marks of a bowlful of embers that a cook had, long ago, let fall into her smock. Indeed, these good parents took no end of precautions. The knives were never sharpened, nor the floors waxed. There were iron grates on the windows and stout bars across the fireplaces. The Homais children, despite their independence, could not move without someone watching them; at the slightest cold, their father would stuff them with cough syrups, and until they were past the age of four, they were all mercilessly made to wear padded caps. True, this was an obsession of Madame Homais's; her husband was privately distressed by it, fearing the effects of such pressure on the organs of the intellect, and he sometimes forgot himself so far as to say to her:

"Are you trying to turn them into Caribs or Botocudos?"

Charles, meanwhile, had tried several times to interrupt the conversation.

"I'd like to talk to you," he had murmured quietly in the ear of the clerk, who started down the stairs ahead of him.

"Could he suspect something?" Léon wondered. His heart began pounding, and his mind was filled with conjectures.

At last, Charles, having closed the door, asked him if he would be so kind as to inquire in person, in Rouen, what the various prices of a good daguerreotype might be; this was a sentimental surprise he was preparing for his wife, a delicate tribute, a portrait of himself in a black suit. But he wanted to know, ahead of time, *what to expect;* such inquiries would surely be no trouble for Monsieur Léon, since he went to town every week, more or less.

For what purpose? Homais suspected it was some *young man's business,* an intrigue. But he was mistaken; Léon was not involved in any love affair. He was more melancholy than ever, and Madame Lefrançois perceived this clearly by the quantity of food he now left on his plate. To find out more about it, she questioned the tax collector; Binet replied, in an arrogant tone, that he *was not in the pay of the police.*

His dinner companion did, however, seem to him quite strange; for often Léon would lie back in his chair, spread his arms wide, and complain vaguely about life.

"The trouble is, you don't have enough distractions," said the tax collector.

"What sort do you mean?"

"Well, in your place, I would have a lathe!"

"But I don't know how to use a lathe," the clerk answered.

"Why, yes, that's true!" said Binet, stroking his jaw with an air of mingled scorn and satisfaction.

Léon was tired of loving without having anything to show for it; then, too, he was beginning to feel the despondency that comes from leading an unvarying life, with no interest to give it direction and no hope to sustain it. He was so bored by Yonville and the people of Yonville that the sight of certain individuals, of certain houses, provoked him until he could not bear it any longer; and the pharmacist, good fellow that he was, was becoming completely intolerable to him. And yet the prospect of a new situation frightened him as much as it attracted him.

This apprehension soon turned into impatience, and at that point Paris beckoned to him, in the distance, with the fanfare of its costume balls and the laughter of its grisettes. Since he had to finish his law studies there, why shouldn't he leave now? What was there to stop him? And he set about making preparations in his imagination: he planned in advance what he would do. In his mind, he furnished a room for himself. There, he would lead the life of an artist! He would take guitar lessons! He would have a dressing gown, a Basque beret, blue velvet slippers! And already he admired the two crossed fencing foils on his mantelpiece, with a skull, and the guitar hanging above.

The difficult thing was his mother's consent; yet nothing seemed more reasonable. Even his employer was urging him to spend time in another law practice, where he could develop himself further. And so, taking a middle course, Léon looked for some position as second clerk in Rouen, could not find one, and at last wrote his mother a long, detailed letter in which he explained the reasons for going to live in Paris at once. She consented.

He did not hurry. Each day, for an entire month, Hivert transported trunks, valises, packages for him from Yonville to Rouen, and from Rouen to Yonville; and when Léon had replenished his wardrobe, reupholstered his three armchairs, bought a supply of silk foulards—in other words, made more preparations than for a trip around the world—still he delayed from week to week, until he received a second letter from his mother pressing him to leave, since he wanted to pass his exam before the vacation.

When the moment came for the farewell embraces, Madame Homais wept; Justin sobbed; Homais, as befitted a strong man, concealed his emotion; he insisted on personally carrying his friend's overcoat to the notary's gate; the latter was to take Léon to Rouen in his carriage. The clerk had just enough time to say his goodbyes to Monsieur Bovary.

When he reached the top of the stairs, he stopped, he felt so out of breath. As he went in, Madame Bovary stood up quickly.

"Here I am again!" said Léon.

"I was sure of it!"

She bit her lips, and a wave of blood rushed under her skin, turning it pink from the roots of her hair to the edge of her collar. She remained standing, leaning with one shoulder against the wood paneling.

"Monsieur isn't here?" he said.

"He's out."

She said again:

"He's out."

Then there was a silence. They looked at each other; and their thoughts, mingling in the same distress, clung to each other like two trembling hearts.

"I would like to give Berthe a kiss, if I could," said Léon.

Emma went down a few steps and called Félicité.

Quickly he looked around at the walls, the shelves, the fireplace, as though to penetrate all of it, carry it all away with him.

But she came back, and the servant brought in Berthe, who was shaking a toy windmill upside down at the end of a string.

Léon kissed her on the neck several times.

"Goodbye, poor child! Goodbye, dear little girl, goodbye!"

And he returned her to her mother.

"Take her away," she said.

They were left alone.

Madame Bovary, her back turned, was resting her face against a windowpane; Léon was holding his cap in his hand and tapping it gently against his thigh.

"It's going to rain," said Emma.

"I have a coat," he answered.

"Ah!"

She turned around, her chin lowered and her forehead toward him. The light slid over it, as though it were marble, as far as the curve of her eyebrows; it was impossible to know what Emma was seeing in the distance or what she was thinking deep inside herself.

"Well, then, goodbye!" he sighed.

She lifted her head abruptly:

"Yes, goodbye . . . Go!"

They moved toward each other; he held out his hand; she hesitated.

"English style, then," she said, surrendering her own hand to him as she forced herself to laugh.

Léon felt it between his fingers, and to him it seemed that the very substance of his entire being was descending into that moist palm.

Then he opened his hand; their eyes met again, and he went.

When he reached the marketplace, he stopped and hid behind a post to contemplate one last time that white house with its four green blinds. He thought he saw a shadow behind the window, in the bedroom; but the curtain, released from its hook as though no one were touching it, slowly stirred its long slanting folds, then sprang fully out and hung down straight and still as a plaster wall. Léon set off at a run.

From a distance, he saw his employer's gig in the road, and next to it a man in an apron holding the horse. Homais and Monsieur Guillaumin were talking together. They were waiting for him.

"Give me a hug," said the apothecary, tears in his eyes. "Here's your overcoat, my good friend; watch out for the cold! Look after yourself! Don't overdo!"

"Come, Léon, jump in!" said the notary.

Homais leaned over the splashboard and, in a voice broken by sobs, pronounced these two sad words:

"Bon voyage!"

"Bon soir," answered Monsieur Guillaumin. "Off we go!" They left, and Homais headed back home.

Madame Bovary had opened her window onto the garden, and she was watching the clouds.

They were piling up in the west, in the direction of Rouen, and swiftly rolling over and over in volutes of black, from behind which long rays of sunlight extended like the golden arrows of a hanging trophy, while the rest of the empty sky was white as porcelain. But a gust of wind bowed the poplars, and suddenly the rain fell, pattering on the green leaves. Then the sun came out again, the hens clucked, sparrows beat their wings in the wet bushes, and puddles of water running over the gravel carried away the pink petals of an acacia.

"Oh, how far off he must be already!" she thought.

Monsieur Homais, as usual, came in at six-thirty, during dinner.

"Well, well," he said, sitting down, "so we've sent our young man on his way, now, have we?"

"So it seems!" answered the doctor.

Then, turning in his chair:

"And what is new at your house?"

"Not much. Only, this afternoon, my wife was a bit upset. Women, you know—the least little thing troubles them! Especially my wife! And one would be wrong to oppose it, since their nervous systems are much more impressionable than ours."

"Poor Léon!" said Charles. "How will he live in Paris? . . . Will he get used to it?"

Madame Bovary sighed.

"Come now!" said the pharmacist, with a tut-tut. "Parties at restaurants! Costume balls! Champagne! He'll have a high old time, I assure you."

"I don't think he'll do anything wrong," objected Charles.

"Nor do I!" Monsieur Homais said quickly; "though he'll have to go along with the others, if he's not to risk looking like a Jesuit. And you don't know the sort of life those young devils lead in the Latin Quarter, with their actresses! Anyway, students are very highly regarded in Paris. If they have any talent at all for making themselves agreeable, they're received in the best circles, and in fact the ladies in the Faubourg Saint-Germain tend to fall in love with them, which gives them the chance, subsequently, to contract some very fine marriages."

"But," said the doctor, "I worry that he may . . . in that place . . ."

"You're right," interrupted the apothecary; "that's the other side of the coin! And you must always keep your hand on your pocket there. For instance, supposing you're in a public park; some fellow comes up to you, well turned out, even decorated, someone you would take for a diplomat; he speaks to you; you get into a conversation with him; he ingratiates himself, offers you a pinch of snuff or picks up your hat for you. Then the two of you become friendlier; he takes you to a café, invites you to his house in the country, introduces you, between one glass and the next, to all sorts of people, and three-quarters of the time, it's only to make off with your purse or entice you into some pernicious adventure."

"That's true," answered Charles; "but I was thinking mainly of diseases—typhoid fever, for example, which students from the country are likely to contract."

Emma shuddered.

"Because of the change in regimen," agreed the pharmacist, "and the resulting perturbation of the whole system. And then, you know, there's the Paris water! And the restaurant meals, all those spicy foods that end by overheating your blood and aren't worth as much, whatever they may say, as a good stew. I myself have always preferred home cooking: it's healthier! For instance, when I was studying pharmacy at Rouen, I stayed in a boardinghouse; I ate with the professors."

And he went on expounding his general opinions and airing his personal predilections until Justin came to get him because an eggnog needed to be made up.

"Not a moment's respite!" he cried. "Always at the grindstone! I can't leave for a minute! I'm made to sweat blood and water, like a workhorse! What eternal drudgery!"

Then, when he was at the door:

"By the way," he said, "have you heard the news?"

"What is it?"

"Well, it's quite likely," said Homais, raising his eyebrows and assuming an expression of extreme gravity, "that the agricultural fair for the Seine Inférieure will be held at Yonville-l'Abbaye this year. At least, that's the rumor that's going around. The paper mentioned something about it this morning. It would be of the utmost importance for our district! But we'll talk about it later. I can see, thank you; Justin has the lantern."

[7]

The next day was, for Emma, a dismal one. Everything seemed enveloped in a black atmosphere that hovered indistinctly over the exterior of things, and sorrow rushed into her soul, moaning softly like the winter wind in abandoned manor houses. It was the sort of reverie you sink into over something that will never return again, the lassitude that overcomes you with each thing that is finished, the pain you suffer when any habitual motion is stopped, when a prolonged vibration abruptly ceases.

As on her return from La Vaubyessard, when the quadrilles whirled around in her head, she was filled with a bleak melancholy, a numb despair. Léon reappeared to her, taller, handsomer, more delightful, less distinct; though gone from her, he had not left her, he was there, and the walls of the house seemed to retain his shadow. She could not take her eyes off the carpet on which he had stepped, the empty furniture on which he had sat. The river still flowed past and slowly nudged its little billows along the shining bank. They had walked there many times, accompanied by the same murmur of the waves, over the moss-covered stones. What lovely sunlight they had enjoyed! What fine afternoons, alone in the shade, at the bottom of the garden! He would read aloud, his head bare, seated on a stool made of dry sticks; the cool wind from the meadow would flutter the pages of the book and the nasturtiums in the arbor . . . Oh! He was gone—the only delight in her life, her only possible hope of happiness! Why hadn't she seized that happiness when it was offered! Why hadn't she held on to it with both hands, on both knees, when it tried to slip away? And she cursed herself for not having loved Léon; she thirsted for his lips. She was seized with a longing to run to him, to throw herself into his arms, to say: "Here I am, I'm yours!" But the difficulties of the undertaking discouraged Emma in advance, and her desires, increased by regret, merely became all the more urgent.

From then on, the memory of Léon occupied the center of her feeling of weariness; there it sparkled more brightly than a fire abandoned by travelers on the snow of a Russian steppe. She would rush up to it, she would crouch down next to it, she would delicately stir its embers, so close to dying out, she would look all around for something that could revive it; and the most distant memories, as well as the most recent events, what she was feeling and what she was imagining, her sensuous desires, which were dissipating, her plans for happiness, which were cracking in the wind like dead branches, her sterile virtue, her disappointed hopes, the litter of her domestic life—she gathered all of it up, took it, and used it to rekindle her sadness.

And yet the flames died down, either because the supply of fuel was exhausted or because too much was piled on. Little by little, love was extinguished by absence, longing smothered by routine; and the incendiary glow that had reddened her pale sky was covered over in shadow and by degrees faded away. In the torpor of her consciousness, she even misunderstood her feelings of repugnance for her husband to be yearnings for her lover, the scorching of hatred for the rekindling of affection; but since the storm continued to rage and her passion burned itself to ashes, and since no help came and no sun appeared, night closed in completely around her, and she remained lost in a terrible, piercing cold.

Then the bad days of Tostes began again. She considered herself far more unhappy now: for along with her experience of sorrow, she now had the certainty that it would never end.

A woman who had required of herself such great sacrifices could surely be permitted to indulge her whims. She bought herself a Gothic prie-dieu, and she spent fourteen francs in one month on lemons for blanching her fingernails; she sent away to Rouen for a dress of blue cashmere; at Lheureux's, she chose the most beautiful of his scarves; she tied it around her waist over her dressing gown; and outfitted in this way, with the shutters closed, she would lie down on a couch with a book in her hand.

She would often change the way she wore her hair: she would arrange it à la Chinoise, or in gentle curls, or intertwined braids; she parted it on the side of her head and rolled it under, like a man's.

She decided to learn Italian: she bought dictionaries, a grammar, a supply of white paper. She attempted some serious reading, in history and philosophy. At night, sometimes, Charles would wake with a start, thinking he was being called to a sickbed.

"I'm coming," he would mumble.

And it was the sound of Emma striking a match to relight the lamp. But it was the same with her reading as with her tapestry-work projects, which, barely begun, crowded her cupboard; she would take them up, leave them off, go on to others.

She had moods in which she could easily have been provoked into extravagant behavior. One day she insisted, in defiance of her husband, that she could indeed drink half a large glass of eau-de-vie, and when Charles foolishly challenged her to do it, she swallowed the eau-de-vie to the last drop.

Despite her flightiness (this was what the townswomen of Yonville called it), Emma did not look happy, and the corners of her mouth were usually marked by those stiff creases that line the faces of old maids and people of failed ambitions. She was pale all over, as white as a sheet; the skin of her nose was stretched tight around the nostrils; her eyes stared at you vaguely. Because she had discovered three gray hairs at her temples, she talked a good deal about growing old.

She often had dizzy spells. One day she even spat blood, and when Charles fussed over her, showing his concern:

"Bah!" she answered, "what does it matter?"

Charles retreated into his office; and he wept, his elbows on the table, sitting in his office chair, under the phrenological head.

Then he wrote to his mother asking her to come, and together they had long conferences on the subject of Emma.

What was the answer? What could they do, since she was refusing all treatment?

"Do you know what your wife needs?" Mère Bovary went on. "She needs to be forced to work, to work with her hands! If she was obliged to earn her living, like so many others, she wouldn't be having these vapors—they come from all the ideas she stuffs her head with, and her idle life."

"She does keep busy, though," said Charles.

"Ah! Busy! With what, pray tell? Reading novels, evil books, books against religion that make fun of the priests with speeches from Voltaire. But all of that has its effect, my poor child, and a person who has no religion always comes to a bad end."

So it was decided that Emma would be prevented from reading novels. The project did not seem an easy one. The good lady took it upon herself: when she passed through Rouen, she would go in person to the proprietor of the lending library and inform him that Emma was terminating her subscription. Wouldn't one have the right to alert the police if, despite this, the bookseller persisted in his business as purveyor of poison?

The farewells between mother-in-law and daughter-in-law were curt. During the three weeks they had been together, they had not exchanged four words, apart from formal greetings and polite inquiries when they encountered each other at the table and at night before going to bed.

Madame Bovary senior left on a Wednesday, which was market day at Yonville.

From morning on, the Square was congested with a line of carts, all tipped up with their shafts in the air, extending along the housefronts from the church to the inn. On the opposite side were canvas booths selling cotton goods, woolen blankets and stockings, halters for horses, and bundles of blue ribbons whose ends flew in the wind. Larger metal goods were spread over the ground, between the pyramids of eggs and the small hampers of cheeses, from which sticky pieces of straw poked out; near the threshers, clucking hens in flat cages thrust their necks through the bars. The people, crowding together in one spot and unwilling to move, at times seemed about to break the pharmacy's front window. On Wednesdays the shop never emptied out, and people pushed their way in not so much to buy medicines as to have consultations, so celebrated was Monsieur Homais's reputation in the surrounding villages. His robust confidence had bewitched the countrypeople. They regarded him as a greater doctor than any real doctor.

Emma was leaning on her elbows at her window (she would often sit there: a window, in the country, takes the place of a theater or a public walk), and she was amusing herself contemplating the mob of rustics, when she saw a gentleman dressed in a green velvet frock coat. He wore yellow gloves, though he was shod in heavy gaiters; and he was headed toward the doctor's house, followed by a countryman walking with bowed head and pensive air.

"May I see Monsieur?" he asked Justin, who was talking on the doorsill with Félicité.

And taking him for the servant of the house:

"Tell him that Monsieur Rodolphe Boulanger, of La Huchette, is here."

It was not out of a landowner's vanity that the new arrival had added "of La Huchette" to his name, but to identify himself more clearly. La Huchette, indeed, was an estate near Yonville whose château he had just acquired, along with two farms that he was cultivating himself, though without taking excessive trouble over them. He was a bachelor and was said to have *at least fifteen thousand livres in income!*

Charles came into the parlor. Monsieur Boulanger introduced his man, who wanted to be bled because he was feeling *ants all up and down his body.*

"It'll clear me out," was his objection to every argument.

So Bovary ordered a bandage and a basin to be brought, and asked Justin to hold it. Then, speaking to the villager, who was already pale:

"Don't be afraid, my good fellow."

"No, no," answered the other, "go ahead!"

And with an air of bravado, he held out his thick arm. At the prick of the lancet, the blood spurted forth and spattered over the mirror.

"Bring the bowl closer!" exclaimed Charles.

"Mark that!" said the countryman. "It's like a little spring coming up! What red blood I have! A good sign, isn't it?"

"Sometimes," said the officer of health, "they don't feel anything at first, then the syncope occurs afterward, especially in people with good constitutions, like this one."

At these words, the countryman let go of the lancet case he had been turning around and around in his fingers. The jolt of his shoulders made the back of the chair creak. His hat fell off.

"I expected as much," said Bovary, applying his finger to the vein.

The basin was beginning to tremble in Justin's hands; his knees wobbled, he turned pale.

"Where's my wife? Emma!" called Charles.

Immediately she came down the stairs.

"Vinegar!" he cried. "Oh, Lord, two at once!"

And he was so agitated that he had trouble applying the compress.

"It's nothing," said Monsieur Boulanger calmly, as he took Justin in his arms.

And he sat him on the table, leaning his back against the wall.

Madame Bovary began removing his cravat. There was a knot in the strings of his shirt; for a few minutes she moved her light fingers around the boy's neck; then she poured some vinegar on her cambric handkerchief; with it she dampened his temples with little pats, and she blew on them softly.

The carter came to; but Justin remained in his faint, and his irises were sinking into the whites, like blue flowers in milk.

"We ought to hide that from him," said Charles.

Madame Bovary took the basin. With the movement she made, bending down to put it under the table, her dress (it was a summer dress with four flounces, yellow, long in the waist, wide in the skirt) flared out around her over the stone floor of the room; —and as Emma, stooping, swayed a little, putting out her arms, the material swelled and subsided here and there, following the contours of her body. She went to get a carafe of water, and she was melting lumps of sugar in it when the pharmacist arrived. The servant had gone to find him in the hubbub; seeing his student with his eyes open, he drew a long breath. Then, walking around him, he looked him up and down.

"Fool!" he said. "You little fool! Really! Fool, spelled f-o-o-l! Quite an event, isn't it—a phlebotomy! A strapping fellow like you, who isn't afraid of anything! Just look at him—like a squirrel, he climbs up to shake the nuts down from dizzying heights. Ah, yes! Speak up, boast about yourself! What a fine natural aptitude you'll have for being a pharmacist later on; you know, you may be called before a tribunal in some serious situation, to enlighten the magistrates; and you'll have to maintain your composure, speak rationally, show yourself to be a man, or else be taken for an imbecile!"

Justin did not answer. The apothecary continued:

"Who asked you to come? You're always bothering Monsieur and Madame! Besides, on Wednesdays, your presence is especially indispensable to me. Right now there are twenty people over at the house. I left everything because of my concern for you. Now, come on! Hurry! Wait for me there and keep an eye on the jars!"

When Justin, who was putting his things back on, had gone, they talked a little about fainting spells. Madame Bovary had never had one.

"That's extraordinary for a lady!" said Monsieur Boulanger. "The fact is, some people are very sensitive. At a duel, for example, I once saw a witness lose consciousness merely at the sound of the pistols being loaded."

"I myself," said the apothecary, "am not in the least affected by the sight of other people's blood; but the very idea of shedding my own would be enough to make me faint, if I thought about it too much."

Meanwhile, Monsieur Boulanger sent his servant away, advising him to set his mind at rest, now that his whim had been gratified.

"It has afforded me the advantage of making your acquaintance," he added.

And he was looking at Emma as he spoke.

Then he laid three francs on the corner of the table, bowed casually, and went off.

He was soon on the other side of the river (this was the path he took back to La Huchette); and Emma saw him in the meadow, walking under the poplars, slowing down from time to time, like someone deep in thought.

"She's very nice!" he was saying to himself; "she's very nice, that doctor's wife! Lovely teeth, dark eyes, a trim little foot, and a figure like a Parisian. Where the devil did she come from? Where did he find her, that gross fellow?"

Monsieur Rodolphe Boulanger was thirty-four years old; his nature was rough and his intelligence keen; he had known many women and was a good judge of them. This one had seemed pretty to him; so he was thinking about her, and about her husband.

"I believe he's very stupid. She's probably tired of him. He has dirty nails and a three-day-old beard. While he trots off to his patients, she stays at home darning socks. And we're bored! We'd like to live in the city, dance the polka every night! Poor little woman! That one's gasping for love like a carp for water on a kitchen table. With three pretty compliments, that one would adore me, I'm sure of it! It would be lovely! Charming! . . . Yes, but how to get rid of the woman afterward?"

And so his glimpse of the hindrances that might stand in the way of his pleasure made him, by contrast, think of his mistress. She was an actress in Rouen whom he was supporting; and as he paused over her image, which gave him, even in recollection, feelings of satiety:

"Ah," he thought, "Madame Bovary is much prettier than she is, and fresher! Virginie is definitely beginning to grow fat. She's so tiresome with her enthusiasms. And what a passion she has for prawns!"

The countryside was deserted, and around him Rodolphe heard only the regular beat of the grass whipping his boots, and far away the chirping of the crickets hiding under the oats; he saw Emma again in that room, dressed as he had seen her, and he undressed her.

"I'll have her!" he cried, striking a clod of earth in front of him with a stick and crushing it.

And he immediately examined the tactical part of the undertaking. He asked himself:

"Where would one meet? How would one manage it? The brat would be constantly hanging around one's neck, and the maid, the neighbors, the husband, every kind of serious bother! Bah!" he said, "It would take too much time!"

Then he began again:

"The thing is, her eyes bore into your heart like gimlets. And that pale complexion! . . . How I love pale women!"

By the time he reached the top of the Argueil hill, he had made up his mind.

"Now it's only a matter of looking for opportunities. Well, I'll stop by there from time to time, I'll send them some game, some poultry; I'll have myself bled, if necessary; we'll become friends, I'll invite them to my house . . . Why, yes! Yes, of course!" he added, "the fair is coming up; she'll be there; I'll see her. We'll make a start, a bold start. That's the surest way."

[8]

It was here at last, the day of the famous Agricultural Fair! On the morning of the solemn occasion, all the townspeople were at their doors talking about the preparations; the pediment of the town hall had been festooned with ivy; a tent for the banquet had been set up in a field; and, in the middle of the Square, in front of the church, a sort of ancient cannon was to signal the arrival of the Prefect and the naming of the prizewinning farmers. The national guard from Buchy (there was none at Yonville) had come to join the fire brigade, of which Binet was captain. On this day he was wearing a collar even higher than usual; and his chest, buttoned up tight in his tunic, was so stiff and motionless that all the vitality of his being seemed to have descended into his two legs, which rose in cadence, in rhythmic steps, with a single motion. Because a rivalry existed between the tax collector and the colonel, each of them, to show off his talents, took his men separately through their maneuvers. The red epaulets and the black breastplates could be seen turn by turn passing back and forth. There was no end to it, and it kept beginning again! Never had there been such a display of magnificence! A number of townspeople, the day before, had washed their houses; tricolored flags were hanging from the half-open windows; all the taverns were full; and in the good weather that prevailed, the starched headdresses, the gold crosses, and the multicolored fichus gleamed whiter than snow, sparkled in the bright sun, and relieved with their scattered hues the somber monotony of the frock coats and blue smocks. The farmwives from the surrounding regions, after descending from their horses, withdrew the large pin with which they had held their dresses tucked up close around their bodies for fear of spots; while their husbands, by contrast, in order to protect their hats, kept a pocket handkerchief over them, holding one corner between their teeth.

The crowd was entering the main street from both ends of the village. They flowed into it from lanes, alleys, houses, and now and then one could hear a knocker falling back against a door behind a townswoman in cotton gloves who was coming out to see the festivities. Particularly admired were two long triangular frames covered with little colored-glass oil lamps that flanked a platform on which the officials were going to sit; and against the four columns of the town hall there were also four polelike affairs, each bearing a little banner of greenish cloth embellished with an inscription in gold letters. One read "Commerce," another "Agriculture," the third "Industry," and the fourth "Fine Arts."

But the jubilation brightening all faces seemed to be casting a gloom over Madame Lefrançois, the innkeeper. Standing on the steps of her kitchen, she was murmuring into her chin:

"What stupidity! What stupidity—them and their piece of canvas! Do they really think the prefect'll enjoy having his dinner out there under a tent like a circus clown? They say all this fuss is for the good of our district! Then why go clear to Neufchâtel for a third-rate cook! And who's it for, anyways—cowherds! riffraff! . . ."

The apothecary came by. He was wearing a black frock coat, nankeen trousers, beaver-skin shoes, and, wonder of wonders, a hat—a low-crowned hat.

"Your servant!" he said; "I beg your pardon, I'm in a hurry."

And when the stout widow asked him where he was going:

"It seems funny to you, doesn't it, seeing as I'm usually locked up in my laboratory tighter than the old man's rat in his cheese."

"What cheese are you talking about?" asked the innkeeper.

"Never mind, never mind! It doesn't matter!" Homais went on. "I was merely trying to express to you, Madame Lefrançois, that I normally remain entirely secluded within my own home. And yet today, given the circumstances, one must really . . ."

"Ah! You're going out there?" she said with a scornful look.

"Yes, I am," replied the pharmacist, surprised; "I'm a member of the advisory committee, aren't I?"

Mère Lefrançois contemplated him for a few moments and then answered with a smile:

"That's different! But what has farming to do with you? Do you know anything about it?"

"Certainly I know something about it, since I am a pharmacist, which is to say a chemist! And since the object of chemistry, Madame Lefrançois, is a knowledge of the reciprocal and molecular action of all natural bodies, it follows that agriculture falls within its domain! And indeed, take the composition of manures, the fermentation of liquids, the analysis of gases, and the influence of noxious emanations—what is all that, I ask you, if not chemistry pure and simple?"

The innkeeper said nothing in reply. Homais continued:

"Do you think that, in order to be an agronomist, you need to till the soil or fatten the poultry yourself? No—but you do need to understand the constitution of the substances involved, the geological strata, the effects of the atmosphere, the quality of soils, minerals, waters, the density of the different bodies, and their capillary attraction! And so forth. And you need to be deeply familiar with all your principles of hygiene, in order to direct and review the construction of the buildings, the regimen of the animals, the feeding of the servants! You must also, Madame Lefrançois, know your botany; be able to distinguish among the plants, you know, tell which are salubrious and which deleterious, which are unproductive and which nutritive, if it's a good idea to pull them up in this spot and resow them over there, propagate these, destroy those others; in short, you need to keep up with the latest science by reading pamphlets and public papers, you must always keep your hand in, be prepared to point out which improvements . . ."

The innkeeper had not stopped staring at the door of the Café Français. The pharmacist continued:

"Would to God our farmers were chemists, or at least that they would pay more attention to the advice of the scientists! For instance, I myself recently wrote a rather powerful little work, a treatise of over seventy-two pages, entitled 'On Cider, Its Fabrication and Its Effects; Followed by a Number of New Reflections on the Subject,' which I sent to the Agronomic Society of Rouen; and which even earned me the honor of being received among its members—agricultural section, pomology division; well, now, if my work had been made available to the public . . ."

But the pharmacist stopped, because Madame Lefrançois seemed so preoccupied.

"Just look at them!" she said; "it's beyond understanding! such a hole-in-the-wall!"

And with shrugs that pulled the stitches of her sweater tight across her chest, she gestured with both hands toward her rival's establishment, out of which now came the sound of singing.

"Anyway, it won't be there much longer," she added; "another few days and that'll be the end of it."

Homais drew back in amazement. She descended her three steps and spoke in his ear:

"What! You don't know? They're going to shut him down this week.

Lheureux's the one that's forcing him to sell. He's killed him with promissory notes."

"What a dreadful catastrophe!" cried the pharmacist, who was always prepared with expressions to fit every imaginable circumstance.

And so the innkeeper began telling him the story, which she had had from Théodore, Monsieur Guillaumin's servant, and even though she despised Tellier, she blamed Lheureux. He was a wheedler, a toady.

"Ah! There—" she said, "there he is now, in the market; he's bowing to Madame Bovary; she's got a green hat on. And she's holding Monsieur Boulanger's arm."

"Madame Bovary!" said Homais. "I must go and pay my respects. Perhaps she'd like to have a seat in the enclosure, under the peristyle."

And without listening to Mère Lefrançois, who was calling him back to tell him more, the pharmacist went off with a quick step, a smile on his lips, and his knees pointing straight ahead, distributing a profusion of greetings right and left and filling a good deal of space with the large skirts of his black coat, which floated in the breeze behind him.

Rodolphe, having spotted him from a distance, had quickened his pace; but Madame Bovary was out of breath; he therefore slowed down and said to her, smiling, in a savage tone:

"I was trying to avoid that coarse fellow—you know, the pharmacist."

She nudged him with her elbow.

"What does that mean?" he wondered.

And he observed her out of the corner of his eye as they walked on.

Her profile was so calm that one could guess nothing from it. It stood out in the bright light, within the oval of her bonnet, whose pale ribbons resembled the leaves of rushes. Her eyes with their long curved lashes were gazing ahead, and, though wide open, they seemed a bit narrowed by her cheekbones, because of the blood that beat gently under her delicate skin. The membrane between her nostrils was of a translucent rose color. She was inclining her head toward her shoulder, and one could see between her lips the nacreous tips of her white teeth.

"Is she making fun of me?" mused Rodolphe.

But that gesture of Emma's had been no more than a warning; for Monsieur Lheureux was walking alongside them, and he spoke to them from time to time, as though to begin a conversation:

"What a splendid day! Everyone is out! The wind is from the east!"

And Madame Bovary scarcely answered him, no more did Rodolphe, while at their slightest motion the dry-goods merchant would draw closer, saying, "I beg your pardon?" and touching his hat.

When they were in front of the blacksmith's, instead of following the road all the way to the gate, Rodolphe abruptly turned aside into a path, drawing Madame Bovary along with him; he cried out:

"Goodbye, Monsieur Lheureux! Nice seeing you!"

"How you dismissed him!" she said, laughing.

"Why," he answered, "should one allow others to push their way in? And since, today, I have the good fortune to be with you . . ."

Emma blushed. He did not finish his sentence. Then he talked about the fine weather and how pleasant it was to walk on the grass. A few late oxeyes had appeared.

"Look at those pretty daisies," he said. "Enough good oracles for all the girls around here who are in love."

He added:

"Should I pick one? What do you think?"

"Are you in love?" she asked, coughing a little.

"Well! Who knows!" answered Rodolphe.

The meadow was beginning to fill, and the housewives would bump into you with their great umbrellas, their baskets, and their small children. One often had to give way before a long file of countrywomen, farm maids in blue stockings, flat shoes, and silver rings, who smelled of milk when one passed near them. They walked holding hands and thus covered the entire length of the meadow, from the row of aspens to the banquet tent. But it was time for the judging, and one after another the farmers were entering a kind of arena formed by a long rope supported on posts.

The animals were there, their noses turned to the rope, their unequal hindquarters forming a ragged line. Drowsy pigs were burrowing in the earth with their snouts; calves were bawling; sheep were bleating; cows, one leg folded in, spread their bellies over the grass and, slowly chewing their cuds, blinked their heavy eyelids under the flies that buzzed around them. Bare-armed carters held the halters of rearing stallions that whinnied with widened nostrils in the direction of the mares, who remained calm, reaching out their heads and hanging manes while their foals rested in their shadow or came now and then to suckle from them; and over the long undulation of all these massed bodies, one could see a white mane rising in the wind, like a wave, or sharp horns thrusting up, and the heads of men running. Off to one side, beyond the enclosure, a hundred paces away, was a big black bull wearing a muzzle and an iron ring in its nose, as motionless as a bronze statue. A child in rags held it by a rope.

Meanwhile, between the two rows, a group of gentlemen were advancing with heavy steps, examining each animal, then conferring with one another in low voices. One of them, who seemed more important, was taking a few notes, as he walked, in a notebook. This was the chairman of the jury: Monsieur Derozerays de la Panville. As soon as he recognized Rodolphe, he came forward briskly and said to him with a friendly smile:

"Why, Monsieur Boulanger, are you deserting us?"

Rodolphe protested that he would be along shortly. But when the chairman had gone off:

"Oh, no," he said. "Indeed I will not be along shortly; I value your company above his any day."

And even as he poked fun at the fair, Rodolphe showed the policeman his blue card so that they could walk about more freely, and he even stopped now and then in front of some handsome *specimen*, which Madame Bovary did not much admire. He noticed this and then began to make jokes about the ladies of Yonville and the way they dressed; then he asked her forgiveness for the carelessness of his own appearance. It was that incoherent mix of the ordinary and the elegant that common people generally take for evidence of an eccentric lifestyle, chaotic passions, the tyrannical dictates of art, and always a certain contempt for social conventions, which either charms or exasperates them. Thus, the breast of his cambric shirt, with its pleated cuffs, swelled as the wind caught it in the opening of his vest of gray twill, and his broad-striped trousers revealed at the ankles his low nankeen boots, vamped in patent leather. They were so highly polished they mirrored the grass; and in them he was trampling the horse dung underfoot, one hand in his jacket pocket and his straw hat tipped to the side.

"Besides," he added, "when you live in the country . . ."

"It's all a waste of effort," said Emma.

"True!" replied Rodolphe. "Just imagine—not one of these good people is capable of understanding even the cut of a coat!"

Then they talked about the mediocrity of provincial life, how stifling it was, how fatal to one's illusions.

"And so I myself," said Rodolphe, "sink into such melancholy . . ."

"You!" she broke in, surprised. "But I thought you were very happy."

"Oh, yes, I seem to be, because when I'm with other people, I'm able to hide my face behind a mask of mockery; and yet how often, at the sight of a cemetery, in the moonlight, have I asked myself if I would not do better to go join those who sleep there . . ."

"Oh! And your friends?" she said. "You're not thinking of them."

"My friends? Which ones? Do I have any? Who cares about me?"

And he accompanied these last words with a kind of whistle between his lips.

But they were obliged to draw apart because of a great tower of chairs that a man was carrying behind them. He was so overburdened that one could see only the tips of his wooden shoes and the ends of his two arms, held straight out in front of him. It was Lestiboudois, the gravedigger, who was transporting the chairs from the church in among the throng of people. Highly imaginative concerning anything to do with his own interests, he had discovered this means of drawing a profit from the fair; and his idea was a success, for he was being accosted on all sides—the villagers, who were hot, were indeed quarreling over these straw-seated chairs with their smell of incense, and they leaned back with a certain veneration against the stout slats soiled by wax from the tapers.

Madame Bovary took Rodolphe's arm again; he continued as though talking to himself:

"Yes! I've missed out on so many things! I've been so alone! Ah! If only I'd had some goal in life, if I'd known some affection, if I'd found someone . . . Oh, I would have expended all the energy I possess, I would have surmounted everything, conquered everything!"

"Yet it seems to me," said Emma, "that you're scarcely to be pitied."

"Oh? You think so?" said Rodolphe.

"Because . . . well . . . ," she went on, "you're free."

She hesitated:

"Rich."

"Don't make fun of me," he answered.

And she was swearing that she was not making fun of him, when a cannon shot resounded; immediately everyone began crowding, in confusion, toward the village.

It was a false alarm. The prefect had not arrived; and the members of the jury were perplexed, not knowing whether to begin the proceedings or continue to wait.

At last, on the far side of the Square, a large hired landau appeared, drawn by two thin horses being fiercely whipped by a coachman in a white hat. Binet had time enough only to shout, "Fall in!" and the colonel to imitate him. There was a rush toward the stacked rifles. They hurled themselves at them. A few even forgot their collars. But the prefect's coach-and-pair seemed to sense the difficulty, and the coupled nags, swaying from side to side on their slender chain, drew up at a slow trot in front of the portico of the town hall just at the moment when the national guard and the fire brigade were deploying there, marching in place to the beat of the drums.

"Mark time!" shouted Binet.

"Halt!" shouted the colonel. "File to the left!"

And after a present-arms in which the rattling of the rifle bands sounded like a copper cauldron tumbling down a flight of stairs, all the rifles were lowered.

They then saw, descending from the carriage, a gentleman dressed in a short coat embroidered in silver, bald over his forehead, his hair tufted on the crown of his head, with a pallid complexion and a most benign expression. He half closed his large, heavy-lidded eyes in order to study the crowd, at the same time lifting his sharp nose and arranging his sunken mouth into a smile. He recognized the mayor by his sash and explained to him that the prefect had been unable to come. He himself was a prefectural councilor. Then he added some excuses; Tuvache responded to these with civilities; the other confessed himself overwhelmed; and they remained thus, face-to-face, their foreheads almost touching, surrounded by the members of the jury, the town council, the local dignitaries, the national guard, and the crowd. The councilor, resting his little black tricornered hat against his chest, reiterated his salutations, while Tuvache, bent like a bow, smiled in turn, stammered, searched for words, protested his devotion to the monarchy and his recognition of the honor that was being bestowed on Yonville.

Hippolyte, the stableboy at the inn, came forward to take the horses by their bridles from the coachman and, limping on his clubfoot, led them through the gateway of the Lion d'Or, where many of the countryfolk had gathered to examine the carriage. The drum rolled, the howitzer boomed, and the gentlemen filed up to sit on the platform in the armchairs of red Utrecht velvet lent by Madame Tuvache.

These men all looked alike. Their soft, fair faces, a little tanned by the sun, were the color of sweet cider, and their fluffy side-whiskers escaped from high, stiff collars held straight by white cravats tied in broad bows. Every vest was of velvet, shawl style; every watch bore, at the end of a long ribbon, some sort of oval seal made of carnelian; and every man rested his hands on his thighs, carefully stretching the crotch of his trousers, whose hard-finished fabric shone more brilliantly than the leather of his stout boots.

The ladies of the party stayed in back, under the portico, between the columns, while the crowd of common folk was opposite, standing, or sitting in chairs. Indeed, Lestiboudois had brought over all those he had moved out of the meadow, and he kept running to the church to get even more, causing such congestion with his commerce that it was very difficult for anyone to reach the little flight of steps up to the platform.

"What I think," said Monsieur Lheureux (addressing the pharmacist, who was passing him on his way to his seat), "is that they should have set up a pair of Venetian masts there: hung with something a bit severe and sumptuous, it would have made a very pretty sight."

"Certainly," answered Homais. "But what can you expect! The mayor took everything into his own hands. He doesn't have much taste, poor Tuvache, and in fact he hasn't a trace of what's called artistic sense."

Meanwhile, Rodolphe, with Madame Bovary, had gone up to the second floor of the town hall, into the *council chamber,* and since it was empty, he had declared that here they would be in a good position to enjoy the spectacle more comfortably. He took three stools from around the oval table, under the bust of the king, and having brought them over to one of the windows, they sat down side by side.

There was some agitation on the platform, prolonged whisperings, confabulations. Finally the Councilor stood up. They now knew that his name was Lieuvain, and this name was repeated from one to another in the crowd. After he had checked over several sheets of paper and applied his eye to them the better to see, he began:

"Gentlemen,

"May I first be permitted (before speaking to you about the object of today's gathering, and this sentiment, I am sure, will be shared by all of you)—may I first be permitted, I say, to pay tribute to the higher administration, the government, the monarch, gentlemen, our sovereign, that beloved king to whom no branch of public or private prosperity is a matter of indifference, and who with a hand at once so firm and so wise guides the Chariot of State amid the unceasing perils of a stormy sea, knowing, moreover, how to command a respect for peace as well as for war, industry, commerce, agriculture, and the fine arts."

"I really ought," said Rodolphe, "to move back a bit."

"Why?" said Emma.

But at this moment, the Councilor's voice rose to an extraordinary pitch. He was declaiming:

"The time is past, gentlemen, when civil discord bloodied our public squares, when the landowner, the businessman, even the worker, drifting off at night into a peaceful sleep, trembled lest he be brutally awakened by the sound of incendiary alarms, when the most subversive of maxims were boldly undermining the foundations . . ."

"Because," Rodolphe went on, "I might be seen from down below; and then I'd have to apologize for the next two weeks, and what with my bad reputation . . ."

"Oh, you're slandering yourself!" said Emma.

"No, no, it's deplorable, I swear."

"But, gentlemen," the Councilor went on, "if I dismiss these dark pictures from my memory and return my gaze to the present situation of our fair nation, what do I see? Commerce and the arts are flourishing everywhere; everywhere new lines of communication, like so many new arteries in the State's body, are establishing new relationships; our great manufacturing centers have resumed their activity; religion, now more firmly established, smiles in every heart; our ports are full, our confidence reborn, and France breathes again at last! . . ."

"Besides," added Rodolphe, "perhaps, from society's point of view, they may be right?"

"How do you mean?" she asked.

"Why, don't you know," he said, "that there exist souls who endure endless torment? They are driven now to dream, now to take action, driven to experience the purest passions, then the most extreme joys, and so they hurl themselves into every sort of fantasy, every sort of folly."

She looked at him, then, the way one contemplates a traveler who has journeyed through mythical lands, and she said:

"We poor women haven't even that diversion!"

"A sad diversion, for one doesn't find happiness in it."

"But can one ever find happiness?" she asked.

"Oh, yes, you happen upon it one day," he answered.

"And this," the Councilor was saying, "is what you have come to realize. You farmers and workers of the fields; you peace-loving pioneers in an endeavor so essential to civilization! You men of progress and morality! You have realized, I say, that the storms of politics are truly even more to be feared than the disturbances of the atmosphere . . ."

"You happen upon it one day," Rodolphe repeated, "one day, suddenly, when you had despaired of it. Then new horizons open out; it's like a voice crying, 'Here it is!' You feel the need to confide your whole life to this person, to give her everything, to sacrifice everything for her! You don't have to explain anything; you sense each other's thoughts. You've seen each other in your dreams." (And he was looking at her.) "Here it is at last, the treasure you've been seeking for so long, here it is before you; it shines, it sparkles. Yet still you doubt it, you don't dare believe in it; you're still dazzled by it, as if you were coming out of the darkness into the light."

And as he finished speaking, Rodolphe added pantomime to his words. He passed his hand across his face, like a man overcome with dizziness; then he let it fall on Emma's hand. She withdrew hers. But the Councilor was still reading:

"And who would be surprised, gentlemen? Only one who is so blind, so deeply immersed (I'm not afraid to say it)—so deeply immersed in the prejudices of another age that he still fails to appreciate the spirit of our farming population. Where, indeed, can one find more patriotism than in rural areas, more devotion to the common good, more—in a word—intelligence? And by intelligence, gentlemen, I do not mean that superficial intelligence, that vain ornament of idle minds, but rather that profound and reasonable intelligence that applies itself above all else to the pursuit of useful goals, contributing thus to the good of every man, to the betterment of all, and to the preservation of the State, fruit of respect for the law and performance of duty . . ."

"Ah! Again!" said Rodolphe. "They're always going on about one's duty—I'm bored to death by the word. They're a bunch of old drivelers in flannel vests, church hens with foot warmers and rosaries forever singing in our ears: 'Duty! Duty!' Lord help me! Our duty is to feel what is great, cherish what is beautiful—not to accept all of society's conventions, with the humiliations it imposes on us."

"And yet . . . and yet . . . ," objected Madame Bovary.

"No! Why rant against the passions? Aren't they the only beautiful thing on earth, the source of heroism, enthusiasm, poetry, music, the arts—everything, in fact?"

"But still," said Emma, "we have to pay some attention to society's opinions and abide by its morality."

"Ah! In fact there are two moralities," he replied. "The petty one, the conventional one, the one devised by men, that keeps changing and bellows so loudly, making a commotion down here among us, in a perfectly pedestrian way, like that gathering of imbeciles you see out there. But the other one, the eternal one, is all around and above us, like the landscape that surrounds us and the blue sky that gives us light."

Monsieur Lieuvain had just wiped his mouth with his pocket handkerchief. He went on:

"And why would I presume, gentlemen, to demonstrate to you here, today, the usefulness of agriculture? Who furnishes us our needs? Who provides our sustenance? Is it not the farmer? The farmer, gentlemen, who sows with his diligent hand the fecund furrows of our countryside, causes the wheat to sprout, which, ground and reduced to powder by ingenious machinery, emerges under the name of flour, and, thence transported to our cities, is soon delivered to the baker, who creates from it a food for the poor man as well as for the rich. Is it not also the farmer who fattens his plentiful flocks in the pastures to provide us with clothing? For how would we clothe ourselves, how would we feed ourselves, without the farmer? In fact, gentlemen, is there any need to go even so far in search of examples? Who among you has not reflected many a time on the great benefit we derive from that modest creature, that ornament of our poultry yards, which furnishes at once a downy pillow for our beds, succulent flesh for our tables, and also eggs? But I would never come to an end if I had to enumerate one after the other all the different products that the earth, when it is well cultivated, lavishes like a generous mother on her children. Here, we have the vineyard; there, the cider orchard; yonder, rapeseed; elsewhere, cheeses; and flax—gentlemen, let us not forget flax! which in recent years has enjoyed a considerable increase, to which I would like most particularly to call your attention."

He did not need to ask for their attention: for every mouth in the crowd hung open, as though to drink in his words. Tuvache, next to him, was listening wide-eyed; Monsieur Derozerays, from time to time, quietly closed his eyelids; and farther off, the pharmacist, with his son Napoléon between his knees, was cupping his hand around his ear in order not to lose a single syllable. The other members of the jury kept slowly dipping their chins into their vests to signal their approval. The members of the fire brigade, below the platform, were leaning on their bayonets; and Binet stood motionless, his elbow out, the tip of his sword in the air. He could perhaps hear, but he could not have seen anything, because the visor of his helmet was descending onto his nose. His lieutenant, Monsieur Tuvache's youngest son, had gone even further with his own; for he was wearing one so enormous that it rocked back and forth on his head, allowing the end of his calico kerchief to protrude. Under it, he was smiling with a quite childlike gentleness, and his pale little face, on which drops of moisture shimmered, wore an expression of drowsy bliss and exhaustion.

The Square was packed right up to the housefronts. People could be seen leaning on their elbows at every window, standing in every doorway, and Justin, in front of the display window of the pharmacy, seemed completely transfixed by the contemplation of what he was gazing at. Despite the silence, Monsieur Lieuvain's voice dissipated in the air. It came to you in shreds of phrases, interrupted now and then by the scraping of the chairs in the crowd; then one would suddenly hear, emanating from behind, the prolonged bellow of an ox, or the bleats of the lambs answering one another at the street corners. For the animals had been driven in that close by the cowherds and shepherds, and they lowed from time to time even as they reached out with their tongues and tore off a scrap of foliage hanging down over their muzzles.

Rodolphe had drawn close to Emma, and he was saying rapidly, in a low voice:

"Doesn't it revolt you, the way society conspires? Is there a single feeling it doesn't condemn? The noblest instincts, the purest sympathies, are persecuted, maligned, and if at last two poor souls should find each other, everything is organized to prevent their coming together. They'll try, all the same, they'll beat their wings, they'll call out to each other. Oh, even so! —sooner or later, in six months, in ten years, they'll come together, they'll love each other, because fate demands it and they were born for each other."

He sat with his arms crossed over his knees, and, lifting his face toward Emma, he looked at her fixedly from very near. She could distinguish in his eyes little lines of gold radiating out all around his black pupils, and she could even smell the scent of the pomade with which his hair was glazed. Then a languor came over her; she recalled the vicomte who had waltzed with her at La Vaubyessard, whose beard had given off the same smell of vanilla and lemon as this hair; and reflexively she half closed her eyelids the better to breathe it in. But as she did this, straightening in her chair, she saw in the distance, on the farthest horizon, the old stagecoach, the *Hirondelle*, slowly descending the hill of Les Leux, trailing a long plume of dust behind it. It was in that yellow carriage that Léon had so often returned to her; and by that very road he had left forever! She believed she could see him across the square, at his window; then everything blurred together, some clouds passed; it seemed to her that she was still circling in the waltz, under the blaze of the chandeliers, in the arms of the vicomte, and that Léon was not far off, that he was coming . . . and yet she could still sense Rodolphe's head next to her. And so the sweetness of this sensation permeated her desires of earlier times, and like grains of sand before a gust of wind, they whirled about in the subtle whiff of the fragrance that was spreading through her soul. Again and again she opened wide her nostrils to breathe in the freshness of the ivy around the capitals. She drew off her gloves, she dried her hands; then, with her handkerchief, she fanned her face, while through the pulsing at her temples she could hear the murmur of the crowd and the voice of the Councilor intoning his phrases.

He was saying:

"Persist! Persevere! Listen neither to the promptings of routine nor to the rash counsels of reckless empiricism! Apply yourselves above all to improving the soil, to enriching manures, to developing fine breeds— equine, bovine, ovine, and porcine! Let this agricultural fair be for you a sort of peaceful arena in which the victor, as he leaves, will hold out his hand to the vanquished and fraternize with him, wishing him better success next time! And you, venerable servants! humble workers in our households, whose arduous labors no government until this day has acknowledged, come forward and receive the recompense for your silent virtues, and be persuaded that the State, henceforth, has its eyes fixed upon you, that it encourages you, that it protects you, that it will accede to your just demands and lighten, insofar as it can, the burden of your arduous sacrifices!"

Then Monsieur Lieuvain sat down; Monsieur Derozerays stood up and began another speech. His was perhaps not as flowery as the Councilor's; but it merited respect for its more positive style, that is, for its more specialized knowledge and loftier considerations. Thus, less space was taken up by praise of the government; religion and agriculture occupied more. Clearly shown was the relationship between the two, and how they had always contributed to civilization. Rodolphe was talking with Madame Bovary about dreams, presentiments, magnetism. Going back to the cradle of human society, the orator was depicting those primitive times in which men lived on acorns deep in the forest. Then they had left off their animal skins, donned cloth, dug furrows, planted vines. Was this a good thing? Weren't there more drawbacks than advantages in this discovery? This was the problem Monsieur Derozerays had set himself. From magnetism, Rodolphe had gradually moved on to affinities, and while the chairman cited Cincinnatus at his plow, Diocletian planting his cabbages, and the emperors of China inaugurating the new year by sowing seed, the young man was explaining to the young woman that these irresistible attractions had their source in some previous existence.

"You and I, for instance—" he was saying, "why did we meet? What chance decreed it? It must be that, like two rivers flowing across the intervening distance and converging, our own particular inclinations impelled us toward each other."

And he grasped her hand; she did not withdraw it.

"For all-around good farming!—" cried the chairman.

"A few days ago, for example, when I came to your house . . ."

"To Monsieur Bizet, of Quincampoix—"

"Did I know that I would be coming here with you?"

"Seventy francs!"

"A hundred times I've tried to leave you, and yet I've followed you, I've stayed with you."

"For manures—"

"As I would stay with you tonight, tomorrow, every day, my whole life!"

"To Monsieur Caron, of Argueil, a gold medal!"

"For never before have I been so utterly charmed by anyone's company."

"To Monsieur Bain, of Givry-Saint-Martin!—"

"So that I'll carry the memory of you away with me . . ."

"For a merino ram . . ."

"Whereas you'll forget me. I will have passed like a shadow."

"To Monsieur Belot, of Notre-Dame . . ."

"No! I will—won't I—have a place in your thoughts, in your life?"

"Porcine breed, prize *ex aequo:* to Messieurs Lehérissé and Cullembourg, sixty francs!"

Rodolphe squeezed her hand, and he felt it warm and trembling like a captive dove that wants to fly away again; but whether because she was trying to free it or because she was responding to that pressure, she moved her fingers; he exclaimed:

"Oh, thank you! You're not rejecting me! How good you are! I'm yours; you know that! Let me look at you, let me gaze at you!"

A gust of wind coming in through the windows ruffled the cloth on the table, and in the Square down below, all the tall headdresses of the countrywomen lifted like the wings of white butterflies fluttering.

"Use of oilseed cakes," continued the chairman.

He was hurrying:

"Liquid manure . . . cultivation of flax . . . drainage . . . long-term leases . . . domestic service."

Rodolphe had stopped speaking. They were gazing at each other. Intense desire made their dry lips quiver; and softly, effortlessly, their fingers intertwined.

"Catherine-Nicaise-Élisabeth Leroux, of Sassetot-la-Guerrière, for fifty-four years of service on the same farm, a silver medal—value twenty-five francs!"

"Where is she—where's Catherine Leroux?" repeated the Councilor.

She did not come forward, and one could hear voices whispering:

"Go on!"

"No."

"To the left!"

"Don't be afraid!"

"Oh, how stupid she is!"

"Well, is she here or not?" shouted Tuvache.

"Yes! . . . Here she is!"

"Well, get her to come up!"

Then they watched as she went up onto the platform: a frightened-looking little old woman who seemed to shrink within her shabby clothes. She had thick wooden clogs on her feet, and a large blue apron over her hips. Her thin face, surrounded with a borderless bonnet, was more creased with wrinkles than a withered pippin, and from the sleeves of her red blouse hung two long hands with gnarled joints. Barn dust, caustic washing soda, and wool grease had so thoroughly encrusted, chafed, and hardened them that they seemed dirty even though they had been washed in clear water; and from the habit of serving, they remained half open, as though offering their own testimony to the great suffering they had endured. A kind of monkish rigidity dignified the expression on her face. Nothing sad or tender softened those pale eyes. Living so much among animals, she had taken on their muteness and their placidity. This was the first time she had ever been surrounded by so many people; and, inwardly terrified by the flags, the drums, the gentlemen in black suits, and the Councilor's Legion of Honor medal, she remained completely motionless, not knowing whether to move forward or run away, nor why the crowd was urging her on or why the members of the jury were smiling at her. Thus did she stand there in front of those beaming citizens—this half century of servitude.

"Come here, venerable Catherine-Nicaise-Élisabeth Leroux!" said the Councilor, who had taken the list of laureates from the chairman's hands.

And examining by turns the sheet of paper and the old woman, he repeated in a fatherly tone:

"Come here, come here!"

"Are you deaf?" said Tuvache, leaping up from his chair.

And he began shouting in her ear:

"Fifty-four years of service! A silver medal! Twenty-five francs! It's for you!"

Then, when she had her medal, she studied it. Finally, a beatific smile spread over her face, and one could hear her murmuring as she went away:

"I'll give it to our curé, so that he will say some masses for me."

"What fanaticism!" exclaimed the pharmacist, leaning toward the notary.

The ceremony was over; the crowd dispersed; and now that the speeches had been read, everyone was resuming his usual rank, and everything was returning to normal: the masters were bullying the servants, and the servants were beating the animals, those indolent conquering heroes heading back to the stables with a green crown between their horns.

Meanwhile, the national guard had gone up to the second floor of the town hall, brioches impaled on their bayonets, the battalion drummer carrying a basket of bottles. Madame Bovary took Rodolphe's arm; he accompanied her back home; they separated in front of her door; then, alone, he strolled about in the meadow, waiting for the banquet to begin.

The feast was long, noisy, badly served; they were packed in together so tightly they had trouble moving their elbows, and the narrow boards that served as benches nearly broke under the weight of the guests. They ate abundantly. Each person helped himself to his fair share. The sweat ran down every forehead; and a whitish vapor, like the mist over a river on an autumn morning, hovered over the table between the hanging lamps. Rodolphe, leaning his back against the canvas of the tent, was thinking so hard about Emma that he heard nothing. Behind him, on the lawn, servants were stacking dirty plates; his neighbors were talking, he did not answer them; someone filled his glass, and a silence settled over his thoughts, despite the increases in the din. He was dreaming of what she had said and of the shape of her lips; her face, as though in so many magic mirrors, shone out from the badges of the shakos; the folds of her dress hung down the walls; and days of love stretched endlessly ahead in the vistas of the future.

He saw her again that evening, during the fireworks; but she was with her husband, Madame Homais, and the pharmacist, who was very worried about the danger of stray rockets; and he kept leaving the others to give Binet a word of advice.

The fireworks sent to Monsieur Tuvache's address had, out of an excess of caution, been locked away in his cellar; so the damp powder barely ignited, and the main piece, which was supposed to represent a dragon biting its tail, failed completely. From time to time, a pitiful Roman candle would go off; then the gaping crowd would erupt in a shout in which were mingled the cries of women being tickled at the waist under cover of the darkness. Emma, silent, was snuggling gently against Charles's shoulder; then, lifting her chin, she would follow the rocket's trail of light through the black sky. Rodolphe was watching her by the glow of the burning oil lamps.

One by one, these went out. The stars appeared. A few drops of rain began to fall. She tied her fichu over her bare head.

At that moment, the Councilor's fiacre emerged from the inn yard. His coachman, who was drunk, immediately dozed off; and from far away one could see the mass of his body, above the hood of the carriage, between the two lanterns, swaying right and left with the pitching of the braces.

"Really," said the apothecary, "drunkenness ought to be severely dealt with! I'd like to see them list on the door of the town hall, every week, on a special board, the names of all those who have intoxicated themselves with alcohol during the week. Also, in terms of statistics, this would provide a sort of public record to which one could, if necessary . . . Excuse me!"

And once again he hurried over to the captain.

The latter was on his way home. He was returning to his lathe.

"Perhaps it wouldn't hurt," Homais said to him, "to send one of your men or go yourself . . ."

"Leave me alone, will you," answered the tax collector. "There's nothing to worry about!"

"No cause for concern," said the apothecary when he was back with his friends. "Monsieur Binet has assured me that all proper measures have been taken. Not a spark has fallen. The pumps are full. Let's go home to bed."

"My faith! I need to," remarked Madame Homais, who was yawning vigorously; "but all the same, we've had a very lovely day for our fair."

Rodolphe repeated softly, with a tender glance:

"Oh, yes! Very lovely!"

And having taken leave of one another, they turned away.

Two days later, in *Le Fanal de Rouen,* there was a long article about the agricultural fair. Homais, inspired, had composed it the very next day:

"Why these festoons, these flowers, these garlands? Whither was it bound, this crowd running like the waves of a raging sea under the torrents of a tropical sun spreading its heat over our fallow fields?"

Next, he talked about the condition of the countrypeople. Certainly the government was doing a good deal, but not enough! "Be bold!" he cried, addressing the administration. "A thousand reforms are indispensable, let us bring them to pass." Then, addressing the arrival of the Councilor, he did not fail to mention "the martial air of our militia," nor "the most spirited women of our village," nor "the bald-headed old men who were present, veritable patriarchs, some of whom, relics of our immortal phalanxes, felt their hearts throb once again to the manly beat of the drums." He mentioned himself among the first of the members of the jury, and he even reminded his readers, in a footnote, that Monsieur Homais, pharmacist, had sent a monograph on cider to the Agronomic Society. When he came to the distribution of the prizes, he depicted the joy of the laureates in dithyrambic lines. "Father embraced son, brother brother, husband wife. More than one proudly showed off his humble medal and, once back in his home, by the side of his good helpmeet, will doubtless have hung it, with tears in his eyes, on the modest wall of his little abode.

"At about six o'clock, a banquet set up in the meadow belonging to Monsieur Liégeard brought together the main participants in the fair. The utmost cordiality prevailed throughout. A number of toasts were offered: By Monsieur Lieuvain, to the monarch! By Monsieur Tuvache, to the prefect! By Monsieur Derozerays, to agriculture! By Monsieur Homais, to those two sisters, industry and the fine arts! By Monsieur Leplichey, to improvements! In the evening, a brilliant display of fireworks suddenly illuminated the heavens. It was a veritable kaleidoscope, a true stage set for an opera, and for a moment we in our little corner of the earth might have believed we had been transported into a dream from *A Thousand and One Nights.*

"Let us note that no untoward event occurred to trouble this family gathering."

And he added:

"Remarked upon, only, was the absence of the clergy. No doubt the vestries interpret progress in a different manner. As you will, apostles of Loyola!"

[9]

Six weeks went by. Rodolphe did not return. At last, one evening, he appeared.

He had said to himself, the day after the fair:

"Better not go back right away—that would be a mistake."

And at the end of the week, he had gone off hunting. After the hunting trip, he had imagined it was too late; then he reasoned it out this way:

"But if she has loved me from the first day, she must be impatient to see me again, and therefore she'll love me all the more. So let's go on!"

And he knew his calculation had been correct when, entering the room, he saw Emma turn pale.

She was alone. Day was falling. The little muslin curtains over the windowpanes thickened the twilight, and the gilding on the barometer, struck by a ray of sun, cast flames over the mirror between the indentations of the coral.

Rodolphe remained standing; and Emma barely responded to his first polite remarks.

"I've had business to see to," he said. "I've been ill."

"Seriously ill?" she exclaimed.

"Well," said Rodolphe, sitting down beside her on a stool, "no! . . . The fact is I didn't want to come back."

"Why?"

"Can't you guess?"

He looked at her again, but with such intensity that she bowed her head, blushing. He went on:

"Emma . . ."

"Monsieur!" she said, moving away slightly.

"Ah! You see," he replied in a melancholy voice, "I was right not to want to come back; because that name, the name that fills my soul and that slipped out of me—you forbid me to use it! Madame Bovary! . . . Oh, everyone calls you that! . . . It's not your name, anyway; it belongs to someone else!"

He said it again:

"Someone else!"

And he hid his face in his hands.

"Yes. I think about you constantly! . . . The memory of you makes me despair! Oh, forgive me! . . . I'll leave you alone . . . Goodbye! . . . I'll go away . . . so far away that you'll never hear of me again! . . . And yet . . . today . . . I don't know what power it was that impelled me to see you! For one can't fight against providence, one can't resist the smiles of an angel! One can't help being carried away by what is beautiful, charming, endearing!"

It was the first time Emma had heard such things said to her; and her pride, like a person relaxing in a steam bath, stretched out languidly in the warmth of the words.

"But though I didn't come to you," he went on, "though I couldn't see you, ah!—at least I could see what was around you. At night, every night, I would get up, I would come here, I would gaze at your house, at the roof shining in the moonlight, at the trees in the garden swaying by your window, and at a little lamp, a gleam of light, shining through the panes of glass in the darkness. Ah! You scarcely knew that out there, so close and yet so far away, was a poor wretch . . ."

She turned to him with a sob.

"Oh! You're so good!" she said.

"No. I love you, that's all! You can't doubt it! Say it to me: one word! Just one word!"

And imperceptibly, Rodolphe let himself slip from the stool to the floor; but they could hear the sound of wooden shoes in the kitchen, and he noticed that the parlor door was not closed.

"It would be very kind of you," he went on, straightening up, "to indulge a whim of mine!"

The whim was to walk through her house; he wanted to see it; and since Madame Bovary had no objection, they were both rising when Charles came in.

"Hello, Doctor," Rodolphe said to him.

The public health officer, flattered at being addressed by this unexpected title, launched into a stream of obsequious remarks, and the other took advantage of this to collect himself a little.

"Madame was telling me," he said then, "about her health . . ."

Charles interrupted him: he was terribly worried, in fact; his wife's fits of breathlessness had started up again. Then Rodolphe asked if exercise in the form of horseback riding would not be good for her.

"Certainly! Excellent, perfect! . . . What a fine idea! You ought to act upon it."

And when she objected that she did not have a horse, Monsieur Rodolphe offered her one of his; she refused his offer; he did not insist; then, to give a reason for his visit, he said that his carter, the man who had been bled, was still having dizzy spells.

"I'll come by," said Bovary.

"No, no, I'll send him to you; we'll come here—it'll be more convenient for you."

"Well, all right! Thank you."

And as soon as they were alone:

"Why won't you accept Monsieur Boulanger's suggestions? He's being so gracious."

She looked cross, contemplated a dozen excuses, and finally declared *that it might seem strange.*

"Well, I really don't care!" said Charles, turning on his heel. "Health comes first! You're quite wrong!"

"Well, how do you expect me to go riding, if I don't have a riding habit?"

"You must order one!" he answered.

The riding habit decided her.

When the outfit was ready, Charles wrote to Monsieur Boulanger that his wife was at his disposition, and that they were grateful for his kindness.

The following day, at noon, Rodolphe arrived in front of Charles's door with two saddle horses. One was wearing pink pom-poms at its ears and a lady's buckskin saddle.

Rodolphe had put on tall boots of soft leather, telling himself that she had probably never seen anything like them; and indeed Emma was charmed by the way he looked when he appeared on the landing in his full velvet coat and his white tricot riding breeches. She was ready; she was waiting for him.

Justin slipped out of the pharmacy to see her, and the pharmacist, too, left his work. He gave Monsieur Boulanger some advice:

"An accident can happen so quickly! Watch out! Your horses may be high-spirited!"

She heard a noise over her head: it was Félicité drumming on the windowpanes to amuse little Berthe. The child sent her a kiss; her mother answered by motioning with the butt of her riding crop.

"Have a good ride!" shouted Monsieur Homais. "But be careful! Be careful!"

And he waved his newspaper as he watched them go off.

As soon as he felt the earth, Emma's horse broke into a gallop. Rodolphe galloped next to her. At times they would exchange a few words. With her face tilted down a little, her hand raised, and her right arm outstretched, she abandoned herself to the cadence of the motion that rocked her in the saddle.

At the base of the hill, Rodolphe loosened his reins; they took off together in a single leap; then, at the top, the horses stopped suddenly, and her long blue veil fell back around her.

It was the beginning of October. There was a haze over the countryside. Mist lay along the horizon, between the outlines of the hills; and elsewhere it tore apart, rose, vanished. Sometimes, through a gap in the haze, one could see the roofs of Yonville under a ray of sunlight in the distance, with its gardens by the water's edge, its courtyards, walls, and church steeple. Emma would half close her eyes so as to distinguish her own house, and never had this poor village where she lived seemed so small to her. From the height on which they were standing, the whole valley appeared to be one vast, pale lake, evaporating into the air. Clumps of trees jutted up at intervals like black rocks; and the tall lines of poplars, rising above the fog, were like its shores, stirred by the wind.

Beside them, among the pine trees, a dusky light eddied above the grass in the warm atmosphere. The reddish earth, the color of snuff, deadened the sound of their steps; and the horses, as they walked, pushed the fallen pinecones before them with the tips of their iron shoes.

Rodolphe and Emma went on along the edge of the wood. She would turn away from time to time to avoid his eyes, and then she would see only the trunks of the pines in rows, the continuous succession of which dizzied her a little. The horses were blowing. The leather of the saddles creaked.

Just as they entered the forest, the sun appeared.

"God is protecting us!" said Rodolphe.

"Do you think so?" she said.

"Let's go on!" he said.

He clicked his tongue. The two animals began to trot.

Tall ferns by the side of the path kept catching in Emma's stirrup. Rodolphe, as he rode, would lean down each time and pull them out. At other moments, to move a branch out of the way, he would come close to her, and Emma would feel his knee brush against her leg. The sky was blue now. The leaves were not moving. There were large clearings full of heather all in bloom; and the expanses of violet alternated with the tangle of trees, which were gray, fawn, or gold depending on their different leaves. Often one would hear a faint beating of wings slipping past under the bushes, or the hoarse, gentle caw of crows flying up into the oaks.

They dismounted. Rodolphe tied up the horses. She walked ahead over the moss, between the ruts.

But her long skirt was getting in her way, even though she carried the end of it, and Rodolphe, walking behind her, kept gazing at her delicate white stocking, which showed between the black cloth and the little black boot and seemed to him to be part of her naked flesh.

She stopped.

"I'm tired," she said.

"Come now, a little farther!" he said. "Take heart—try!"

Then, a hundred steps farther on, she stopped again; and through her veil, which fell obliquely from her man's hat down over her hips, her face could be seen in a bluish transparency, as though she were swimming under azure waves.

"Where are we going?"

He did not answer. She was breathing unevenly. Rodolphe was glancing around him and biting his mustache.

They came to a larger open space, where some saplings had been cleared. They sat down on a felled tree trunk, and Rodolphe began talking to her about his love.

He did not frighten her, at first, with compliments. He was calm, serious, melancholy.

Emma listened to him with her head bowed, stirring the wood chips on the ground with the toe of her boot.

But when he said:

"Our destinies are bound together now, aren't they?"

"No!" she answered. "You know that perfectly well. It can't be."

She stood up to leave. He seized her by the wrist. She stopped. Then, after looking at him for a few moments with tearful, loving eyes, she said quickly:

"Oh, come, let's not talk about it anymore . . . Where are the horses? Let's go back."

He made a gesture of anger and weariness. She repeated:

"Where are the horses? Where are the horses?"

Then, smiling a strange smile, his eyes unmoving, his teeth clenched, he moved toward her with open arms. She backed away trembling. She stammered:

"Oh, you're frightening me! You're upsetting me! Let's go."

"If we must," he said, changing his expression.

And he immediately became respectful again, tender, timid. She gave him her arm. They turned back. He said:

"Now, what was the matter? What happened? I don't understand! You must be misjudging me. Within my soul you're like a madonna on a pedestal, in an exalted place, secure, immaculate. But I need you if I am to live! I need your eyes, your voice, your thoughts. Be my friend, my sister, my angel!"

And he reached out his arm and put it around her waist. She tried gently to free herself. He held her that way as they walked.

But they could hear the two horses, who were browsing on leaves.

"Oh, just a little longer!" said Rodolphe. "Let's not go yet. Stay here!"

He drew her farther on, around a little pond, where duckweed made a patch of green on the water. Faded water lilies lay motionless among the rushes. At the sound of their steps in the grass, frogs leaped away to conceal themselves.

"I'm wrong, I'm wrong," she said. "I'm insane to listen to you."

"Why? . . . Emma! Emma!"

"Oh, Rodolphe! . . . ," the young woman said slowly, leaning on his shoulder.

The material of her riding habit caught on his velvet coat. She tipped back her head, her white throat swelled with a sigh; and weakened, bathed in tears, hiding her face, with a long tremor she gave herself up to him.

The evening shadows were coming down; the horizontal sun, passing between the branches, dazzled her eyes. Here and there, all around her, patches of light shimmered in the leaves or on the ground, as if hummingbirds in flight had scattered their feathers there. Silence was everywhere; something mild seemed to be coming forth from the trees; she could feel her heart beginning to beat again, and her blood flowing through her flesh like a river of milk. Then, from far away beyond the woods, on the other hills, she heard a vague, prolonged cry, a voice that lingered, and she listened to it in silence as it lost itself like a kind of music in the last vibrations of her tingling nerves. Rodolphe, a cigar between his teeth, was mending with his penknife one of the bridles, which had broken.

They returned to Yonville by the same path. They saw the prints of their horses in the mud, side by side, and the same bushes, the same stones in the grass. Nothing around them had changed; and yet, for her, something had happened that was more momentous than if mountains had moved. Rodolphe would lean over, from time to time, and take up her hand to kiss it.

She was charming, on horseback! Upright, with her slender waist, her knee bent against her horse's mane, and a little rosy from the fresh air, in the ruddy light of the evening.

As she entered Yonville, she pranced on the paving stones. People were watching her from the windows.

Her husband, at dinner, thought she looked well; but she seemed not to hear him when he asked about her outing; and she sat still with her elbow at the edge of her plate, between the two burning candles.

"Emma!" he said.

"What?"

"Well, I spent this afternoon with Monsieur Alexandre; he has an old filly that's still quite fine, only a little broken in the knees; she could be had, I'm sure, for about a hundred ecus . . ."

He added:

"In fact, thinking you would be pleased, I secured her . . . I bought her . . . Did I do right? Now tell me."

She nodded her head in agreement; then, a quarter of an hour later:

"Are you going out this evening?" she asked.

"Yes. Why?"

"Oh, nothing! Nothing, dear."

And as soon as she was rid of Charles, she went upstairs and shut herself in her room.

At first, it was like a kind of dizziness; she saw the trees, the paths, the ditches, Rodolphe, and she could still feel his arms holding her while the leaves quivered and the rushes whistled.

But catching sight of herself in the mirror, she was surprised by her face. Her eyes had never been so large, so dark, or so deep. Something subtle had spread through her body and was transfiguring her.

She said to herself again and again: "I have a lover! A lover!" reveling in the thought as though she had come into a second puberty. At last she would possess those joys of love, that fever of happiness of which she had despaired. She was entering something marvelous in which all was passion, ecstasy, delirium; a blue-tinged immensity surrounded her, heights of feeling sparkled under her thoughts, and ordinary life appeared only in the distance, far below, in shadow, in the spaces between those peaks.

Then she recalled the heroines of the books she had read, and this lyrical throng of adulterous women began to sing in her memory with sisterly voices that enchanted her. She herself was in some way becoming an actual part of those imaginings and was fulfilling the long daydream of her youth, by seeing herself as this type of amorous woman she had so much envied. Besides, Emma was experiencing the satisfaction of revenge. Hadn't she suffered enough? But now she was triumphing, and love, so long contained, was springing forth whole, with joyful effervescence. She savored it without remorse, without uneasiness, without distress.

The next day passed in a new sweetness. They exchanged vows. She confided her sorrows. Rodolphe kept interrupting her with his kisses; and she, gazing at him with her eyes half closed, would ask him to call her by her name again and tell her again that he loved her. They were in the forest, as on the day before, in a hut used by sabot makers. Its walls were of straw, and its roof came down so low that one had to stoop. They sat close together, on a bed of dry leaves.

From that day on, they wrote to each other regularly every evening. Emma would take her letter to the bottom of the garden, by the stream, to a crack in the terrace wall. Rodolphe would come look for it there and in its place put another, which she would always complain was too short.

One morning, when Charles had gone out before dawn, she was seized by the urge to see Rodolphe that very instant. She could get to La Huchette quickly, stay there one hour, and be back in Yonville while everyone was still asleep. The thought made her breathe hard with longing, and she soon found herself in the middle of the meadow, walking with quick steps, not looking behind her.

Day was breaking. From far away, Emma recognized her lover's house, with its two swallow-tailed weather vanes standing out black against the pale twilight.

Beyond the farmyard was a main building that had to be the château. She entered it as if the walls, at her approach, had parted of their own accord. A broad straight staircase rose to a hallway. Emma turned the latch of a door, and at once, at the far end of the bedroom, she saw a man asleep. It was Rodolphe. She cried out.

"It's you! You're here!" he said again and again. "How did you manage to get here? . . . Oh, your dress is wet!"

"I love you!" she answered, putting her arms around his neck.

This first bold venture having been a success, now each time Charles went out early, Emma would dress quickly and steal down the short flight of steps that led to the edge of the water.

But when the plank bridge for the cows had been raised, she would have to follow the walls that lined the stream; the bank was slippery; to keep from falling, she would cling to the clumps of faded wallflowers. Then she would strike out across the plowed fields, sinking down, stumbling, and catching her thin little boots. Her scarf, tied over her head, would flutter in the wind in the pastures; she was afraid of the cattle, she would start running; she would arrive out of breath, her cheeks pink, her whole body exhaling a cool fragrance of sap, leaves, and fresh air. Rodolphe, at that hour, was still asleep. She was like a spring morning coming into his bedroom.

The yellow curtains, over the windows, gently let in a heavy flaxen light. Emma would grope her way forward, blinking, while the dewdrops suspended in her bands of hair made a sort of halo of topazes all around her face. Rodolphe, laughing, would draw her to him and hold her against his heart.

Afterward, she would examine the room, she would open the drawers of the furniture, she would comb her hair with his comb and look at herself in the shaving mirror. Often, she would even place between her teeth the stem of a large pipe that lay on the night table among the lemons and sugar lumps, next to a carafe of water.

It took them a good quarter of an hour to say goodbye. Then Emma would weep; she wished she never had to leave Rodolphe. Something stronger than she was kept impelling her to go to him, until one day, seeing her come unexpectedly, he frowned as though annoyed.

"What's wrong?" she said. "Are you in pain? Speak to me!"

At last he declared gravely that her visits were becoming reckless and that she was compromising herself.

[10]

Little by little, these fears of Rodolphe's took possession of her. Love had intoxicated her at first, and she had thought of nothing beyond it. But now that it was indispensable to her life, she was afraid of losing some part of it, or even of disturbing it. As she was returning from his house, she would glance uneasily all around, observing every figure that passed on the horizon and every dormer in the village from which she could be seen. She would listen to the footsteps, the shouts, the sound of the plows; and she would stop short, paler and more tremulous than the leaves of the poplars swaying over her head.

One morning, as she was coming back in this state of mind, she suddenly thought she saw the long bore of a rifle pointing at her. It was sticking out at an angle above the rim of a small barrel half buried in the grass, by the edge of a ditch. Emma, though nearly fainting from terror, continued to walk on forward, and a man emerged from the barrel like a jack-in-the-box. He wore gaiters buckled up to the knees, a cap pulled down as far as his eyes, his lips were trembling, and his nose was red. It was Captain Binet, lying in wait for wild duck.

"You should have called out, from a good distance!" he cried. "When you see a gun, you should always give warning."

The tax collector, in saying this, was trying to conceal the fright he had just suffered: Because a prefectural decree prohibited duck hunting except from a boat, Monsieur Binet, despite his respect for the law, found himself in violation. And so, from one minute to the next, he would believe he heard the gamekeeper approaching. But this worry only sharpened his pleasure, and, alone in his barrel, he would congratulate himself on his good luck and his cunning.

At the sight of Emma, he seemed relieved of a great weight, and immediately opened a conversation:

"Not very warm, is it—*quite nippy!*"

Emma did not answer. He went on:

"And you're out good and early, aren't you?"

"Yes," she said, stammering; "I'm coming from the wet nurse, where my child is."

"Ah, very good, very good! As for me, here I've been where you see me now, ever since daybreak; but the weather is so foul that unless you have the bird right at the end of your . . ."

"Good day, Monsieur Binet," she broke in, turning away from him.

"Your servant, madame," he answered dryly.

And he went back inside his barrel.

Emma regretted having left the tax collector so abruptly. He was probably going to make unfavorable conjectures. The story of the nurse was the worst excuse, since everyone in Yonville knew perfectly well that the Bovary child had been back in her parents' home for the past year. What was more, no one lived near there; the path led only to La Huchette; Binet had therefore guessed where she was coming from, and he would not keep quiet, he would talk, that was certain! All day long she racked her brains devising every imaginable lie, with the image constantly before her of that imbecile with his game bag.

After dinner, Charles, seeing that she was anxious, tried to distract her by taking her to the pharmacist's house; and the first person she saw in the pharmacy was him again—the tax collector! He was standing at the counter, in the glow of the red glass jar, and he was saying:

"Please be so good as to give me half an ounce of vitriol."

"Justin," shouted the apothecary, "bring us the sulfuric acid."

Then, to Emma, who was about to go up to Madame Homais's room:

"No, stay here, don't bother, she'll be coming down. Go warm yourself at the stove while you're waiting . . . Excuse me . . . Hello, Doctor" (for the pharmacist took great pleasure in pronouncing that word, "doctor," as though in addressing someone else by the title, he caused some of the glory it held for him to be reflected on himself) . . . "Justin, be careful not to upset the mortars! No, no—get the chairs from the little parlor instead; you know very well we never move the drawing-room armchairs."

And Homais was hurrying out from behind the counter to put his armchair back in its place, when Binet asked him for half an ounce of sugar acid.

"Sugar acid?" asked the pharmacist scornfully. "I don't know what that is—no idea! Maybe what you want is oxalic acid? You mean oxalic acid, don't you?"

Binet explained that he needed a corrosive in order to make up some metal polish to take the rust off parts of his hunting gear. Emma gave a start. The pharmacist began to say:

"Indeed, the weather is not very propitious, because of the damp."

"Nevertheless," the tax collector went on with a sly look, "some people don't seem to mind it."

She felt she was suffocating.

"And could you also give me . . ."

"He's never going to leave!" she was thinking.

"A half ounce of rosin and the same of turpentine, four ounces of beeswax, and three half ounces of bone black, please, to clean the patent leather on my gear."

The apothecary was beginning to carve the wax when Madame Homais appeared with Irma in her arms, Napoléon by her side, and Athalie following her. She went and sat down on the velvet bench by the window, and the boy crouched on a stool, while his older sister prowled around the jujube box near her little papa. The latter was filling funnels and corking bottles, gluing labels, tying up parcels. Everyone around him was silent; and one could hear only, from time to time, the clink of the weights in the scale, along with a few quiet words from the pharmacist as he gave advice to his pupil.

"And how's your little one?" Madame Homais asked suddenly.

"Silence!" exclaimed her husband, who was entering figures in his calculations notebook.

"Why didn't you bring her along?" she went on in a low voice.

"Shh! Shh!" said Emma, pointing to the apothecary.

But Binet, entirely occupied with reading the column of figures, had probably heard nothing. At last he went out. Then Emma, relieved, sighed deeply.

"How hard you're breathing!" said Madame Homais.

"Oh! It's just that it's a bit warm," she answered.

And so, the next day, they talked about how to arrange their meetings; Emma wanted to bribe her maid with a gift; but it would be better to find some out-of-the-way house in Yonville. Rodolphe promised to look for one.

All winter long, three or four times a week, he would come to the garden in the dead of night. Emma, quite deliberately, had taken the key from the gate, and Charles thought it was lost.

To signal her, Rodolphe would throw a handful of sand against the shutters. She would rise with a start; but sometimes she had to wait, because Charles had a habit of talking by the fireside, and he would go on and on. She would be consumed with impatience; if her eyes had had the power to do it, they would have flung him out the window. At last she would begin preparing for bed; then she would take up a book and read quite tranquilly, as if this reading entertained her. But Charles, who was in bed, would call out to her.

"Come, now, Emma," he would say, "it's time."

"Yes, I'm coming!" she would answer.

Meanwhile, because the candles dazzled him, he would turn to the wall and fall asleep. She would make her escape holding her breath, smiling, trembling, wearing almost nothing.

Rodolphe had a large cloak; he would wrap her in it, and, putting his arm around her waist, silently lead her to the bottom of the garden.

It was to the arbor that they went, to that same bench made of rotten sticks from which Léon had once gazed at her so lovingly on summer evenings. She hardly thought of him now.

The stars shone through the branches of the leafless jasmine. They could hear the stream flowing behind them, and from time to time, on the bank, the clacking of dry reeds. Mounds of shadow loomed here and there in the darkness, and sometimes they would quiver with a single motion, rise up, and bend over like immense black waves advancing to submerge them. The cold of the night made them clasp each other all the more tightly; the sighs on their lips seemed to them deeper; their eyes, which they could barely glimpse, seemed larger; and in the midst of the silence, the words they spoke so quietly dropped into their souls, echoing and reechoing with a crystalline sonority in multiplied vibrations.

When the night was rainy, they would take refuge in the consulting room, between the shed and the stable. She would light a kitchen candle that she had hidden behind the books. Rodolphe would settle there as though he were in his own home. The sight of the bookcase and the desk, of the whole room, in fact, aroused his hilarity; and he could not stop himself from making one joke after another about Charles, which embarrassed Emma. She would have liked to see him more serious, and even, on occasion, more dramatic, as when she thought she heard the sound of footsteps approaching in the alley.

"Someone's coming!" she said.

He blew out the light.

"Do you have your pistols?"

"What for?"

"Why . . . to defend yourself," said Emma.

"From your husband? Oh, that poor fellow!"

And Rodolphe ended his comment with a gesture that meant: "I could annihilate him with a flick of my finger."

She was amazed by his fearlessness, even though she sensed in it a coarseness and naïve vulgarity that shocked her.

Rodolphe thought hard about that episode involving the pistols. If she had spoken in earnest, it was quite ridiculous, he thought, even abhorrent, for he himself had no reason to hate that good man, Charles, since he was not consumed by jealousy, as people put it; —and indeed, concerning this, Emma had made him a solemn vow that he also found not in the best taste.

Besides, she was becoming quite sentimental. They had had to exchange miniatures, they had cut off handfuls of their hair, and now she was asking for a ring, a veritable wedding band, as a symbol of everlasting union. She often spoke to him about the evening church bells or the *voices of nature;* then she would talk about her mother, and his. Rodolphe had lost his mother twenty years before. Nonetheless, Emma would console him in affected language, as one would have consoled a bereaved child, and even said to him sometimes, gazing at the moon:

"I'm sure that somewhere up there, they are together and they approve of our love."

But she was so pretty! And he had possessed few women as ingenuous as she! This love, so free of licentiousness, was a new thing for him and, drawing him out of his easy ways, both flattered his pride and inflamed his sensuality. Emma's rapturous emotion, which his bourgeois common sense disdained, seemed charming to him in his heart of hearts, since he was the object of it. And so, certain of being loved, he stopped making any effort, and imperceptibly his manner changed.

He no longer spoke those sweet words to her that had once made her weep, nor did he offer her those fervent caresses that had once driven her wild; so that their great love, in which she lived immersed, seemed to be seeping away under her, like the waters of a river being absorbed into its own bed, and she could see the mud. She did not want to believe it; she redoubled her affection; and Rodolphe made less and less of an effort to hide his indifference.

She did not know if she was sorry she had yielded to him, or if, on the contrary, she longed to cherish him even more. The humiliation of feeling so weak was turning into a resentment tempered by sensuous pleasure. It was not an attachment; it was a kind of permanent seduction. He was subjugating her. She was almost afraid of it.

Outward appearances, nevertheless, were more serene than ever, Rodolphe having succeeded in managing the affair as he pleased; and after six months, by the time spring came, they found themselves behaving toward each other like a married couple calmly tending a domestic flame.

It was the time of year when old Rouault sent his turkey, in memory of his mended leg. The gift would always arrive with a letter. Emma cut the string tying it to the basket, and read the following:

My dear children,

I hope these lines find you in good health and that this one will be as good as the others; it seems to me a little more tender, if I dare say so, and denser. But next time, for a change, I'll give you a cock, unless you'd rather keep getting the picots; *and please send the hamper back to me, along with the last two. I've had an unfortunate mishap with my cart shed, one night when the wind was high, the roof flew off into the trees. The harvest wasn't much to speak of either. Well, I don't know when I'm going to come see you. It's so hard for me to leave the house now that I'm on my own, my poor Emma!*

And here there was a gap between the lines, as if the old fellow had let his pen drop and daydreamed for a while.

As for me, I'm well, except for a cold I caught the other day at the Yvetot fair, where I went to hire a shepherd, having sacked mine as a consequence of his being too particular concerning his food. How much there is to complain of with these highway robbers! Besides that, he was also dishonest.

I heard from a peddler who was traveling through your part of the country this winter and had a tooth pulled that Bovary was still working hard. That doesn't surprise me, and he showed me his tooth; we had a coffee together. I asked him if he had seen you, he said no, but he had seen two horses in the stable, from which I concluded that business is good. Glad to hear it, my dear children, and may the good Lord send you all imaginable happiness.

It grieves me that I don't yet know my beloved granddaughter Berthe Bovary. I have planted a tree for her in the garden under your bedroom window, it's a plum tree that bears in September, and I won't let anyone touch it except to make compotes for her later, which I will keep in the cupboard, just for her, when she comes.

Goodbye, my dear children. I kiss you, my daughter; you, too, my son-in-law, and the little one, on both cheeks.

I am, with my very best wishes,
    Your affectionate father,
        THÉODORE ROUAULT

She sat for a few minutes holding the coarse paper between her fingers. The letter was a tangle of spelling mistakes, and Emma followed the gentle thought that clucked its way through them like a hen half hidden in a hedge of thorns. The writing had been dried with ashes from the fireplace, for a little gray powder slid from the letter onto her dress, and she thought she could almost see her father bending toward the hearth to grasp the tongs. How long it was since she used to sit next to him, on the stool, by the fire, burning the end of a stick in the big flame of crackling furze! . . . She thought back to summer evenings flooded with sunlight. The colts would whinny when you walked by, and they would gallop and gallop . . . There was a hive of honeybees under her window, and now and then the bees, circling in the light, would tap against the panes like bouncing balls of gold. How happy those days had been! How free! How full of hope! How rich in illusions! There were none left now! She had spent them in all the different adventures of her soul, in all those successive stages she had gone through, in her virginity, her marriage, and her love; —losing them continuously as her life went on, like a traveler who leaves some part of his wealth at every inn along his road.

But what was making her so unhappy? Where was the extraordinary catastrophe that had overturned her life? And she lifted her head and looked around, as though seeking the cause of what hurt her so.

A ray of April sunshine shimmered over the china on the shelves of the cabinet; the fire was burning; she could feel, under her slippers, the softness of the carpet; the day was clear, the air warm, and she could hear her child bursting into peals of laughter.

In fact, the little girl was rolling around on the lawn, in the midst of the grass that was being dried for hay. She was lying flat on her stomach on top of one of the piles. The servant was holding on to her by the skirt. Lestiboudois was raking close by, and every time he came up, she would lean out, beating the air with her arms.

"Bring her to me!" said her mother, hurrying over to give her a kiss. "How much I love you, my poor child! How much I love you!"

Then, noticing that the tips of the child's ears were a little dirty, she quickly rang for warm water and cleaned her, changed her underclothes, her stockings, her shoes, asked a thousand questions about her health, as though just back from a trip; and finally, kissing her again and weeping a little, she handed her back to the maid, who was standing there quite astonished at this excess of tenderness.

That night, Rodolphe found her more serious than usual.

"It will pass," he supposed; "it's just a whim."

And he missed three of their rendezvous in succession. When he returned, she was cold and almost disdainful.

"Ah! You're wasting your time, my pet . . ."

And he appeared not to notice her melancholy sighs, nor the handkerchief she kept bringing out.

It was then that Emma repented!

She even asked herself why she despised Charles, and if it would not have been better to be able to love him. But he did not offer much of an opening for this renewal of affection, so that she was quite foiled in her momentary inclination for sacrifice, when the apothecary happened to provide her with a timely opportunity.

[11]

He had recently read an article singing the praises of a new method of correcting clubfeet; and since he was a partisan of progress, he conceived the patriotic idea that Yonville, too, in order *to keep abreast of the times,* ought to be performing operations on strephopodia.

"After all," he said to Emma, "what risk is there? Look" (and he enumerated on his fingers the advantages of the attempt): "almost certain success, relief and improved appearance for the patient, immediate celebrity for the surgeon. Why wouldn't your husband, for example, want to help out poor Hippolyte, over at the Lion d'Or? Note that the boy would be sure to tell the story of his cure to all the travelers, and also" (Homais lowered his voice and looked around) "what would prevent me from sending the newspaper a little piece about it? My Lord! An article gets around . . . people talk about it . . . the thing ends up snowballing! And who knows? Who knows?"

Indeed, Bovary might make a success of it; Emma had no reason to think he was not skillful, and what a satisfaction it would be for her to have started him on a path that would increase both his reputation and his fortune? All she wanted, now, was to be able to lean on something more solid than love.

Charles, urged by her and by the apothecary, allowed himself to be persuaded. He sent to Rouen for the volume by Doctor Duval, and every evening, his head in his hands, he immersed himself in reading it.

While Charles was studying pes equinus, varus, and valgus, that is, strephocatopodia, strephendopodia, and strephexopodia (or, to be more exact, the various malformations of the foot, downward, inward, and outward), along with strephypopodia and strephanopodia (in other words, downward torsion and upward straightening), Monsieur Homais, by every kind of argument, was exhorting the innkeeper's stableboy to submit to the operation.

"You may possibly feel just a slight pain; it's a simple prick like a mild bloodletting, less than the extirpation of certain types of corns."

Hippolyte, as he thought about it, was rolling his eyes in bewilderment.

"In any case," the pharmacist went on, "this has nothing to do with me! I'm thinking of you! Out of pure humanity! I would like to see you relieved, my friend, of your hideous claudication, along with that swaying of the lumbar region, which, though you claim otherwise, must prove a considerable obstacle to you in the exercise of your vocation."

Then Homais described how much nimbler and more vigorous he would feel afterward, and even implied that he might be more pleasing to women; and the stableboy began to smile foolishly. Then he attacked him through his vanity:

"Aren't you a man, by heaven! What if you had had to serve in the army, follow your flag into battle? . . . Ah! Hippolyte!"

And Homais would walk away, declaring that he could not understand such stubbornness, such blindness in refusing the benefits of science.

The poor fellow gave in, for it was a kind of general conspiracy. Binet, who never meddled in other people's affairs, Madame Lefrançois, Artémise, the neighbors, and even the mayor, Monsieur Tuvache everyone urged him, lectured him, shamed him; but what decided him, in the end, was that *it wouldn't cost him anything*. Bovary even undertook to provide the apparatus for the operation. This piece of generosity had been Emma's idea; and Charles agreed to it, telling himself in his heart of hearts that his wife was an angel.

And so, with suggestions from the pharmacist, and after starting over three times, he had the carpenter, with the help of the locksmith, build him a sort of box weighing about eight pounds and containing ample quantities of iron, wood, sheet metal, leather, screws, and nuts.

However, in order to know which of Hippolyte's tendons should be cut, it was necessary to find out first what sort of clubfoot he had.

His foot formed an almost straight line with his leg, which did not prevent it from also being turned inward, so that it was a pes equinus mixed with a little of the varus, or a slight varus strongly marked by the pes equinus. But with this pes equinus, as broad, in fact, as a horse's hoof, with its roughened skin, stringy tendons, large toes, and black toenails representing the nails of the horseshoe, the strephopod would gallop, from morning to night, like a deer. One was always seeing him in the square, skipping around the carts, thrusting his unequal limb out in front of him. In fact, he seemed stronger on that leg than on the other. Through having served so long, it had developed something like the moral qualities of patience and energy, and when he was given a heavy piece of work to do, he would throw his weight on that leg by preference.

Now, since it was a pes equinus, it was necessary to cut the Achilles tendon, only later tackling the anterior tibial muscle so as to get rid of the varus; for the doctor did not dare risk both operations at once, and in fact he was quaking already, for fear of assaulting some important part of the foot with which he was unfamiliar.

Neither Ambroise Paré, applying a ligature directly to an artery for the first time since Celsus, fifteen centuries before; nor Dupuytren, about to open an abscess through a thick layer of encephalon; nor Gensoul, when he performed the first ablation of the superior maxilla, had a heart that pounded so, a hand so tremulous, a mind so tense as Monsieur Bovary approaching Hippolyte, his *tenotomy knife* in his hand. And as in a hospital, one saw, on a table to one side, a pile of lint, some waxed threads, a great many bandages, a pyramid of bandages, all the bandages that could be found in the apothecary. It was Monsieur Homais who had been organizing all these preparations since early morning, as much in order to dazzle the crowd as to delude himself. Charles pierced the skin; a sharp snap could be heard. The tendon was cut, the operation was done. Hippolyte could not get over his surprise; he took Bovary's hands and covered them with kisses.

"Now, now, calm down," said the apothecary. "You'll have a chance later on to show your benefactor how grateful you are!"

And he went downstairs to describe the result to five or six curious bystanders who had taken up positions in the courtyard and who imagined that Hippolyte would reappear walking upright. Then Charles, having buckled his patient into the mechanical-motion device, returned home, where Emma, very anxious, was waiting for him at the door. She threw her arms around him; they sat down at the table; he ate a great deal; and, at dessert, he even asked for a cup of coffee, a bit of intemperance he usually permitted himself only on Sundays when they had company.

The evening was delightful, full of conversation and shared dreams. They talked about their future wealth, improvements to be made in the household; he saw his reputation growing, his prosperity increasing, his wife loving him forever; and she was happy to find herself reinvigorated by a new sentiment, a healthier, better one, a feeling of some affection for this poor man who cherished her so. The thought of Rodolphe passed through her mind for a moment; but her eyes returned to Charles: she even noticed with surprise that his teeth weren't bad at all.

They were in bed when Monsieur Homais, despite the cook, abruptly entered their room, holding in his hand a freshly written sheet of paper. It was the notice he was going to send to *Le Fanal de Rouen.* He was bringing it for them to read.

"Read it to us," said Bovary.

He read:

"'Despite the prejudices that still cover a part of the face of Europe like a web, the light is nevertheless beginning to penetrate into our countryside. Thus, on Tuesday last, our little city of Yonville found itself the theater for a surgical experiment that was at the same time an act of pure philanthropy. Monsieur Bovary, one of our most distinguished practitioners . . .'"

"Oh! That's going too far! Too far!" said Charles, suffocating with emotion.

"No, not at all! Come now! . . . 'Operated on a clubfoot . . .' I didn't use the scientific term because, you know, in a newspaper . . . perhaps not everyone would understand; the common people must . . ."

"Indeed, yes," said Bovary. "Go on."

"I'll continue," said the pharmacist. "'Monsieur Bovary, one of our most distinguished practitioners, operated on a clubfoot by the name of Hippolyte Tautain, stableboy for the past twenty-five years at the Lion d'Or hotel, kept by Madame Widow Lefrançois, on the Place d'Armes. The novelty of the undertaking and the interest felt in the patient had attracted such a gathering of the population that there was a veritable crush on the threshold of the establishment. The operation, what is more, was performed as though by magic, and only a few drops of blood appeared on the skin, as if to announce that the rebellious tendon had at last yielded to the efforts of art. The patient, strange to say (we affirm this *de visu*), professed no pain. His condition, up to the present, is all that could be hoped for. There is every indication that his convalescence will be brief; and who knows but what, at the next village fair, we may see our good Hippolyte, amid a chorus of gay blades, taking part in the bacchanalian dances, thus proving to all eyes, by his verve no less than his entrechats, how fully he has recovered? All honor, therefore, to our generous men of science! All honor to those tireless intellects who devote their waking hours to the betterment or relief of their fellow men! All honor to them! All honor thrice over! Can we not now cry out that the blind shall see, the deaf shall hear, and the lame shall walk? But what fanaticism once promised to its chosen few, science now accomplishes for all men! We shall keep our readers informed of the successive stages of this most remarkable cure.'"

Which did not stop Mère Lefrançois from coming by five days later, frightened to death and shouting:

"Help! He's dying! . . . I'm going out of my mind!"

Charles hurried to the Lion d'Or, and the pharmacist, seeing him pass through the square without a hat, left the pharmacy. He himself turned up breathless, red-faced, worried, and asking everyone who was climbing the stairs:

"What's the matter with our interesting strephopod?"

The strephopod was thrashing about in dreadful convulsions, so much so that the mechanical apparatus in which his leg was enclosed was striking the wall hard enough to stave it in.

With many precautions so as not to disturb the position of the leg, they therefore removed the box, and a horrifying sight met their eyes. The shape of the foot had disappeared within a swelling so extreme that the skin seemed about to split, and the entire surface was covered with ecchymoses caused by the much-vaunted machine. Hippolyte had complained before this that it was hurting him; no one had paid any attention; they had to admit he had not been entirely wrong; and they left him free for a few hours. But scarcely had the edema gone down a little than the two experts deemed it advisable to return the limb to the apparatus, tightening it further in order to speed things up. At last, three days later, Hippolyte being unable to endure it any longer, they removed the contrivance again, and were quite astonished at the result they observed. A livid tumefaction was now spreading up the leg, with phlyctenae here and there from which a black liquid was seeping out. Things were taking a serious turn.

Hippolyte was becoming despondent, and Mère Lefrançois moved him into the small parlor, next to the kitchen, so that he would at least have some distraction.

But the tax collector, who dined there every day, complained bitterly at such companionship. So they transported Hippolyte into the billiards room.

There he lay, whimpering under his coarse blankets, pale, unshaven, hollow-eyed, now and then turning his sweaty head on the dirty pillow where flies kept landing. Madame Bovary would come to see him. She would bring cloths for his poultices and comfort him, encourage him. He had no lack of company, in any case, especially on market days, when he was surrounded by countryfolk knocking the billiard balls, sparring with the cue sticks, smoking, drinking, singing, shouting.

"How are you?" they would say, slapping him on the shoulder. "Ah, you don't look too good! But it's your own fault. You should have done this, you should have done that."

And they would tell him stories about people who had all been cured by remedies different from his own; then they would add, by way of consolation:

"The thing is, you're cosseting yourself! You should get up! You pamper yourself like royalty! Oh, never mind, you old wag! How vile you smell!"

Indeed, the gangrene was climbing higher and higher. Bovary himself felt sick about it. He would come by at any hour, from one moment to the next. Hippolyte would look at him with eyes full of terror and, sobbing, would stammer:

"When will I be cured? . . . Oh, save me! . . . How miserable I am! How miserable I am!"

And the doctor would go away again, always advising a restricted diet.

"Don't listen to him, my boy," Mère Lefrançois would say; "haven't they tormented you enough already, as it is? You'll only make yourself weaker. Here, swallow this!"

And she would offer him some good broth, a slice of roast mutton, a piece of bacon, and now and then a small glass of eau-de-vie, which he did not feel strong enough to bring to his lips.

The Abbé Bournisien, learning that he was getting worse, asked to see him. He began by sympathizing with him over his illness, at the same time declaring that he should rejoice in it, since it was the will of the Lord, and lose no time taking advantage of the opportunity to reconcile himself with heaven.

"For," said the clergyman in a fatherly tone, "you were neglecting your duties a little; one rarely saw you at the divine service; how many years has it been since you approached the holy altar? I understand that your occupations, the hustle and bustle of the world, may have distracted you from tending to your salvation. But now it's time to reflect on it. Do not despair, however; I have known some great sinners who, when they were about to appear before God (you've not yet reached that point, I'm well aware), implored His mercy and certainly died in the best of situations. Let us hope that, like them, you will set us a good example! For instance, as a precaution, why not recite a 'Hail Mary, full of grace' and an 'Our Father, who art in heaven' every morning and every evening? Yes! Do this for me, to oblige me. What will it cost you? . . . Will you promise?"

The poor devil promised. The curé came back on the following days. He would chat with the innkeeper and even tell anecdotes full of jokes and puns that Hippolyte did not understand. Then, as soon as the situation allowed, he would revert to religious subjects, his face assuming a suitable expression.

His zeal appeared to be succeeding; for the strephopod soon evinced a desire to go on a pilgrimage to Bon-Secours if he should recover: to which Monsieur Bournisien answered that he saw no objection to that; two precautions were worth more than one. *One risked nothing.*

The apothecary was furious at what he called *the priest's scheming;* it would interfere, he claimed, with Hippolyte's convalescence, and he kept saying to Madame Lefrançois:

"Leave him alone! Leave him alone! You're disturbing his peace of mind with your mysticism!"

But the good woman would not listen to him. He was *the cause of everything.* In a spirit of contrariness, she even hung a full basin of holy water by the patient's bedside, along with a sprig of boxwood.

Yet religion appeared to be of no more help to him than the surgery, and the invincible rot continued to rise from his extremities toward his abdomen. It was no use their varying the potions and changing the poultices, the muscles dissolved more every day, and at last Charles responded with an affirmative nod when Mère Lefrançois asked him if she could not, as a last resort, send for Monsieur Canivet, of Neufchâtel, who was a celebrity.

A medical doctor, fifty years old, who enjoyed a good position and was full of self-assurance, the colleague did not scruple to laugh in scorn when he uncovered the leg, gangrenous up to the knee. Then, after declaring bluntly that it would have to be amputated, he went off to the pharmacist to rail against the donkeys who had managed to reduce an unfortunate man to such a state. Shaking Monsieur Homais by the button of his frock coat, he expostulated in the pharmacy:

"These are inventions originating in Paris! They're notions belonging to those gentlemen from the Capital! Like strabismus, chloroform, lithotrity—a collection of monstrosities that ought to be outlawed by the government! But they want to look smart, and they cram you with remedies without worrying about the consequences. We out here aren't as clever as that; we're not scientists, dandies, ladies' men; we're practitioners, healers, and we would never consider operating on someone who was in marvelous health! Correct a clubfoot? How do you correct a clubfoot? It would be like trying to straighten a hunchback, for example!"

Homais was pained, listening to this speech, and he concealed his suffering under an obsequious smile, since he needed to humor Monsieur Canivet, whose prescriptions sometimes came as far as Yonville; he therefore did not take up Bovary's defense, but refrained from making any comment at all, and, abandoning his principles, sacrificed his dignity to the more serious interests of his business.

It was a considerable event in the village, this midthigh amputation by Doctor Canivet! All the inhabitants, that day, had risen earlier than usual, and the Grande-Rue, though full of people, had something ominous about it, as though an execution were about to take place. In the grocery, people were talking about Hippolyte's illness; the shops were selling nothing; and Madame Tuvache, the mayor's wife, did not budge from her window, so impatient was she to see the surgeon appear.

He arrived in his cabriolet, which he was driving himself. But because over time the springs on the right side had yielded under the weight of his corpulence, the carriage tipped a little to one side as it came on, and one could see, on the other cushion, next to him, an enormous chest covered in red sheep leather whose three brass fastenings shone magisterially.

When he had passed like a whirlwind under the porch of the Lion d'Or, the doctor, shouting loudly, ordered them to unharness his horse; then he went into the stable to see if it was really being given oats to eat; for whenever he arrived at the home of one of his patients, he would first look after his mare and his cabriolet. People even said, because of this: "Ah! Monsieur Canivet—what a character!" And he was all the more respected for his unshakable self-possession. The universe might have perished down to the last man, and he would not have neglected the least of his habits.

Homais came up to him.

"I'm counting on you," said the doctor. "Are we ready? Off we go!"

But the apothecary, blushing, confessed that he was too sensitive to be present at such an operation.

"When one is a mere onlooker," he said, "one's imagination, you know, becomes overexcited! And my nervous system is so . . ."

"Bah!" interrupted Canivet. "On the contrary, you seem to me disposed to apoplexy. And what's more, that doesn't surprise me; because you gentlemen, you pharmacists, are always cooped up in your kitchens, which must end by altering your constitutions. Now, look at me: Every day I get up at four in the morning, I shave in cold water (I'm never cold), and I don't wear flannel, I never catch cold, I'm sound in wind and limb! I eat sometimes one way, sometimes another, and accept it philosophically, taking my meals where I can. That's why I'm not delicate like you, and it's all the same to me whether I cut up a good Christian or some chicken that's put in front of me. It's all a matter of habit, you'll say . . . , just habit! . . ."

Then, without any regard for Hippolyte, who was sweating with anguish under his bedclothes, the two gentlemen embarked on a conversation in which the apothecary compared the coolness of a surgeon to that of a general; and this comparison was agreeable to Canivet, who launched into some remarks on the demands of his art. He looked upon it as a sacred calling, though the officers of health brought dishonor to it. At last, returning to the patient, he examined the bandages Homais had brought, the same ones that had appeared at the time of the clubfoot operation, and asked for someone to hold the limb for him. They sent for Lestiboudois, and Monsieur Canivet, having rolled up his sleeves, went into the billiards room, while the apothecary remained with Artémise and the innkeeper, both of them whiter than their aprons and straining their ears toward the door.

Bovary, during this time, did not dare move from his house. He stayed downstairs, in the parlor, sitting by the cold fireplace, his chin on his chest, his hands joined, his eyes fixed. What a mishap! he was thinking, what a disappointment! And yet he had taken every precaution imaginable. Fate had had a hand in it. Even so! —if Hippolyte should die later, he was the one who would have killed him. And then, what reason would he give during his visits to patients, when they asked him? Maybe, though, he had made a mistake somewhere? He searched his mind, found nothing. But even the most famous surgeons certainly made mistakes. That's what people never wanted to believe! No—instead, they were going to laugh at him, talk about him! The news would spread as far as Forges! Neufchâtel! Rouen! All over! Who could tell if his colleagues wouldn't write against him? There would be a controversy; he would have to answer in the newspapers. Hippolyte himself might sue him. He saw himself dishonored, ruined, lost! And his imagination, assaulted by a multitude of possibilities, pitched back and forth among them like an empty cask carried out to sea and rolling about in the waves.

Emma, sitting opposite, was watching him; she did not share his humiliation, she was experiencing a humiliation of a different sort: that she had imagined such a man could be worth something, as though twenty times over she had not already been sufficiently convinced of his mediocrity.

Charles paced back and forth in the room. His boots were creaking on the parquet floor.

"Sit down," she said. "You're annoying me!"

He sat down again.

Really, how had she (she who was so intelligent!) managed to misjudge things yet again? And through what lamentable folly had she spoiled her life this way, with one sacrifice after another? She recalled all her natural fondness for luxury, all the privations of her soul, the sordid details of marriage, housekeeping, her dreams falling in the mud like wounded swallows, everything she had desired, everything she had denied herself, everything she could have had! And for what! For what!

In the midst of the silence that hung over the village, a harrowing cry rang out through the air. Bovary turned so white he seemed about to faint. Her brows contracted in a nervous gesture, then she went on. Yet it was for him, for this creature, for this man who understood nothing, who felt nothing! —for there he was, quite calm, not even suspecting that from now on, the ridicule attached to his name was going to soil her as well as him. She had made efforts to love him, and she had repented in tears for having yielded to another.

"Why, perhaps it was a valgus!" exclaimed Bovary suddenly, meditating.

At the unexpected shock of that sentence falling upon her thoughts like a lead ball on a silver plate, Emma, with a shudder, lifted her head to try to understand what he meant; and they looked at each other in silence, almost dumbfounded to see each other there, so far apart had their thoughts taken them. Charles was contemplating her with the clouded gaze of a drunken man, even as he listened, motionless, to the amputee's last cries, which followed one another in lingering modulations punctuated by sharp shrieks, like the howling of some animal whose throat is being cut in the distance. Emma was biting her pale lips, and, as she rolled in her fingers one of the fragments of coral she had broken off, she fastened on Charles the burning points of her eyes, like two arrows of fire about to be loosed. Everything about him irritated her now—his face, his clothes, what he was not saying, his entire person, his very existence. She repented her past virtue as though it had been a crime, and what remained of it crumbled under the furious blows of her pride. She relished all the wretched ironies of triumphant adultery. The memory of her lover returned to her with dizzying enticements: she flung her soul at it, swept away toward that image by a new fervor; and Charles seemed to her as detached from her life, as forever absent, as impossible and annihilated, as if he were about to die and were suffering his death throes before her eyes.

There was a sound of footsteps on the sidewalk. Charles looked out; and through the lowered blind, he saw by the edge of the market, in the full sun, Doctor Canivet wiping his forehead with his kerchief. Homais, behind him, was carrying in his hands a large red box, and they were both heading in the direction of the pharmacy.

Then, in sudden tenderness and discouragement, Charles turned to his wife, saying:

"Kiss me, my dear!"

"Leave me alone!" she said, red with anger.

"What is it? What is it?" he said, stupefied. "Calm yourself! Don't be upset! . . . You know how much I love you! . . . Come to me!"

"Stop!" she shouted with a terrible look.

And rushing out of the room, Emma shut the door so hard that the barometer leaped from the wall and shattered on the floor.

Charles sank back in his chair, overwhelmed, trying to think what could be wrong with her, imagining a nervous illness, weeping, with the vague sense that in the air around him was something deadly and incomprehensible.

That night, when Rodolphe came into the garden, he found his mistress waiting for him at the bottom of the flight of steps, on the lowest step. They fell into each other's arms, and all their animosity melted away like snow in the heat of that kiss.

[12]

Their love had been reawakened. Often, Emma would even write to him suddenly in the middle of the day; then, through the windowpane, she would signal to Justin, who, quickly untying his apron, would fly off to La Huchette. Rodolphe would come; what she wanted to tell him was that she was bored, that her husband was hateful and her life hideous!

"How can I do anything about it?" he exclaimed one day, impatient.

"Oh! If you wanted to! . . ."

She was sitting on the ground, between his knees, her hair loosened, her gaze absent.

"Well, what?" said Rodolphe.

She sighed.

"We could go live somewhere else . . . somewhere . . ."

"You're really mad!" he said, laughing. "Did you really say that?"

She returned to the idea; he seemed not to understand, and changed the direction of the conversation.

What he did not understand was all this disturbance over such a simple thing as love. She had a motive, a reason, a sort of auxiliary force strengthening her passion for him.

This affection, indeed, grew each day with her aversion for her husband. The more fully she gave herself to the one, the more she despised the other; Charles had never appeared to her so unpleasant, with such square fingers, such clumsy wit, such common manners, as when they happened to be together after her meetings with Rodolphe. Then, even as she played at being the wife and virtuous woman, she would become inflamed at the thought of that head with its black hair turning in a curl over the suntanned forehead, of that body at once so robust and so elegant, of that man so experienced in his judgment, so passionate in his desire! It was for him that she would file her nails with the care of an engraver, and that there was never enough *cold cream* on her skin, nor patchouli on her handkerchiefs. She would load herself with bracelets, rings, necklaces. When he was coming, she would fill her two large blue glass vases with roses, and arrange her room and herself like a courtesan waiting for a prince. The maid had to launder her linens constantly; and so all day long, Félicité would not move from the kitchen, where young Justin, who often kept her company, would watch her as she worked.

His elbow on the long board where she was ironing, he would stare avidly at all these women's things spread out around him: the dimity petticoats, the fichus, the collars, and the drawstring pantalets, vast at the hips and narrowing lower down.

"What's this for?" the boy would ask, running his hand over the crinoline or the hooks and eyes.

"Have you never seen a thing?" Félicité would answer, laughing; "as if your own mistress, Madame Homais, don't wear just the same sort."

"Well, yes! Madame Homais!"

And he would add in a meditative tone:

"Is she a lady like Madame?"

But Félicité would lose patience when he hovered around her like this. She was six years older, and Théodore, Monsieur Guillaumin's servant, was beginning to court her.

"Leave me in peace!" she would say, moving her jar of starch. "Go grind your almonds; you're always poking your nose into women's affairs; don't get mixed up in all that till you have some hair on your chin, you wicked scamp."

"Oh, don't get mad. I'm going to go and *do her boots* for you."

And immediately he would reach up to the mantelpiece for Emma's boots, which were caked in mud—the mud from her rendezvous; it would fall away as dust under his fingers, and he would watch it rising gently in a ray of sunlight.

"How frightened you are of harming them!" said the servant, who took no such care when cleaning them herself, since as soon as the material had lost its freshness, Madame would pass them on to her.

Emma had a quantity of them in her cupboard, and she went through them one after another, without Charles ever allowing himself the slightest comment.

In the same way, he laid out three hundred francs for a wooden leg that she felt ought to be given to Hippolyte as a gift. The leg was lined with cork and had joints with springs; it was a complicated mechanism covered with a black pant leg ending in a patent leather boot. But Hippolyte, not daring to use such a handsome leg every day, begged Madame Bovary to procure him another that would be more convenient. The doctor, of course, covered the expense of this acquisition, too.

And so the stableboy gradually resumed his job. One would see him passing through the village as he used to, and when from far away Charles heard the sharp rap of his stick on the paving stones, he would quickly change his route.

It was Monsieur Lheureux, the dry-goods merchant, who had taken charge of the order; this provided him with an opportunity to visit Emma. He would chat with her about the new goods from Paris, about the dozens of novelties for women, he would make himself very agreeable, and he never asked for money. Emma let herself fall into this easy way of satisfying all her whims. For instance, she wanted to have, in order to give it as a gift to Rodolphe, a very lovely riding crop that was to be found in Rouen in an umbrella store. Monsieur Lheureux, the following week, set it down on her table.

But the next day he appeared at her house with a bill for 270 francs, not counting the centimes. Emma was very embarrassed: all the drawers in the secretary desk were empty; they owed more than two weeks to Lestiboudois, two trimesters to the servant; there were a quantity of other debts as well; and Bovary was waiting impatiently for the remittance from Monsieur Derozerays, who was in the habit, each year, of paying it around Saint Peter's Day.

She succeeded at first in putting Lheureux off; finally he lost patience: people were hounding him, his capital was tied up elsewhere, and if he did not recover some of it, he would be forced to take back all the articles she had.

"Well, take them back!" said Emma.

"Oh, I'm joking!" he replied. "Only, I do wish I had that riding crop back. Yes! I'll ask Monsieur to return it."

"No, no!" she said.

"Ah! I've got you!" thought Lheureux.

And, sure of his discovery, he went out repeating softly with his customary little whistle:

"All right! We'll see! We'll see!"

She was musing about how she could extricate herself, when the servant entered the room and deposited on the mantelpiece a little scroll of blue paper, *from Monsieur Derozerays.* Emma leaped on it, opened it up. It contained fifteen napoleons. It was the account. She heard Charles on the stairs; she threw the gold into the back of her drawer and took the key.

Three days later, Lheureux reappeared.

"I have an arrangement to propose to you," he said. "If, instead of pay-ing the agreed-upon sum, you would like to take . . ."

"Here it is," she said, placing fourteen napoleons in his hand.

The draper was stupefied. Then, to conceal his disappointment, he launched into a stream of apologies and offers of service, all of which Emma refused; then she stood there for a few minutes fingering in her apron pocket the two one-hundred-sous coins he had given back to her. She promised herself she would economize, so that later she could repay . . .

"Bah!" she thought. "He'll never give it another thought."

Besides the riding crop with its silver-gilt knob, Rodolphe had received a signet ring with the motto *Amor nel cor,* a scarf to use as a muffler, and lastly a cigar case just like the Vicomte's, the one that Charles had once picked up from the road and that Emma had kept. Yet he found these gifts humiliating. He refused several of them; she insisted; and in the end Rodolphe gave in, finding her tyrannical and overly intrusive.

And she had odd notions:

"When midnight strikes," she would say, "think of me!"

And if he confessed that he had not thought of her, there would be a torrent of reproaches, always ending with the eternal question:

"Do you love me?"

"Yes, of course I love you!" he would answer.

"Very much?"

"Certainly!"

"You've never loved anyone else, have you?"

"Do you think I was a virgin when you met me?" he would exclaim, laughing.

Emma would weep, and he would make an effort to comfort her, enlivening his protestations with puns.

"Oh! It's just that I love you!" she would go on; "I love you so much I can't do without you, do you know that? I sometimes long so much to see you again that I'm torn apart by all the fury of my love. I wonder: 'Where is he? Maybe he's talking to another woman? She's smiling at him, he's walking up to her . . .' No! There isn't anyone else that you like, is there? Some other women may be more beautiful, but I'm better at loving you! I'm your servant and your concubine! You're my king, my idol! You're good! You're handsome! You're intelligent! You're strong!"

He had heard these things said to him so often that for him there was nothing original about them. Emma was like all other mistresses; and the charm of novelty, slipping off gradually like a piece of clothing, revealed in its nakedness the eternal monotony of passion, which always assumes the same forms and uses the same language. He could not perceive—this man of such broad experience—the difference in feelings that might underlie similarities of expression. Because licentious or venal lips had murmured the same words to him, he had little faith in their truthfulness; one had to discount, he thought, exaggerated speeches that concealed mediocre affections; as if the fullness of the soul did not sometimes overflow in the emptiest of metaphors, since none of us can ever express the exact measure of our needs, or our ideas, or our sorrows, and human speech is like a cracked kettle on which we beat out tunes for bears to dance to, when we long to move the stars to pity.

But with the critical superiority possessed by anyone who remains aloof, whatever the relationship, Rodolphe saw other pleasures this love affair might offer. He deemed any sort of modesty to be inconvenient. He treated her carelessly. He made her into something compliant and corrupt. Hers was a sort of idiotic attachment full of admiration for him, of sensual pleasure for her, a bliss that numbed her; and her soul sank into this intoxication and drowned in it, shriveled like the Duke of Clarence in his butt of malmsey.

Solely from the effect of her amorous habits, Madame Bovary's behavior now changed. Her glances became bolder, her speech freer; she was even so unseemly as to take a walk with Monsieur Rodolphe with a cigarette between her lips, *as though flouting the whole world;* at last, those who had still doubted no longer did so when they saw her step down from the *Hirondelle* one day with her waist tightly buttoned up in a vest like a man; and Madame Bovary senior, who, after a dreadful scene with her husband, had come to take refuge in her son's home, was as scandalized as any of the townswomen. Many other things displeased her: first of all, Charles had not listened to her advice about forbidding novels; then, she did not like *the way the house was run;* she permitted herself some observations, and they became angry, on one occasion especially, with regard to Félicité.

Madame Bovary senior, the night before, as she was going down the hall, had surprised her in the company of a man, a man with brown chin whiskers, about forty years old, who, at the sound of her footsteps, had quickly fled the kitchen. At this, Emma burst out laughing; but the good lady flew into a rage, declaring that unless one cared nothing for morals, one had to keep an eye on those of one's servants.

"What sort of world do you come from?" said her daughter-in-law, with such an impertinent look that Madame Bovary asked her if she wasn't perhaps defending herself.

"Get out!" said the young woman, leaping to her feet.

"Emma! . . . Mama! . . ." cried Charles, trying to get them to make up.

But they had both fled the room in their rage. Emma kept stamping her foot with fury, saying over and over:

"Oh! What nice manners she has! The peasant!"

He ran to his mother; she was in a paroxysm, stammering:

"What a snip! What a featherbrain! Maybe worse!"

And she intended to leave immediately, if the other did not come apologize. Charles therefore returned to his wife and begged her to give in; he went down on his knees; in the end she answered:

"All right! I'll do it."

And indeed, she held out her hand to her mother-in-law with the dignity of a marquise, saying:

"Forgive me, madame."

Then, back in her room, Emma threw herself facedown on her bed and cried like a child, her head buried in the pillow.

They had agreed, she and Rodolphe, that in case something extraordinary happened, she would attach a little scrap of white paper to the shutter, so that if by chance he happened to be in Yonville, he could come quickly to the lane behind the house. Emma put up the signal; she had been waiting three-quarters of an hour when suddenly she saw Rodolphe in the corner of the market. She was tempted to open the window and call out to him; but he had already disappeared. She fell back in despair.

Soon, however, she thought she heard someone coming along the sidewalk. Surely it was he; she went downstairs, crossed the yard. He was there, outside. She threw herself in his arms.

"Take care, would you," he said.

"Oh, if you only knew!" she said.

And she began to tell him everything, hastily, incoherently, exaggerating the facts, inventing a few things, and with such an abundance of parenthetical digressions that he understood nothing.

"Come now, my poor angel, be brave, cheer up, be patient!"

"But for four years now I've been patient and I've suffered! . . . A love like ours ought to be confessed before heaven itself! They're trying to torture me. I can't bear it any longer! Save me!"

She was clinging to Rodolphe. Her eyes, full of tears, sparkled like flames underwater; her chest rose and fell rapidly; never had he loved her so much, so that he lost his head and asked:

"What should we do? What do you want?"

"Take me away!" she cried. "Oh, take me away from here! . . . I beg you!"

And she pressed her mouth on his, as though to snatch from it the unexpected consent that was exhaled in a kiss.

"But . . . ," said Rodolphe.

"What?"

"What about your daughter?"

She pondered for a few moments, then answered:

"We'll take her—it can't be helped!"

"What a woman!" he said to himself as he watched her go away.

For she had slipped into the garden. They were calling her.

Mère Bovary was very surprised, during the following days, by her daughter-in-law's metamorphosis. Emma was indeed more docile, carrying deference to the point of asking her for a recipe for pickling gherkins.

Was this the better to deceive them? Or did she wish, through a sort of voluptuous stoicism, to experience more profoundly the bitterness of what she was going to leave behind? But on the contrary, she took no notice; she lived as though engrossed in the anticipated enjoyment of her coming happiness. This was an eternal subject of conversation with Rodolphe. She would lean on his shoulder, she would murmur:

"Just think, when at last we're in the mail coach! . . . Can you imagine? Is it possible? The moment I feel the carriage start forward, I think it'll be as if we were going up in a balloon, as if we were rising into the clouds. Do you know that I'm counting the days? . . . Are you?"

Never had Madame Bovary been as lovely as she was during this time; hers was that indefinable beauty that comes from joy, enthusiasm, success, and that is nothing more than a harmony of temperament and circumstances. Her desires, her sorrows, her experience of pleasure, and her ever-youthful illusions had had the same effect as manure, rain, wind, and sun on a flower, developing her by degrees, and she was at last blooming in the fullness of her nature. Her eyelids seemed shaped expressly for those long, loving glances in which her pupils would disappear, while a heavy sigh would widen her delicate nostrils and lift the fleshy corners of her lips, shadowed, in the light, by a trace of dark down. Some artist skilled in depravity might have arranged the coil of her hair over the nape of her neck; it was looped in a heavy mass, carelessly, according to the chance dictates of her adulterous affair, which loosened it every day. Her voice now took on softer inflections, her body, too; something subtle and penetrating emanated even from the folds of her dress and the arch of her foot. Charles, as in the early days of his marriage, found her delicious and quite irresistible.

When he returned home in the middle of the night, he did not dare wake her. The porcelain night-light cast a trembling round glow on the ceiling, and the closed curtains of the little cradle formed a sort of white hut that rose up in the darkness by the side of the bed. Charles gazed at them. He thought he could hear the shallow breath of his child. She would be growing now; each season would quickly bring with it another advance. He could already see her coming home from school at the close of the day, wreathed in laughter, her little blouse spotted with ink, carrying her basket on her arm; then she would have to be sent to boarding school, that would cost a good deal; how would they do it? He would ponder this. He thought he might rent a small farm in the area, which he would oversee himself, every morning, on his way to visit his patients. He would save the income, he would put it in a savings bank; then he would buy some shares somewhere, it didn't matter where; in addition, his clientele would increase—he was counting on that, because he wanted Berthe to be well brought up, accomplished, learn to play the piano. Ah, how pretty she would be, later, when she was fifteen, when, resembling her mother, she would, like her, wear large straw hats in summer! From a distance, people would take them for two sisters. He pictured her working in the evening near them, in the lamplight; she would embroider some slippers for him; she would look after the household; she would fill the whole house with her sweetness and gaiety. Eventually, they would think of getting her settled: they would find her some decent boy with a solid profession; he would make her happy; it would last forever.

Emma was not sleeping, she was pretending to be asleep; and while he dozed off next to her, she would grow more wakeful, dreaming other dreams.

Four galloping horses had been bearing her off, for a week now, toward a new country from which they would never return. They went on and on, their arms entwined, without speaking. Often, from the top of a mountain, they suddenly caught sight of splendid city with domes, bridges, ships, groves of lemon trees, and cathedrals of white marble on whose sharp steeples storks were nesting. They slowed to a walk, because of the large paving stones, and on the ground lay bouquets of flowers being offered by women wearing laced red bodices. One could hear bells ringing, and mules whinnying, along with the murmur of guitars and the splash of fountains, whose flying spray cooled the mounds of fruit arranged in pyramids at the feet of pale statues smiling under the jets of water. And then, one evening, they would arrive at a village of fishermen, where brown nets were drying in the wind along the cliff and the line of shanties. It was here that they would stay and make a life for themselves; they would live in a low house, with a flat roof, shaded by a palm tree, at the far end of a bay, by the edge of the sea. They would go out in a gondola, they would swing in a hammock; their life would be as easy and ample as their silken clothing, all warm and starry like the soft nights on which they would gaze. And yet in the immensity of that future that she created for herself, nothing in particular stood out; the days, all of them magnificent, resembled one another like waves; and all of this hovered on the horizon, infinite, harmonious, blue, and bathed in sunlight. But the child would begin coughing in her cradle, or Bovary would snore more loudly, and Emma would not fall asleep until morning, when the dawn was whitening the windowpanes, and already young Justin, on the square, was opening the pharmacy shutters.

She had sent for Monsieur Lheureux and had said to him:

"I will be needing a cloak, a large cloak, with a broad collar, lined."

"Are you going off on a trip?" he asked.

"No! But . . . never mind, I can count on you, can't I? And quickly!"

He bowed.

"I will also need," she went on, "a trunk . . . not too heavy . . . roomy."

"Yes, yes, I understand, about ninety-two centimeters by fifty, the way they're making them nowadays."

"And an overnight bag."

"Clearly," thought Lheureux, "there's some sort of quarrel behind this."

"And here," said Madame Bovary, drawing her watch from her belt, "take this; you can pay yourself out of it."

But the merchant exclaimed that that was not right; they knew each other; did he doubt her? What childishness! She insisted, however, that he take the chain at least, and Lheureux had already put it in his pocket and was on his way out when she called him back.

"You can keep it all in your shop. As for the cloak"—she seemed to be thinking it over—"don't bring that either; just give me the tailor's address and ask them to have it ready for me."

They were to make their escape the following month. She would leave Yonville as though to run some errands in Rouen. Rodolphe would have reserved their seats, acquired passports, and even written to Paris, in order to have the coach to themselves as far as Marseille, where they would buy a barouche and, from there, continue without stopping along the Genoa route. She would take care to send her luggage to Lheureux's, whence it would be loaded directly onto the *Hirondelle* so that no one would suspect anything; and in all of this, the subject of her child never came up. Rodolphe avoided talking about it; perhaps she was not thinking about it.

He wanted another two weeks, in order to finish making some arrangements; then, at the end of one week, he asked for two more; then he said he was ill; after that he went on a trip; the month of August passed; and after all these delays, they settled irrevocably on September 4, a Monday.

At last Saturday arrived, two days before the Monday.

Rodolphe came that night, earlier than usual.

"Is everything ready?" he asked her.

"Yes."

Then they strolled around a flower bed, and went to sit near the terrace, on the edge of the wall.

"You're sad," said Emma.

"No, why?"

And yet he was looking at her strangely, with tenderness.

"Is it because you're going away?" she went on, "because you're leaving the things you love, because you're leaving your life here? Oh, I understand! . . . But in the whole world I have nothing. You're everything to me. And I'll be everything to you, I'll be your family, your homeland; I'll take care of you, I'll love you."

"How enchanting you are!" he said, taking her in his arms.

"Am I really?" she said with a laugh of voluptuous pleasure. "Do you love me? Now, swear you do!"

"Do I love you? Do I love you? I adore you, my love!"

The moon, perfectly round and deep red, was rising straight from the earth, at the far end of the meadow. It climbed quickly among the branches of the poplars, which hid it in places like a black curtain full of holes. Then it appeared in the empty sky, dazzling white, filling it with light; and, slowing, it spread over the river a wide stain that formed an infinity of stars; and the gleam of silver seemed to twist all the way down to the bottom, like a headless snake covered with luminous scales. It resembled, too, some monstrous candelabra streaming all down its length with molten drops of diamond. The mild night opened out around them; layers of shadow filled the leaves. Emma, her eyes half closed, inhaled with deep sighs the cool breeze that was blowing. They did not speak to each other, so lost were they in their pervasive reveries. The affection of earlier days returned to their hearts, as abundant and silent as the flowing river, as soft as the perfume borne to them by the mock-orange flowers, and cast over their memories shadows more colossal and more melancholy than those of the motionless willows that lay across the grass. Often some nocturnal creature, a hedgehog or weasel, setting off on its hunt, would disturb the leaves, or now and then they would hear a single ripe peach dropping from the espalier.

"What a lovely night!" said Rodolphe.

"We'll have many more!" said Emma.

And, as though talking to herself:

"Yes, it will be good to travel . . . Yet why is my heart so sad? Is it fear of the unknown . . . ? Or the effect of leaving my familiar ways . . . ? Or . . . ? No, it's because I'm too happy! How weak I am, aren't I? Forgive me!"

"There's still time!" he cried. "Think about it carefully, you might be sorry."

"Never!" she said impetuously.

And, moving close to him:

"What harm can come to me, after all? There's not a desert, not a precipice, not an ocean that I wouldn't cross with you. When we're living together, our life will be like an embrace that becomes closer and more complete every day! There'll be nothing to bother us, no worries, nothing in our way! We'll be alone together, we'll be everything to each other, forever . . . Say something, answer me."

He answered at regular intervals: "Yes . . . yes! . . ." She had slipped her fingers into his hair, and she kept repeating in a childlike voice, despite the large tears that were flowing from her eyes:

"Rodolphe! Rodolphe! . . . Ah! Rodolphe, dear little Rodolphe!"
Midnight struck.

"Midnight!" she said. "Now it's tomorrow! One more day!"

He stood up to leave; and as if this motion of his were the signal for their departure, Emma, suddenly cheerful, said:

"You have the passports?"

"Yes."

"You haven't forgotten anything?"

"No."

"You're sure?"

"Of course."

"The Hôtel de Provence—that's where you'll be waiting for me? . . . At noon?"

He nodded.

"Till tomorrow, then!" said Emma with a last caress.

And she watched him walk away.

He did not turn around. She ran after him, and, leaning over by the water's edge between the bushes:

"Till tomorrow!" she cried.

He was already on the other side of the stream, walking quickly across the meadow.

After a few minutes, Rodolphe stopped; and when he saw her in her white dress gradually vanish into the darkness like a phantom, his heart began to pound so hard that he leaned against a tree to keep from falling.

"What an idiot I am!" he said with a dreadful oath. "Well, it doesn't matter; she was a lovely mistress!"

And immediately, Emma's beauty, and all the pleasures of their love, reappeared before him. At first he softened, then he turned against her.

"Because, really," he exclaimed, gesticulating, "I can't abandon my own country. I can't assume responsibility for a child."

He was saying these things to strengthen himself in his resolve.

"And besides—the difficulties, the expense . . . Oh, no! No, no, no! It would have been too stupid!"

[1 3]

As soon as Rodolphe arrived home, he sat down quickly at his desk under the stag's head that hung as a trophy on the wall. But once the pen was in his hand, he could not think of anything, so, leaning on his elbows, he began to reflect. Emma seemed to him to have receded into a distant past, as if the decision he had just made had suddenly placed an immense gap between them.

To recapture something of her, he went to the cupboard by the head of his bed and took out an old Reims cookie tin in which he was in the habit of putting the letters women sent to him, and there escaped from it a smell of damp dust and withered roses. First he saw a pocket handkerchief covered with pale droplets. It was one of hers, from when she had had a nosebleed, once when they were out together; he had forgotten. Near it, knocking against the corners of the box, was the miniature Emma had given him; he found her clothing pretentious and her *sidelong gaze* most pitiful in its effect; then, because he had been studying this picture and summoning up a recollection of its original, Emma's features gradually became confused in his memory, as if the living face and the painted face, rubbing together, had obliterated each other. Finally he read some of her letters; they were full of explanations concerning their trip, as short, technical, and urgent as business letters. He wanted to look at the long ones again, the ones from earlier times; in order to find them at the bottom of the tin, Rodolphe disturbed all the others; and mechanically he began rummaging through the pile of papers and other things, rediscovering in disarray some bouquets, a garter, a black mask, pins, and hair—hair!— brown, blond, some of which, even, caught on the iron fittings of the box and broke when it was opened.

Thus idling through his souvenirs, he examined the handwriting and the styles of the letters, as varied as their spelling. They were tender or jolly, facetious, melancholy; there were some that demanded love and others that demanded money. A single word would cause him to recall certain faces, certain gestures, the sound of a voice; sometimes, however, he recalled nothing.

Indeed, these women, flocking into his thoughts all at the same time, impeded and diminished one another, as though leveled by the sameness of his love. And picking up fistfuls of the disordered letters, he amused himself for a few minutes letting them fall in cascades from his right hand into his left. At last, bored, sleepy, Rodolphe carried the tin back to the cupboard, saying to himself:

"What a load of nonsense! . . ."

Which summed up his opinion; for his pleasures, like schoolchildren in a schoolyard, had so trampled his heart that nothing green grew there, and whatever passed through it, more heedless than the children, did not even leave behind its name, as they did, carved on the wall.

"Come, now," he said to himself, "let's get started!"

He wrote:

Be brave, Emma! Be brave! I don't want to ruin your life . . .

"That's true, after all," thought Rodolphe; "I'm acting in her interest; I'm being honest."

Did you weigh your decision carefully? Were you aware of the abyss into which I was drawing you, my poor angel? You weren't, were you? You were going ahead, foolishly trusting, believing in happiness, in the future . . . Oh, poor wretches that we are! Lunatics!

Rodolphe stopped at this point, looking for some good excuse.

"What if I told her I'd lost my entire fortune? . . . Oh, no! Anyway, that wouldn't put a stop to anything. I'd just have to go through the whole thing again later. Can one ever make women of that sort listen to reason?"

He reflected, then added:

I will never forget you, believe me, and I will continue to be deeply devoted to you; but one day, sooner or later, this ardor would no doubt have diminished (such being the destiny of all things human)! We would have had moments of weariness, and who knows, even, if I would not have suffered the atrocious pain of witnessing your remorse and partaking of it myself, since I would have been the cause of it. The very idea of the sorrows that burden you is torture to me, Emma! Forget me! Why did I ever have to meet you? Why were you so beautiful? Is it my fault? Oh, Lord, no! Fate is to blame, only fate!

"There's a word that always has a nice effect," he said to himself.

Oh, if you had been one of those women with a frivolous heart—who certainly exist—I could have selfishly experimented without putting you at risk. But the delicious exaltation of feeling that is at once your charm and your torment has prevented you from understanding, adorable woman that you are, the falseness of our future position. I, too, did not think about it at first, and I lay down to rest in the shade of that ideal happiness, as in the poisonous shade of the fatal manchineel tree, without foreseeing the consequences.

"Perhaps she'll think I'm giving this up out of greed . . . Oh, well, too bad! It doesn't matter, I must be done with it!"

The world is cruel, Emma. Wherever we had gone, it would have pursued us. You would have had to submit to indiscreet questions, calumny, scorn, perhaps insult. You, insulted! Oh! . . . When my wish is that I might seat you on a throne! When I will carry the thought of you away with me like a talisman! For I am punishing myself by exile for all the harm I have done you. I am going away. Where? I have no idea—I have lost my reason! Adieu! Be good always! Preserve the memory of the wretch who lost you. Teach my name to your child, so that she may repeat it in her prayers.

The wicks of the two candles were flickering. Rodolphe stood up to go close the window and, when he had sat down again, said:

"I think that's all. Oh! One more thing, for fear that she'll come *pester me.*"

I will be far away when you read these sad lines; for I am determined to flee as quickly as possible in order to avoid the temptation of seeing you again. This is no time for weakness! I will come back; and perhaps, in time to come, we will talk together quite calmly of our old love. Adieu!

And there was one last adieu, separated into two words: *A Dieu!* which he judged to be in excellent taste.

"Now, how shall I sign it?" he asked himself. "Your devoted? . . . No. Your friend? . . . Yes, that's it."

Your friend.

He reread his letter. It seemed good to him.

"Poor little woman!" he thought with emotion. "She'll think I have no more feeling than a stone; there should have been a few tears on it; but I can't cry; it's not my fault." Then, having poured some water into a glass, Rodolphe dipped his finger in it and let fall from above a fat drop, which made a pale blot on the ink; finally, looking to seal the letter, he came upon the *Amor nel cor* signet ring.

"This is scarcely appropriate under the circumstances . . . Oh, well! It doesn't matter!"

After which he smoked three pipes and went to bed.

The next day, when he got up (at about two o'clock—he had slept late), Rodolphe sent for a servant to gather a basket of apricots for him. He placed the letter in the bottom, under some vine leaves, and at once ordered Girard, his plowboy, to take it carefully to Madame Bovary. This was the means he used to correspond with her, sending her either fruit or game, according to the season.

"If she asks about me," he said, "you will answer that I've gone on a trip. You must give the basket only to her, put it into her own hands . . . Go on now, and take care!"

Girard put on his new smock, tied his handkerchief around the apricots, and, walking with long, heavy strides in his thick hobnailed clogs, tranquilly set off down the path to Yonville.

When he reached her house, Madame Bovary was arranging a bundle of linens on the kitchen table with Félicité.

"Here," said the servant. "Our master sends you this."

She was seized by a feeling of dread, and while searching for some coins in her pocket, she gazed at the boy with wild eyes, as he in turn looked at her with amazement, not understanding how such a gift could upset someone so much. At last he went out. Félicité was still there. She could not endure it any longer, she hurried into the parlor as though to put the apricots there, overturned the basket, tore the leaves apart, found the letter, opened it, and, as if an inferno were blazing behind her, fled up to her room, overcome with terror.

Charles was there, she saw him; he spoke to her, she heard nothing, and she continued hastily climbing the stairs, breathless, frenzied, beside herself, and still holding that horrible piece of paper, which rattled in her fingers like a sheet of metal. On the third floor, she stopped in front of the door to the attic, which was closed.

Then she tried to calm herself; she remembered the letter; she had to finish it; she did not dare. Anyway, where? How? Someone would see her.

"Oh, no—here!" she thought; "I'll be all right in here."

Emma pushed open the door and went in.

The slate tiles of the roof admitted a sultry heat that dropped straight down, pressing against her temples and stifling her; she dragged herself to the shuttered dormer window; she pulled back the bolt, and the dazzling light sprang in.

Before her, above the rooftops, the open countryside spread out as far as the eye could see. Down below, beneath her, the village square was empty; the stones of the sidewalk sparkled, the weather vanes on the houses stood motionless; at the street corner, from a lower story, came a kind of whirring noise with strident changes of tone. It was Binet at his lathe.

She had leaned against the frame of the window, and she was rereading the letter, now and then giving an angry, derisive laugh. But the more steadily she fixed her attention on it, the more confused her thoughts became. She saw him again, she heard him, she put her arms around him; and her heartbeats, striking her chest like the great blows of a battering ram, came faster and faster one after another, at unequal intervals. She cast her eyes about her, wishing the earth would cave in. Why not put an end to it all? What was holding her back? She was free. And she moved forward, she looked down at the paving stones, saying to herself:

"Go on! Go on!"

The ray of light that rose directly up to her from below was pulling the weight of her body down toward the abyss. It seemed to her that the ground in the village square was swaying back and forth and rising along the walls, and that the floor was tipping down at the end, like a vessel pitching. She was standing right at the edge, almost suspended, surrounded by a great empty space. The blue of the sky was coming into her, the air circulating inside her hollow skull, she had only to give in, to let herself be taken; and the whirring of the lathe never stopped, like a furious voice calling her.

"Emma! Emma!" Charles shouted.

She stopped.

"Where are you? Come here!"

The idea that she had just escaped death almost made her faint from terror; she closed her eyes; then she started at the touch of a hand on her sleeve: it was Félicité.

"Monsieur is waiting for you, madame; the soup is on the table."

And she had to go down! She had to sit down to dinner!

She tried to eat. The pieces of food made her choke. Then she unfolded her napkin as though to examine the places where it had been darned, and really tried to apply herself to this work, counting the threads of the weave. Suddenly she remembered the letter again. Had she lost it? How would she ever find it? But her mind was so exhausted that she would never have been able to invent a pretext for leaving the table. And she had become a coward; she was afraid of Charles; he knew everything, she was sure! Indeed, oddly enough, he spoke these words:

"It will be some time, so it seems, before we see Monsieur Rodolphe again."

"Who told you that?" she asked, starting.

"Who told me that?" he replied, a little surprised at her abrupt tone; "it was Girard; I met him just now at the door of the Café Français. He's gone off on a trip, or he's about to go off."

She gave a sob.

"Why should you be so surprised? He does go away like that now and then for his own enjoyment, and my faith! I approve. If you have a little money and you're not married! . . . Besides, he knows how to have a good time, our friend does! He's quite the wag. Monsieur Langlois told me once how . . ."

He fell silent for the sake of decency, because the servant was coming in.

She put back in the basket the apricots that lay scattered over the étagère; Charles, without noticing how flushed his wife was, asked for them, took one, and bit into it.

"Oh, it's perfect!" he said. "Here, taste one."

And he held out the basket, which she pushed gently away.

"Smell them, then: what a fragrance!" he said, passing them under her nose several times.

"I can't breathe!" she cried, leaping to her feet.

But through an effort of will, she conquered the spasm; then:

"It's nothing!" she said, "it's nothing! It's just nerves! Sit down, eat!"

For she dreaded being questioned, fussed over, never left alone.

Charles, obeying her, had sat down again, and he was spitting the apricot stones into his hand and then depositing them on his plate.

Suddenly a blue tilbury crossed the square at a fast trot. Emma cried out and fell straight over backward onto the floor.

Indeed, Rodolphe, after a good deal of reflection, had decided to leave for Rouen. However, since there is no other route from La Huchette to Buchy but the Yonville road, he had had to drive through the village, and Emma had recognized him by the gleam of the lanterns that sliced like a flash of lightning through the dusk.

The pharmacist, at the sound of the commotion, rushed to the house. The table, along with all the plates, had been overturned; the sauce, the meat, the knives, the saltcellar, and the oil cruet lay strewn about the room; Charles was calling for help; Berthe, frightened, was shrieking; and Félicité, her hands shaking, was unlacing Madame, whose entire body was racked with convulsions.

"I'll just run," said the apothecary, "to my laboratory for some aromatic vinegar."

Then, when she opened her eyes, breathing from the flask:

"I was sure of it," he said; "this stuff would wake a dead man."

"Speak to us!" Charles was saying. "Speak to us! Wake up! It's me, your Charles, who loves you! Do you recognize me? Here now, here's your little girl: now give her a kiss, won't you!"

The child held out her arms toward her mother to clasp them around her neck. But Emma, turning her head away, said brokenly:

"No, no . . . no one!"

She fainted again. They carried her to her bed.

She remained lying there, her mouth open, her eyelids closed, her hands flat beside her, motionless, and as white as a wax statue. From her eyes trickled two streams of tears onto the pillow.

Charles, standing, stayed at the back of the alcove, and the pharmacist, next to him, maintained that meditative silence suitable for the more serious occasions of life.

"Don't worry," he said, pressing his elbow, "I think the paroxysm has passed."

"Yes, she's resting a little now!" answered Charles, who was watching her sleep. "Poor woman! . . . Poor woman! . . . She's had a relapse!"

Then Homais asked how this accident had happened. Charles answered that she had been stricken suddenly while eating apricots.

"Extraordinary! . . ." said the pharmacist. "Why, it's quite possible that the apricots brought on the syncope! Some people are so naturally impressionable when coming into contact with certain odors! And this would actually be a nice topic to study, from the point of view of both its pathology and its physiology. The priests recognize its importance; they've always brought aromatics into their ceremonies. They do it to stupefy the understanding and provoke a state of ecstasy, which, of course, is easy enough to achieve in persons of the female sex, who are more delicate than the others. Cases have been cited of women fainting at the smell of burned horn, fresh bread . . ."

"Take care not to wake her!" said Bovary softly.

"And," continued the apothecary, "it's not only humans who are vulnerable to these anomalies, but animals, too. For instance, you're surely aware of the singular aphrodisiac effect produced by *Nepeta cataria,* vulgarly known as catnip, on the feline tribe; and again, to mention an example I guarantee to be authentic, Bridoux (one of my old schoolmates, presently established in the rue Malpalu) has a dog that falls into convulsions if one offers it a snuffbox. He frequently performs the experiment in front of his friends, at his summerhouse in Bois-Guillaume. Who would ever think that a simple sternutative could work such havoc in a quadruped's organism? It's extremely curious, don't you find?"

"Yes," said Charles, who was not listening.

"This just proves to us," the other went on, smiling with an air of benign complacency, "how innumerable are the irregularities of the nervous system. As regards Madame, she has always seemed to me, I confess, a genuinely sensitive case. Thus, I would not recommend, my good friend, any of those so-called remedies that, under the pretext of attacking the symptoms, attack the constitution. No, no idle medication! A regimen, and nothing else! Sedatives, emollients, dulcifiers. And also, don't you think it might be a good thing to rouse her imagination?"

"In what way? How?" asked Bovary.

"Ah! That's the problem! Such, indeed, is the problem: *That is the question!*" he quoted in English—"as I was reading in the paper the other day."

But Emma, waking, cried out:

"The letter! The letter!"

They thought she was delirious; and she was, from midnight on: a brain fever had set in.

For forty-three days, Charles did not leave her side. He abandoned all his patients; he no longer went to bed; he was continually taking her pulse, applying mustard plasters, cold-water compresses. He sent Justin to Neufchâtel to get ice; the ice melted on the way home; he sent him back. He called in Monsieur Canivet for a consultation; he had Doctor Larivière, his old teacher, come from Rouen; he was in despair. What frightened him the most was Emma's prostration; for she did not speak, heard nothing, and even seemed not to be in pain—as if both her body and her soul were resting from all their suffering.

Toward the middle of October, she was able to sit up in bed with some pillows behind her. Charles wept when he saw her eat her first slice of bread and jam. Her strength returned to her; she would get up for a few hours during the afternoon, and one day when she was feeling better, he tried to induce her to go out, leaning on his arm, for a stroll in the garden. The sand on the paths was disappearing under the dead leaves; she walked one step at a time, dragging her slippers; and, leaning her shoulder against Charles, she smiled the whole time.

In this way they went to the far end, close to the terrace. She straightened up slowly, put her hand above her eyes, in order to look out; she looked into the distance, the far distance; but there was nothing on the horizon except great grass fires, smoking on the hills.

"You're going to tire yourself out, dear," said Bovary.

And, nudging her gently, to induce her to go into the arbor:

"Sit down on the bench: you'll be all right here."

"Oh, no! Not there, not there!" she said in a faltering voice.

She was overcome by dizziness, and that evening, her illness returned, though in a more uncertain guise and with more complex characteristics. Sometimes she felt a pain in her heart, sometimes in her chest, then in her head, then in her arms and legs; she had fits of vomiting in which Charles believed he saw the first symptoms of cancer.

And on top of this, poor man, he had money worries!

[14]

First of all, he did not know how he was going to compensate Monsieur Homais for all the medicaments that had come from his pharmacy; and although, as a doctor, he could have chosen not to pay, nevertheless he felt a little ashamed at incurring that obligation. Then the household expenses, now that the servant was in charge, were becoming frightening; the notes were raining down on the house; the tradespeople were complaining; Monsieur Lheureux, above all, was harassing him. Indeed, at the height of Emma's illness, Lheureux, profiting from the circumstances to pad his bill, had promptly brought over the coat, the overnight bag, two trunks instead of one, an abundance of other things as well. It was in vain that Charles said he did not need them; the merchant answered arrogantly that all these articles had been ordered from him and that he would not take them back; besides, it would be upsetting to Madame during her convalescence; Monsieur should think it over; in short, he was resolved to pursue him in a court of law rather than give up his rights and take back his merchandise. Charles afterward ordered everything to be sent back to the shop; Félicité forgot; he had other worries; it was not thought of again; Monsieur Lheureux returned to the attack and, by turns threatening and complaining, maneuvered in such a way that in the end Bovary signed a note payable in six months. But scarcely had he signed this note, than a bold idea struck him: to borrow 1,000 francs from Monsieur Lheureux. And so he asked, with a look of embarrassment, if there was not some means of obtaining this amount, adding that it would be for one year and at any rate of interest he liked. Lheureux hurried to his shop, brought back the ecus, and dictated another note, whereby Bovary undertook to pay to his order, on September 1 next, the sum of 1,070 francs; which, with the 180 already stipulated, came to exactly 1,250. Thus, lending at 6 percent, augmented by a quarter's commission and a profit of a good third at least on the goods, the whole thing should, in twelve months, yield a profit of 130 francs; and he hoped the matter would not end there, that the notes would not be paid, that they would be renewed, and that his meager capital, having been well nourished in the doctor's home as though in a private sanatorium, would return to him, one day, considerably plumper, large enough to split open the bag.

Everything, moreover, was going well for him. He was the contracting party for supplying cider to the Neufchâtel hospital; Monsieur Guillaumin had promised him some shares in the Grumesnil peat bogs; and he was thinking of setting up a new coach service between Argueil and Rouen, which would soon, no doubt, spell the end of that old rattletrap at the Lion d'Or and, being faster, costing less, and carrying larger loads, would thus put all the Yonville trade into his hands.

Charles often asked himself how he was going to be able to pay back so much money the following year; and he would search his mind, imagine various expedients, such as appealing to his father or selling something. But his father would have turned a deaf ear, and he himself had nothing he could sell. And he encountered so many difficulties that he would quickly put such unpleasant reflections out of his mind. He would reproach himself for forgetting Emma; as if all his thoughts belonged to her and he was stealing from her if he failed to think about her all the time.

The winter was harsh. Madame's convalescence was a long one. When the weather was fine, they would push her in her armchair up to the window, the one that looked out over the square; for she now had an aversion to the garden, and the shutters on that side always remained closed. She wanted the horse to be sold; what she had once loved, she no longer liked. All her thoughts seemed to be confined to looking after herself. She would stay in bed eating light meals, ring for the servant to ask about her tisanes or to chat with her. Meanwhile, the snow on the roof of the covered market would cast its motionless white reflection into the room; then, later in the season, the rain would fall. And every day Emma would wait, with a kind of anxiety, for the unfailing recurrence of trivial events, little though they mattered to her. The most important of these was the arrival, in the evening, of the *Hirondelle*. Then the innkeeper would shout and other voices would reply, while Hippolyte's lantern, as he lifted the trunks down from the roof of the coach, was like a star in the darkness. At noon, Charles would return home; then he would go out; later, she would have some broth; and toward five o'clock, at the end of the day, the children, on their way home from school, dragging their wooden shoes along the sidewalk, would strike the hooks of the shutters, one after the other, with their rulers.

It was at this hour that Monsieur Bournisien would come to see her. He would inquire about her health, bring her news, and urge her to piety in a coaxing little conversation that was not without charm. The very sight of his cassock would comfort her.

One day at the height of her illness, when she believed she was dying, she had asked to be given Communion; and as her room was prepared for the sacrament, as the chest of drawers crowded with syrups was transformed into an altar and Félicité scattered dahlia flowers over the floor, Emma felt some powerful force pass over her that rid her of all her suffering, of all perception, of all feeling. Her flesh, relieved, no longer weighed her down; a new life was beginning; it seemed to her that her whole being, ascending toward God, would dissolve in that love as burning incense dissipates into smoke. Holy water was sprinkled over the sheets of the bed; the priest withdrew the white host from the holy ciborium; and, fainting with heavenly joy, she put her lips forward to receive the proffered body of the Savior. The curtains of her alcove swelled out softly around her, like clouds, and the rays from the two wax tapers burning on the chest seemed to her like dazzling halos. Then she let her head fall back, thinking she could hear, through the vastnesses of space, the music of seraphic harps, and could see in an azure sky, on a throne of gold, surrounded by the saints holding fronds of green palm, God the Father in all His brilliant majesty, who with a sign sent angels with flaming wings down to the earth to carry her away in their arms.

This splendid vision lingered in her memory as the most beautiful thing she could ever have dreamed; so that now she kept striving to recapture the sensation of it, which persisted in a less all-encompassing manner but with a sweetness as profound. Her soul, exhausted by pride, was at last reposing in Christian humility; and, savoring the pleasure of being weak, Emma watched within herself the destruction of her will, which was to open wide the way for incursions of grace. So there existed greater delights in place of mere happiness, a love above all other loves, without interruption and without end, one that would continue to increase through all eternity! She could glimpse, among the illusions born of her hopes, a state of purity floating above the earth, merging with heaven, and this was where she aspired to be. She wanted to become a saint. She bought rosaries, she carried amulets; she wished she had a reliquary studded with emeralds in her room, by the head of her bed, so that she could kiss it every night.

The curé marveled at these tendencies, although he felt that Emma's piety might in the end, because of its fervor, verge on heresy and even nonsense. But not being very well versed in these matters once they went beyond certain bounds, he wrote to Monsieur Boulard, Monseigneur's bookseller, to send him *something particularly good, for a female of high intelligence.* The bookseller, with as much indifference as if he were dispatching cheap trinkets to black Africans, packaged up a hodgepodge of everything then current in the religious book trade. Included were slim handbooks in the form of questions and answers, haughty-toned pamphlets in the manner of Monsieur de Maistre, and novels of a certain sort in pink paperboards and a sickly-sweet style fabricated by troubadour seminarists or repentant bluestockings. There was *Think On It Well; The Man of the World at Mary's Feet, by Monsieur de ***, decorated with many orders; The Errors of Voltaire, Intended for the Young,* etc.

Madame Bovary's mind was not yet clear enough for her to apply herself seriously to anything; what was more, she undertook these readings too hastily. She was irritated by the regulations governing worship; the condescension of the polemical writings displeased her by their relentless pursuit of people she had never heard of; and the secular stories spiced with religion seemed to her written in such ignorance of the world that they imperceptibly distanced her from the very truths she was hoping to see confirmed. She persisted nonetheless, and when the volume fell from her hands, she believed she was filled with the most refined Catholic melancholy ever conceived by an ethereal soul.

As for the memory of Rodolphe, she had thrust it down into the depths of her heart; and there it remained, as solemn and still as a king's mummy in an underground chamber. From this great embalmed love rose an emanation that permeated everything, imparting a fragrance of tenderness to the atmosphere of spotless purity in which she wanted to live. When she knelt at her Gothic prie-dieu, she would address the Lord with the same sweet words she used to murmur to her lover in the ecstatic transports of her adultery. This she did to induce faith to come to her; but no rapture descended from heaven, and she would get to her feet, her arms and legs tired, with the vague sense that it was all an immense hoax. This quest was, she thought, but an added merit; and in her pride at her devoutness, Emma would compare herself to those great ladies of earlier times over whose glory she had daydreamed before a portrait of La Vallière, and who, trailing behind them so majestically the spangled trains of their long gowns, would withdraw to a lonely spot to shed at Christ's feet all the tears of a heart wounded by life.

Then she plunged into excessive acts of charity. She would sew clothing for the poor; she would send firewood to women in childbirth; and Charles, on returning home one day, found three shiftless fellows at the kitchen table eating soup. She arranged for her little girl to be brought back to the house; her husband, during her illness, had sent the child to the nurse. She tried to teach her to read; though Berthe wept, she no longer became annoyed. It was a decision she had made—to adopt an attitude of resignation, of indulgence toward all. Her language, on all subjects, was full of lofty expressions. She would say to her child:

"Is your stomachache gone, my angel?"

The elder Madame Bovary found nothing with which to reproach her, except perhaps this mania for knitting camisoles for orphans instead of mending her dish towels. But, exhausted by the quarrels in her own home, the good woman was happy in this peaceful house, and she even stayed until after Easter to avoid the sarcastic remarks of the elder Bovary, who never failed, on Good Friday, to order himself a chitterling sausage.

Besides the company of her mother-in-law, who steadied her somewhat because of her rectitude of judgment and her sober ways, Emma also received, nearly every day, other visitors. There was Madame Langlois, Madame Caron, Madame Dubreuil, Madame Tuvache, and, regularly from two to five o'clock, the excellent Madame Homais, who had never wanted to believe any of the ill-natured gossip that people retailed about her neighbor. The Homais children would also come to see her; Justin would bring them. He would accompany them up to the bedroom, and he would remain standing by the door without moving or speaking. Often, indeed, Madame Bovary, taking no notice, would begin to dress. She would start by taking out her comb and shaking her head briskly; and the first time he saw that full mane of hair with its black ringlets tumbling down to her knees, it was for him, poor boy, like suddenly entering something new and extraordinary, something whose splendor frightened him.

Emma probably did not notice his silent eagerness nor his timidity. She never suspected that love, which had disappeared from her life, was pulsating there, near her, beneath that shirt of coarse linen, in that adolescent heart so open to the emanations of her beauty. Moreover, she now enveloped everything in such indifference, her words were so affectionate and her glances so haughty, her behavior so changeable, that one could no longer distinguish selfishness from charity, nor corruption from virtue. One evening, for instance, she lost her temper with the maid, who, when asking permission to go out, stammered as she tried to think of an excuse; then, all of a sudden:

"So you love him?" Emma said.

And without waiting for an answer from Félicité, who was blushing, she added sadly:

"Well, go on, then, run to him! Enjoy yourself!"

In early spring, she had the garden completely redone, from one end to the other, despite Bovary's comments; he was happy, however, to see her showing any sort of spirit at last. She gave more and more evidence of this as her health returned. First, she found a way to get rid of Mère Rolet, the nurse, who had fallen into the habit, during Emma's convalescence, of coming to the kitchen all too often with her two nurslings and her boarder, whose appetite was more robust than a cannibal's. Then she distanced herself from the Homais family, dismissed all the other visitors one by one, and even attended church with less diligence, eliciting the hearty approval of the apothecary, who said to her amiably:

"You were beginning to look a bit like a priest yourself!"

Monsieur Bournisien would drop by every day, as he had done before, upon leaving catechism class. He preferred to remain outdoors, taking the air *deep in the grove,* as he called the arbor. This was the time of day when Charles came home. They were hot; sweet cider would be brought out; and together they would drink to Madame's full recovery.

Binet was there, too, down below them, that is, against the terrace wall, fishing for crayfish. Bovary would invite him to have a drink, and he was a perfect expert at uncorking the cider jugs.

"First," he would say, gazing with satisfaction all around him and out to the far edge of the countryside, "you must hold the bottle upright on the table, like this, and then, after cutting the strings, you push the cork up a little at a time, gently, gently, the way they open Seltzer water in restaurants."

But the cider, during his demonstration, would often spurt out in their faces, and then the clergyman, with his throaty laugh, never failed to offer this pleasantry:

"Its excellence certainly leaps to the eye!"

He was a decent sort, really, and was not even scandalized one day when the pharmacist advised Charles to take Madame, as a distraction, to the theater in Rouen to see the famous tenor Lagardy. Homais, surprised at his silence, asked his opinion, and the priest declared that he considered music less dangerous to morality than literature.

But the pharmacist took up the defense of letters. The theater, he claimed, served to attack prejudice and, in the guise of pleasure, inculcate virtue.

"*Castigat ridendo mores,* Monsieur Bournisien! For instance, look at most of Voltaire's tragedies; they're cleverly scattered with philosophical reflections that constitute a veritable school of morality and diplomacy for the common people."

"Well," said Binet, "I once saw a play called *The Urchin of Paris* that has one outstanding character in it, an old general, who's really first-rate! He lays into the son of a wealthy family who's seduced a seamstress, and at the end she . . ."

"Of course," continued Homais, "there's bad literature just as there's bad pharmacy! But to make a blanket condemnation of the most important of the fine arts seems to me a piece of stupidity, a barbarity worthy of that abominable age when they locked up Galileo."

"I'm quite aware," objected the Curé, "that good works exist, and good authors; nevertheless, wouldn't it be the case that people of different sexes coming together in an enchanting hall decorated with worldly pomp, and then the heathenish disguises, the makeup, the footlights, the effeminate voices—all of this must in the end encourage a certain licentiousness of spirit and put unseemly thoughts and impure temptations into one's head? Such, at least, is the opinion of all the Fathers. Well," he added, suddenly assuming an exalted tone and rolling a pinch of snuff on his thumb, "if the Church condemned spectacles, it must have been right to do so; we must submit to her decrees."

"Why," asked the apothecary, "does the Church excommunicate actors? After all, in the old days they participated openly in the ecclesiastical ceremonies. Yes, they performed, they put on, right in the middle of the choir, a species of farce called a mystery, which often offended the laws of decency."

The clergyman merely groaned in answer, and the pharmacist went on:

"It's the same in the Bible; there are . . . you know . . . some rather spicy . . . details, things . . . that are really . . . daring!"

And, when Monsieur Bournisien made a gesture of annoyance:

"Ah! You would agree that it is not a book to put in the hands of a young person, and I would be cross if Athalie . . ."

"But it's the Protestants," the other cried out impatiently, "and not we, who recommend the Bible!"

"Doesn't matter!" said Homais. "I'm surprised that these days, in these enlightened times, anyone should still persist in prohibiting a form of intellectual entertainment that is harmless, morally uplifting, and even, sometimes, healthful—isn't that so, Doctor?"

"Quite possibly," answered the doctor noncommittally, either because, having the same opinion, he did not want to give offense, or because he had no opinion.

The conversation seemed to be over, when the pharmacist saw fit to make one last thrust.

"I've known a few priests who would dress in ordinary clothes and go see dancing girls fling their legs in the air."

"Come now!" the curé said.

"Yes! I've known a few!"

And separating the syllables, Homais said again:

"I've—known—a—few."

"Well, now! They were wrong," said Bournisien, resigned to hearing it all.

"Lord! There's plenty more they do!" exclaimed the apothecary.

"Monsieur! . . ." the clergyman retorted with a look so ferocious that the pharmacist was intimidated.

"I only mean to say," he then replied in a milder tone, "that tolerance is the surest way of attracting souls to religion."

"That's true! That's true!" conceded the good fellow, sitting back down in his chair.

But he remained there for only a couple of minutes longer. Then, as soon as he had gone, Monsieur Homais addressed the doctor:

"Now, that's what they call a stinger! I licked him, you saw it—how I licked him! . . . Now, really, do take Madame to the theater, even if only to get a rise out one of those blackcoats for once in your life, for heaven's sake. If I could find someone to replace me, I'd go with you myself. And don't delay! Lagardy's giving only one performance; he's booked in England for a considerable sum of money. Oh, they say he's a case! He's rolling in money! He takes three mistresses along with him, as well as his chef! All these great artists burn the candle at both ends; they need a dissolute sort of life to give a little spark to their imagination. But they die in the poorhouse, because they hadn't the sense, when they were young, to save some of their money. Well, bon appétit; see you tomorrow!"

This idea of the theater quickly germinated in Bovary's mind; for he at once communicated it to his wife, who at first refused, pleading the fatigue, the bother, the expense; but exceptionally, Charles did not give in, so convinced was he that this diversion would do her good. He saw nothing standing in the way of it; his mother had sent them three hundred francs that he had given up hope of getting, their current debts were not enormous, and the due date of the notes to be paid to Sieur Lheureux was still so far off that he did not have to think about them. Besides, imagining that she was merely being tactful about this, he continued to insist; so that in the end, because of his importunity, she decided to do it. And the next day, at eight o'clock in the morning, they bundled themselves into the *Hirondelle*.

The apothecary, who had nothing keeping him in Yonville, but who thought himself duty bound never to stir from it, sighed as he watched them leave.

"Well, have a good trip!" he said to them. "Happy mortals that you are!"

Then, addressing Emma, who was wearing a blue silk dress with four flounces:

"You're as pretty as a picture! You'll *shine* in Rouen."

The coach set them down at the Hôtel de la Croix Rouge, on the place Beauvoisine. It was one of those inns such as exist on the outskirts of every provincial city, with large stables and small bedrooms, where you see hens in the middle of the stable yard pecking at oats under the mud-spattered gigs of traveling salesmen—good old hostelries with worm-eaten wooden balconies that creak in the wind on winter nights, which are always full of people, noise, and food, their dark tables sticky from *glorias*, their thick windowpanes yellowed by flies, their damp napkins spotted blue with wine, and which, smelling always of the village, like farmhands dressed in town clothing, have a café on the street, and, on the side facing the fields, a vegetable garden. Charles immediately went off on his errand. He confused the stage boxes with the balconies, the parterre with the loges, asked for explanations, failed to understand them, was sent off by the box office to the manager, went back to the inn, returned to the box office, and in this way walked the entire length of the city several times over, from the theater to the boulevard.

Madame bought herself a hat, some gloves, a bouquet. Monsieur was very afraid of missing the beginning; and without having had time enough even to swallow a bowl of soup, they arrived at the theater, whose doors were still closed.

[15]

The crowd was standing against the wall, penned symmetrically between the railings. At the corners of the neighboring streets, gigantic posters repeated in baroque letters: "*Lucie de Lammermoor* . . . Lagardy . . . Opéra . . . etc." It was a fine evening; everyone was hot; sweat trickled through ringlets of hair, and handkerchiefs were being taken out of pockets to mop rosy foreheads; and now and then a warm breeze, blowing from the river, would gently stir the edges of the canvas awnings that hung over the tavern doors. A little farther down the street, however, people were cooled by a current of glacial air that smelled of tallow, leather, and oil. It emanated from the rue des Charrettes, with its large dark warehouses and rolling casks.

For fear of seeming ridiculous, Emma wanted to take a stroll down to the port before going in, and Bovary prudently kept the tickets in his hand, inside his pants pocket, which he pressed against his abdomen.

Her heart began to pound even in the lobby. She smiled involuntarily with satisfaction as she saw the crowd hurry off to the right down the other corridor while she climbed the staircase to the *first-tier boxes*. Like a child, she took pleasure in pushing the broad padded doors with her finger; she inhaled deeply, with her whole chest, the dusty smell of the corridors, and when she was seated in her box, she straightened her back with the casual grace of a duchess.

The hall was beginning to fill, people were taking opera glasses out of their cases, and the holders of season tickets, catching sight of one another from a distance, were exchanging bows. They had come here seeking relaxation in the fine arts from the anxieties of commerce; but not actually forgetting *business,* they were still talking cotton, proof spirits, or indigo. The heads of old men, expressionless and calm, with grayish white hair and skin, resembled silver medals tarnished by lead vapor. The young dandies were strutting about the parterre, displaying, in the opening of their vests, their pink or apple-green cravats; and Madame Bovary was admiring them from above as they rested the taut palms of their yellow gloves on the gold knobs of their canes.

Meanwhile, the orchestra's candles were lit; the chandelier came down from the ceiling, the radiance of its faceted crystal pouring a sudden gaiety out into the hall; then the musicians entered one after another, and there was first a prolonged din of double basses rumbling, violins squeaking, cornets trumpeting, flutes and flageolets piping. But three knocks were heard from the stage; the kettledrums began to roll, the brasses sounded a few chords, and the curtain rose on a country scene.

It was a crossroads in a forest, on the left a spring shaded by an oak. Countryfolk and lords, their plaids on their shoulders, were singing a hunting song together; then a captain entered and invoked the spirit of evil, raising his arms to heaven; another appeared; they went away, and the hunters resumed their song.

She was back in the books she had read in her youth—deep in Sir Walter Scott. She imagined she could hear, through the mist, the sound of Scottish bagpipes echoing over the heather. Her recollection of the novel also made it easier for her to understand the libretto; she could follow the plot phrase by phrase, while the elusive thoughts that kept returning to her were dissipated immediately by the gusts of music. She gave herself up to the lulling melodies and felt her whole being vibrate as if the bows of the violins were running over her very nerves. She did not have eyes enough to take in the costumes, the sets, the characters, the painted trees that quivered at every footstep, and the velvet caps, the cloaks, the swords, all these fantasies rustling within the music as though in the atmosphere of another world. But now a young woman came forward, tossing a purse to a squire in green. She remained there alone, and then came the sound of a flute like the murmuring of a spring or the warbling of a bird. Gravely Lucie entered upon her cavatina in G major; she lamented her love, she asked for wings. Emma, too, would have liked to escape from life and fly off in an embrace. Suddenly, Edgar Lagardy appeared.

He had the splendid sort of pallor that imparts something of the majesty of marble to the ardent races of the South. His muscular torso was tightly encased in a brown doublet; a small engraved dirk swung against his left thigh; and he rolled his eyes languorously about him while displaying his white teeth. People said that a Polish princess, hearing him sing one evening on the beach at Biarritz, where he was repairing longboats, had fallen in love with him. She had ruined herself for him. He had abandoned her for other women, and inevitably his fame as a lover had merely enhanced his reputation as an artist. Shrewd ham actor that he was, he even took care always to slip into the notices a poetic phrase about the charm of his personality and the sensitivity of his soul. A beautiful voice, imperturbable poise, more temperament than intelligence, and more bombast than lyricism combined to enhance that admirable charlatan nature, in which there was a touch of both the hairdresser and the toreador.

From the very first scene, he enthralled them. He clasped Lucie in his arms, he left her, he came back, he seemed in despair: he had outbursts of anger, then moments of infinitely sweet elegiac huskiness, and the notes that slipped from his bare throat mingled with sobs and kisses. Emma leaned forward to watch him, scratching the velvet of her box with her fingernails. She absorbed into her heart the melodious laments that drifted along to the accompaniment of the double basses like the cries of the shipwrecked in the tumult of a storm. She recognized all the intoxicating delights, all the agonies, that had nearly killed her. Lucie's voice seemed the echo of Emma's own consciousness, and the illusion that so charmed her, something from her own life. But no one on earth had loved her with such a love. *He* had not wept, as Edgar was weeping, on that last evening, in the moonlight, when they had said to each other: "Tomorrow; tomorrow! . . ." The hall shook with shouts of "Bravo"; they began the entire stretto again; the lovers sang about the flowers on their graves, about their vows, their exile, their destiny, their hopes; and when they uttered their final farewell, Emma gave a sharp cry that merged with the vibrations of the closing chords.

"Now, why," asked Bovary, "is that lord persecuting her so?"

"But he isn't!" she answered; "he's her lover."

"But he swears he'll take his revenge on her family, whereas the other one, the one who came on a little while ago, said: 'I love Lucie and I believe she loves me.' Besides, he walked off arm in arm with her father. Because that was her father, wasn't it, the ugly little man with a cock's feather in his hat?"

Despite Emma's explanations, beginning with the recitative duet in which Gilbert describes his abominable machinations to his master Ashton, Charles, seeing the false engagement ring that was to deceive Lucie, believed it was a love token sent by Edgar. He confessed, what was more, that he could not follow the story, because of the music—which interfered greatly with the words.

"What does it matter?" said Emma; "be quiet!"

"It's just that, as you know," he went on, leaning over her shoulder, "I do like to understand."

"Be quiet! Be quiet!" she said impatiently.

Lucie was coming forward, half borne up by her women, a wreath of orange blossoms in her hair, and paler than the white satin of her dress. Emma was dreaming of her own wedding day; and she saw herself back there again, surrounded by wheat fields, on the little path, when they were walking toward the church. Why hadn't she, like this woman, resisted, pleaded? On the contrary, she had been full of joy, unaware of the abyss into which she was rushing . . . Ah! if only, in the freshness of her beauty, before the defilement of marriage and the disillusionment of adultery, she could have set down her life upon some great, solid heart, then virtue, tenderness, desire, and duty would all have joined together, and she would never have descended from such lofty felicity. But that happiness, no doubt, was a lie imagined in despair of all desire. She knew, now, how paltry were the passions exaggerated by art. So, endeavoring to turn her thoughts away from this, Emma now determined to regard this replication of her sufferings as nothing more than a vivid fantasy for the entertainment of the eye, and she was even smiling to herself in disdainful pity, when at the back of the stage, from behind the velvet curtains, appeared a man in a black cloak.

A single gesture sent his broad-brimmed Spanish hat to the floor; immediately the instruments and the singers began the sextet. Edgar, glittering with fury, dominated all the others with his brighter voice. Ashton in deep tones hurled his murderous provocations at him, Lucie uttered her sharp lament, Arthur, standing apart, sang in a modulating middle register, and the minister's bass-baritone boomed like an organ, while the voices of the women, repeating his words, started up again in a delicious chorus. They stood in a single line, gesticulating; and anger, vengeance, jealousy, terror, pity, and stupefaction issued simultaneously from their half-open mouths. The outraged lover was brandishing his naked sword; his lace collar jerked up with each movement of his chest, and he strode to the right and to the left in his soft flared boots, clanking his silver-gilt spurs on the boards. His love, she was thinking, must be inexhaustible, for him to pour it out on the crowd in such large floods. All her impulses to denigrate vanished as she was invaded by the poetry of the role, and, drawn to the man by the illusion of the character, she tried to picture his life to herself, that vibrant, extraordinary, splendid life, which she, too, could nevertheless have led if chance had so willed it. They would have met, they would have fallen in love! With him, she would have traveled through all the kingdoms of Europe, from capital to capital, sharing his troubles and his triumphs, gathering the flowers people threw to him, embroidering his costumes herself; then each evening, sitting far back in her box, behind the gilt lattice, she would absorb with all her being the effusions of that soul that sang for her alone; from the stage, even while he was acting, he would be looking at her. But a kind of madness came over her: he was looking at her now, she was sure of it! She wanted to run into his arms, take refuge in his strength, as in the incarnation of love itself, and say to him, cry out to him: "Lift me up, take me away, let us go away! All my passion and all my dreams are yours, yours alone!"

The curtain came down.

The smell of gas mingled with people's breath; the breeze from the waving fans made the atmosphere even more stifling. Emma tried to go out, but the crowd was blocking the corridors, and she fell back into her seat with palpitations that made it hard for her to breathe. Charles, afraid of seeing her faint, hurried to the refreshment bar to get her a glass of barley water.

He had great difficulty returning to his seat, for people were bumping his elbows at every step because of the glass he was holding in his hands, and in fact he spilled three-quarters of it over the shoulders of a Rouen woman in short sleeves, who, feeling the cold liquid run down her back, began to screech like a peacock, as though she were being murdered. Her husband, the owner of a spinning mill, flew into a rage against the clumsy fellow; and while with her handkerchief she was mopping the spots on her beautiful cherry-red taffeta dress, he kept muttering in surly tones the words "compensation," "cost," "reimbursement." At last Charles reached his wife, saying breathlessly:

"Heavens, I thought I'd never get back! There's such a crowd! . . . Such a crowd! . . ."

He added:

"Now, guess who I ran into up there. Monsieur Léon!"

"Léon?"

"Himself! He'll be coming along to pay you his respects."

And as he finished speaking, the former clerk from Yonville entered the box.

He held out his hand with a gentlemanly informality; and Madame Bovary, without thinking, offered her own, no doubt yielding to the attraction of a stronger will. She had not felt it since that spring evening when the rain was falling on the green leaves as they said goodbye to each other, standing beside the window. But quickly recalling herself to the proprieties of the situation, with an effort she shook off the indolence of her memories and began to stammer a few hurried phrases.

"Why, good evening! . . . What a surprise! . . ."

"Quiet!" cried a voice from the parterre, for the third act was beginning.

"So you're here in Rouen now?"

"Yes."

"Since when?"

"Shh! Go outside! Out!"

People were turning toward them; they fell silent.

But from that moment on, she no longer listened; and the chorus of guests, the scene between Ashton and his servant, the great duet in D major—for her, it all took place at a distance, as if the instruments had become less resonant and the characters more remote; she was remembering the card party at the pharmacist's house, and the walk to the wet nurse's, the reading in the arbor, the intimate conversations by the fireside, the whole course of that modest love, so tranquil and so prolonged, so discreet, so tender, which she had nevertheless forgotten. Now why had he come back? What combination of events was bringing him back into her life? He was standing behind her, leaning his shoulder against the partition wall; and from time to time, she felt herself shiver under the warm breath from his nostrils that stirred her hair.

"Are you enjoying this?" he asked, bending over so close to her that the tip of his mustache brushed her cheek.

She answered nonchalantly:

"Oh, my Lord, no! Not particularly."

Then he suggested that they leave the theater and go somewhere for an ice.

"Oh, not yet! Let's stay!" said Bovary. "She's let her hair down: something tragic's probably about to happen."

But the mad scene was not at all interesting to Emma, and the heroine's acting seemed to her exaggerated.

"She's shrieking too loudly," she said, turning to Charles, who was listening.

"Yes . . . perhaps . . . a little," he replied, torn between his frank enjoyment and the respect he had for his wife's opinions.

Then Léon said, sighing:

"It's so warm. It's quite . . ."

"Unbearable! Yes."

"Are you uncomfortable?" asked Bovary.

"Yes, I'm stifling; let's go."

Monsieur Léon carefully laid her long lace shawl over her shoulders, and the three of them went down to the port, where they sat in the open air in front of the windows of a café.

First they talked about her illness, although Emma interrupted Charles from time to time, afraid, she said, that Monsieur Léon might be bored; and Léon told them he had come to Rouen to spend two years in a busy practice, so as to accustom himself to the business, which was different in Normandy from the sort he had handled in Paris. Then he asked after Berthe, the Homais family, Mère Lefrançois; and since, in the presence of the husband, they had no more to say to each other, the conversation soon died.

People coming from the theater passed by on the sidewalk, humming or bawling at the top of their lungs: *O bel ange, ma Lucie!* Then Léon, to show off his passion for the arts, began to talk music. He had seen Tamburini, Rubini, Persiani, Grisi; and compared to them, Lagardy, for all his grand outbursts, was nothing.

"And yet," interrupted Charles, who was taking little bites of his rum sorbet, "they say that in the last act he's really wonderful; I'm sorry we left before the end, because I was beginning to enjoy it."

"Oh, well," the clerk went on, "he'll be giving another performance soon enough."

But Charles answered that they were leaving the next day.

"Unless," he added, turning to his wife, "you'd like to stay on alone, my pet?"

And, changing tactics in the face of this unexpected opportunity to see his hopes answered, the young man began praising Lagardy in the last song. It was something superb, sublime! At that, Charles insisted:

"You'd go back on Sunday. Come now, make up your mind to do it! You'd be wrong not to, if you have the least suspicion that it would do you good."

Meanwhile, the tables around them were emptying; a waiter came and discreetly stationed himself near them; Charles understood and drew out his purse; the clerk held him back by the arm and even remembered to leave another two silver coins, which he clinked down on the marble.

"Really," murmured Bovary, "I don't like you to spend your money . . ."

The other made a dismissive gesture full of cordiality, and, taking up his hat:

"It's settled, then? Tomorrow, at six o'clock?"

Charles exclaimed again that he could not be away any longer; but nothing prevented Emma . . .

"It's just that . . . ," she stammered with an odd smile, "I'm not really sure . . ."

"Well! We'll see, you'll think it over, you'll know better in the morning . . ."

Then to Léon, who was walking along with them:

"Now that you're in our neighborhood again, I hope you'll come by, from time to time, and stay for dinner?"

The clerk declared that he certainly would, since he needed to go to Yonville anyway on a matter concerning his firm. And they parted by the passage Saint-Herbland, just as eleven-thirty was striking at the cathedral.

PART III

[1]

Monsieur Léon, while pursuing his legal studies, had quite often frequented La Chaumière, where in fact he enjoyed quite nice successes among the grisettes, who found him *distinguished*. He was the most seemly of students: he wore his hair neither too long nor too short, did not squander all of his quarter's allowance on the first of the month, and kept on good terms with his professors. As for excesses, he had always refrained from committing them, as much from timidity as from fastidiousness.

Often, when he remained in his room reading, or sat in the evening under the lime trees of the Luxembourg, he would let his Code fall to the ground, and the memory of Emma would come back to him. But little by little, his feeling weakened, and other desires accumulated on top of it, though it still persisted through them; for Léon had not lost all hope, and for him a sort of uncertain promise hovered in the future, like a golden fruit hanging from some fantastic leafy bough.

Then, when he saw her again after an absence of three years, his passion reawakened. He must at last resolve, he thought, to attempt to possess her. What was more, his shyness had worn away from contact with wild companions, and he returned to the provinces scornful of all who had not stepped with a patent-leather foot on the asphalt of the boulevards. Before a Parisienne in lace, in the salon of some illustrious physician, a person of importance with medals and a carriage, the poor clerk, no doubt, would have trembled like a child; but here in Rouen, by the quay, with the wife of this small country practitioner, he felt at ease, certain in advance that he would dazzle her. Self-confidence depends upon surroundings: one does not speak the same way in a grand apartment as in a garret, and a rich woman seems to have all her banknotes about her, guarding her virtue, like a cuirass, in the lining of her corset.

Upon taking leave of Monsieur and Madame Bovary the night before, Léon had followed them, at a distance, down the street; then, having seen them stop at the Croix Rouge, he had turned back and spent the whole night devising a plan.

The next day at about five o'clock, therefore, he entered the kitchen of the inn, his throat tight, his cheeks pale, with the resolve of the timid man who will be stopped by nothing.

"Monsieur is not here," answered a servant.

This seemed to him a good omen. He went up.

She was not disturbed that he had come; on the contrary, she apologized for having forgotten to tell him where they were staying.

"Oh! I guessed," Léon said.

"How?"

He claimed that a kind of instinct had guided him to her, by chance. She began to smile, and immediately, in order to rectify his blunder, Léon told her he had spent his morning looking for her in every hotel in the city, one after another.

"So you decided to stay?" he added.

"Yes," she said, "and I was wrong. One shouldn't accustom oneself to impractical pleasures when one is surrounded by so many demands . . ."

"Oh! I can imagine . . ."

"Oh, no, you can't! Because you're not a woman."

But men had their troubles, too, and the conversation began with some philosophical reflections. Emma went on at length about the wretchedness of earthly affections and the eternal isolation in which the heart remains entombed.

To show himself to good advantage, or quite naturally imitating her melancholy, which was inspiring his own, the young man declared that he had been prodigiously bored throughout his studies. Legal procedure irritated him, other vocations attracted him, and his mother, in her letters, never stopped tormenting him. For they were becoming more and more specific about the causes of their unhappiness, both, as they spoke, growing more ardent as this progressive unburdening continued. But they would sometimes stop before the complete disclosure of a thought and would then try to imagine a phrase that could express it anyway. She did not confess her passion for another man; he did not say that he had forgotten her.

Perhaps he no longer remembered those suppers following the costume balls, with girls dressed as stevedores; and she probably did not recall the meetings of earlier days, when she would run through the grass in the morning to her lover's château. The sounds of the city barely reached them; and the room seemed small, as if designed to draw their solitude in more closely around them. Emma, in a dimity dressing gown, leaned her chignon against the back of the old armchair; the yellow wallpaper made a sort of golden ground behind her; and her bare head was repeated in the mirror, with its white parting in the middle and the lobes of her ears showing below the bands of her hair.

"Oh, forgive me," she said. "This is wrong of me! I'm boring you with my eternal complaints!"

"No, never! Never!"

"If only you knew," she went on, raising her lovely, tear-filled eyes to the ceiling, "all that I had dreamed of."

"I, too! Oh, how I suffered! Often, I would go out, I would walk, I would wander along the quays, dizzying myself with the noise of the crowd, without being able to drive away the obsession that was hounding me. In a print shop on the boulevard, there's an Italian engraving showing one of the Muses. She's draped in a tunic and looking at the moon, with her hair down and forget-me-nots in it. Something kept compelling me to go there; I would stay for hours at a time."

Then, his voice trembling:

"She looked a little like you."

Madame Bovary turned her head away so that he would not see the irresistible smile she felt appearing on her lips.

"Often," he went on, "I would write letters to you and then tear them up."

She did not answer. He went on:

"I would fancy that some chance event might bring you to me. I thought I recognized you on street corners; and I would run after a cab if I saw a shawl, a veil like yours, floating at the window . . ."

She seemed determined to let him talk without interrupting him. Crossing her arms and bowing her head, she was contemplating the bows on her slippers and making little movements in the satin, now and then, with her toes.

At last, she sighed:

"The most pitiful thing, don't you think, is to drag out one's life uselessly, the way I do. If only our suffering could benefit someone, we could find consolation in the thought of sacrifice!"

He began to extol virtue, duty, and silent renunciation, he himself having an incredible need for selfless dedication that he could not satisfy.

"I would very much like," she said, "to belong to an order of nursing sisters."

"Alas!" he replied, "men have no such sacred missions, and I see no calling . . . except perhaps that of doctor . . ."

With a slight shrug, Emma interrupted him to lament the illness during which she had nearly died; what a shame!—she would no longer be suffering now. Léon immediately envied *the tranquillity of the grave,* and one night he had even written out his will, requesting that he be buried in that beautiful coverlet, with its bands of velvet, that she had given him; for this was the way they would have liked to be—they were both creating for themselves an ideal against which they were now adjusting their past lives. Besides, speech is a rolling press that always extends one's emotions.

But at this invention concerning the coverlet:

"Why?" she asked.

"Why?"

He hesitated.

"Because I loved you so much!"

And, applauding himself for having gotten past the difficulty, Léon watched her expression out of the corner of his eye.

It was like the sky, when a gust of wind drives away the clouds. The accumulation of sad thoughts that had darkened her blue eyes seemed to withdraw from them; her entire face was radiant.

He was waiting. At last she answered:

"I always thought so . . ."

Then they told each other about the little happenings of that far-off life, whose delights and sorrows they had just evoked in a single word. He recalled the arbor of clematis, the dresses she had worn, the furniture in her room, her entire house.

"And our poor cactuses, where are they?"

"The cold killed them this winter."

"Ah! You know, I often thought of them. I would see them again as I used to, when the sun would strike the shutters on summer mornings . . . and I would see your two bare arms moving about among the flowers."

"My poor friend!" she blurted, holding her hand out to him.

Léon quickly pressed his lips to it. Then, when he had taken a deep breath:

"For me, in those days, you were a kind of incomprehensible force that held my life captive. There was one time, for example, when I came to your house; but you probably don't remember this?"

"Yes, I do," she said. "Go on."

"You were downstairs, in the hall, about to go out, standing on the bottom step; —you were even wearing a hat with little blue flowers on it; and though you hadn't invited me, I went with you in spite of myself. Yet every minute I was more and more aware of how foolish I'd been, and I went on walking near you, not quite daring to follow you, and not wanting to leave you. When you entered a shop, I'd stay out in the street; I'd watch you through the window as you undid your gloves and counted out the change on the counter. Then you rang at Madame Tuvache's, they opened the door, and I stayed there like an idiot in front of that great, heavy door after it fell shut behind you."

As she listened, Madame Bovary marveled at how old she was; all these things as they reappeared seemed to extend her life; it was as though immense expanses of feeling were opened up, upon which she could look back; and from time to time, she would say softly, her eyes half closed:

"Yes, it's true! . . . It's true! . . . . It's true . . ."

They heard eight o'clock strike from the different clocks in the Beauvoisine district, which is full of boarding schools, churches, and large mansions now abandoned. They were no longer talking; but as they stared at each other, they felt a murmuring in their heads, as if something audible were escaping from one to the other through their steady gazes. They had just taken each other by the hand; and the past, the future, their reminiscences, and their dreams were all now merged in the sweetness of their ecstasy. The darkness was growing denser along the walls; still gleaming, half lost in shadow, were the garish colors of four prints representing four scenes from *The Tower of Nesle,* with legends below in Spanish and French. Through the sash window, one could see a patch of dark sky between peaked roofs.

She stood up to light two candles on the dresser, then came and sat down again.

"Well . . . ," Léon said.

"Well?" she answered.

And he was trying to think how to resume the interrupted conversation, when she said:

"Why is it that no one, before now, has ever expressed such feelings to me?"

The clerk exclaimed that idealistic natures were difficult to understand. He had loved her the moment he first saw her; and he was filled with despair when he thought what happiness might have been theirs if, by good fortune, meeting earlier, they had been joined together by an indissoluble bond.

"I've sometimes thought about that," she answered.

"What a dream!" murmured Léon.

And, delicately fingering the blue border of her long white belt, he added:

"What's to prevent us from beginning again now? . . ."

"No, my dear," she answered. "I'm too old . . . you're too young . . . forget me! Others will love you . . . and you'll love them."

"Not as I love you!" he cried.

"You child! Come now, let's be sensible! That's what I want!"

She pointed out to him all the reasons their love was impossible, and why they would have to remain, as they used to be, merely friends, like brother and sister.

Did she mean it when she said this? Probably Emma herself did not know, completely occupied as she was by the charm of the seduction and the need to resist it; and, contemplating the young man with a fond gaze, she gently pushed away the timid caresses his trembling hands were attempting.

"Oh, forgive me," he said, drawing back.

And Emma was seized by a vague alarm in the face of this timidity, which was more dangerous to her than Rodolphe's boldness when he came up to her with open arms. Never had any man seemed to her so handsome. His whole bearing radiated an exquisite candor. He had lowered his long, fine, curving eyelashes. The smooth skin of his cheek was flushed, with desire—she thought—for her, and Emma felt an irresistible longing to put her lips to it. Then, leaning toward the clock as though to see the time:

"Heavens, how late it is!" she said; "how we've talked!"

He understood the hint and picked up his hat.

"I even forgot the opera! Poor Bovary—and he left me here just for that! Monsieur Lormeaux, in the rue Grand-Pont, was supposed to take me with his wife."

And the opportunity was lost, for she was leaving the next day.

"Really?" said Léon.

"Yes."

"But I must see you again," he went on; "I wanted to tell you . . ."

"What?"

"Something . . . important, something serious. Oh, no! You mustn't go, you can't! If you knew . . . Listen . . . Didn't you understand what I was saying? Couldn't you guess? . . ."

"And yet you express yourself very clearly," said Emma.

"Ah! Now you're joking with me! Please don't! Take pity on me, let me see you again . . . once . . . just once."

"Well . . ."

She stopped; then, as though thinking better of it:

"Oh, not here!"

"Wherever you like."

"Do you want to . . ."

She seemed to think it over; then, tersely:

"Tomorrow, at eleven o'clock, in the cathedral."

"I'll be there!" he exclaimed, seizing her hands, which she disengaged.

And as they were now both standing, he behind her and Emma bowing her head, he leaned over and gave her a long kiss on the nape of her neck.

"You're crazy! Ah!—you're quite crazy!" she said with little peals of laughter as he kissed her again and again.

Then, leaning his face forward over her shoulder, he seemed to be searching her eyes for her consent. They looked at him full of an icy majesty.

Léon took a few steps back, preparing to leave. He stopped on the doorsill. Then he whispered in a tremulous voice:

"Till tomorrow."

She answered with a nod and vanished like a bird into the next room.

Emma, that evening, wrote the clerk an endless letter canceling their appointment: it was all over now, and for the sake of their own happiness, they must never meet again. But when the letter was finished, since she did not have Léon's address, she found herself quite perplexed.

"I'll give it to him myself," she said; "he's sure to come."

The next day, Léon, his window open, singing softly on his balcony, polished his dress shoes himself with several layers of polish. He drew on a pair of white pants, some thin socks, a green coat, poured into his handkerchief everything he owned in the way of scent, then, having had his hair curled, took the curl out of it again, so as to give his hair a more natural elegance.

"It's still too early!" he thought, looking at the barber's cuckoo clock, which pointed to nine.

He read an old fashion magazine, went out, smoked a cigar, walked up three streets, imagined it was time, and headed briskly toward the parvis of Notre-Dame.

It was a beautiful summer morning. Silver gleamed in the windows of the gold- and silversmiths, and the light that fell obliquely on the cathedral shimmered in the cracks of the gray stones; a flock of birds circled in the blue sky around the trefoiled pinnacle turrets; the square, echoing with cries, smelled of the flowers that bordered its pavement—roses, jasmine, carnations, narcissus, and tuberoses unevenly interspersed with damp greenery, catnip, and chickweed; the fountain, in the middle, was gurgling; and under broad umbrellas, among pyramids of cantaloupes, bareheaded flower-women were twisting bunches of violets in paper.

The young man took one. It was the first time he had bought flowers for a woman; and as he inhaled their fragrance, his chest swelled with pride, as though this homage, which he intended for someone else, had been redirected toward him.

Yet he was afraid of being seen; he went resolutely into the church.

The verger, just then, was standing on the threshold, in the center of the left-hand portal, under the *Marianne Dancing,* a plume on his head, a rapier by his calf, a staff in his fist, more majestic than a cardinal and gleaming like a sacred ciborium.

He advanced toward Léon, and with that smile of unctuous benignity assumed by ecclesiastics when questioning children:

"Monsieur is perhaps from out of town? Monsieur would like to be shown the special features of the church?"

"No," said the other.

And first he walked all the way around the side aisles. Then he came and looked out at the square. Emma was not in sight. He walked back as far as the choir.

The nave was mirrored in the brimming holy-water basins, along with the lower parts of the ogives and some portions of the stained glass. But the reflections of the images, breaking at the marble rims, continued beyond, over the flagstones, like a gaudy carpet. The broad daylight of the outdoors extended into the church in three enormous beams through the three open portals. Now and then, deep inside the church, a sacristan would pass the altar, making that oblique genuflection practiced by the devout when in a hurry. The crystal chandeliers hung motionless. In the choir, a silver lamp was burning; and from the side chapels, from the darker parts of the church, there sometimes issued a sort of effluence of sighs, along with the sound of a grille closing, sending its echo up under the lofty vaults.

Léon, with a sober step, was walking close to the walls. Never had life seemed so good to him. Any minute now she would appear, charming, agitated, glancing behind her at the eyes that were following her, —in her flounced dress, her gold lorgnette, her thin little boots, all kinds of elegant refinements he had never had a taste of before, and with all the ineffable seductiveness of virtue yielding. The church, like a gigantic boudoir, was arranging itself around her; the vaults were leaning down to gather up, in the shadows, the confession of her love; the windows shone resplendent to illuminate her face; and the censers burned so that she might appear like an angel, amid clouds of perfume.

Yet still she did not come. He took a seat, and his eyes happened upon a blue window that shows boatmen carrying baskets. He looked at it for a long time, attentively, and he counted the scales on the fish and the buttonholes on the doublets, while his thoughts wandered in search of Emma.

The verger, standing to one side, was raging inwardly at this person who permitted himself to admire the cathedral on his own. He was behaving monstrously, he felt, stealing from him, in a way, and almost committing a sacrilege.

But a rustling of silk on the flagstones, the brim of a hat, a black hooded cloak . . . It was she! Léon stood up and hurried to meet her.

Emma was pale. She was walking quickly.

"Read this!" she said, handing him a piece of paper . . . "No, no!"

And abruptly she drew back her hand and went into the Lady Chapel, where, kneeling against a chair, she began to pray.

The young man was irritated by this overly pious whim; but then he found a certain charm in seeing her thus, in the middle of an assignation, lost in prayer like some Andalusian marquise; then he quickly grew bored, for she was going on and on.

Emma was praying, or rather endeavoring to pray, in the hope that some sudden resolution would descend upon her from heaven; and in order to attract divine assistance, she was filling her eyes with the splendors of the tabernacle, breathing in the fragrance of the white stock in full bloom in their tall vases, and listening to the silence of the church, which only increased the tumult in her heart.

She was standing up again, and they were about to leave, when the verger approached them smartly, saying:

"Madame is perhaps from out of town? Madame would like to be shown the special features of the church?"

"No, no!" exclaimed the clerk.

"Why not?" she said.

For with her wavering virtue she was clinging to the Virgin, to the sculptures, to the tombs, to every chance opportunity.

Then, so that they might proceed *in the right order,* the verger led them to the entrance close to the square, where, pointing with his staff to a great circle of black paving stones without inscription or engraving:

"That," he declared majestically, "is the circumference of the beautiful Amboise bell. It weighed forty thousand pounds. There was not its like in all of Europe. The workman who cast it died of joy . . ."

"Let's go," said Léon.

The fellow walked on; then, having returned to the Lady Chapel, he stretched out his arms in an all-embracing gesture of revelation, and, prouder than a country landowner showing you his espaliered trees:

"Under this simple stone lies Pierre de Brézé, Lord of the Varenne and of Brissac, Grand Marshal of Poitou, and Governor of Normandy, who died in the battle of Montlhéry, July sixteenth, 1465."

Léon, biting his lips, tapped his feet impatiently.

"And to the right, this gentleman, clad in steel, on the rearing horse, is his grandson Louis de Brézé, Lord of Breval and of Montchauvet, Count of Maulevrier, Baron of Mauny, Chamberlain to the King, Knight of the Order, and likewise Governor of Normandy, who died on July twenty-third, 1531, a Sunday, as the inscription tells us; and below him, that man about to descend into the grave shows you the very same person. It is not possible to imagine, don't you agree, a more perfect representation of the void?"

Madame Bovary raised her lorgnette. Léon, motionless, was looking at her, no longer even trying to say a single word, or make a single motion, so discouraged did he feel in the face of this twofold persistence of volubility and indifference.

Their eternal guide was continuing:

"This woman on her knees at his side and weeping is his wife, Diane de Poitiers, Countess of Brézé, Duchess of Valentinois, born in 1499, died in 1566; and to the left, the one carrying a child, the Holy Virgin. Now, turn this way: here are the tombs of the Amboises. They were both cardinals and archbishops of Rouen. That one over there was a minister to King Louis XII. He was a great benefactor to the Cathedral. They found that in his will he had left thirty thousand gold ecus to the poor."

And without pausing, still continuing to talk, he urged them into a chapel cluttered with balustrades, moved some of them aside, and revealed a sort of block, which could well have been a poorly made statue.

"At one time," he said with a deep sigh, "this used to adorn the tomb of Richard the Lionhearted, King of England and Duke of Normandy. It was the Calvinists, monsieur, who reduced it to its present condition. They buried it, for spite, in the ground under Monseigneur's episcopal throne. Look—here's the door by which Monseigneur reaches his residence. Now let us go on and see the Gargoyle windows."

But Léon quickly drew a silver coin from his pocket and seized Emma by the arm. The verger was quite stupefied, puzzled by this untimely munificence when there remained so many things for the stranger still to see. And so, calling him back:

"Eh, monsieur! The steeple! The steeple! . . ."

"Thank you, no," said Léon.

"Monsieur is making a mistake! You'll see that it's four hundred and forty feet high, nine feet less than the great pyramid of Egypt. It's made entirely of cast iron, it . . ."

Léon was fleeing; for it seemed to him that his love, which for nearly two hours now had been immobilized inside the church like the very stones, was about to evaporate, like a puff of smoke, up that sort of truncated pipe, that oblong cage, that openwork chimney, which perches so perilously and so grotesquely on top of the cathedral, like the extravagant experiment of some whimsical metalworker.

"Where are we going?" she said.

Without answering, he was walking on at a rapid pace, and Madame Bovary was already dipping her finger in the holy water, when they heard behind them the sound of heavy panting regularly punctuated by the tapping of a stick. Léon turned around.

"Monsieur!"

"What?"

And he recognized the verger, carrying under his arm and balancing against his stomach about twenty stout paperbound volumes. They were books *dealing with the cathedral.*

"Fool!" muttered Léon, dashing out of the church.

A street urchin was loitering about on the parvis:

"Go get me a cab!"

The child set off like a shot up the rue des Quatre-Vents; now they were left alone for a few minutes, face-to-face and a little embarrassed.

"Oh, Léon! . . . Really . . . I don't know . . . if I should . . . !"

She was simpering. Then, in a serious tone:

"It's quite improper, you know."

"In what way?" replied the clerk. "They do it in Paris!"

And that remark, like an irresistible argument, decided her.

Yet the cab was nowhere in sight. Léon was afraid she would go back inside the church. At last the cab appeared.

"Go out by the north door, at least!" cried the verger, who had remained on the threshold. "So that you can see the Resurrection, the Last Judgment, Paradise, King David, and the Souls of the Damned burning in the flames of hell!"

"Where does Monsieur wish to go?" asked the coachman.

"Wherever you like!" said Léon, thrusting Emma into the carriage.

And the heavy vehicle started off.

It went down the rue Grand-Pont, crossed the place des Arts, the quai Napoléon, and the Pont Neuf, and stopped short in front of the statue of Pierre Corneille.

"Keep going!" said a voice issuing from the interior.

The carriage set off again and, gathering speed on the downward slope from the carrefour La Fayette, came up to the railway station at a fast gallop.

"No! Straight on!" cried the same voice.

The cab went out through the gates and soon, having reached the promenade, trotted quietly between the lines of tall elms. The coachman wiped his forehead, put his leather hat between his legs, and urged the carriage on beyond the side avenues to the water's edge, by the grass.

It went along the river, on the towpath with its surface of dry pebbles, and, for a long time, toward Oyssel, beyond the islands.

But all of a sudden, it dashed in one leap across Quatremares, Sotteville, the Grande-Chaussée, the rue d'Elbeuf, and made its third stop in front of the Jardin des Plantes.

"Keep going!" shouted the voice more furiously.

And immediately starting off again, it went past Saint-Sever, along the quai des Curandiers, along the quai aux Meules, once again over the bridge, by the place du Champ-de-Mars, and behind the gardens of the home for the elderly, where old men in black jackets walk in the sun along a terrace all green with ivy. It went back up the boulevard Bouvreuil, along the boulevard Cauchoise, then down the entire length of Mont-Riboudet as far as the Deville hill.

It turned back; and then, without any fixed plan or direction, at random, it wandered. It was seen at Saint-Pol, at Lescure, at Mont Gargan, at the Rouge-Mare, and in the place du Gaillardbois; in the rue Maladreric, the rue Dinanderie, in front of Saint-Romain, Saint-Vivien, Saint-Maclou, Saint-Nicaise—in front of the Customs House—at the Basse Vieille-Tour, at Trois-Pipes, and at the Cimetière Monumental. From his seat the coachman now and again glanced at a tavern with a despairing eye. He could not understand what mania for locomotion was compelling these individuals to refuse to stop. He would sometimes try, and he would immediately hear exclamations of rage behind him. Then he would lash his two sweating nags all the harder, but with no regard for bumps, catching a wheel on one side or the other, not caring, demoralized, and almost weeping from thirst, fatigue, and gloom.

And at the harbor, among the drays and great barrels, and in the streets, at the corners by the guard stones, the townspeople would stare wide-eyed in amazement at this thing so unheard of in the provinces, a carriage with drawn blinds that kept appearing and reappearing, sealed tighter than a tomb and tossed about like a ship at sea.

Once, at midday, out in the countryside, when the sun was beating down most fiercely against the old silver-plated lamps, a bare hand passed under the little blinds of yellow canvas and threw out some torn scraps of paper, which scattered in the wind and alighted, at a distance, like white butterflies, on a field of red clover all in bloom.

Then, toward six o'clock, the carriage stopped in a lane in the Beauvoisine district, and a woman stepped down from it and walked away, her veil lowered, without turning her head.

[2]

When she reached the inn, Madame Bovary was surprised not to see the stagecoach. Hivert, after waiting fifty-three minutes for her, had in the end driven away.

Nothing really obliged her to leave; but she had given her word that she would return that evening. Besides, Charles was waiting for her; and already she felt in her heart that craven docility that is, for many women, at once the punishment for their adultery, and the price they pay to redeem it.

Quickly she packed her bag, paid the bill, hired a gig in the courtyard, and, urging on the driver, encouraging him, asking him every minute what time it was and how many kilometers they had gone, managed to overtake the *Hirondelle* near the first houses of Quincampoix.

Scarcely seated in her corner, she closed her eyes, opening them again at the bottom of the hill, where from a distance she recognized Félicité, watching for her in front of the blacksmith's. Hivert reined in his horses, and the cook, stretching up to the carriage window, said mysteriously:

"Madame, you must go to Monsieur Homais's house right away. It's urgent."

The village was silent as usual. At the street corners, little pink mounds were steaming in the air, for it was jam time, and everyone in Yonville was confecting his own provision on the same day. But in front of the pharmacist's shop, people were admiring a much larger mound, and one that surpassed the others with the superiority that a chemist's dispensary is bound to have over ordinary stoves, a general need over individual whims.

She went in. The large armchair was overturned, and even *Le Fanal de Rouen* was on the floor, lying between the two pestles. She pushed open the hall door; and in the middle of the kitchen, among the brown jars full of loose currants, grated sugar, lump sugar, scales on the table, pans on the fire, she saw the entire Homais family, big and little, wearing aprons that rose up to their chins and holding forks in their hands. Justin was standing with bowed head, and the pharmacist was shouting:

"Who told you to go get it from the capharnaum?"

"What is it? What's the matter?"

"What's the matter?" answered the apothecary. "We're making jam; it's cooking; but it was about to overflow because it was boiling too fast, and I called for another pan. Then, because he's slothful, because he's lazy, he goes to my laboratory and takes, from the nail where it hangs—the key to the capharnaum!"

This was the apothecary's name for a small room under the eaves filled with the utensils and supplies of his profession. Often he would spend long hours there alone, labeling, decanting, repackaging; and he considered it not a mere storeroom, but a veritable sanctuary, from which would then issue, transformed by his own hands, all kinds of pills, boluses, infusions, lotions, and potions, which were destined to spread his renown through the surrounding area. Not another soul ever set foot in there; and he had such a high regard for it that he would sweep it out himself. If the pharmacy, open to all comers, was the spot where he proudly exhibited his skill, the capharnaum was the refuge where, selfishly withdrawing from the world, Homais would rapturously indulge his predilections; thus, Justin's thoughtlessness seemed to him monstrously irreverent; and, redder than the currants, he said again:

"Yes, the key to the capharnaum! The key for locking away the acids and the caustic alkalis! To go and take one of the spare pans!—a pan with a lid!—one I may never use! Each thing has its own importance in the delicate operations of our art! What the devil! One must make distinctions, one mustn't employ for quasi-domestic purposes something intended for pharmaceuticals! It's as if one were to cut up a chicken with a scalpel, as if a magistrate . . ."

"There, now, calm down, dear!" Madame Homais was saying.

And Athalie, pulling him by his frock coat:

"Papa! Papa!"

"No! Leave me alone!" the apothecary went on. "Leave me alone! Blast! I might as well go into business as a grocer, upon my word of honor! Go on! Respect nothing! Break it all! Shatter it all! Let the leeches out! Burn the mallow! Marinate pickles in the apothecary jars! Cut up the bandages!"

"But you had . . . ," said Emma.

"In a minute!— Do you know the risk you were taking? . . . Didn't you notice something in the corner, on the left, on the third shelf? Speak, answer, articulate something!"

"I don't . . . know," stammered the boy.

"Ah! You don't know! Well, I *do* know! You saw a bottle, a blue glass bottle, sealed with yellow wax, with white powder in it, on which I have in fact written: *Dangerous!* And do you know what's in it? Arsenic! —and you were going to touch that? Take a pan that's right next to it!"

"Right next to it!" exclaimed Madame Homais, joining her hands. "Arsenic? You could poison us all!"

And the children began to cry out, as though they were already feeling atrocious pains in their bowels.

"Or poison a patient!" continued the apothecary. "So you wanted me to appear on the criminals' bench, in the court of assizes? See me dragged to the gallows? Don't you know the care I take in handling everything, even though I'm so utterly practiced in it? I even frighten myself, often, when I think of my responsibility! —for the government persecutes us, and the absurd legislation that restricts us hangs like a veritable sword of Damocles over our heads!"

Emma was no longer thinking of asking what they wanted from her, and the pharmacist continued breathlessly:

"This is how you acknowledge the kindness I've shown you! This is how you repay me for the completely fatherly care I lavish on you! For without me, where would you be? What would you be doing? Who provides you with your food, your education, your clothes, all the means by which you may one day enter with honor the ranks of society! But for that you have to pull hard on the oar, you have to get calluses on your hands, as they say. *Fabricando fit faber, age quod agis.*"

He was so angry he was quoting Latin. He would have quoted Chinese or Greenlandic, had he known those languages; for he was in the throes of the sort of crisis in which one's entire soul shows indiscriminately what it contains, just as the Ocean, during a storm, gapes open from the seaweed on its shore to the sand in its abysses.

And he went on:

"I'm beginning to repent terribly having taken you into my care! I'd certainly have done better to leave you to squat in your misery, back then, in the filth you were born in! You'll never be good for anything but looking after horned animals! You have no aptitude for the sciences! You barely know how to glue on a label! And you live here, in my house, gorging yourself like a monk or a fighting cock!"

But Emma, turning toward Madame Homais:

"They told me to come . . ."

"Oh! My Lord!" interrupted the good lady with a sad look; "how can I possibly tell you? . . . It's a dreadful thing!"

She broke off. The apothecary was thundering on:

"Empty it! Scour it! Take it back! Hurry up, can't you!"

And as he shook Justin by the collar of his smock, a book fell out of the pocket.

The boy bent down. Homais was quicker, and, having picked up the volume, he studied it, his eyes wide, his jaw gaping.

"*Conjugal . . . Love!*" he said slowly, separating the two words. "Oh! Very good! Very good! Very nice! With engravings, too! . . . Ah! this is too much!"

Madame Homais stepped forward.

"No, don't touch it!"

The children wanted to see the pictures.

"Leave the room!" he said imperiously.

And they left.

At first he paced back and forth with long strides, keeping the volume open between his fingers, rolling his eyes, breathless, swollen, apoplectic. Then he walked straight over to his pupil, and, planting himself before him with his arms crossed:

"Well, so you have all the vices, do you, you little wretch? . . . Watch out, you're on a downward slope! . . . I don't suppose it has occurred to you that this sordid book of yours might fall into the hands of my children, strike a spark in their minds, tarnish Athalie's purity, corrupt

Napoléon! Physically, he's already a man. Are you quite sure, at least, that they haven't read it? Can you guarantee me . . . ?"

"Now, really, monsieur," Emma said. "Didn't you have something to tell me . . . ?"

"Yes, I did, madame . . . Your father-in-law is dead!"

Indeed, the elder Monsieur Bovary had died two days before, suddenly, from an attack of apoplexy, as he was leaving the table; and out of an excessive concern for Emma's sensibility, Charles had asked Monsieur Homais to inform her with the greatest tact of this horrible news.

The pharmacist had pondered his announcement, he had rounded it, polished it, cadenced it; it was a masterpiece of discretion and transitions, of subtle phrasing and delicacy; but rage had swept away rhetoric.

Emma, despairing of hearing any details, therefore left the pharmacy; for Monsieur Homais had resumed the trend of his vituperations. He was calming down, however, and was now grumbling in a fatherly tone, all the while fanning himself with his fez:

"It's not that I disapprove of the book altogether! The author was a doctor. There are certain scientific aspects of it that are not bad for a man to know, that, indeed, I would venture to say, a man should know. But later, later! At least wait till you're a man yourself and your character's formed."

At the sound of the door knocker, Charles, who was waiting for her, came forward with his arms open and said with tears in his voice:

"Oh, my dearest! . . ."

And he leaned over gently to kiss her. But at the touch of his lips, the memory of the other one seized her, and she passed her hand over her face, shuddering.

Yet she answered:

"Yes, I know . . . I know . . ."

He showed her the letter in which his mother described the event without any sentimental hypocrisy. She was only sorry that her husband had not received the succor of religion, since he had died at Doudeville, in the street, on the doorsill of a café, after a patriotic meal with former officers.

Emma gave him back the letter; then, at dinner, for the sake of form, she affected some reluctance. But since he urged her several times, she began resolutely to eat, while Charles, opposite her, remained motionless in a posture of dejection.

From time to time, lifting his head, he would give her a long look of distress. Once, he sighed:

"I would have liked to see him one more time!"

She said nothing. Finally, realizing that she ought to say something:

"How old was he—your father?"

"Fifty-eight!"

"Ah!"

And that was all.

A quarter of an hour later, he added:

"My poor mother! . . . What will become of her now?"

She conveyed with a gesture that she did not know.

Seeing her so reserved, Charles supposed that she was grieving, and he forced himself to say nothing so as not to reawaken this sorrow, which moved him. Nevertheless, shaking off his own:

"Did you have good time yesterday?" he asked.

"Yes."

When the tablecloth was removed, Bovary did not get up, nor did Emma; and as she contemplated him, the monotony of the spectacle gradually drove all compassion from her heart. He seemed to her puny, weak, worthless, in fact a poor man in every way. How could she get rid of him? What an interminable evening! She felt numbed, as though by something stupefying like the fumes of opium.

They heard from the hall the dry sound of a stick striking the floorboards. It was Hippolyte bringing Madame's bags. In order to set them down, he laboriously described a quarter of a circle with his wooden leg.

"He doesn't even think about it anymore!" she said to herself as she looked at the poor devil, whose thick red hair was dripping with sweat.

Bovary was searching for a small coin in the bottom of his purse; and without appearing to realize how much humiliation there was for him in the very presence of this man, standing there like a living reproach for his incorrigible ineptitude:

"Oh! what a pretty bouquet you have there!" he said, noticing Léon's violets on the mantelpiece.

"Yes," she said indifferently; "I bought it earlier . . . from a beggar woman."

Charles picked up the violets, and, cooling his tear-reddened eyes against them, he gently inhaled their fragrance. She took them quickly from his hand and went to put them in a glass of water.

The next day, the elder Madame Bovary arrived. She and her son wept a good deal. Emma, under the pretext of having orders to give, disappeared.

The day after, they had to decide, together, about their mourning clothes. They went to sit down, with their workbaskets, by the water's edge, under the arbor.

Charles was thinking about his father, and he was surprised to feel so much affection for the man, whom up to then he had believed he had loved only halfheartedly. The elder Madame Bovary was thinking about her husband. The worst days of the past as they reappeared to her seemed enviable. Everything was eclipsed by her instinctive grief for the loss of a long-enduring habit; and from time to time, as she worked her needle, a large tear would run down the length of her nose and remain hanging there for a moment. Emma was thinking that scarcely forty-eight hours ago, they had been together, far away from the world, deeply intoxicated, without eyes enough to gaze at each other. She was trying to recapture even the imperceptible details of that vanished day. But the presence of her mother-in-law and her husband interfered. She wished she could hear nothing, see nothing, so as not to disturb the recollection of her love, which was steadily vanishing, no matter what she did, under external sensations.

She was unstitching the lining of a dress, the scraps of which lay scattered about her; Mère Bovary, without raising her eyes, was plying a pair of squeaky scissors; and Charles, in his list slippers and the old brown frock coat that served him as a dressing gown, had his hands in his pockets and was not speaking either; near them, Berthe, in a little white apron, was scraping the sand in the paths with her spade.

Suddenly they saw Monsieur Lheureux, the dry-goods merchant, entering by the gate.

He was coming to offer his services, *in view of the melancholy circumstances*. Emma answered that she believed she could do without them. The merchant did not consider himself defeated.

"A thousand apologies," he said; "I would like to have a word in private."

Then, in a low voice:

"It's about that matter . . . You know?"

Charles turned crimson to his ears.

"Ah! Yes! Of course."

And in his disturbance, turning to his wife:

"My dear . . . Could you take care of . . . ?"

She seemed to understand, for she stood up, and Charles said to his mother:

"It's nothing! Probably some household trifle."

He did not want her to know about the note, afraid of what she would say.

As soon as Emma was alone with Monsieur Lheureux, he began by congratulating her, in quite clear terms, on the inheritance, then went on to chat about indifferent things—the espaliers, the harvest, and his own health, which was always *so-so, fair to middling.* Indeed, he worked like a dog, even though, despite what people said, he did not make enough even to put butter on his bread.

Emma was letting him talk. She had been so prodigiously bored the last two days!

"And you're quite well again now?" he went on. "My faith, I could see that your poor husband was in a real state! He's a good fellow, though we did have our difficulties, he and I."

She asked what they were, for Charles had hidden from her the dispute over her purchases.

"But you know very well!" retorted Lheureux. "It was over those little whims of yours—the luggage."

He had lowered his hat over his eyes, and with both hands behind his back, smiling and whistling under his breath, he was looking her full in the face in an insufferable manner. Did he suspect something? She became lost in apprehension. At last, however, he went on:

"We've made it up now, and I came back to suggest an arrangement to him."

It was to renew the note signed by Bovary. Of course, Monsieur should do as he saw fit; he should not let it worry him, especially now that he was going to have a host of other troubles.

"And he would do even better to hand it over to someone else, to you, for example; with a power of attorney, it would be easy, and then you and I could take care of these matters together . . ."

She did not understand. He fell silent. Then, going on to speak of his trade, Lheureux declared that Madame should not fail to order something from him. He would send her a length of black barege, twelve meters, to make up a dress.

"The one you have there is good enough for the house. You need another for visiting. I saw that right away when I came in. I have the eye of an American."

He did not send the material, he brought it. Then he came again to take the measurements; he came again on other pretexts, each time trying to make himself amiable, helpful, pledging his loyalty like a vassal, as Homais would have put it, and always slipping to Emma some words of advice about the power of attorney. He never mentioned the note. She did not think about it; Charles, at the beginning of her convalescence, had indeed told her something about it; but her mind had been so agitated that she no longer remembered. What was more, she refrained from broaching any discussion of money; Mère Bovary was surprised by this and attributed her change of disposition to the religious sentiments she had developed when she was ill.

But as soon as she had left, Emma lost no time amazing Bovary with her practical good sense. They were going to have to make inquiries, check the mortgages, see if there ought to be a sale by auction or a liquidation. She used technical terms at random; she uttered important words such as "order," "the future," "foresight," and continually exaggerated the complications of the inheritance; and then one day she showed him the draft of a general authorization to "manage and administer his affairs, negotiate all loans, sign and endorse all notes, pay all sums, etc." She had profited from Lheureux's lessons.

Charles, naïvely, asked her where this paper had come from.

"From Monsieur Guillaumin."

And with the greatest composure in the world, she added:

"I don't trust him very much. Notaries have such a bad reputation! We ought perhaps to consult . . . We know only . . . Oh, there's no one!"

"Unless Léon . . . ," replied Charles, who was thinking.

But it was hard to explain matters by letter. So she offered to make the trip. He thanked her but would not let her. She insisted. Each tried to outdo the other with considerate attentions. At last, she cried out in a tone of affected rebellion:

"No, you must let me—I must go."

"How good you are!" he said, kissing her on the forehead.

The very next day, she set off in the *Hirondelle* for Rouen to consult Monsieur Léon; and she stayed there three days.

[3]

They were three full, exquisite, splendid days, a real honeymoon.

They stayed at the Hôtel de Boulogne, on the harbor. And there they lived with shutters closed and doors locked, flowers on the floor and fruit drinks on ice, which were brought up to them from morning on.

Toward evening, they would hire a covered boat and go have dinner on an island.

It was the hour when, from along the dockside, one can hear the echo of the caulkers' mallets striking the hulls of the ships. Smoke from the tar would rise from between the trees, and on the river one saw broad patches of oil undulating unevenly beneath the crimson glow of the sun, like floating sheets of Florentine bronze.

They would go down among the moored boats, whose long oblique cables would gently graze the top of their own.

The noises of the city would imperceptibly recede: the rumbling of carts, the tumult of voices, the yapping of dogs on the decks of ships. She would untie her hat, and they would land on their island.

They would sit in the low-ceilinged room of a tavern with black nets hanging at its door. They would eat fried smelts, cream, and cherries. They would lie down in the grass; they would go off and kiss under the poplars; and they would wish that, like two Robinson Crusoes, they could live forever in that little spot, which seemed to them, in their bliss, the most magnificent on earth. It was not the first time they had seen trees, blue sky, or lawn, or that they had heard water trickling and the breeze blowing through the leaves; but they had never before admired all of this, it was as if nature had not existed before, or as if it had begun to be beautiful only once they had slaked their desires.

At night, they would leave again. The boat would follow the shoreline of the islands. They would remain deep inside, the two of them hidden by the darkness, without talking. The square oars would creak between the iron thole pins; and this would mark the silence like the beat of a metronome, while at the stern the mooring rope that trailed behind them never ceased its soft little lapping in the water.

One time, the moon appeared; then inevitably they spoke of it in flowery phrases, finding the star melancholy and full of poetry; she even began to sing:

"One evening—dost thou recall?—we were sailing . . ." etc.

Her weak, melodious voice died away over the water; and the breeze carried off the vocal flourishes that Léon heard passing, like the fluttering of wings, around him.

She was sitting opposite him, leaning against the bulkhead, where the moon entered through one of the open flaps. Her black dress, whose folds spread wide in a fan, made her look slimmer, taller. Her head was raised, her hands joined, and her eyes looked up toward the sky. At times the shadows of the willows would hide her altogether; then she would reappear suddenly, like a vision, in the light from the moon.

Léon, in the bottom of the boat beside her, found under his hand a ribbon of flame-red silk.

The boatman examined it and finally said:

"Ah! Maybe it belongs to a party I took out the other day. They was a crowd of wags, all right, gentlemen and ladies both, with their cakes, champagne, trumpets, the works! One of 'em especially, he was a tall, good-looking fella with a little mustache, very droll! And they all kept after him: 'Come on, tell us a story . . . Adolphe'—or Dodolphe, I think it was."

She shivered.

"Are you uncomfortable?" asked Léon, moving closer to her.

"Oh, it's nothing! Just the chill of the night air, probably."

"And he would've had no shortage of female company, either," added the old sailor softly, believing he was saying something polite to the stranger.

Then, spitting into his hands, he took up his oars again.

But they had to part! Their farewells were sad. He was to send his letters to Mère Rolet's; and she gave him such precise instructions concerning the double envelope that he greatly admired her cunning in love.

"So you swear to me that everything's in order?" she said as they kissed for the last time.

"Yes, of course!" —But why in the world, he mused afterward, returning alone through the streets, is she so dead set on this power of attorney?

[4]

Léon soon began to give himself airs in front of his fellow clerks, avoided their company, and neglected the briefs completely.

He would wait for her letters; he would read them over and over. He would write to her. He would conjure up her image with all the strength of his desire and his memories. Instead of diminishing in her absence, this longing to see her again grew, so much so that one Saturday morning he fled from the office.

When, from the top of the hill, he saw the church steeple in the valley below with its tin flag turning in the wind, he felt the same pleasure, compounded of triumphant vanity and egotistical affection, that a millionaire must experience when returning to his native village.

He went and prowled around her house. A light was shining in the kitchen. He watched for her shadow behind the curtains. Nothing appeared.

Mère Lefrançois, when she saw him, exclaimed loudly, finding him "taller and thinner," while Artémise, on the contrary, found him "fatter and darker."

He dined in the little parlor, as in the old days, but alone, without the tax collector; for Binet, *tired* of waiting for the *Hirondelle,* had permanently advanced his mealtime by one hour, and he now dined at five o'clock sharp, though he quite often claimed that *the old timepiece was slow.*

Léon, however, plucked up his resolve; he went and knocked at the door of the doctor's house. Madame was in her room, from which she did not come down until a quarter of an hour later. Monsieur seemed delighted to see him again; but he did not stir from the house that whole evening, or the whole of the following day.

He saw her alone, that night, very late, behind the garden, in the lane; —in the lane, where she had seen the other! There was a thunderstorm, and they talked under an umbrella, in the glare of the lightning.

To be apart was becoming intolerable.

"I'd rather die!" Emma was saying.

She was moving restlessly about in his arms and weeping.

"Goodbye! . . . Goodbye! . . . When will I see you again?"

They turned back to kiss each other again, and it was then that she promised him she would soon find an opportunity, by whatever means, for them to see each other freely and regularly, at least once a week. Emma was certain of this. She was, what was more, full of hope. Some money would be coming her way.

And so she bought, for her bedroom, a pair of yellow curtains with broad stripes whose low price Monsieur Lheureux had recommended to her; she dreamed of a carpet, and Lheureux, assuring her that "she wouldn't have to swallow the whole sea to get it," politely undertook to provide her with one. She could no longer do without his services. Twenty times in the course of the day, she would send for him, and he would immediately drop whatever he was doing, without permitting himself a murmur of protest. Nor was it clear to anyone why Mère Rolet came to have lunch at her house every day and even saw her in private.

It was at about this time, that is, toward the beginning of winter, that she seemed to be seized by a great passion for music.

One evening when Charles was listening, she started the same piece over again four times in succession, each time becoming annoyed, while, without noticing any difference, he would cry out:

"Bravo! . . . Very good! . . . You're mistaken! Go on!"

"No! It's dreadful! My fingers are so rusty."

The next day, he begged her *to play something for him again.*

"All right, just to please you!"

And Charles admitted that she had fallen off somewhat. She mixed up the staves, stumbled; then, stopping abruptly:

"Oh, it's no use! I ought to take lessons; but . . ."

She bit her lip and added:

"Twenty francs an hour is too expensive!"

"Yes, it is . . . a little . . . ," said Charles, giving a foolish, skeptical laugh. "But it seems to me you could perhaps get someone for less; because there must be musicians with no reputation who are better than the famous ones."

"Well, go find them," said Emma.

The next day, when he came home, he gazed at her with a sly look, and at last could not help remarking:

"How obstinate you are sometimes! I was in Barfeuchères today. Well, Madame Liégeard assured me that her three girls, who are at the Misé-ricorde, are taking lessons for a charge of fifty sous per session, and from a marvelous teacher!"

She shrugged and did not open her instrument again.

But whenever she walked by it (if Bovary happened to be there), she would sigh:

"Ah, my poor piano!"

And if someone came to see her, she would always remark that she had given up her music and could not go back to it now, for compelling reasons. Then one would pity her. It was too bad! She had such a lovely talent! People even talked about it to Bovary. They made him feel ashamed, especially the pharmacist:

"You're making a mistake! One should never allow the natural faculties to lie fallow. Besides, keep in mind, my good friend, that by encouraging Madame to take lessons, you will be economizing later on your child's musical training! I myself believe that mothers ought to teach their children themselves. This is an idea of Rousseau's; it's perhaps a little new still, but it'll end by prevailing, I'm sure, like mothers breast-feeding, and vaccination."

And so Charles returned once more to the question of the piano. Emma answered sourly that it would be better to sell it. That poor piano, which had so often given him a proud gratification—to see it go would somehow be, for Bovary, like seeing her kill a part of herself!

"If you wanted . . . one lesson," he would say, from time to time, "it wouldn't really ruin us, after all."

"But lessons don't do any good," she would reply, "unless they're kept up."

And that is how she managed to obtain from her husband permission to go to the city, once a week, to see her lover. It was even thought, after a month, that she had made considerable progress.

[5]

It was Thursday. She would rise and dress silently so as not to wake Charles, who would have commented on the fact that she was getting ready too early. Then she would pace back and forth; she would stand in front of the windows, she would look out at the Square. The first light of the day would creep in among the posts of the marketplace, and on the pharmacist's house, whose shutters were closed, could be seen, in the pale tints of dawn, the capital letters of its sign.

When the clock showed quarter past seven, she would go off to the Lion d'Or, whose door Artémise, yawning, would come to open for her. The servant would uncover for Madame the coals buried under the ashes. Emma would remain alone in the kitchen. From time to time, she would go outside. Hivert would be harnessing the horses at a leisurely pace, while listening to Mère Lefrançois, who, putting her head, in its nightcap, out a little window above, was charging him with commissions and giving him explanations that would have bewildered a different sort of man. Emma would tap the soles of her little boots on the paving stones of the courtyard.

At last, when he had eaten his soup, put on his heavy cloak, lit his pipe, and seized his whip, he would settle himself calmly on his seat.

The *Hirondelle* would set off at a gentle trot and for three-quarters of a league would stop here and there to take on passengers who were watching for it, standing by the side of the road, in front of the gates of their farmyards. Those who had left word the day before would make it wait for them; a few, even, were still in bed inside their houses; Hivert would call, shout, curse, then get down from his seat and go pound on the door. The wind would blow in through the cracked windows of the carriage.

The four outside seats, however, would fill up, the carriage would roll on, lines of apple trees would pass one after another; and the road, between its two long ditches full of yellow water, would keep narrowing toward the horizon.

Emma knew it from one end to the other; she knew that after a pasture came a signpost, then an elm tree, a barn, or a road mender's hut; sometimes, even, in order to create surprises for herself, she would close her eyes. But she never lost her clear sense of how much distance there was still to be covered.

At last, the brick houses would come closer together, the ground would reverberate under the wheels, the *Hirondelle* would glide between gardens in which one could see, through a fence, statues, a knoll surmounted by an arbor, clipped yews, and a child's swing. Then, in a single glance, the city would appear.

Descending in an amphitheater, and drowned in mist, it broadened out untidily beyond the bridges. Then the open country rose again in a monotonous sweep, until in the distance it touched the uncertain lower edge of the pale sky. Seen thus from above, the entire landscape had the stillness of a painting; the ships at anchor were piled together in one corner; the river curved round the foot of the green hills; and the islands, oblong in shape, resembled great black fish that had come to a stop on the water. The factory chimneys expelled immense brown plumes that flew off at the tips. One could hear the rumbling of the foundries along with the clear chimes of the churches that rose through the fog. The leafless trees along the boulevards were like thickets of violet among the houses, and the roofs, all gleaming with rain, sparkled unequally, according to the heights of the neighborhoods. Now and then a gust of wind would carry the clouds off toward the Sainte-Catherine hill, like aerial waves breaking in silence against a cliff.

For her, something dizzying emanated from those closely crowded lives, and her heart would swell hugely with it, as if all of the hundred twenty thousand souls throbbing down there had transmitted to her, at the same moment, the vapor of the passions she supposed they harbored. Her love would grow larger in the presence of this vastness and fill with tumult at the indistinct hum that ascended from below. She would pour this love back out, onto the squares, the promenades, the streets, and in her eyes, the old Norman city would spread before her like some immense capital, some Babylon she was entering. She would lean on both hands out through the carriage window, inhaling the air; the three horses would gallop on, the stones would grind in the mud, the coach would sway, and Hivert would shout ahead to the carts along the road, while the townsmen who had slept in Bois-Guillaume would descend the hillside peacefully in their little family carriages.

They would stop at the city gate; Emma would unbuckle her clogs, put on different gloves, straighten her shawl; and twenty paces farther on, she would leave the *Hirondelle*.

The city, at that hour, was just waking up. Clerks in tasseled caps were polishing the shop windows, and women holding baskets on their hips uttered a resounding cry from time to time at the street corners. She walked with her eyes on the ground, keeping close to the walls and smiling with pleasure under her lowered black veil.

For fear of being seen, she would usually not take the shortest route. She would plunge into dark alleys, and she would emerge all in a sweat at the bottom of the rue Nationale, close to the fountain that stands there. This is the neighborhood of the theater, full of bars and prostitutes. Often a cart would pass by near her, carrying a wobbling stage set. Waiters in aprons were scattering sand over the paving stones, between green shrubs. There was a smell of absinthe, cigars, and oysters.

She would turn down a street; she would recognize him by the curls escaping from under his hat.

Léon would continue on down the sidewalk. She would follow him to the hotel; he would go up, he would open the door, he would go in . . . How they would hold each other!

Then, after their kisses, the words would pour out. They would tell each other about the difficulties of the past week, their forebodings, their worries about the letters; but now everything would be forgotten, and they would look into each other's eyes, laughing with sensual delight and calling each other by pet names.

The bed was a large mahogany one in the form of a gondola. The curtains of red Levantine silk, which descended from the ceiling, were looped back too low near the flaring headboard; —and nothing in the world was as lovely as her brown hair and white skin standing out against that crimson, when, in a gesture of modesty, she would bring her two bare arms together, hiding her face in her hands.

The warm room, with its subdued carpet, its playful ornaments, and its tranquil light, seemed perfectly suited to the intimacies of passion. The arrow-tipped rods of the canopy, the brass curtain hooks, and the great knobs on the andirons would gleam suddenly if the sun came in. On the mantelpiece, between the candelabras, were two of those large pink shells in which you can hear the sound of the sea when you put them to your ear.

How they loved that dear room, so full of gaiety despite its somewhat faded splendor! They would always find the furniture in its place, and sometimes a few hairpins she had forgotten the previous Thursday under the base of the clock. They would lunch by the fireside, at a little pedestal table inlaid with rosewood. Emma would carve, prattling all sorts of affectionate nonsense as she put the pieces on his plate; and she would laugh a deep, voluptuous laugh when the froth from the champagne overflowed the rim of the delicate glass onto the rings of her fingers. They were so completely lost in their possession of each other that they believed they were in their own private house and were destined to live there till they died, as an eternally young husband and wife. They would say "our room," "our carpet," "our chairs," she would even speak of "my slippers," a gift from Léon, a whim she had had. They were slippers of pink satin, trimmed with swansdown. When she sat on his knees, her leg, now too short to reach the floor, would swing in the air; and the dainty slipper, which had no back to it, would dangle from the toes of her bare foot.

He was savoring for the first time the inexpressible delicacy of feminine refinements. Never had he encountered this grace in language, this reserve in clothing, these drowsy, dovelike postures. He admired the sublimity of her soul and the lace on her petticoat. What was more, wasn't she *a woman of the world,* and a married woman! —a real mistress, in other words?

Because her moods were so various, by turns mystical and joyful, garrulous, taciturn, fiery, casual, she woke in him a thousand desires, stirring his instincts or his memories. She was the beloved of every novel, the heroine of every drama, the vague *she* of every volume of poetry. He rediscovered on her shoulders the warm amber color of the *bathing odalisque;* she had the long waist of the feudal châtelaines; she resembled, as well, the *pale beauty of Barcelona,* but above all she was an Angel!

Often, as he looked at her, it seemed to him that his soul, fleeing to her, spread like a wave over the contours of her head and was then drawn down into the whiteness of her chest.

He would kneel in front of her; and, with his elbows on her knees, he would gaze at her with a smile, his forehead held up to her.

She would lean down to him and murmur, as though breathless with intoxication:

"Oh, don't move! Don't say anything! Look at me! There is something so sweet in your eyes; it does me so much good!"

She would call him "child":

"Child, do you love me?"

And she would scarcely hear his answer, so quickly did his lips rise to her mouth.

On the clock there was a simpering little bronze Cupid cradling a gilt wreath in its arms. They often laughed at it; but when the moment came for parting, everything seemed serious to them.

Motionless, face-to-face, they would say over and over:

"Till Thursday! . . . Till Thursday!"

Then she would abruptly take his head in her hands, kiss him quickly on the forehead, crying, "Goodbye!" and run out into the stairwell.

She would go down the rue de la Comédie, to a hairdresser's, to have her bands of hair arranged. Night would be falling; they would light the gas in the shop.

She would hear the theater's little bell summoning the players to the performance; and across the street she would see white-faced men and women in faded clothing walking past and entering the stage door.

It was warm in that small room with its too-low ceiling, where the stove hummed amid the wigs and pomades. The smell of the curling irons, along with those plump hands at work on her head, would soon make her drowsy, and she would doze a little in her smock. Often the assistant, as he arranged her hair, would offer her tickets to the masked ball.

Then she would set out! She would walk back through the streets; she would reach the Croix Rouge; she would retrieve her clogs, which she had hidden that morning under a seat, and squeeze into her place among the impatient passengers. Some of them would get out at the bottom of the hill. She would remain alone in the carriage.

At each bend, more and more of the city lights would come into view, forming a broad layer of luminous mist over the mass of houses. Emma would kneel on the cushions and let her eyes wander over that radiance. She would sob, call out to Léon, and send him tender messages and kisses that were lost in the wind.

On the hillside, there was a poor devil wandering along with his stick amid all the coaches. Layers of rags covered his shoulders, and an old staved-in beaver hat, pulled down into a bowl shape, hid his face; but when he took it off, he revealed, in place of eyelids, two gaping, bloody sockets. His flesh was shredding off in red tatters; and from it oozed liquid that dried in green crusts down to his nose, where his black nostrils sniffled convulsively. When he spoke to you, he would tip his head far back with an idiotic laugh; —then his bluish eyes, rolling incessantly around, would keep coming up, near his temples, against the edges of the open sores.

He would sing a little song as he followed the carriages:

Oft in the warmth of a summer's day
A maiden's thoughts to love will stray

And the rest of it was all about birds, sunshine, and leaves.

Sometimes he would appear abruptly behind Emma, bareheaded. She would draw back with a cry. Hivert liked to tease him. He would urge him to take a booth at the Saint-Romain fair or, with a laugh, ask how his girlfriend was.

Often, they would be moving steadily along when his hat would suddenly come into the coach through the little window, while he held fast with his other arm, standing on the footboard between the spattering wheels. His voice, weak at first, and wailing, would grow shrill. It would linger in the darkness, like the indistinct lamentation of some vague distress; and, heard through the ringing of the harness bells, the murmur of the trees, and the rumbling of the hollow body of the coach, it had something distant about it that would overwhelm Emma. It would descend into the depths of her soul like a whirlwind into an abyss and would carry her away into the spaces of a boundless melancholy. But Hivert, noticing the counterbalancing weight, would lash out at the blind man with long strokes of his whip. The tip would sting him on his sores, and he would drop off into the mud, howling.

Then the passengers on the *Hirondelle* would at last fall asleep, some with their mouths open, others with their chins lowered, leaning against a neighbor's shoulder, or with an arm through the strap, swaying rhythmically with the motion of the carriage; and the glimmer of the lamp swinging outside over the rumps of the shaft horses, penetrating into the interior through the curtains of chocolate calico, would cast blood-red shadows over all those motionless individuals. Emma, drunk with sadness, would shiver in her clothes; and her feet would grow colder and colder, death in her soul.

Charles, at the house, would be waiting for her; the *Hirondelle* was always late on Thursdays. Finally, Madame was here! She would barely kiss the child. Dinner was not ready, but it didn't matter! —she made excuses for the cook. Now, it seemed, the girl was allowed to do anything.

Often her husband, noticing her pallor, would ask if she was not ill.

"No," Emma would say.

"But," he would reply, "you seem so strange this evening!"

"Oh, it's nothing, it's nothing!"

There were even days when she had no sooner come in than she would go up to her room; and Justin, who happened to be there, would move about with silent steps, cleverer at serving her than an excellent lady's maid. He would set out the matches, the candlestick, a book, arrange her bed jacket, fold back the bedclothes.

"All right," she would say, "that'll do, off you go now!"

For he would still be standing there, his hands hanging at his sides and his eyes wide open, as though enmeshed in the myriad strands of a sudden reverie.

The next day was awful, and the following ones even more intolerable, because of Emma's impatience to recapture her happiness—hers was a sharp lust inflamed by familiar images, which, on the seventh day, would explode freely under Léon's caresses. His own raptures were hidden within effusions of wonder and gratitude. Emma would taste that love in a discreet and concentrated way, sustaining it by all the artifices of her affection, a little afraid that it might one day vanish.

Often she would say to him gently, in her melancholy voice:

"Ah, one day you'll leave me, I know! . . . You'll get married! . . . You'll be just like the others."

He would ask:

"What others?"

"Oh—men, you know," she would answer.

Then she would add, languidly thrusting him away:

"You're all vile creatures!"

One day when they were talking philosophically about their disillusionment with the world, she happened to say (testing his jealousy, or perhaps yielding to too strong a need to unburden herself) that in the past, before him, she had loved someone else—"not the way I love you!" she quickly added, swearing on her daughter's head that *nothing had happened.*

The young man believed her but nevertheless questioned her to find out what *he* did.

"He was a ship's captain, my dear."

Did she not say this in order to keep him from trying to find out more, and at the same time to put herself in a very lofty position, by claiming to have exerted such a fascination over a man who had to be by nature both aggressive and accustomed to deferential treatment?

The clerk felt, then, the lowliness of his own position; he longed for epaulets, medals, titles. She must like all that: he suspected it because of her expensive habits.

However, Emma was silent about a great many of her extravagant ideas, such as her desire to have a blue tilbury, harnessed with an English horse and driven by a groom in top boots, to take her to Rouen. It was Justin who had inspired her with this whim, by pleading with her to take him on as footman in her household; and if this privation did not diminish, at each of her meetings with Léon, the pleasure of her arrival, it certainly augmented the bitterness of her return home.

Often when they were talking about Paris, she would end by murmuring:

"Ah! how good it would be for us, living there!"

"Aren't we happy?" the young man would reply gently, running his hand over her bands of hair.

"Yes, it's true," she would say. "I'm being foolish; kiss me!"

She was more charming than ever to her husband; she would make him pistachio creams and play waltzes after dinner. So he believed he was the most fortunate of mortals, and Emma's life was free of worry, when one evening, suddenly:

"It is Mademoiselle Lempereur, isn't it, who's giving you lessons?"

"Yes."

"Well, I just saw her," Charles went on, "at Madame Liégeard's. I mentioned you to her; she doesn't know you."

It was like a thunderbolt. But she replied with a natural air:

"Oh! She's probably forgotten my name."

"But perhaps at Rouen," said the doctor, "there are several Demoiselles Lempereur who teach piano?"

"It's possible!"

Then quickly:

"But I have her receipts! Here, look!"

And she went to the secretary desk, rummaged in all the drawers, mixed up all the papers, and in the end became so confused that Charles urged her vehemently not to go to so much trouble over those wretched receipts.

"Oh, I'll find them," she said.

Indeed, the very next Friday, Charles, as he was putting on one of his boots in the small, windowless room where his clothes were kept, felt a piece of paper between the leather and his sock; he took it out and read:

Received, for three months of lessons, in addition to various supplies, the sum of sixty-five francs. FÉLICIE LEMPEREUR, *Music Instructor.*

"How in the world did this get into my boot?"

"It probably fell out of that old box of invoices," she answered, "on the edge of the shelf."

From that moment on, her life was no more than a confection of lies in which she wrapped her love, as though in veils, to hide it.

Lying became a need, a mania, a pleasure, to the point that if she said she had gone down the right side of the street yesterday, one could be sure she had gone down the left.

One morning when she had just set off, as was her habit, rather lightly dressed, there was a sudden snowfall; and as Charles was watching the weather out the window, he caught sight of Monsieur Bournisien in the *boc* belonging to Sieur Tuvache, who was driving him to Rouen. So he went downstairs to entrust the clergyman with a thick shawl so that he might deliver it to Madame, as soon as he should reach the Croix Rouge. Scarcely had he arrived at the inn than Bournisien asked where the wife of the Yonville doctor was. The hotel keeper answered that she spent very little time at her establishment. And so, that evening, when he recognized Madame Bovary in the *Hirondelle,* the curé told her about his difficulty, without appearing, however, to attach any importance to it; for he commenced singing the praises of a preacher who at that time was performing wonders in the cathedral and whom all the ladies were rushing to hear.

It did not matter that he had not asked for explanations, others might later prove less discreet. And so she felt it useful to get out at the Croix

Rouge, each time, so that the good people of her village who saw her on the stairs would not suspect anything.

One day, however, Monsieur Lheureux encountered her as she was leaving the Hôtel de Boulogne on Léon's arm; and she was afraid, imagining that he would talk. He was not so stupid.

But three days later, he entered her room, closed the door, and said: "I'm afraid I need some money."

She declared that she could not give him any. Lheureux complained profusely and recalled all the kindnesses he had shown her.

Indeed, of the two notes signed by Charles, Emma had so far paid only one. As for the second, the shopkeeper, upon her entreaty, had consented to replace it by two others, which themselves had been renewed for quite a long term. Then he drew from his pocket a list of goods not paid for, namely the curtains, the carpet, the material for the armchairs, several dresses, and various toilet articles, whose value amounted to the sum of two thousand francs, more or less.

She bowed her head; he went on:

"But if you have no cash, you have *possessions*."

And he mentioned a wretched, tumbledown cottage situated in Barneville, near Aumale, which did not bring in much. It had once been part of a little farm sold by the elder Monsieur Bovary—for Lheureux knew everything, even its area in hectares and the name of the neighbors.

"In your place," he was saying, "I would liquidate the debt, and I would still have whatever money was left over."

She pleaded the difficulty of finding a buyer; he offered the hope of locating one; but she asked what she would have to do so that she would be able to sell it.

"Don't you have the power of attorney?" he answered.

The words came to her like a gust of fresh air.

"Leave me the note," said Emma.

"Oh, it's not worth the bother!" Lheureux said.

He came back the following week and boasted that, after some effort, he had in the end discovered a certain Langlois who, for a long time now, had been coveting the property without making known his price.

"The price doesn't matter!" she cried.

On the contrary, it was necessary to wait, to sound the fellow out. The thing was worth the trouble of a trip, and as she could not make that trip, he offered to go to the place in person to confer with Langlois. On his return, he announced that the buyer was proposing four thousand francs.

Emma beamed at this news.

"Frankly," he added, "that's a good price."

She received half the sum immediately, and when she was about to settle his account, the merchant said to her:

"To be perfectly honest, it pains me to see you hand over such a *significant* sum all at once."

Then she looked at the banknotes; and, dreaming of the infinite numbers of meetings represented by those two thousand francs:

"Why . . . What . . . ?" she stammered.

"Oh!" he replied, laughing good-naturedly, "one can put whatever one likes on a bill. Don't you think I know something about household affairs?"

And he looked at her fixedly, all the while holding two long pieces of paper in his hand and sliding them back and forth between his fingertips. At last, he opened his billfold and spread out on the table four promissory notes, each for a thousand francs.

"Sign these for me," he said, "and keep all of it."

She cried out, shocked.

"But if I give you the surplus," answered Monsieur Lheureux shamelessly, "aren't I actually doing you a service?"

And, taking a pen, he wrote at the bottom of the bill: "Received from Madame Bovary, four thousand francs."

"What are you worried about, since in six months you'll be receiving the balance on your shack, and I'm making the last note fall due after that payment?"

Emma was becoming a little confused by his calculations, and she felt a ringing in her ears as if gold coins were bursting out of their sacks and clinking on the floor all around her. At last Lheureux explained that he had a friend named Vinçart, a banker at Rouen, who would discount these four notes, and then he himself would return the surplus of the real debt to Madame.

But instead of two thousand francs, he brought only eighteen hundred, because this friend Vinçart (as was *only right*) had taken a deduction of two hundred, to cover commission and discount.

Then he casually requested a receipt.

"You understand . . . in business . . . sometimes . . . And with the date, please, the date."

A vista of attainable fantasies then opened before Emma. She had enough prudence to put aside a thousand ecus, with which the first three notes, when they fell due, were paid; but the fourth, by chance, arrived at the house on a Thursday, and Charles, stunned, waited patiently for his wife's return to hear her explanations.

If she had not told him about this note, it was to spare him domestic worries; she sat down on his knee, caressed him, talked lovingly to him, made a long enumeration of all the indispensable things she had taken on credit.

"So you'll have to agree that, considering how many things there were, that wasn't so expensive."

Charles, at his wits' end, soon had recourse to the eternal Lheureux, who promised to calm things down, if Monsieur would sign two notes to him, one of which would be for seven hundred francs, payable in three months. To put himself in a position to do this, he wrote his mother a touching letter. Instead of sending an answer, she came herself; and when Emma wanted to know if he had gotten anything from her:

"Yes," he answered. "But she's asking to see the bill."

The next day, at dawn, Emma hurried to Monsieur Lheureux to beg him to draw up another note, which would not be for more than a thousand francs; for if she were to show the one for four thousand, she would have had to say that she had paid off two-thirds of it and confess, consequently, to the sale of the building, the negotiation of which was skillfully handled by the merchant and actually not made known until later.

Despite the very low price of each article, the elder Madame Bovary did not fail to find the expenditure unduly high.

"Couldn't you do without a carpet? Why replace the fabric on the armchairs? In my day, they had just one armchair in a house, for the old people—at least, it was like that in my mother's house, and she was a respectable woman, I can assure you. Not everyone can be rich! No fortune can hold out against constant wastefulness! I would blush to pamper myself the way you do! and yet I'm an old woman, I need care and attention . . . What a lot! what a lot of frills and frippery! What! silk for lining, at two francs! . . . whereas you can find muslin at ten sous, even at eight sous, that does the job perfectly."

Emma, lying back in the love seat, replied with the greatest calm:

"Oh, madame, that's enough! that's enough! . . ."

The other continued to lecture her, predicting that they would end up in the poorhouse. Anyway, it was Bovary's fault. Fortunately, he had promised to cancel that power of attorney . . .

"What?"

"Ah! He swore to me he would," the good woman went on.

Emma opened the window, called out to Charles, and the poor fellow was forced to confess the promise extracted from him by his mother.

Emma vanished, then quickly returned, majestically handing her a large piece of paper.

"I thank you," said the old woman.

And she threw the power of attorney into the fire.

Emma burst into a strident, harsh laughter that went on and on: she was having an attack of hysterics.

"Oh, my God!" cried Charles. "You're at fault, too! You come and make trouble for her! . . ."

His mother, shrugging, claimed *it was all just playacting*.

But Charles, rebelling for the first time, took up his wife's defense, so that the elder Madame Bovary made up her mind to leave. She went off the very next day, and on the doorsill, when he tried to hold her back, she replied:

"No, no! You love her more than me, and you're right, that's as it should be. As for the rest, it's just too bad! You'll see! . . . Take care of yourself! . . . because I'm not about to come back soon, making trouble for her, as you say."

Charles remained nonetheless very shamefaced with Emma, who did not hide the resentment she still felt against him for his lack of trust; many entreaties were necessary before she consented to take back her power of attorney, and he even went with her to Monsieur Guillaumin to have him draw up a second one, exactly the same.

"I understand," said the notary; "a man of science can't be expected to trouble himself with the practical details of life."

And Charles felt soothed by this unctuous reflection, which gave his weakness the appearance of a preoccupation with higher things.

What an eruption, the following Thursday, at the hotel, in their room, with Léon! She laughed, wept, sang, danced, sent for sorbets, insisted on smoking cigarettes, seemed to him extravagant, but adorable, splendid.

He did not know what reaction was driving her to plunge deeper and deeper, with her whole being, into the pursuit of pleasure. She was becoming irritable, greedy, and voluptuous; and she would walk with him in the streets, her head high—unafraid, she would say, of compromising herself. Sometimes, however, Emma would shudder at the sudden thought of meeting Rodolphe; for it seemed to her, even though they had separated forever, that she was not completely free of his domination.

One evening, she did not return to Yonville at all. Charles grew frantic, and little Berthe, not wanting to go to bed without her mama, was sobbing as though her heart would break. Justin had set off on a haphazard search down the road. Monsieur Homais had left his pharmacy.

Finally, at eleven o'clock, unable to bear it any longer, Charles harnessed his *boc,* leaped into it, whipped up his horse, and arrived toward two o'clock in the morning at the Croix Rouge. No one there. He thought the clerk might have seen her; but where did he live? Charles, fortunately, recalled the address of his employer. He rushed there.

Day was beginning to break. He made out some metal nameplates above a door; he knocked. Someone, without opening, shouted out the information he had asked for, adding a number of insults against people who disturbed others at night.

The house where the clerk lived had no doorbell, no knocker, no porter. Charles pounded with his fist on the shutters. A policeman happened to be passing; then he became afraid and went away.

"I'm crazy," he was saying to himself; "they probably kept her for dinner at Monsieur Lormeaux's."

The Lormeaux family no longer lived in Rouen.

"She must have stayed to look after Madame Dubreuil. Oh! Madame Dubreuil has been dead ten months! . . . Well, where is she?"

An idea came to him. He asked, in a café, for the *Directory* and searched quickly for the name of Mademoiselle Lempereur, who lived in the rue de la Renelle-des-Maroquiniers, at number 74.

As he was entering that street, Emma herself appeared at the other end; he did not so much embrace her as fling himself on her, exclaiming:

"What kept you yesterday?"

"I was taken ill."

"From what? . . . Where? . . . How? . . ."

She ran her hand over her forehead and answered:

"At Mademoiselle Lempereur's."

"I was sure of it! I was on my way there."

"Oh, it's not worth the trouble!" said Emma. "She's just gone out; but in the future, don't be uneasy. I'm not free, don't you see, if I know that the slightest delay upsets you like this."

She was giving herself a kind of permission not to be hampered in her escapades. And, quite freely, she took full advantage of it. Whenever she was seized by a desire to see Léon, she would leave under any pretext at all, and, as he was not expecting her that day, she would go looking for him at his office.

It was a great delight the first few times; but soon he no longer hid the truth, namely, that his employer was complaining loudly about these disruptions.

"Oh, nonsense! Come on," she would say.

And he would slip out.

She wanted him to dress all in black and grow a little pointed beard on his chin so that he would resemble the portraits of Louis XIII. She wanted to see his rooms, found them mediocre; he blushed at that; she took no notice, then advised him to buy curtains like her own; and when he objected to the expense:

"Oh, you do hold tight to your little ecus, don't you!" she said, laughing.

Léon would have to tell her, each time, everything he had done since they last met. She asked for verses, verses composed for her, *a love poem* in her honor; he could never manage to find the rhyme for the second line, and in the end he copied a sonnet from a keepsake album.

He did this less out of vanity than with the sole aim of pleasing her. He did not question her ideas; he accepted all her tastes; he was becoming her mistress more than she was his. She said tender things to him and gave him kisses that transported his soul. Where could she have learned this depravity, so deep and so dissembled that it was almost incorporeal?

[6]

On his trips to see her, Léon had often dined at the home of the pharmacist, and he had felt obliged, out of politeness, to invite him in return.

"With pleasure!" Monsieur Homais had responded. "I need to revitalize myself a bit, in any case, for I'm getting into a rut here. We'll go to the theater, eat in a restaurant, treat ourselves to a real fling!"

"Ah! My dearest!" murmured Madame Homais tenderly, dismayed by the unknown perils he was preparing to risk.

"Well, what is it? Don't you think I'm already ruining my health as it is by living amid the continual emanations from the pharmacy! Such, however, is the nature of women: they're jealous of Science, then oppose one's enjoying the most legitimate amusement. Never mind, you can count on me; one of these days, I'll turn up in Rouen and together we'll make the *monacos* fly."

In earlier times, the apothecary would have carefully avoided such an expression; but he was now inclined toward a playful Parisian style, which he found in better taste; and, like his neighbor Madame Bovary, he would examine the clerk inquisitively about the customs of the capital; he even used slang to dazzle . . . the bourgeoisie, saying *"turne"* (digs), *"bazar"* (stuff), *"chicard"* (classy), *"chicandard"* (most classy), *"Breda-street"* (red-light district), and *"Je me la casse"* (I'm hoofing it) for "I'm going now."

And so, one Thursday, Emma was surprised to encounter Monsieur Homais in the kitchen of the Lion d'Or wearing traveling clothes, that is, draped in an old cloak that no one knew he owned, and carrying in one hand a suitcase, and in the other the footmuff from his shop. He had not confided his plan to anyone, for fear of worrying the public by his absence.

The idea of revisiting the places where he had spent his youth no doubt excited him, for he did not stop discoursing all the way there; then, scarcely arrived, he leaped smartly from the carriage and set off in search of Léon; and though the clerk struggled, Monsieur Homais dragged him out to the large Café de Normandie, which he entered majestically without doffing his hat, deeming it very provincial to bare his head in a public place.

Emma waited for Léon three-quarters of an hour. Finally she hurried to his office, and, lost in conjectures of every kind, accusing him of indifference and reproaching herself for her weakness, she spent the afternoon with her forehead pressed to the windowpane.

At two o'clock they were still at the table, face-to-face. The large room was emptying; the stovepipe, in the form of a palm tree, spread out over the white ceiling in a gold fan; and near them, behind the window, in the full sun, a small jet of water gurgled into a marble basin where, among watercress and asparagus, three torpid lobsters extended their claws toward a heap of quail lying on their sides.

Homais was thoroughly enjoying himself. Although he was even more intoxicated by luxury than by a sumptuous meal, still, the Pommard was exciting his faculties a little, and, when the rum omelet appeared, he began to advance certain immoral theories concerning women. What captivated him above all was *chic.* He adored an elegant toilette in a well-furnished room, and, as for the bodily attributes, he was not averse to a *dainty morsel.*

Léon was gazing at the clock in despair. The apothecary was drinking, eating, talking.

"You must be feeling quite bereft," he said suddenly, "here in Rouen. But then your love doesn't live too far away."

And when the other blushed:

"Come now, be frank! You won't deny that in Yonville . . ."

The young man began to stammer.

"At Madame Bovary's, weren't you courting . . ."

"Well, who?"

"The servant girl!"

He was not joking; but, vanity prevailing over discretion, Léon protested in spite of himself. Besides, he liked only dark-haired women.

"I agree with you," said the pharmacist; "they're more hot-blooded."

And leaning over to his friend's ear, he indicated the signs by which one could recognize a hot-blooded woman. He even launched into an ethnographic digression: German women were moody, French women licentious, Italian women passionate.

"And what about Negro women?" asked the clerk.

"That's a taste cultivated by artists," said Homais. "—Waiter! Two demitasses."

"Shall we go?" said Léon at last, becoming impatient.

"Yes," said Homais in English.

But before going, he asked to see the head of the establishment and offered him his congratulations.

Then the young man, in the hope of being left alone, alleged that he had some business to take care of.

"Ah! I'll escort you!" said Homais.

And as he walked along the streets with him, Homais talked about his wife, his children, their future, and his pharmacy, describing the state of decline it had once been in and the degree of perfection to which he had raised it.

Having arrived in front of the Hôtel de Boulogne, Léon left him abruptly, climbed the stairs, and found his mistress highly emotional.

When she heard the pharmacist's name, she flew into a rage. Yet he was piling one good excuse upon the next: It was not his fault. Didn't she know Monsieur Homais? Could she believe that he preferred his company? But she turned away; he held her back; and, sinking to his knees, he put his arms around her waist in a languorous posture full of desire and supplication.

She stood there; her great fiery eyes were gazing at him soberly in a way that was almost terrifying. Then they darkened with tears, her rosy eyelids lowered, she yielded her hands, and Léon was just bringing them to his lips when a servant appeared and informed Monsieur that someone was asking for him.

"Are you going to come back?" she asked.

"Yes."

"When?"

"Right away."

"It was a *dodge,*" said the pharmacist when he saw Léon. "I wanted to interrupt this appointment of yours, which I thought you didn't seem too pleased about. Let's go to Bridoux's and have a glass of garus."

Léon swore he had to return to his office. Then the apothecary made some jokes about paperwork and legal proceedings.

"Forget about Cujas and Bartole for a little while—what the devil! What's to stop you? Be a bold fellow! Come to Bridoux's; you'll have a look at his dog. It's very odd!"

And when the clerk persisted:

"Then I'll come, too. I'll read a newspaper while I wait, or dip into one of the Codes."

Léon, stunned by Emma's anger, Monsieur Homais's chatter, and perhaps the heaviness of his lunch, remained undecided, as though bewitched by the pharmacist, who kept repeating:

"Come to Bridoux's! It's only a couple of steps away, in the rue Malpalu."

And so, out of cowardice, out of stupidity, out of that shameful feeling that entices us into the most antipathetic actions, he let himself be taken off to Bridoux's; and they found him in his little courtyard, overseeing three waiters who were panting as they turned the large wheel of a machine for making Seltzer water. Homais gave them some advice; he embraced Bridoux; they had their garus. Twenty times over, Léon tried to go; but the pharmacist held him back by the arm, saying:

"In a minute! I'm leaving. We'll stop by *Le Fanal de Rouen* and see those gentlemen. I'll introduce you to Thomassin."

He got rid of him, however, and raced back to the hotel. Emma was no longer there.

She had just left, enraged. She hated him now. That broken promise at their rendezvous seemed to her an insult, and she sought yet more reasons to separate from him: he was incapable of heroism, he was weak, ordinary, softer than a woman, and also greedy and timid.

Then, growing calmer, she came to see that she had probably disparaged him unjustly. But vilifying those we love always detaches us from them a little. We should not touch our idols: their gilding will remain on our hands.

Now they talked more often about things unconcerned with their love; and the letters Emma sent him were full of flowers, verses, the moon and the stars, as she naïvely attempted to revive her weakened passion with external stimulants. She kept promising herself that on her next trip, she would be profoundly happy; then she would admit that she had not felt anything extraordinary. This disappointment would fade quickly in the presence of fresh hope, and Emma would return to him more ardent, more avid. She would undress roughly, tearing the thin string of her corset, which would whistle around her hips like a slithering snake. She would stand on the tips of her bare toes to see one more time that the door was locked, then drop all her clothes in a single motion; —and, pale, speechless, solemn, she would collapse against his chest with a long shudder.

But on that forehead beaded with cold droplets, on those stammering lips, in those wild eyes, in the clasp of those arms, there was something extreme, undefined, and bleak that seemed to Léon to slip subtly between them as though to separate them.

He did not dare question her; but, understanding how experienced she was, he would say to himself that she must have passed through every ordeal of suffering and pleasure. What had once charmed him he now found a little frightening. Moreover, he rebelled against the way his personality was absorbed by her more and more each day. He resented Emma for this perpetual victory. He even attempted to stop loving her; then, at the creak of her little boots, he would feel how cowardly he was, like a drunkard at the sight of strong liquor.

True, she unfailingly lavished on him attentions of every kind, from delicacies for the table to her stylish clothing and her dreamy glances. She would bring roses from Yonville in her bosom and toss them in his face; she would worry over his health, give him advice about how to conduct himself; and in order to keep a firmer hold on him, hoping that heaven would perhaps intervene, she hung around his neck a medal of the Blessed Virgin. She informed herself, like a virtuous mother, about his friends. She would say to him:

"Don't see them, don't go out, think only about us, love me!"

She would have liked to be able to keep a constant eye on him, and it occurred to her to have him followed in the streets. Near the hotel, there was a sort of tramp who was always accosting travelers and who would not refuse . . . But her pride rebelled.

"Oh, too bad! If he's deceiving me, what do I care! Does it matter to me?"

One day when they had left each other early, and she was walking back alone down the boulevard, she caught sight of the walls of her convent; she sat down on a bench, in the shade of the elms. How peaceful those days had been! How she had longed for the indescribable feelings of love that she had tried, with the help of her books, to imagine for herself!

The first months of her marriage, her horseback rides in the forest, the Vicomte waltzing, and Lagardy singing, all passed before her eyes again . . . And suddenly Léon appeared to her as far away as the others.

"And yet I love him!" she said to herself.

It didn't matter! She was not happy and never had been. Why was life so inadequate, why did the things she depended on turn immediately to dust? . . . Yet if somewhere there existed a strong, handsome being, with a valorous nature, at once exalted and refined, with the heart of a poet in the shape of an angel, a lyre with strings of brass, sounding elegiac epithalamiums to the heavens, then why mightn't she, by chance, find him? Oh, how impossible! And anyway, nothing was worth the difficulty of such a search; everything was a lie! Every smile hid a yawn of boredom, every joy a malediction, every pleasure its own disgust, and the sweetest kisses left on your lips no more than a vain longing for a more sublime pleasure.

A prolonged metallic rattle whirred through the air and four strokes sounded from the convent bell. Four o'clock! and it seemed to her that she had been there on that bench for all eternity. But an infinity of passions can be contained within a minute, like a crowd of people in a small space.

Emma's life was completely occupied by her passions, and she worried no more about money than an archduchess.

One day, however, a sickly-looking man, red-faced and bald, entered her house declaring that he had been sent by Monsieur Vinçart of Rouen. He withdrew the pins fastening the side pocket of his long green frock coat, stuck them in his sleeve, and politely held out a piece of paper.

It was a note for seven hundred francs, signed by her, which Lheureux, despite all his protestations, had endorsed over to Vinçart.

She sent her servant to his house. He was unable to come.

Then the stranger, who had remained standing, glancing curiously to the right and left under the cover of his thick blond eyebrows, asked with a naïve air:

"What answer will I give Monsieur Vinçart?"

"Well," answered Emma, "tell him . . . that I don't have it . . . It'll have to be next week . . . He should wait . . . Yes. Next week."

And the fellow went off without uttering a word.

But the next day, at noon, she received a protest of nonpayment; and the sight of the official document, on which were displayed, in several places and in large letters, the words "Maître Hareng, Bailiff at Bucy," frightened her so much that she ran in all haste to the dry-goods merchant.

She found him in his shop, tying up a parcel.

"Your servant!" he said; "what can I do for you?"

Yet Lheureux went on with his task, helped by a slightly hunchbacked girl of about thirteen, who served him as both shop assistant and cook.

Then, his wooden shoes clattering on the floorboards of the shop, he preceded Madame up to the second floor and showed her into a cramped office where a large pine desk supported several ledgers secured by a transverse padlocked iron bar. Against the wall, under some lengths of calico, a strongbox could be seen, of such dimensions, however, that it had to contain something other than promissory notes and cash. Indeed, Monsieur Lheureux was a pawnbroker, and it was here that he had put Madame Bovary's gold chain, along with some earrings belonging to poor Père Tellier, who, having at last been obliged to sell, had bought a struggling grocery business in Quincampoix, where he was dying of his catarrh, his face yellower than the candles that surrounded him.

Lheureux sat down in his large straw armchair, saying:

"What is it now?"

"Here."

And she showed him the paper.

"Well, what can I do about it?"

Then she flew into a rage, reminding him of the promise he had given her not to circulate her notes; he admitted it.

"But I was forced to do it. I had a knife at my throat."

"And what's going to happen now?" she went on.

"Oh, it's very simple: a court order, and then seizure . . . ; no help for it!"

Emma had to restrain herself from striking him. She asked quietly if there was no way to appease Monsieur Vinçart.

"Oh, yes . . . appease Vinçart. You don't know him; he's fiercer than an Arab."

But Monsieur Lheureux simply had to intervene.

"Listen! It seems to me that, up to now, I've been quite good to you."

And, opening one of his ledgers:

"Here!"

Then, going up the page with his finger:

"Let's see . . . let's see . . . On August third, two hundred francs . . . On June seventeenth, one hundred fifty . . . March twenty-third, forty-six . . . In April . . ."

He stopped, as though afraid of doing something foolish.

"And I'm not saying anything about the notes signed by Monsieur, one for seven hundred francs, another for three hundred! As for your little payments on account, and the interest, there's no end to all of that, it's a real muddle. I'm not getting mixed up in it anymore!"

She was weeping; she even called him her "good Monsieur Lheureux." But he kept laying the blame on that "cunning dog Vinçart." Anyway, he himself didn't have a centime; no one was paying him at the moment; people were eating the wool off his back; a poor shopkeeper like him couldn't offer advances.

Emma fell silent; and Monsieur Lheureux, who was nibbling the barbs of a quill pen, probably began to worry about her silence, for he went on:

"Of course, if, one of these days, I were to receive some payments . . . I could possibly . . ."

"After all," she said, "as soon as the balance on Barneville . . ."

"What? . . ."

And, learning that Langlois had not yet paid, he seemed very surprised. Then, in a honey-smooth voice:

"And you say we can agree . . ."

"Oh, whatever you like!"

Then he closed his eyes in order to think, wrote down a few figures, and, declaring that it would be very hard for him, that the thing was risky and that he was *bleeding himself white,* he dictated four notes of 250 francs each, with due dates falling at intervals one month apart.

"Provided Vinçart is willing to listen to me! Anyway, we're agreed, I'm not trifling with you, I'm straight as an arrow."

Then he casually showed her several pieces of new merchandise, though not one of them, in his opinion, was worthy of Madame.

"Just think—here's dress goods for seven sous a meter, and certified dye-fast! And yet they swallow that! They don't get told different, you may well believe," wishing, by this confession that he swindled others, to convince her of his utter honesty.

Then he called her back, to show her three ells of point lace he had just picked up "at auction."

"Isn't it fine!" said Lheureux; "it's very much used nowadays, for antimacassars—it's the style."

And quicker than a conjurer, he wrapped the lace in blue paper and put it in Emma's hands.

"At least, could you let me know . . . ?"

"Ah! Later," he said, turning on his heels.

That evening, she pressed Bovary to write his mother and ask her to send them the balance of the inheritance at once. Her mother-in-law answered that she had nothing more: the settlement was done, and what was left for them, apart from Barneville, was six hundred livres yearly income, which she would pay out to them punctually.

Then Madame sent bills to two or three clients and soon made liberal use of this expedient, which was successful. She was always careful to add, as a postscript: "Don't speak of this to my husband, you know how proud he is . . . My apologies . . . Your servant . . ." There were a few complaints; she intercepted them.

To make some money for herself, she began selling her old gloves, her old hats, the old scrap iron; and she haggled rapaciously, —her peasant blood driving her to make a profit. Then, on her trips to the city, she would trade with secondhand dealers for knickknacks that Monsieur Lheureux, if no one else, would certainly buy from her. She bought herself ostrich feathers, Chinese porcelain, and round-topped chests; she borrowed from Félicité, from Madame Lefrançois, from the landlady of the Croix Rouge, from anyone, anywhere. Out of the money she received at last from Barneville, she paid two notes; the remaining fifteen hundred francs melted away. She signed new notes, and so it went on!

Sometimes, it is true, she would attempt some calculations; but she would discover things so exorbitant that she could not believe them. So she would begin again, quickly become muddled, drop it all at that point, and think no more about it.

The house was certainly dismal now! Tradesmen could be seen leaving with furious looks on their faces. Handkerchiefs were draped over the stoves; and little Berthe, to the great indignation of Madame Homais, wore stockings with holes in them. If Charles timidly ventured a comment, she would answer roughly that it was not her fault!

Why these fits of anger? He blamed it all on her old nervous complaint; and, reproaching himself for having mistaken her infirmities for defects of character, he would accuse himself of selfishness, and would want to rush over and take her in his arms.

"Oh, no!" he would say to himself. "I would only annoy her!"

And he would stay where he was.

After dinner, he would walk alone in the garden; he would take little Berthe on his knees, and, spreading out his medical journal, try to teach her to read. The child, who had never been given any schooling, would soon open wide her large, sad eyes and begin to cry. Then he would comfort her; he would go get some water for her in the watering can to make rivers in the sand, or break off branches of the privet hedge to plant trees in the flower beds, which hardly spoiled the garden, choked as it was with tall grass; they owed so many days' pay to Lestiboudois! Then the child would feel chilly and ask for her mother.

"Call your nanny, my dearest," Charles would say. "You know very well your mama doesn't like to be disturbed."

Autumn was beginning and already the leaves were falling, like two years ago, when she was so ill! When would it end! . . . And he would go on walking, his hands behind his back.

Madame was in her room. One did not go upstairs. She would remain there all day long, listless, half dressed, and, from time to time, burning pastilles of incense that she had bought in Rouen in a shop belonging to an Algerian. So as not to have that man lying there next to her at night asleep, she managed, by the unpleasant faces she made, to relegate him to the third floor; and till morning she would read lurid books full of orgies and scenes of bloodshed. Often she would become terrified, she would cry out, Charles would come running.

"Oh, go away!" she would say.

Or, at other times, burning more hotly with that secret flame that adultery had revived, breathless, agitated, consumed by desire, she would open her window, breathe in the cold air, toss her too-heavy mane of hair in the wind, and, looking at the stars, long for princely loves. She would think of him, of Léon. At such moments she would have given anything for a single one of those meetings with him, which so satiated her.

Those were her gala days. She wanted them to be splendid! And when he could not pay all the expenses himself, she would liberally make up the difference, which happened almost every time. He tried to persuade her that they would be just as happy elsewhere, in a more modest hotel; but she found objections.

One day, she drew from her bag six little silver-plated spoons (they were

Père Rouault's wedding present) and asked him to take them immediately to the pawnbroker for her; and Léon complied, though he did not like doing it. He was afraid of compromising himself.

Then, as he thought about it afterward, he felt that his mistress was behaving strangely and that people were perhaps not wrong to want to separate him from her.

Indeed, someone had sent his mother a long anonymous letter, warning her that he was *ruining himself with a married woman;* and right away the good lady, having visions of that eternal bogey of family life, that ill-defined, pernicious creature, that siren, that fantastic monster inhabiting the depths of love, wrote to Maître Dubocage, his employer, who behaved perfectly in this matter. He detained him for three-quarters of an hour, trying to unseal his eyes, to warn him of the chasm before him. Such an intrigue would later hurt his chances of establishing himself. He entreated him to break it off, and, if he would not make the sacrifice in his own interest, at least to do it for him, Dubocage!

In the end, Léon had sworn not to see Emma again; and he reproached himself for not having kept his word, considering all that this woman might still draw down upon him in the way of trouble and talk, not to mention the jokes his fellow clerks traded around the stove every morning. Besides, he was about to be made head clerk: the time had come to be serious. And so he gave up the flute, exalted sentiments, and the fancies of the imagination; —for in the heat of his youth, every bourgeois man has believed, if only for a day, for a minute, that he is capable of boundless passions, lofty enterprises. The most halfhearted libertine has dreamed of sultans' wives; every notary carries within him the remains of a poet.

He became bored, now, when Emma suddenly burst into sobs on his chest; and, like people who cannot endure more than a certain dose of music, his heart would grow drowsy with indifference at the din raised by a love whose refinements he could no longer see.

They knew each other too well to experience, in their mutual possession, that wonder which multiplies the joy of it a hundred times over. She was as weary of him as he was tired of her. Emma was rediscovering in adultery all the platitudes of marriage.

But how could she get rid of him? And then, though she might feel humiliated at the baseness of such a happiness, she clung to it out of habit or depravity; and every day, she pursued it more eagerly, exhausting all pleasure by wanting it to be too great. She blamed Léon for her disappointed hopes, as if he had betrayed her; and she even longed for some catastrophe that would cause them to separate, since she did not have the courage to resolve to do it herself.

Yet she continued to write him loving letters, believing in the principle that a woman must always write to her lover.

But as she wrote, she saw a different man, a phantom created out of her most ardent memories, the most beautiful things she had read, her strongest desires; and in the end he became so real, and so accessible, that she would tremble, marveling, and yet be unable to imagine him clearly, so lost was he, like a god, under the abundance of his attributes. He inhabited that blue-tinted land where silken ladders sway from balconies, amid the breath of flowers, in the moonlight. She would sense him near her; he was going to come and sweep her away in a single kiss. Then she would fall back, shattered; for these transports of vague love tired her more than prolonged debauchery.

She was experiencing, now, a general and constant aching exhaustion. Often, Emma would receive summonses, official stamped documents that she would scarcely look at. She wished she could stop living, or sleep all the time.

On Mid-Lent Day, she did not return to Yonville; in the evening she went to a masked ball. She wore velvet breeches and red stockings, a wig with a queue, and a cocked hat over one ear. She leaped about all night to the frenetic sounds of the trombones; people gathered around her in a circle; and in the morning she found herself in the portico of the theater with five or six masqueraders, stevedores and sailors, friends of Léon's, who were talking about going somewhere for supper.

The cafés in the neighborhood were full. Down by the harbor, they spotted a very mediocre restaurant whose proprietor opened a small room for them on the fifth floor.

The men whispered in a corner, doubtless conferring about the cost. There were a clerk, two medical students, and a shop assistant: what company for her! As for the women, Emma quickly realized from the quality of their voices that they had to be, almost all of them, of the lowest class. She felt frightened, then, pushed back her chair and lowered her eyes.

The others began to eat. She did not eat; her forehead was burning, her eyelids were tingling, and her skin was icy cold. In her head she could still feel the dance floor rebounding under the rhythmic pulsation of the thousand dancing feet. Then she grew dizzy from the smell of the punch and the smoke from the cigars. She fainted; they carried her to the window.

Day was beginning to break, and a large patch of crimson was widening in the pale sky toward Sainte-Catherine hill. The livid surface of the river was shivering in the wind; the bridges were deserted; the streetlights were going out.

She revived, however, and by chance thought of Berthe, asleep back there in her nanny's room. But a cart full of long strips of iron went by, casting a deafening metallic vibration against the walls of the houses.

She abruptly slipped away from the place, got rid of her costume, told Léon she had to go home, and was at last alone in the Hôtel de Boulogne. Everything seemed unbearable to her, even herself. She wished she could escape like a bird, go recapture her youth somewhere far, far away, in the immaculate reaches of space.

She went out, she crossed the boulevard, the place Cauchoise, and the outskirts of the city, coming to a street in the open that overlooked some gardens. She was walking quickly; the fresh air quieted her; and gradually the faces of the crowd, the masks, the quadrilles, the chandeliers, the meal afterward, those women—everything disappeared like mist blown off by the wind. Then, back at the Croix Rouge, she threw herself on her bed, in the little room on the third floor with the prints of *The Tower of Nesle*. At four o'clock in the afternoon, Hivert woke her.

When she returned home, Félicité showed her a gray sheet of paper behind the clock. She read:

"In accordance with the written instrument, in formal execution of a judgment . . ."

What judgment? In fact, another paper had been delivered the day before, of which she had no knowledge; and so she was stupefied by the following words:

"Madame Bovary is hereby commanded by order of the king, the law, and the courts . . ."

Then, skipping a few lines, she saw:

"Within not more than twenty-four hours."—What? "To pay the total sum of eight thousand francs." And there was even, lower down: "To this she shall be constrained by every legal recourse, and notably by the seizure of her furniture and effects."

What was she to do? . . . Within twenty-four hours; tomorrow! Lheureux, she thought, no doubt wanted to frighten her again; for she suddenly understood all his maneuvers, the purpose behind his obliging manner. What reassured her was the very exaggeration of the sum.

Yet, by dint of buying, never paying, borrowing, signing notes, then renewing those notes, which increased each time they came due, she had ended by amassing for Sieur Lheureux a capital that he was awaiting impatiently, to use in his speculations.

She presented herself at his shop with a casual air.

"Do you know what's happened to me? It must be a joke!"

"No."

"What do you mean?"

He turned away slowly and said, crossing his arms:

"Did you think, my dear lady, that I was going to serve as your outfitter and banker for all eternity simply for the love of God? I must recover my outlay—let's be fair!"

She exclaimed over the debt.

"Too bad! The court has acknowledged it! There's been a judgment! You were notified! Besides, it isn't me, it's Vinçart."

"But couldn't you possibly . . ."

"Not a thing!"

"But . . . still . . . let's talk it over."

And she cast about for excuses; she had known nothing . . . it was a surprise . . .

"Whose fault is that?" said Lheureux, bowing to her ironically. "I slave like a Negro, and you're out kicking up your heels."

"Ah! Don't moralize!"

"It never hurts," he replied.

She was craven, she begged him; and she even laid her pretty long, white hand on the merchant's knee.

"Don't touch me! One would think you were trying to seduce me!"

"You're a scoundrel!" she cried.

"Oh, oh! How you do go on!" he answered, laughing.

"I'll tell everyone what you are. I'll tell my husband . . ."

"Well, I have something to show him—your husband!"

And Lheureux took from his strongbox the receipt for eighteen hundred francs that she had given him at the time of the Vinçart discount.

"Do you think," he added, "that he won't understand your little theft, the poor dear fellow?"

She collapsed, more stunned than if she had been hit over the head with a club. He was walking back and forth between the window and the desk, saying over and over:

"Oh, I'll show it to him . . . I'll show it to him . . ."

Then he approached her, and, in a soft voice:

"It's not funny, I know; yet no one has ever died of it, and since it's the only way you have left to pay me back my money . . ."

"But where will I find it?" said Emma, wringing her hands.

"Oh, nonsense! With as many friends as you have . . . !"

And he gave her a look so shrewd and so terrible that she shuddered to the depths of her being.

"I promise you," she said, "I'll sign . . ."

"I've had enough of your signatures!"

"I'll sell . . ."

"Come now!" he said, shrugging his shoulders, "you've nothing left."

And he called through the peephole that opened into the shop:

"Annette! Don't forget the three remnants of number fourteen."

The servant appeared; Emma understood and asked how much money he would need to stop all the proceedings.

"It's too late!"

"But what if I brought you a few thousand francs, a quarter of the sum, a third, almost all of it?"

"No! It's no use!"

He pushed her gently toward the stairs.

"I beg you, Monsieur Lheureux, just a few more days!"

She was sobbing.

"Ah, that's good! Tears!"

"You're driving me to despair!"

"I really don't care!" he said, closing the door behind her.

[7]

She was stoical, the next day, when Maître Hareng, the bailiff, presented himself at her house with two witnesses to draw up the inventory of the seizure.

They began with Bovary's consulting room and did not write down the phrenological head, which was considered a *tool of his profession;* but in the kitchen they counted the plates, the pots, the chairs, the candlesticks, and, in her bedroom, every knickknack on the étagère. They examined her dresses, the linen, the dressing room; and her life itself, down to its most private recesses, was spread out at full length, like a cadaver being autopsied, under the eyes of these three men.

Maître Hareng, buttoned up in a thin black coat, wearing a white cravat and very tight shoe straps, repeated from time to time:

"If you'll allow me, madame? If you'll allow me?"

He often exclaimed:

"Charming! . . . Very pretty!"

Then he would go back to writing, dipping his pen in the horn inkwell he held in his left hand.

When they were finished with the other rooms, they went up to the attic.

She kept a desk there in which Rodolphe's letters were locked up. It had to be opened.

"Ah! A correspondence!" said Maître Hareng with a discreet smile. "But if you'll allow me . . . ! For I must make sure the box does not contain anything else."

And he tilted the papers slightly, as though to make some napoleons fall out of them. She was seized with indignation at the sight of that thick, red hand, its fingers soft as slugs, resting on those pages in which her very heart had beaten.

At last they left! Félicité came back. She had sent her to keep watch and intercept Bovary; and they quickly installed the bailiff's watchman up under the roof, where he swore he would remain.

During the evening, Charles seemed to her careworn. Emma studied him with an anguished gaze, believing she could read accusations in the wrinkles on his face. Then, when her eyes rested again on the mantelpiece decorated with Chinese screens, on the wide drapes, the armchairs, all those things that had sweetened the bitterness of her life, she would be overcome with remorse, or, rather, with a vast regret that stimulated her passion rather than killing it. Charles placidly poked the fire, his feet on the andirons.

At one moment the watchman, probably growing bored in his hiding place, made a slight noise.

"Is someone walking around up there?" said Charles.

"No!" she answered. "An attic window's been left open, it's blowing in the wind."

She set off for Rouen the following day, a Sunday, in order to call on all the bankers whose names she knew. They were in the country or away on a trip. She did not give up; and those whom she was able to meet, she asked for money, protesting that she needed it, that she would pay it back. Some of them laughed in her face; all of them refused her.

At two o'clock, she hurried to Léon's place, knocked on his door. No one opened. At last he appeared.

"What brings you here?"

"Does it bother you?"

"No . . . but . . ."

And he confessed that the landlord did not like them to entertain "women."

"I have to talk to you," she said.

Then he reached for his key. She stopped him.

"No! At our place."

And they went to their room at the Hôtel de Boulogne.

As soon as she got there, she drank a large glass of water. She was very pale. She said:

"Léon, you have to do me a favor."

And, shaking him by his two hands, which she was squeezing tight, she added:

"Listen, I need eight thousand francs!"

"You're out of your mind!"

"Not yet!"

And immediately, telling him all about the seizure, she revealed the trouble she was in; for Charles was ignorant of everything, her mother-in-law detested her, Père Rouault could do nothing; but he, Léon, must set about finding this indispensable sum . . .

"How do you expect me to . . . ?"

"How spineless you're being!" she exclaimed.

Then he said stupidly:

"You're exaggerating how bad it is. Perhaps with a thousand ecus your man would calm down."

All the more reason to try something; they couldn't possibly fail to locate three thousand francs. Besides, Léon could sign for it instead of her.

"Go on! Try! You must! Hurry! . . . Oh, try! Try! I will love you so much!"

He went out, came back after an hour, and said with a solemn face:

"I went to three people . . . no use!"

They sat face-to-face, on either side of the fireplace, motionless, silent. Emma was shrugging her shoulders and tapping her feet impatiently. Then he heard her murmur:

"If I were in your place, I would certainly know where to find it!"

"Well, where?"

"In your office!"

And she looked at him.

A diabolical boldness emanated from her burning eyes, and her lids lowered in a lascivious and encouraging manner; —so that the young man felt himself weakening under the mute will of this woman who was urging him to commit a crime. Then he was afraid, and, in order to avoid further explanations, he struck himself on the forehead, exclaiming:

"Morel is supposed to come back tonight! He won't refuse me, I hope." (This was one of his friends, the son of a wealthy businessman.) "And I'll bring it to you tomorrow," he added.

Emma did not seem to greet this hope with as much joy as he had imagined. Did she suspect he was lying? Blushing, he went on:

"But if you don't see me by three, don't wait any longer, dear. I have to go, forgive me. Goodbye!"

He clasped her hand, but it felt quite inert to him. Emma no longer had the strength to feel anything.

Four o'clock chimed; and she rose to go back to Yonville, obeying, like an automaton, the force of her habits.

The weather was fine; it was one of those clear, raw March days when the sun shines from a pure, cloudless sky. The people of Rouen in their

Sunday best were out for a walk, looking happy. She reached the place du Parvis. People were coming from vespers; the crowd was pouring out through the three doors like a river through the three arches of a bridge, and among them, stiller than a rock, stood the verger.

Then she remembered the day when, anxious and full of hope, she had entered that great nave, which, extending before her, was not as deep as her love; and she walked on, weeping under her veil, dazed, faltering, nearly fainting.

"Look out!" shouted a voice from behind a carriage gate as it opened.

She stopped to make way for a black horse that came out prancing between the shafts of a tilbury driven by a gentleman in sable furs. Who was it? She knew him . . . The carriage plunged forward and disappeared.

Why, it was he, the Vicomte! She turned back: the street was deserted. And she was so stricken, so sad, that she leaned against a wall to keep from falling.

Then she thought she had been mistaken. The truth was, she had no idea. Everything, within and outside her, was abandoning her. She felt lost, tumbling haphazardly through indefinable chasms; and it was almost with joy that she saw, when she reached the Croix Rouge, good old Homais watching as a large box full of pharmaceutical supplies was loaded onto the *Hirondelle.* In his hand he held, wrapped in a scarf, six *cheminots* for his wife.

Madame Homais was very fond of these heavy little turban-shaped loaves that are eaten with salted butter during Lent: a last relic of Gothic food, dating back perhaps to the century of the Crusades, and one with which the robust Normans used to stuff themselves, believing that before them on the table, in the light of their yellow torches, between the jugs of hippocras and the giant slabs of pork, lay the heads of Saracens waiting to be devoured. The apothecary's wife would chomp them heroically, like the Normans, despite her deplorable set of teeth; and so, each time Monsieur Homais went to town, he did not fail to bring some back to her, buying them always from the great baker in the rue Massacre.

"Charmed to see you!" he said, offering Emma his hand to help her into the *Hirondelle.*

Then he hung the *cheminots* from the thin straps of the baggage net and sat there bareheaded, his arms folded, in a posture both pensive and Napoleonic.

But when the Blind Man appeared as usual at the foot of the hill, he exclaimed:

"I can't understand why the authorities continue to tolerate such dishonest occupations! These unfortunate creatures ought to be locked up and forced to do some sort of work! Progress, upon my word, moves at the pace of a tortoise! We're wallowing in utter barbarity!"

The Blind Man was holding out his hat, and it swung to and fro at the edge of the carriage window like a pucker of tapestry that had come loose from its tack.

"That," said the pharmacist, "is a scrofulous disease!"

And though he knew the poor devil, he pretended to be seeing him for the first time, murmured the words "cornea," "opaque cornea," "sclerotic," "facies," then asked him in a fatherly tone:

"Have you had this dreadful infirmity for long, my friend? Instead of getting drunk in cafés, you'd do better to follow a regimen."

He urged him to take only good wine and good beer and to eat good roast meat. The Blind Man continued his song; he seemed, in fact, nearly imbecilic. At last, Monsieur Homais opened his purse.

"Here—here's a sou; give me back two liards; and don't forget my advice; you'll find you're better off for it."

Hivert allowed himself to voice some doubts as to its efficacy. But the apothecary guaranteed he would cure the man himself, with an antiphlogistic salve of his own making, and he gave his address:

"Monsieur Homais, near the market, well enough known thereabouts."

"Now, in return for our trouble," said Hivert, "you'll *perform your act.*"

The Blind Man crouched down on his haunches, threw back his head, and, rolling his greenish eyes and sticking out his tongue, rubbed his stomach with both hands while uttering a sort of muffled howl, like a famished dog. Emma, filled with disgust, tossed him a five-franc coin over her shoulder. It was her entire fortune. She felt it was a grand gesture to throw it away like that.

The carriage had started off again when suddenly Monsieur Homais leaned out the window and shouted:

"Nothing farinaceous and no dairy products! Wear wool against your skin and expose the diseased areas to juniper-berry smoke!"

The sight of things she knew filing past before her eyes gradually distracted Emma from her present pain. An intolerable weariness overcame her, and she reached home stupefied, dispirited, almost asleep.

"Let whatever happens, happen!" she said to herself.

And anyway, who could tell—why shouldn't something extraordinary occur at any moment? Lheureux might even die.

She was awakened at nine o'clock the next morning by the sound of voices in the square. A crowd had gathered in the market to read a large notice stuck to one of the poles, and she saw Justin climb up on a guard stone and tear the notice down. But at that moment, the rural policeman seized him by the collar. Monsieur Homais came out of the pharmacy, and Mère Lefrançois, in the middle of the crowd, seemed to be holding forth.

"Madame! Madame!" exclaimed Félicité as she came inside; "it's scandalous!"

And the poor girl, very upset, handed her a sheet of yellow paper she had just ripped from the door. With a quick glance, Emma read that all her goods were to be sold.

Then they contemplated each other in silence. The two of them, servant and mistress, had no secrets from each other. At last Félicité sighed:

"If I was you, Madame, I would go see Monsieur Guillaumin."

"Do you think . . . ?"

And that question meant:

"You know the household through the manservant—do you think the master might sometimes have talked about me?"

"Yes, go there—you'd best go."

She dressed, putting on her black gown and her bonnet with the jet beads; and so that no one would see her (there were still many people in the square), she headed out of the village by the path along the water.

She was out of breath when she reached the notary's gate; the sky was dark, and a little snow was falling.

At the sound of the bell, Théodore, in a red vest, appeared on the front steps; he came to open the gate for her almost familiarly, as though for someone he knew well, and showed her into the dining room.

A large porcelain stove hummed under a cactus plant that filled the niche, and in frames of black wood, against the oak-grained wallpaper, hung Steuben's *Esmeralda* and Schopin's *Potiphar*. The laid table, the two silver chafing dishes, the crystal doorknobs, the parquet floor, and the furniture, all gleamed with a meticulous, English cleanliness; the windowpanes were decorated, at each corner, with colored glass.

"This," Emma was thinking, "is the kind of dining room I ought to have."

The notary came in wearing a dressing gown printed with palm trees, which he pressed against his body with his left arm, while with his right hand he doffed and then quickly replaced his maroon velvet toque, pretentiously positioned on the right side; from it emerged the ends of three strands of fair hair that, starting at the back of his head, encircled his bald skull.

After he had offered her a seat, he sat down to breakfast, apologizing profusely for his impoliteness.

"Monsieur," she said, "I would like to ask you . . ."

"What, madame? I'm listening."

She began to describe her situation.

Maître Guillaumin was aware of it, having a secret association with the dry-goods merchant, from whom he regularly acquired the capital for the mortgage loans that he was asked to contract.

So he knew (even better than she) the long history of those notes, very small at first, bearing various names as endorsers, with due dates spaced out at long intervals and renewed continually, until the day when, gathering up all the writs of nonpayment, the merchant had entrusted his friend Vinçart with taking the necessary legal actions in his own name, not wanting to be viewed as a monster by his fellow villagers.

She punctuated her story with recriminations against Lheureux, recriminations to which the notary responded from time to time with a meaningless word. Eating his cutlet and drinking his tea, he lowered his chin into his sky-blue cravat, which was stuck with two diamond pins linked by a small gold chain; and he was smiling a singular smile, sickly-sweet and equivocal. But noticing that her feet were damp:

"Do move closer to the stove . . . put them higher up . . . against the porcelain."

She was afraid of dirtying it. The notary continued gallantly:

"Pretty things never do any harm."

Then she tried to move him to sympathy and, becoming emotional herself, told him about her household's slender means, her troubles, her needs. He understood—such an elegant woman!—and, without interrupting his meal, he had turned right around toward her, so that his knee brushed against her boot, whose sole was curled, steaming, against the stove.

But when she asked him for a thousand ecus, he tightened his lips, then declared that he was very sorry not to have had the management of her capital earlier, for there were a hundred convenient ways, even for a lady, of increasing her funds. In the peat bogs of Grumesnil or the lands around Le Havre, one could have ventured excellent speculations, with almost sure results; and he allowed her to consume herself with rage at the thought of the fantastic sums she could certainly have made.

"How was it," he went on, "that you never came to me?"

"I don't really know," she said.

"Why? Eh? . . . Were you perhaps afraid of me? I'm the one who should be complaining! We hardly know each other! Yet I'm deeply devoted to you; you don't doubt that now, I hope?"

He reached out his hand, took hers, pressed a greedy kiss upon it, then kept it on his knee; and he played with her fingers delicately, murmuring a thousand sweet things to her.

His toneless voice whispered on like a running brook; a spark leaped from his eye through the glittering lens of his glasses; and his hands moved up inside Emma's sleeve, to knead her arm. Against her cheek she felt the touch of his uneven breath. The man was bothering her horribly.

She sprang to her feet and said:

"Monsieur, I'm waiting!"

"For what?" cried the notary, suddenly growing extremely pale.

"The money!"

"But . . ."

Then, yielding to an overpowering surge of desire:

"Well, yes, all right! . . ."

He was dragging himself toward her on his knees, without concern for his dressing gown.

"For mercy's sake! Don't go! I love you!"

He seized her around the waist.

A flood of crimson rushed into Madame Bovary's face. She recoiled with a terrible look and cried:

"It's shameless of you to take advantage of my distress, monsieur! I'm to be pitied, but I'm not for sale!"

And she went out.

The notary remained quite stupefied, his eyes fixed on his handsome carpet slippers. They had been the gift of a lover. The sight of them finally consoled him. Besides, he was thinking, such an adventure would have taken him too far.

"What a scoundrel! What a boor! . . . What a foul thing to do!" she was saying to herself, fleeing with a quick step under the aspens that lined the road. Disappointment at her lack of success added force to the indignation she felt at the insult to her modesty; it seemed to her that Providence was pursuing her relentlessly, and, filled with pride at this thought, never had she felt so much esteem for herself nor so much contempt for others. Some fighting spirit was transporting her. She longed to strike out at all men, spit in their faces, crush every one of them; and she walked rapidly straight on, pale, trembling, enraged, searching the empty horizon with tearful eyes, as though reveling in the hatred that was suffocating her.

When she caught sight of her house, she felt suddenly numb. She could not go on; and yet she had to; besides, where could she run away to?

Félicité was waiting for her on the doorstep.

"Well?"

"No!" said Emma.

And for a quarter of an hour, the two of them conferred about the various people in Yonville who might be willing to help her. But each time Félicité named someone, Emma would reply:

"Impossible! They wouldn't!"

"And Monsieur will be coming home!"

"I know, I know . . . Leave me, I want to be alone."

She had tried everything. There was nothing left now; and so when Charles appeared, she was going to say to him:

"Go back outside. That carpet you're walking on isn't ours anymore. Not a thing in your house belongs to you anymore, not a stick of furniture, not a pin, not a piece of straw, and I'm the one who has ruined you, you poor man!"

Then he would give a great sob, then he would weep and weep, and at last, after his surprise had passed, he would forgive her.

"Yes," she muttered, clenching her teeth, "he'll forgive me. He! —whereas even if he gave me a million it wouldn't be enough to induce me to forgive him for having known me . . . Never! Never!"

The thought of Bovary's superiority over her enraged her. And whether or not she confessed, he would at any moment now, soon, tomorrow, learn about the catastrophe; therefore, she would have to wait for the dreadful scene and suffer the burden of his magnanimity. She felt a desire to return to Lheureux's shop: what was the use? To write to her father; it was too late. And perhaps she was regretting, now, that she had not yielded to the other man, when she heard a horse trotting down the alley. It was he, he was opening the gate, he was paler than the plaster wall. Rushing down the stairs, she fled through the square; and the mayor's wife, who was chatting with Lestiboudois in front of the church, saw her go into the tax collector's house.

Madame Tuvache hurried off to tell Madame Caron. The two ladies went up into the attic; and, concealed by some linen laid over the drying racks, they positioned themselves comfortably where they could see the whole interior of Binet's place.

He was alone, in his mansard room, busily copying, in wood, one of those ivory ornaments impossible to describe, composed of crescents and of spheres carved one inside the other, the whole standing erect like an obelisk and useful for nothing; and he was just cutting into the last part, he was reaching the end! In the chiaroscuro of his workshop, the blond dust flew up from his tool like a plume of sparks under the iron shoes of a galloping horse; the two wheels were turning, droning; Binet was smiling, his chin lowered, his nostrils wide; and he seemed lost in that state of complete happiness induced, most probably, only by a mediocre occupation that entertains the mind with easy challenges and gratifies it with a success beyond which there is nothing further to aspire to.

"Ah! There she is!" said Madame Tuvache.

But it was hardly possible, because of the lathe, to hear what she was saying.

At last, the ladies believed they could distinguish the word "francs," and Mère Tuvache breathed very softly:

"She's asking him for an extension in paying her taxes."

"It would seem so!" said the other.

They saw her pacing back and forth, examining the napkin rings, the candlesticks, the banister knobs displayed against the walls, while Binet stroked his beard with satisfaction.

"Has she perhaps come to order something from him?" asked Madame Tuvache.

"But he never sells anything!" objected her neighbor.

The notary seemed to be listening, at the same time widening his eyes as if he did not understand. She went on, her manner affectionate and supplicating. She moved closer to him; her breast was heaving; they were no longer talking.

"Is she making advances to him?" asked Madame Tuvache.

Binet was flushed all the way to his ears. She took his hands.

"Ah! This is too much!"

And no doubt she was proposing something scandalous; for the tax collector—though he was a brave man, had fought at Bautzen and at Lützen, had taken part in the French campaign, and had even been *proposed for the Legion of Honor*—suddenly recoiled well back from her, as though he had seen a snake, and exclaimed:

"Madame! What can you be thinking? . . ."

"Such women ought to be whipped!" said Madame Tuvache.

"Now where is she?" said Madame Caron.

For she had disappeared while they were speaking; then they spotted her going down the Grande-Rue and turning right, as though heading toward the cemetery, and they lost themselves in conjectures.

"Mère Rolet," she said, when she reached the wet nurse's house, "I can't breathe! . . . Undo my laces."

She collapsed on the bed; she was sobbing. Mère Rolet covered her with a petticoat and remained standing by her. Then, when she did not answer, the good woman moved away, took up her spinning wheel, and began spinning some flax.

"Oh! Stop it!" she murmured, thinking she heard Binet's lathe.

"What's bothering her?" the nurse wondered. "Why has she come here?"

She had rushed there, impelled by a kind of terror that drove her from her house.

Lying on her back, motionless, her eyes fixed, she could discern things only indistinctly, though she applied her attention to them with an absurd persistence. She stared at the flakes of plaster on the walls, two sticks of firewood smoking end to end, and a large spider above her head walking in a cleft in the beam. At last she gathered her thoughts. She remembered . . . One day, with Léon . . . Oh, how distant it was! . . . The sun was shining on the river, and the clematis smelled lovely . . . Then, swept along by her memories as though by a boiling torrent, she soon recalled the previous day.

"What time is it?" she asked.

Mère Rolet went outside, held up the fingers of her right hand toward the brightest part of the sky, and slowly came back in, saying:

"Almost three o'clock."

"Oh! Thank you, thank you!"

For he would come. She was sure of it! He would have got some money. But perhaps he would go down to her house, without suspecting that she was here; and she ordered the nurse to run to her house and get him.

"Hurry!"

"But my dear lady, I'm going! I'm going!"

She was surprised, now, that she had not thought of him right away; yesterday, he had given his word, he would not break it; and already she saw herself at Lheureux's, spreading out the three banknotes on his desk. Then she would have to invent a story to explain things to Bovary. What would it be?

Meanwhile, the nurse was taking a long time returning. But as there was no clock in the cottage, Emma was afraid she might be exaggerating how much time had passed. She began to take little walks around the garden, step by step; she went down the path along the hedge and returned quickly, hoping the good woman might have come home another way. At last, tired of waiting, assailed by suspicions that she thrust away, no longer knowing if she had been there for a hundred years or a minute, she sat down in a corner and closed her eyes and blocked her ears. The gate creaked: she leaped up; before she could speak, Mère Rolet said:

"There's nobody at your house!"

"What?"

"No! No one! And Monsieur is weeping. He's calling you. They're looking for you."

Emma did not answer. She was breathing hard and staring wildly all around, while the countrywoman, frightened by her face, was instinctively backing away, thinking she was mad. Suddenly she struck her forehead and cried out, for the memory of Rodolphe, like a great bolt of lightning on a dark night, had entered her mind. He was so good, so sensitive, so generous! And besides, if he should hesitate to do her this service, she would know quite well how to force him by reminding him, with a single glance, of their lost love. She therefore set off toward La Huchette, quite unaware that she was hastening to yield to the very thing that had, only recently, so enraged her, nor in the least suspecting that she was prostituting herself.

[8]

She asked herself, as she walked: "What am I going to say? Where will I begin?" And as she came closer, she recognized the shrubs, the trees, the furze on the hill, the château beyond. She found herself experiencing once again the sensations of her first love, and her poor, contracted heart swelled with affection. A warm wind was blowing in her face; the snow, melting, fell drop by drop from the buds onto the grass.

She entered, as she used to, by the little gate into the park, then came to the main courtyard, which was bordered by a double row of thick-leaved lime trees. Their branches swayed, whistling. The dogs in the kennel all began to bark, and though the explosion of their voices echoed and reechoed, no one appeared.

She went up the broad, straight staircase, with its wooden banisters, that led to the hallway paved with dusty flagstones onto which many bedrooms opened, one after another, as in a monastery or an inn. His was at the end, at the very back, on the left. When she put her fingers on the latch, her strength suddenly abandoned her. She was afraid he would not be there, she almost wished he would not be, and yet this was her only hope, her last chance for salvation. She collected herself for a minute, and then, strengthening her resolve with a sense of the present necessity, she went in.

He was in front of the fire, his feet against the mantel, smoking a pipe.

"Why, it's you!" he said, standing up abruptly.

"Yes, it's me! . . . Rodolphe, I need your advice."

And despite all her efforts, it was impossible for her to unclench her teeth.

"You haven't changed, you're as charming as ever!"

"Oh—my charms!" she said bitterly. "They must be wretched enough, my dear friend, since you chose to reject them."

Then he started in upon an explanation of his behavior, excusing himself in vague terms, since he could not invent something better.

She allowed herself to be persuaded by his words, even more by his voice and by the sight of his person, so much so that she pretended to believe, or perhaps did believe, the excuse he gave for their break: it was a secret on which the honor and even the life of a third person depended.

"It doesn't matter!" she said, looking at him sadly. "I suffered a good deal!"

He answered philosophically:

"Life is like that!"

"Has it been good to you, at least," Emma went on, "since we separated?"

"Oh! Neither good . . . nor bad . . ."

"Perhaps it would have been better if we'd never left each other."

"Yes . . . perhaps!"

"Do you think so?" she said, moving closer to him.

And she sighed:

"Oh, Rodolphe! If you only knew! . . . I really loved you!"

It was then that she took his hand, and they remained for some time with their fingers intertwined—as on the first day, at the Agricultural Fair! Pride was making him struggle against his feelings of tenderness. But, leaning against his chest, she said to him:

"How did you expect me to live without you? One can't break the habit of being happy, you know! I was desperate! I thought I was going to die! I'll tell you about it; you'll see how it was. And you . . . you stayed away from me! . . ."

Because he had indeed carefully avoided her, for the past three years, out of that natural cowardice characteristic of the stronger sex; and Emma went on, with enchanting little motions of her head, more winning than an amorous cat:

"You've loved other women, admit it. Oh, I understand them, you know! I forgive them; you probably seduced them, the way you seduced me. You're a man! Everything about you would make a woman cherish you. But you and I will start all over again, won't we? We'll love each other! See, I'm laughing, I'm happy! . . . Say something, won't you?"

And she was ravishing to look at, a tear trembling in her eye like water from a rainstorm in the blue chalice of a flower.

He drew her down on his knees, and with the back of his hand he caressed her smooth bands of hair, where, in the light of dusk, a last ray of sunlight gleamed like an arrow of gold. She bowed her head; at last he kissed her on the eyelids, very gently, with the tips of his lips.

"But you've been crying!" he said. "Why?"

She burst into sobs. Rodolphe thought it was from the violence of her love; when she said nothing, he took that silence for a last feeling of modesty, and he exclaimed:

"Ah, forgive me! You're the only one I care about. I've been idiotic and wicked! I love you, I'll always love you! . . . What's the matter? Please tell me!"

He was on his knees.

"Well, then . . . I'm ruined, Rodolphe! You must lend me three thousand francs!"

"But . . . but . . . ," he said, slowly getting to his feet, a grave expression coming over his features.

"You know," she went on quickly, "my husband had placed the whole of his fortune with a notary; he ran off. We borrowed; the patients weren't paying. In fact, the settlement of the estate isn't done yet; we'll have something later. But today, because we don't have three thousand francs, they're taking possession of our things; it's happening now, at this very instant; and so, counting on your friendship, I've come to you."

"Ah!" thought Rodolphe, suddenly turning very pale. "That's why she came!"

At last he said calmly:

"I don't have it, dear lady."

He was not lying. If he had had it, he would probably have given it, unpleasant though it usually is to make such handsome gestures: a request for money, of all the tempests that may descend upon love, being the coldest and most profoundly destructive.

At first she went on staring at him for a long moment.

"You don't have it!"

She said it again several times:

"You don't have it! . . . I ought to have spared myself this final humiliation. You never loved me! You're no better than the rest!"

She was giving herself away, she was destroying herself.

Rodolphe broke in, declaring that he was "hard up" himself.

"Oh, I'm sorry for you!" said Emma. "I'm so sorry for you! . . ."

And, her eyes falling on a damascened rifle shining in a display of arms:

"But when you're as poor as that, you don't put silver on the stock of your rifle! You don't buy a clock with tortoiseshell inlays!" she went on, pointing to the Boulle clock. "Or silver-gilt whistles for your whips"—she touched them—"or watch charms for your watch chain! Oh! he lacks for nothing! There's even a liqueur stand in his bedroom; for you pamper yourself, you live well, you have a château, farms, woods; you hunt, you travel to Paris . . . Oh! even these—" she exclaimed, taking his cuff links from the mantelpiece, "the least of your foolish things!—can be turned into money! . . . Oh! But I don't want them!—keep them!"

And she hurled the cuff links from her, their gold chain snapping as they struck the wall.

"But I—I would have given you everything, I would have sold everything, I would have worked with my hands, I would have begged by the roadside, for a smile, for a glance, just to hear you say 'Thank you!' And you sit there quietly in your chair, as if you hadn't already made me suffer enough? Without you, you know very well, I could have been happy! What made you do it? Was it a wager? Yet you loved me, you used to say so . . . And just now you said it again . . . Ah! you'd have done better to throw me out! My hands are still warm from your kisses, and here's the very place, on the carpet, where you crouched at my knees and swore you'd love me forever. You made me believe it: for two years, you enticed me along in the most magnificent, the sweetest of dreams! . . . Oh, yes! and our plans for going away, do you remember? Oh, your letter! Your letter tore my heart to pieces! . . . And then, when I come back to him—and he's rich, and happy, and free!—to implore him for help, help that anyone in the world would give, when I come begging, bringing back all my love, he rejects me, because it would cost him three thousand francs!"

"I don't have it!" answered Rodolphe with that perfect calm with which resigned anger covers itself like a shield.

She went out. The walls were trembling, the ceiling was crushing her; and she walked back down the long avenue, stumbling over the piles of dead leaves that were scattering in the wind. At last she reached the ditch in front of the gate; she broke her nails on the latch, so frantic was she to open it. Then, a hundred paces farther on, breathless, nearly falling, she stopped. And, turning, she once again saw the impassive château, with its park, its gardens, its three courtyards, the many windows of its façade.

She stood there lost in a daze, no longer aware of herself except through the beating of her arteries, which she thought she could hear outside herself like some deafening music filling the countryside. The earth beneath her feet was softer than a wave, and the furrows seemed to her like immense brown billows unfurling. All that her mind contained of memories and thoughts was pouring out at once, in a single burst, like the thousand parts of a firework. She saw her father, Lheureux's office, their room back there, another landscape. Madness was stealing over her; she grew frightened and managed to take hold of herself again, though confusedly; for she did not remember the cause of her horrible state of mind, namely, the question of the money. She was suffering only because of her love, and she felt her soul slipping away through the memory of it, just as the wounded, in their last agony, feel the life going out of them through their bleeding wounds.

Night was falling, rooks were flying overhead.

It seemed to her suddenly that little flame-colored globes were exploding in the air like bullets bursting and flattening, and spinning over and over, then melting on the snow, among the branches of the trees. In the center of each, Rodolphe's face appeared. They were multiplying, coming together, penetrating her; everything vanished. She recognized the lights of the houses, shining from a distance through the mist.

At once her situation, like an abyss, appeared before her. She was panting as if her ribs might break. Then, in an ecstasy of heroism that filled her almost with joy, she ran down the hillside, across the plank bridge, on down the path and the alley, and across the marketplace, and came to the front of the pharmacist's shop.

No one was there. She was about to go in; but, at the sound of the shop's bell, someone might come; and so, slipping through the gate, holding her breath, feeling her way along the walls, she went as far as the door to the kitchen, where a candle set on the stove was burning. Justin, in shirtsleeves, was carrying out a dish.

"Ah! They're having dinner. Wait."

He returned. She tapped on the window. He came outside.

"The key! The one for upstairs, where the . . ."

"What?"

And he looked at her, astonished by the pallor of her face, which stood out white against the black background of the night. She seemed to him extraordinarily beautiful, and as majestic as a phantom; without understanding what she wanted, he had a foreboding of something terrible.

But she went on quickly, in a low voice, a voice that was soft, melting:

"I want it! Give it to me."

The wall was thin, and one could hear the clattering of the forks on the plates in the dining room.

She claimed she needed to kill some rats that were stopping her from sleeping.

"I ought to let Monsieur know."

"No! Stay here!"

Then, with a casual air:

"Oh, it's not worth bothering, I'll tell him myself later. Come on, light the way for me!"

She went into the hallway onto which the laboratory door opened. Hanging against the wall was a key labeled *capharnaum.*

"Justin!" shouted the apothecary, who was growing impatient.

"Let's go up!"

And he followed her.

The key turned in the lock, and she went straight to the third shelf, so well did her memory guide her, seized the blue jar, wrenched out the cork, thrust in her hand, and, withdrawing it full of white powder, began to eat it.

"Stop!" he cried, throwing himself on her.

"Be quiet! Someone might come . . ."

He was in despair and wanted to call out.

"Don't say anything about it. All the blame would fall on your master!"

Then she turned away, suddenly at peace, almost serene, as though she had done her duty.

When Charles, overwhelmed by the news of the seizure, returned to the house, Emma had just left. He shouted, he wept, he fainted, but she did not return. Where could she be? He sent Félicité to Homais's, to Monsieur Tuvache's, to Lheureux's, to the Lion d'Or, everywhere; and in the intervals when his anguish subsided, he saw his reputation destroyed, their fortune lost, Berthe's future blighted! What was the cause? . . . Not a word! He waited until six o'clock that evening. At last, unable to bear it any longer, and imagining she had gone to Rouen, he went out onto the big road, walked for half a league, met no one, waited a little longer, and came back.

She had returned.

"What happened? . . . Why? . . . Explain it to me! . . ."

She sat down at her desk and wrote a letter, which she sealed slowly, adding the day's date and the hour. Then she said in a solemn tone:

"You'll read this tomorrow; until then, I beg you, don't ask me a single question! . . . No, not one!"

"But . . ."

"Oh, leave me alone!"

And she lay down at full length on her bed.

An acrid taste in her mouth woke her. She caught sight of Charles and closed her eyes again.

She was observing herself curiously, to see if she was in pain. But no! Nothing yet. She could hear the ticking of the clock, the sound of the fire, and Charles breathing as he stood by her bed.

"Ah! It's a small thing, really—death!" she thought; "I'll fall asleep, and everything will be over!"

She drank a mouthful of water and turned to the wall.

That hideous taste of ink persisted.

"I'm thirsty! . . . Oh, I'm so thirsty!" she said with a sigh.

"What's the matter with you?" said Charles, who was holding out a glass to her.

"It's nothing! . . . Open the window . . . I'm suffocating!"

And she was overcome by a wave of nausea so sudden that she scarcely had time to snatch her handkerchief from under the pillow.

"Take it away!" she said quickly. "Throw it out!"

He questioned her; she did not answer. She was keeping still, for fear that the least disturbance would make her vomit. Meanwhile, she felt an icy cold rising within her from her feet to her heart.

"Ah! Now it's beginning!" she murmured.

"What did you say?"

She rolled her head from side to side with a gentle motion full of anguish, at the same time opening her jaws again and again, as though she were holding something very heavy on her tongue. At eight o'clock, the vomiting began again.

Charles observed that in the bottom of the basin there was a sort of white gravel clinging to the porcelain sides.

"How extraordinary! How curious!" he kept saying.

But she said loudly:

"No. You're wrong!"

Then, delicately, almost caressingly, he passed his hand over her stomach. She gave a sharp cry. He drew back, alarmed.

Then she began to moan, weakly at first. Her shoulders were shaken by a violent shudder, and she turned paler than the sheet in which her clenched fingers were buried. Her uneven pulse was almost imperceptible now.

Beads of sweat stood out on her face, which was tinged with blue and almost rigid, as though frozen by the exhalation of some metallic vapor. Her teeth were chattering, her dilated eyes gazed vaguely around her, and to each question her only answer was to move her head back and forth; she even smiled two or three times. Gradually, her moans grew louder. A muffled howl escaped her; she claimed she was feeling better and would soon get up. But she was seized with convulsions; she cried out:

"Oh! It's awful. My God!"

He flung himself to his knees by her bed.

"Speak to me! What did you eat? Answer, in heaven's name!"

And he looked at her with a love in his eyes that she had never seen before.

"Well . . . There . . . over there! . . ." she said in a faltering voice.

He leaped to the desk, broke the seal, and read aloud: " 'No one should be blamed . . .' " He stopped, passed his hand over his eyes, and read it again.

"What! . . . Help! Oh, help!"

And he could do nothing but say that word over and over again: "Poisoned! Poisoned!" Félicité ran to Homais, who uttered it loudly in the square; Madame Lefrançois heard it at the Lion d'Or; several people got out of bed to let their neighbors know; and all night the village was awake.

Perplexed, stammering, close to collapse, Charles walked around the room. He stumbled against the furniture, tore at his hair; and the pharmacist had never imagined there could be so dreadful a spectacle.

He returned to his house to write to Monsieur Canivet and Doctor Larivière. He was flustered; he composed more than fifteen drafts. Hippolyte went off to Neufchâtel, and Justin spurred Bovary's horse so hard that he had to leave it on the hill at Bois-Guillaume, foundered and three-quarters dead.

Charles tried to leaf through his medical dictionary; he could not see, the lines were dancing.

"Calm down!" said the apothecary. "It's just a question of administering some powerful antidote. Which poison was it?"

Charles showed him the letter. It was arsenic.

"Well, then," Homais went on, "an analysis must be done."

For he knew that in cases of poisoning an analysis always had to be done; and Charles, not understanding, answered:

"Ah! Do it! Do it! Save her . . ."

Then, returning to her side, he sank down on the carpet, and he stayed there resting his head against the edge of her bed, sobbing.

"Don't cry!" she said to him. "I won't be tormenting you much longer!"

"Why? What made you do it?"

She replied:

"I had to, my dear."

"Weren't you happy? Is it my fault? And yet I did everything I could!"

"Yes . . . that's true . . . You're good. You are!"

And she ran her hand through his hair slowly. The gentleness of that sensation was more than his sadness could bear; he felt his entire being give way to despair at the thought of having to lose her, just when she was admitting more love for him than ever before; and he could think of nothing; he knew nothing, dared nothing; the urgent need for an immediate decision was enough to overwhelm him.

She was done, she was thinking, with all the betrayals, the atrocities, and the endless cravings that had tormented her. She hated no one now; a twilight confusion was descending on her thoughts, and of all earthly sounds Emma now heard only the intermittent lamentation of that poor heart, soft and indistinct, like the last echo of a symphony moving away into the distance.

"Bring me little Berthe," she said, raising herself on her elbow.

"You're not worse, are you?" asked Charles.

"No! No!"

The child came in, in the arms of her nanny, wearing a long night-gown from which her bare feet emerged, her expression serious, still half dreaming. She gazed in surprise at the disordered room and blinked her eyes, dazzled by the candles burning here and there on the furniture. They probably reminded her of the morning of New Year's Day or Mid-Lent, when, wakened early in this same way by candlelight, she would be brought into her mother's bed to be given her presents, for she began to say:

"Where is it, Mama?"

And when no one spoke:

"But I don't see my little shoe!"

Félicité held her over the bed, while she was still looking toward the fireplace.

"Was it nurse that took it?" she asked.

And at that word, which carried her back in memory to her adulteries and her misfortunes, Madame Bovary turned her head away, as though in revulsion at another, stronger poison that was rising into her mouth. Berthe, meanwhile, was still on the bed.

"Oh, how big your eyes are, Mama! How pale you are! You're sweating! . . ."

Her mother looked at her.

"I'm frightened!" said the little girl, drawing back.

Emma took her hand to kiss it; she struggled.

"That's enough! Take her away!" cried Charles, who was sobbing in the alcove.

Then the symptoms stopped for a moment; she seemed less agitated;

and with each meaningless word she spoke, with each slightly calmer breath that came from her chest, he gained new hope. At last, when Canivet entered, he threw himself into his arms, weeping.

"Ah! It's you! Thank you! You're so kind! But things are going better now. Here, look at her . . ."

His colleague was not at all of that opinion, and *not beating about the bush,* as he put it, he prescribed an emetic to empty the stomach completely.

She was soon vomiting blood. Her lips pressed together more tightly. Her limbs were contracted, her body was covered with brown spots, and her pulse was slipping under their fingers like a taut thread, like a harp string about to snap.

Then she began to scream horribly. She cursed the poison, swore at it, implored it to be quick, and with her stiffened arms pushed away everything that Charles, in greater agony than she, tried to make her drink. He was standing, his handkerchief at his lips, his breath rasping in his throat, weeping and choked by sobs that shook him down to his heels; Félicité was rushing here and there in the room; Homais, motionless, kept sighing heavily; and Monsieur Canivet, though still maintaining his composure, was beginning to feel troubled.

"The devil! . . . and yet . . . she has been purged, and once the cause is removed . . ."

"The effect should cease," said Homais; "it's self-evident."

"Well, save her!" exclaimed Bovary.

And so, without listening to the pharmacist, who was venturing the hypothesis that "this might be a salutary paroxysm," Canivet was about to administer some theriaca when they heard the crack of a whip; all the windowpanes rattled, and a berlin drawn by three horses straining against their breast straps and spattered with mud up to their ears emerged in a single bound from the corner of the marketplace. It was Doctor Larivière.

The sudden appearance of a god would not have aroused more emotion. Bovary raised his hands, Canivet stopped short, and Homais removed his fez well before the doctor came in.

He belonged to that great school of surgery inspired by Bichat, to that now-vanished generation of philosopher-practitioners who cherished their art with a fanatical love and practiced it with enthusiasm and sagacity!

The entire hospital shook when he flew into a rage, and his pupils revered him so deeply that as soon as they established themselves, they would endeavor to imitate him as closely as possible; thus, in the surrounding towns, one would recognize, on their backs, his long quilted merino overcoat and his ample black tailcoat, whose unbuttoned cuffs partly covered his fleshy hands—his very fine hands, always gloveless, as though to be more prepared to plunge into human suffering. Disdainful of medals, titles, and academies, hospitable, generous, fatherly toward the poor, and practicing virtue without believing in it, he would almost have passed for a saint had not the shrewdness of his mind made him feared like a devil. His gaze, keener than his lancet, would descend straight into your soul, past your excuses and your reticence, and disarticulate your every lie. And so he went on from day to day, full of the easy majesty that comes from an awareness of great talent, from wealth, and from forty years of an irreproachable life of hard work.

He frowned even in the doorway, seeing Emma's cadaverous face as she lay on her back, her mouth open. Then, while appearing to listen to Canivet, he ran his forefinger under his nostrils and said several times:

"Good, good."

But he gave a slow shrug of his shoulders. Bovary observed it; they looked at each other; and this man, though so used to the sight of grief, could not stop a tear from falling on his ruffled shirtfront.

He wanted to take Canivet into the next room. Charles followed him.

"She's very bad, isn't she? What if we applied mustard plasters—I don't know! You must think of something—you who have saved so many lives!"

Charles put his arms around him and gazed at him in fear and entreaty, nearly fainting against his chest.

"Come now, my poor fellow, be brave! There's nothing more to be done."

And Doctor Larivière turned away.

"You're leaving?"

"I'll be back."

He went out as though to give an order to the postilion, accompanied by Sieur Canivet, who was no more anxious than he was to see Emma die in his hands.

The pharmacist joined them on the square. He was incapable, by temperament, of staying away from a famous person. And so he beseeched Monsieur Larivière to do him the signal honor of being his guest at lunch.

They quickly sent for pigeons from the Lion d'Or, whatever the butcher had in the way of cutlets, cream from Tuvache, eggs from Lestiboudois, and the apothecary himself helped with the preparations while Madame Homais, tugging at the laces of her bodice, said:

"Please forgive us, monsieur; here in this desolate spot, if we don't have a day's warning . . ."

"The stemmed glasses!!!" hissed Homais.

"If we lived in the city, at least we'd be able to fall back on stuffed pigs' feet."

"Be quiet! . . . Please sit down, Doctor!"

He felt it appropriate, after the first few bites, to provide some details about the catastrophe:

"First we had a feeling of siccity in the pharynx, then intolerable pains in the epigastrium, then superpurgation and coma."

"How did she poison herself?"

"I don't know, Doctor—I'm not even sure where she could have procured the arsenious oxide."

Justin, who was just then carrying in a stack of plates, was seized with a fit of trembling.

"What's the matter with you?" asked the pharmacist.

At that question, the young man let everything fall to the floor with a great crash.

"Imbecile!" cried Homais. "Clumsy lout! Pathetic ass!"

But, abruptly controlling himself:

"I wanted, Doctor, to attempt an analysis, and *primo,* I carefully inserted into a tube . . ."

"It would have been better," said the surgeon, "to insert your fingers into her throat."

His colleague said nothing, having just a short time before received, in private, a severe rebuke concerning his emetic, so that this worthy Canivet, so arrogant and long-winded in the case of the clubfoot, was today very modest; he smiled without pause, in an approving manner.

Homais was blossoming with pride in his role as Amphitryon, and the distressing thought of Bovary contributed vaguely to his pleasure, by causing him to reflect selfishly on his own situation. Moreover, the presence of the doctor intoxicated him. He was displaying his erudition, making confused and hasty references to cantharides, the upas tree, the manchineel, the viper.

"And I've even read, Doctor, about certain people who were discovered to have been poisoned—quite struck down—by blood sausages that had been too thoroughly fumigated! At least, so says a very fine report composed by one of our leading pharmaceutists, one of our masters, the illustrious Cadet de Gassicourt!"

Madame Homais reappeared, carrying one of those unsteady contrivances heated with spirits of alcohol; for Homais insisted on making his coffee at the table, having, moreover, torrefied it himself, triturated it himself, and compounded it himself.

"*Saccharum,* Doctor," he said, offering some sugar.

Then he sent for all his children to come downstairs, curious to hear the surgeon's opinion of their constitutions.

At last, as Monsieur Larivière was about to leave, Madame Homais asked him for a consultation concerning her husband. His blood was thickening because he fell asleep every evening after dinner.

"Oh! It isn't his *blood* that's thick."

And smiling a little at this joke, which went unnoticed, the doctor opened the door. But the pharmacy was teeming with people; and he had great difficulty managing to free himself of Sieur Tuvache, who was afraid his wife would get an inflammation of the lungs because of her habit of spitting in the ashes; then Monsieur Binet, who sometimes experienced keen hunger pangs, and Madame Caron, who had tingling sensations; Lheureux, who had dizzy spells; Lestiboudois, who had rheumatism; Madame Lefrançois, who had acidity of the stomach. At last the three horses dashed away, and it was generally felt that he had not been at all obliging.

The attention of the public was distracted by the appearance of Monsieur Bournisien, who was crossing the market with the holy oil.

Homais, in deference to his principles, likened priests to crows attracted by the smell of the dead; the sight of a clergyman was personally unpleasant to him, for a soutane made him think of a shroud, and he detested the one partly out of a horror of the other.

Nevertheless, not shrinking from what he called *his mission,* he returned to Bovary's house in company with Canivet, whom Monsieur Larivière, before leaving, had strongly urged to stay, and had it not been for his wife's remonstrances, he would even have taken his two sons along with him, in order to accustom them to grave situations, so that they would have a lesson, an example, a solemn tableau that would later remain in their minds.

The bedroom, when they entered, was full of a melancholy solemnity. On the sewing table, now covered with a white napkin, there were five or six little balls of cotton in a silver dish, near a large crucifix between two lighted candlesticks. Emma's chin was sunk against her chest, her eyes inordinately wide open; and her poor hands wandered over the sheets with that hideous gentle motion of the dying, who seem already to be trying to cover themselves with their shrouds. Pale as a statue, his eyes red as coals, Charles, no longer weeping, stood facing her at the foot of the bed, while the priest, resting on one knee, was mumbling some words in a low voice.

She slowly turned her face and seemed overcome with joy at the sudden sight of the violet stole, no doubt reexperiencing, in the midst of this extraordinary feeling of peace, the lost ecstasy of her first mystical yearnings, alongside the first visions of eternal beatitude.

The priest rose to take up the crucifix; at that, she strained her neck forward like someone who is thirsty, and, pressing her lips to the body of the Man-God, she laid upon it with all her expiring strength the most passionate kiss of love she had ever given. Then he recited the *Misereatur* and the *Indulgentiam,* dipped his right thumb in the oil, and began the unctions: first on the eyes, which had so coveted all earthly splendors; then on the nostrils, so greedy for mild breezes and the smells of love; then on the mouth, which had opened to utter lies, which had moaned with pride and cried out in lust; then on the hands, which had so delighted in the touch of smooth material; and lastly on the soles of the feet, which had once been so quick when she hastened to satiate her desires and which now would never walk again.

The curé wiped his fingers, threw the oil-soaked bits of cotton into the fire, and returned to sit down beside the dying woman to tell her that she should now join her sufferings with those of Jesus Christ and give herself up to divine mercy.

Finishing his exhortations, he tried to put a blessed taper into her hand, symbol of the heavenly glories by which she would soon be surrounded. Emma was too weak and could not close her fingers; had it not been for Monsieur Bournisien, the taper would have fallen to the floor.

Yet she was no longer as pale, and her face bore an expression of serenity, as if the sacrament had cured her.

The priest did not fail to point this out; he even explained to Bovary that the Lord would sometimes prolong people's lives when He judged it advisable for their salvation; and Charles remembered another day when, as now, she had been close to dying and had received Communion.

"Perhaps one shouldn't give up hope," he thought.

Indeed, she looked all around her, slowly, like someone waking from a dream; then, in a distinct voice, she asked for her mirror, and she remained bent over it for some time, until large tears ran down from her eyes. Then she tipped her head back with a sigh and sank down onto the pillow.

At once her chest began rising and falling rapidly. Her tongue protruded at full length from her mouth; her rolling eyes grew paler, like the globes of two lamps about to go out, so that one would have thought she was already dead, except for the frightening, accelerating motion of her ribs, which were shaken by her furious breathing, as if her soul were leaping up to break free. Félicité knelt in front of the crucifix, and even the pharmacist bent a little at the knees, while Monsieur Canivet looked vaguely out at the square. Bournisien had resumed praying, his face leaning against the edge of the bed, his long black soutane trailing out behind him into the room. Charles was on the other side, on his knees, his arms reaching out to Emma. He had taken her hands and he was squeezing them, shuddering at each beat of her heart as at the tremors of a collapsing ruin. As the death rattle grew louder, the clergyman hastened his prayers; they mingled with Bovary's muffled sobs; and at times everything seemed drowned out by the muted murmur of the Latin syllables, which tolled like a passing bell.

Suddenly they heard the noise of heavy wooden shoes on the sidewalk below and the scraping of a stick; and a voice rose, a harsh voice, singing:

How oft the warmth of the sun above
Makes a pretty young girl dream of love.

Emma sat up like a corpse galvanized, her hair loose, her eyes fixed and wide open.

Behind the harvesting scythe,
Gathering she goes,
My Nanette bending to the wheat
Down the generous rows.

"The Blind Man!" she cried out.

And Emma began to laugh a horrible, frantic, despairing laugh, thinking she saw the hideous face of the wretched man looming like terror itself in the darkness of eternity.

The wind blew good and hard that day,
And snatched her petticoat away!

A convulsion flung her down on the mattress. They all drew near. She had ceased to exist.

[9]

After a person dies, a sort of stupefaction settles in, always, so difficult is it to comprehend this sudden advent of nothingness and to resign oneself to believing in it. But when he saw how still she was, Charles threw himself on her crying:

"Goodbye! Goodbye!"

Homais and Canivet took him out of the room.

"Control yourself!"

"All right," he said, struggling, "I'll be reasonable, I won't do any harm. But leave me alone! I want to see her! She's my wife!"

And he wept.

"Weep," said the pharmacist. "Let nature take its course. It will bring you relief!"

Now weaker than a child, Charles allowed himself be led downstairs, into the parlor, and soon Monsieur Homais returned home.

On the Square, he was accosted by the Blind Man, who had dragged himself all the way to Yonville in hope of the antiphlogistic salve and was asking each person who passed where the apothecary lived.

"Come, now! As if I didn't have other dogs to whip! It's just too bad—come back another time!"

And he hurried into the pharmacy.

He had to write two letters, prepare a calmative potion for Bovary, think of a lie that could hide the poisoning, and compose an article about it for *Le Fanal,* not to mention the people who were waiting for news from him; and when the Yonvillians had all heard his story, of how she had mistaken arsenic for sugar while making a vanilla custard, Homais returned once more to Bovary's house.

He found him alone (Monsieur Canivet had just left), sitting in the armchair by the window and staring with an idiotic gaze at the stone floor of the room.

"What you've got to do now," said the pharmacist, "is decide on a time for the ceremony."

"Why? What ceremony?"

Then, in a frightened stammer:

"Oh, no! Really—no! I want to keep her."

Homais, to cover his embarrassment, took a carafe from the étagère and began watering the geraniums.

"Oh, thank you!" said Charles. "You're so kind!"

And he broke off, suffocating under the abundance of memories that the pharmacist's gesture recalled.

Then, to distract him, Homais thought it appropriate to talk a little horticulture; plants needed humidity. Charles bowed his head in agreement.

"Anyway, the warm weather will be returning now."

"Ah!" said Bovary.

The apothecary, out of ideas, quietly parted the little curtains at the window.

"Why, there's Monsieur Tuvache going by."

Charles repeated mechanically:

"Monsieur Tuvache going by."

Homais did not dare talk to him again about the funeral arrangements; it was the clergyman who managed to resign him to it.

He shut himself in his office, took up a pen, and, after having sobbed for some time, he wrote:

I want her to be buried in her wedding dress, with white shoes on, and a wreath. Her hair is to be spread over her shoulders; three coffins, one of oak, one of mahogany, one of lead. No one is to say anything to me, I will be strong enough. Cover her entirely with a large piece of green velvet. This is what I want. Do it.

The gentlemen were very surprised by Bovary's romantic ideas, and the pharmacist immediately went to him and said:

"The velvet seems to me supererogatory. Not to mention the expense . . ."

"Is it any concern of yours?" exclaimed Charles. "Leave me alone! You didn't love her! Get out!"

The clergyman took him by the arm and led him out for a walk around the garden. He discoursed on the vanity of earthly things. God was great, God was good; one should submit without a murmur to his decrees, one should even thank him.

Charles burst out in blasphemies.

"I loathe him—your God!"

"The spirit of rebellion is still in you," said the clergyman with a sigh.

Bovary was far away. He was striding along the wall next to the espalier, and he was grinding his teeth, looking up at heaven with curses in his eyes; but not even a leaf moved.

A light rain was falling. Charles, whose chest was bare, finally began to shiver; he went back inside and sat down in the kitchen.

At six o'clock, a rattling sound could be heard in the Square: it was the *Hirondelle* arriving; and he remained there with his forehead against the windowpanes, watching all the passengers get out one after the other. Félicité put a mattress down for him in the parlor; he threw himself on it and slept.

Though a rationalist, Monsieur Homais respected the dead. And so, without harboring any resentment toward poor Charles, he returned that evening to watch beside the body, bringing three books with him, and a portfolio, in order to take notes.

Monsieur Bournisien was already there, and two tall tapers were burning by the side of the bed, which had been pulled out of the alcove.

The apothecary, who found the silence oppressive, soon offered a few laments concerning the "unfortunate young woman"; and the priest answered that all one could do now was pray for her.

"Still," said Homais, "it's one of two things: either she died in a state of grace (as it is expressed by the church) and therefore has no need of our prayers; or she died impenitent (that is, I think, the ecclesiastical expression), in which case . . ."

Bournisien interrupted him, replying in a surly tone that one had to pray all the same.

"But," objected the pharmacist, "since God is aware of all our needs, what can be the use of prayer?"

"What!" exclaimed the clergyman. "Prayer! So you're not a Christian?"

"Forgive me!" said Homais. "I admire Christianity. In the first place, it freed the slaves, it introduced a moral code into the world . . ."

"It's not about that! All the texts . . ."

"Oh! Oh! The texts! Just open your history book; everyone knows they were falsified by the Jesuits."

Charles came in and, walking to the bed, he slowly pulled back the curtains.

Emma's head was leaning on her right shoulder. The corner of her mouth, which was open, made a sort of black hole in the lower part of her face; her thumbs were bent in toward the palms of her hands; a kind of white dust was sprinkled over her lashes; and her eyes were beginning to disappear in a viscous pallor that resembled a thin cloth, as if spiders had been spinning cobwebs over them. The sheet sagged from her breasts to her knees, rising again at the tips of her toes; and it seemed to Charles that an infinite mass, an enormous weight, was pressing down on her.

The church clock struck two. The deep murmur of the stream could be heard as it flowed past in the darkness at the bottom of the terrace. Monsieur Bournisien, from time to time, would blow his nose loudly, and Homais's pen was scratching over the paper.

"Come now, my good friend," he said, "you mustn't stay. The sight of her is tearing you apart!"

When Charles had gone, the pharmacist and the curé resumed their arguments.

"Read Voltaire!" one was saying; "read d'Holbach, read the *Encyclopedia*!"

"Read the *Letters of Some Portuguese Jews*!" the other was saying; "read the *Proof of Christianity*, by the former magistrate Nicholas!"

They were becoming heated, they were red in the face, they were both talking at once without listening to each other; Bournisien was scandalized by such audacity; Homais marveled at such stupidity; and they were almost on the point of trading insults when Charles suddenly reappeared. He was drawn by a sort of fascination. He kept coming back up the stairs.

He positioned himself facing her so as to see her better, and he sank into a contemplation so profound that it was no longer painful.

He recalled stories about catalepsy, about the miracles of magnetism; and he told himself that by straining his will to the utmost, he could perhaps succeed in reviving her. Once he even leaned over toward her and cried out very softly: "Emma! Emma!" His breath, forcefully expelled, made the candle flames flicker against the wall.

At first light, the elder Madame Bovary arrived; when Charles embraced her, he overflowed in tears again. She tried, as the pharmacist had, to say something to him about the funeral expenses. He flew into such a rage that she fell silent, and he even told her to go into the city immediately to buy what was needed.

Charles remained alone all afternoon: Berthe had been taken to Madame Homais; Félicité was staying upstairs, in the bedroom, with Mère Lefrançois.

In the evening, he received visitors. He would stand up, shake them by the hand, incapable of speaking; then each would sit down next to the others, forming a wide semicircle in front of the fireplace. Faces bowed and legs crossed, they would bob their feet, uttering a heavy sigh from time to time; and all of them were bored beyond measure; yet none would be the first to leave.

When Homais returned at nine o'clock (for the past two days he had been seen constantly crossing the Square), he was carrying a supply of camphor, benzoin, and aromatic herbs. He had also brought a vase full of chlorine, to drive out the miasmas. Just then, the servant, Madame Lefrançois, and Mère Bovary were circling around Emma, finishing dressing her; now they lowered the long, stiff veil, which covered her down to her satin shoes.

Félicité was sobbing:

"Oh, my poor mistress! My poor mistress!"

"Look at her," the innkeeper was saying with a sigh. "How pretty she is, still! You'd swear she'd be getting up any moment now."

Then they leaned over to put on her wreath.

They had to lift her head a little, and at that a stream of black liquid ran out of her mouth like vomit.

"Oh, my Lord! The dress—be careful!" exclaimed Madame Lefrançois. "Help us, can't you!" she said to the pharmacist. "You're not afraid, are you?"

"I, afraid?" he replied, shrugging. "Well, now! I've seen others before this, at the Hôtel Dieu, when I was studying pharmacy! We used to make punch in the dissection hall! The void doesn't frighten a rationalist; in fact, as I often say, I intend to leave my body to the hospitals, so that later I can be of service to Science."

When he arrived, the Curé asked how Monsieur was doing; and at the apothecary's reply he said:

"The shock, you understand, is still too recent!"

Then Homais congratulated him on not being exposed, like other men, to the risk of losing a beloved companion; whence there followed a discussion about the celibacy of priests.

"After all," said the pharmacist, "it's not natural for a man to do without women! We've all heard of crimes . . ."

"Well, hang it!" exclaimed the clergyman. "How do you expect an individual involved in a marriage to preserve the secrets of the confessional, for example?"

Homais attacked confession. Bournisien defended it; he expatiated on the acts of restitution that resulted from it. He cited various anecdotes concerning thieves who had suddenly turned honest. Soldiers, approaching the tribunal of penitence, had felt the scales fall from their eyes. In Fribourg there was a minister . . .

His companion was asleep. Then, as he felt a little short of breath, the air in the room being so heavy, he opened the window, which woke the pharmacist.

"Here, have a pinch of snuff!" he said. "Take it, it clears the head."

There was a steady barking somewhere off in the distance.

"Do you hear a dog howling?" asked the pharmacist.

"They can smell the dead, people say," answered the clergyman. "It's the same with bees: they fly from their hives when people die." Homais did not challenge these superstitions, for he had fallen asleep again.

Monsieur Bournisien, being more resistant, went on moving his lips very softly for some time; then, imperceptibly, he lowered his chin, let go of his thick black book, and began to snore.

They sat opposite each other, their stomachs out, their faces swollen, both scowling, after so much dissension united, at last, in the same human weakness; and they moved no more than the corpse by their side, which seemed to be asleep.

When Charles came in, he did not wake them. It was the last time. He had come to say his goodbyes to her.

The aromatic herbs were still smoking, and swirls of bluish vapor mingled at the edge of the casement with the mist that was entering. There were a few stars, and the night was mild.

The wax from the tapers was falling in great teardrops onto the sheets of the bed. Charles was watching them burn, tiring his eyes in the radiance of their yellow flames.

The watered satin of her dress was shimmering, as white as moonlight. Emma was disappearing beneath it; and it seemed to him she was spreading out beyond herself, confusedly melting into the things around her, into the silence, the night, the wind passing through, the damp smells rising.

Then, suddenly, he saw her in the garden at Tostes, on the bench, against the thorn hedge, or in the streets of Rouen, on the doorsill of their house, in the farmyard at Les Bertaux. Once again he heard the laughter of the high-spirited boys dancing under the apple trees; the bedroom was full of the fragrance of her hair; and her dress rustled in his arms with a sound of sparks. It was this same dress!

He spent a long time like this, remembering all his vanished happiness, her way of sitting and standing, her gestures, the timbre of her voice. One feeling of despair would be followed by another, on and on, inexhaustibly, like the waves of an overflowing tide.

A terrible curiosity came over him: slowly, with the tips of his fingers, his heart pounding, he lifted her veil. But he cried out in horror, waking the other two. They took him downstairs into the parlor.

Then Félicité came up to say that he was asking for some of her hair.

"Cut some!" replied the apothecary.

And since she did not dare, he stepped forward himself, the scissors in his hand. He was shaking so hard that he punctured the skin of the temples in several places. At last, stiffening himself against his emotion, Homais made two or three large cuts at random, leaving white marks in that lovely head of black hair.

The pharmacist and the curé immersed themselves once again in their occupations, not without dozing off from time to time, something for which they reproached each other each time they woke. Then Monsieur Bournisien would sprinkle the room with holy water and Homais would toss a little chlorine on the floor.

Félicité had taken care to set out for them, on the chest of drawers, a bottle of eau-de-vie, a cheese, and a large brioche. And so the apothecary, who could hold out no longer, said, toward four in the morning, sighing:

"I must confess, I would be happy to partake of a bit of sustenance!"

The clergyman did not need to be coaxed; he went out to say his Mass, came back; then they ate and clinked glasses, chuckling a little, without knowing why, excited by that vague sort of elation that follows periods of sadness; and with the last small glass, the priest said to the pharmacist, patting him on the shoulder:

"We'll end up being friends yet, one day!"

Downstairs, in the front hall, they met the workers coming in. For two hours, Charles had to submit to the torture of the hammer resounding on the wooden boards. Then they brought her down in her oak coffin, which they set inside the other two; but as the coffin was too wide, they had to fill the gaps with wool from a mattress. At last, when the three covers had been planed, nailed, soldered, she was placed on display before the door; they opened wide the house, and the people of Yonville began to flow in.

Père Rouault arrived. He fainted in the Square when he saw the black cloth.

[10]

He had not received the pharmacist's letter until thirty-six hours after the event; and out of respect for his sensitivity, Monsieur Homais had written it in such a fashion that it was impossible to know what to think.

First the good fellow had collapsed as though stricken by apoplexy. Then he realized that she was not dead. But she could be . . . At last he had put on his smock, taken up his hat, buckled a spur on his shoe, and ridden off at full speed; and all along the road, Père Rouault, gasping for breath, was consumed with anxiety. Once he even had to get down from his horse. He could no longer see anything, he was hearing voices all around him, he felt he was going mad.

Day dawned. He saw three black hens asleep in a tree; he shuddered, terrified by this omen. Then he promised the Holy Virgin three chasubles for the church and vowed to walk barefoot from the cemetery at Les Bertaux to the chapel in Vassonville.

He entered Maromme hailing the people at the inn, burst open the door with a blow from his shoulder, bounded over to the bag of oats, poured a bottle of sweet cider into the manger, and got back up on his nag, making the sparks fly up from under its hooves.

He told himself they would surely save her; the doctors would certainly find a cure. He recalled all the miraculous recoveries he had heard described.

Then she appeared to him, dead. She was there, in front of him, lying on her back, in the middle of the road. He pulled up on the reins, and the hallucination disappeared.

At Quincampoix, to keep up his courage, he drank three coffees one after the other.

He imagined they had gotten the name wrong when they wrote to him. He looked for the letter in his pocket, felt it, but did not dare open it.

It occurred to him eventually that it was perhaps a *joke*, someone's revenge, something dreamed up by some fellow who had had one too many; after all, if she had died, wouldn't he know it? But no! there was nothing extraordinary about the countryside: the sky was blue, the trees were swaying, a flock of sheep went past. He caught sight of the village; they saw him racing ahead, hunched over his horse; he was whipping it hard, and its girth was dripping blood.

When he regained consciousness, he fell weeping into Bovary's arms:

"My daughter! Emma! My child! Tell me . . ."

And the other answered, sobbing:

"I don't know, I don't know! It's a curse!"

The apothecary separated them.

"The horrible details are pointless. I'll explain it to Monsieur. People are coming. Have some dignity, for goodness' sake! Be rational!"

The poor fellow wanted to appear strong, and he said several times:

"Yes . . . Be brave!"

"Well, all right, then," exclaimed the old man, "I will, great God in heaven! I'll be with her all the way to the end."

The bell was tolling. Everything was ready. It was time to set out.

And sitting side by side in a choir stall, they watched the three choristers cross back and forth in front of them, chanting. The serpent player was blowing with all his might. Monsieur Bournisien, in full apparel, was singing in a shrill voice; he bowed to the tabernacle, raised his hands, extended his arms. Lestiboudois was circulating through the church with his whalebone staff; near the lectern, the coffin lay between four rows of candles. Charles wanted to get up and put them out.

And yet he was trying to awaken a feeling of piety in himself, to rise to the hope of a future life in which he would see her again. He imagined that she had gone off on a voyage, very far away, a long time ago. But then, when he thought that she was here, under all of this, and that it was all over, that she would be taken away and buried, he was filled with a savage, dark, despairing rage. At moments he thought he no longer felt anything; and he relished the easing of his pain, even as he blamed himself for being a wretch.

Something like the sharp sound of an iron-tipped walking stick was heard striking the flagstones at regular intervals. It came from the back and stopped short in the side aisles of the church. A man in a coarse brown jacket knelt down with difficulty. It was Hippolyte, the stableboy at the Lion d'Or. He had put on his new leg.

One of the choristers came through the nave to take up the collection, and the heavy sous clattered one after another into the silver dish.

"Hurry up, would you! I'm suffering so!" exclaimed Bovary, angrily tossing him a five-franc coin.

The churchman thanked him with a long bow.

They sang, they knelt, they got up again, it was endless! He remembered that once, in the early days, they had attended Mass together, and they had sat on the other side, on the right, against the wall. The bell began tolling again. There was a great movement of chairs. The bearers slipped their three poles under the bier, and everyone left the church.

At that moment Justin appeared in the doorway of the pharmacy. He went back inside suddenly, pale, unsteady.

People stood at their windows to see the procession go past. Charles, at the head, stood very straight. He was putting on a brave front and greeted with a nod those who, emerging from lanes or doorways, joined the ranks of the crowd.

The six men, three on either side, were walking with small steps and panting a little. The priests, the choristers, and the two altarboys were reciting the *De profundis;* and their voices went out into the countryside, rising and falling in waves. Now and then they would disappear at a bend in the path; but the great silver cross always rose up between the trees.

The women followed, covered in black cloaks with the hoods folded back; each carried a thick, burning taper in one hand; and Charles felt faint at the endless repetition of prayers and flames, amid the sickening smells of wax and soutanes. A fresh breeze was blowing, the rye and rapeseed were turning green, little dewdrops trembled at the roadside on the thorn hedges. Joyful sounds of all kinds filled the air: the distant rattle of a cart rolling along a rutted road, the crowing of a cock, repeated again and again, or the gallop of a colt running away under the apple trees. The pure sky was dappled with pink clouds; spirals of bluish smoke trailed down over thatched cottages covered in iris; Charles, as he passed, recognized the farmyards. He remembered mornings like this one, when, after visiting some patient, he would come outside and return to her.

The black pall, spangled with white teardrops, lifted from time to time, uncovering the coffin. The tired bearers were slowing down, and the bier moved forward in little jolts, like a boat pitching with every wave.

They arrived.

The men continued on to the far end, to a place in the turf where the grave had been dug.

They ranged themselves all around it; and while the priest was speaking, the red earth, thrown up onto the edges, trickled down at the corners, continuously, noiselessly.

Then, when the four ropes were in position, they pushed the bier onto them. He watched it go down. It was still going down.

At last they heard a thud; the ropes, creaking, came back up. Then Bournisien took the spade that Lestiboudois was holding out to him; with his left hand, as he continued to sprinkle the holy water with his right, he vigorously pushed in a large spadeful; and the pebbles striking the wood of the coffin made that terrible sound that seems to us like the reverberation of eternity itself.

The clergyman passed the aspergillum to his neighbor. It was Monsieur Homais. He shook it gravely, then held it out to Charles, who sank to his knees in the earth and threw in great handfuls of it, crying out: "Goodbye!" He blew her kisses; he dragged himself toward the grave so that he might be swallowed up in it along with her.

They led him away; and he soon calmed down, perhaps feeling, like everyone else, the vague satisfaction of being done with it.

On the way back, Père Rouault began calmly smoking a pipe; something that Homais privately judged to be hardly proper. He likewise noticed that Monsieur Binet had refrained from making an appearance, that Tuvache "had taken off" after the Mass, and that Théodore, the notary's servant, was wearing a blue coat, "as if he couldn't find a black one, seeing as it's the custom, for goodness' sake!" And he went from one group to another, communicating his observations. They were deploring Emma's death, especially Lheureux, who had not failed to attend the burial.

"That poor little lady! How painful for her husband!"

The apothecary said:

"If it hadn't been for me, you may be quite sure, he'd have made a fatal attempt upon himself!"

"Such a good person! To think, though, that I saw her just last Saturday in my shop!"

"I did not have the leisure," said Homais, "to prepare a few words to speak over her grave."

At home, Charles took off his funeral clothes, and Père Rouault put back on his blue smock. It was new, and as he had often wiped his eyes with the sleeves on his way there, the dye had come off on his face; and his tears had made little tracks in the layer of dust that soiled it.

The elder Madame Bovary was with them. All three were quiet. At last the old man said with a sigh:

"You remember, my friend, I came to Tostes once, when you had just lost your first wife. I was able to console you in those days! I could think of something to say; but now . . ."

Then, with a long moan that lifted his whole chest:

"Ah! It's the end for me, you know! I've seen my wife go . . . my son after her . . . and now, today, my daughter!"

He intended to return to Les Bertaux right away, saying that he could not sleep in that house. He even refused to see his granddaughter.

"No, no! It would cause me too much grief. Only, give her a big kiss for me! Goodbye! . . . You're a good fellow! And never fear, I'll not forget," he said, slapping his thigh. "You'll still get your turkey."

But when he reached the top of the hill, he turned around, as he had turned around once before on the road to Saint-Victor, when he was leaving her. The windows of the village were all on fire under the slanting rays of the sun, which was setting beyond the meadow. He shaded his eyes with his hand; and on the horizon he saw a walled enclosure where trees stood in dark clumps here and there among the white stones; then he continued on his way, at a slow trot, for his nag was limping.

Charles and his mother remained together for a very long time talking, that night, despite their fatigue. They spoke about the old days and about the future. She would come live in Yonville, she would keep house for him, they would never again be parted. She was clever and ingratiating, and rejoiced at winning back an affection that had been denied her for so many years. Midnight struck. The village, as usual, was silent, and Charles, awake, was still thinking of *her*.

Rodolphe, who had been hunting in the woods all day by way of distraction, was sleeping peacefully in his château; and Léon, far away, was asleep too.

One other person, at that hour, was not sleeping.

On the grave among the pine trees, a boy knelt weeping, his chest, racked by sobs, heaving in the darkness, oppressed by an immense grief gentler than the moon and more unfathomable than the night. Suddenly the gate creaked. It was Lestiboudois; he had come in search of his spade, which he had forgotten earlier. He recognized Justin scaling the wall, and then he knew the truth about the scoundrel who had been stealing his potatoes.

[11]

The next day, Charles had the child brought back. She asked for her mama. They answered that she was away, that she would bring back some toys for her. Berthe talked about her again several times; then at length she stopped thinking about her. The child's gaiety cut Bovary to the heart, and in addition he had to submit to the pharmacist's intolerable commiserations.

Money troubles soon began again, Monsieur Lheureux urging on his friend Vinçart as before, and Charles signed for some exorbitant sums; for he would never consent to selling the least of the things that had belonged to *her*. His mother was incensed by this. He became angrier than she. He had changed completely. She left the house for good.

Then everyone set out to *profit* from him. Mademoiselle Lempereur claimed six months of lessons, even though Emma had never taken a single one (despite the receipted bill she had shown Bovary): the two women had had an agreement; the lending library claimed three years' subscription fees; Mère Rolet claimed postage on some twenty letters; and when Charles asked for an explanation, she had the discretion to answer:

"Ah! I know nothing about it! It was business."

With every debt he paid, Charles thought he had come to the end of them. Others kept coming in, constantly.

He tried to collect long-outstanding payments for professional visits. He was shown the letters his wife had sent. Then he had to apologize.

Félicité was now wearing Madame's dresses; not all of them, for he had kept a few, and he would go look at them in her dressing room, locking himself in; she was more or less her size, and often when he saw her from behind, Charles would be prey to an illusion and would cry out:

"Oh! stay! stay!"

But at Pentecost, she absconded from Yonville, carried off by Théodore and stealing all that was left of the wardrobe.

It was at about this time that the Widow Dupuis had the honor to inform him of "the marriage of Monsieur Léon Dupuis, her son, notary at Yvetot, to Mademoiselle Léocadie Leboeuf, of Bondeville." Charles, among the congratulations that he addressed to her, wrote this sentence:

"How happy my poor wife would have been!"

One day, when, wandering aimlessly through the house, he had gone up to the attic, he felt under his slipper a little wad of thin paper. He opened it and read: "Be brave, Emma! Be brave! I don't want to ruin your life." It was Rodolphe's letter, which had fallen to the floor among some boxes and remained there, and which the wind from the attic window had just blown toward the door. And Charles stood there openmouthed, without moving, in that same spot where once, even paler than he, Emma, in despair, had longed to die. At last, he discovered a small *R* at the bottom of the second page. Who was it? He recalled Rodolphe's constant attentions, his sudden disappearance, and his constrained manner when meeting her afterward two or three times. But he was deceived by the respectful tone of the letter.

"Perhaps they loved each other platonically," he said to himself.

In any case, Charles was not one who liked to get to the bottom of things: he recoiled before the proofs, and his tentative jealousy vanished in the immensity of his grief.

They must have adored her, he thought. Surely all men had coveted her. Now she seemed to him all the more beautiful; and this thought awakened in him a constant, raging desire that inflamed his despair and had no limits because now it could never be satisfied.

To please her, as though she were still alive, he adopted her tastes, her ideas; he bought himself patent-leather boots, he took up the habit of wearing white cravats. He put brilliantine on his mustache; like her, he wrote promissory notes. She was corrupting him from beyond the grave.

He was obliged to sell the silver, piece by piece; then he sold the parlor furniture. All the rooms were stripped; but the bedroom, her room, remained as it used to be. After dinner, Charles would go up there. He would push the round table up to the fire, and he would pull forward *her* armchair. He would sit opposite. A candle burned in one of the gilt candlesticks. Berthe sat beside him coloring printed pictures.

It pained the poor man to see her so shabbily dressed, her ankle boots missing their laces and the armholes of her smocks torn down to the hips—because the woman who came in to clean hardly took any notice of her. But she was so gentle, so sweet, and she bent her little head so gracefully, letting her lovely blond hair fall over her pink cheeks, that he was filled with an infinite pleasure, a delight permeated with bitterness like those badly made wines that smell of resin. He would mend her playthings, make jumping jacks for her out of cardboard, or sew up the torn stomachs of her dolls. Then, if his eye fell on the sewing box, on a trailing ribbon or even a pin caught in a crack in the table, he would sink into a reverie, and he looked so sad that she, too, like him, would grow sad.

No one came to see them now; for Justin had fled to Rouen, where he became a grocery boy, and the apothecary's children visited the little girl less and less often, since Monsieur Homais preferred, given the difference in their social status, that the association not be prolonged.

The Blind Man, whom he had not been able to cure with his salve, had returned to the hill at Bois Guillaume, where he told travelers the story of the pharmacist's vain attempt, with the result that Homais, when he went to the city, would conceal himself behind the curtains of the *Hirondelle* to avoid encountering him. He loathed him; and wanting, in the interests of his own reputation, to be rid of him at all costs, he launched against him a hidden campaign that revealed both the depth of his intelligence and the wickedness of his vanity. Thus, for six consecutive months, one could read in *Le Fanal de Rouen* paragraphs like the following:

"Anyone wending his way toward the fertile fields of Picardy will no doubt have noticed, on the hill at Bois-Guillaume, a wretched individual afflicted with a horrible lesion of the face. He importunes every traveler, persecutes him, and exacts a veritable tax on him. Are we still living in the monstrous days of the Middle Ages, when vagabonds were permitted to display, in our public places, the leprosy and scrofula they brought back from the Crusades?"

Or:

"Despite the laws against vagrancy, the approaches to our large cities continue to be infested by gangs of paupers. Some, too, are seen going about on their own, and these, perhaps, are not the least dangerous. What can our magistrates be thinking?"

Then Homais began inventing anecdotes:

"Yesterday, on the hill at Bois-Guillaume, a skittish horse . . ." And there followed the tale of an accident occasioned by the presence of the Blind Man.

He was so effective that the Blind Man was incarcerated. But they released him. He started up again, and Homais, too, started up again. It was a battle. The victory went to Homais; for his enemy was condemned for life to an asylum.

This success emboldened him; and from then on, whenever a dog was run over in the district, or a barn burned down, or a woman got beaten, he immediately let the public know about it, guided always by a love of progress and a hatred of priests. He drew comparisons between the primary schools and the Ignorantine friars, to the detriment of the latter, recalled Saint Bartholemew's Day in connection with an allocation of a hundred francs to the church, denounced abuses, and hurled witticisms. That was his word for it. Homais was undermining the foundations; he was becoming dangerous.

Yet he was suffocating within the narrow limits of journalism, and soon he felt the need to produce a book, a "work"! And so he composed a *General Statistics of the Canton of Yonville, Followed by Some Climatological Observations,* and statistics led him to philosophy. He became preoccupied by major questions: social reform, inculcating morality in the poor, fish breeding, rubber, railroads, and so forth. He now blushed at being a bourgeois. He affected the manners of the *artistic type;* he smoked! He bought himself two *chic* Pompadour statuettes to decorate his parlor.

He did not abandon pharmacy at all; on the contrary! He kept up with the latest discoveries. He followed the great chocolate movement. He was the first to bring *cho-ca* and *revalentia* to the Seine-Inférieure. He waxed enthusiastic over Pulvermacher hydroelectric belts; he wore one himself; and at night, when he took off his flannel vest, Madame Homais was quite dazzled by the sight of the golden spiral in which he was almost lost to view, and she felt a redoubling of her passion for this man, bound tighter than a Scythian and as splendid as a Magian priest.

He had some handsome ideas for Emma's tomb. First he proposed a broken column with drapery, next a pyramid, then a Temple of Vesta, a sort of rotunda . . . or perhaps "a pile of ruins." And in every plan, Homais doggedly included a weeping willow, which he considered the obligatory symbol of melancholy.

Charles and he went to Rouen together to see some tombstones at a monument maker's—accompanied by a painter, one Vaufrylard, a friend of Bridoux's who spouted puns the entire time. At last, after examining a hundred or so drawings, ordering an estimate, and making a second trip to Rouen, Charles decided on a mausoleum whose two principal sides were to portray "a guardian spirit bearing an extinguished torch."

As for the inscription, Homais could find nothing as beautiful as: *Sta viator,* and he could get no further; he racked his brains; he kept repeating *Sta viator* . . . At last, he discovered: *amabilem conjugem calcas*! And this was adopted.

One strange thing was that Bovary, though he thought about Emma continually, was forgetting her; and he despaired as he felt her image slip from his memory even in the midst of his efforts to hold on to it. Every night, however, he would dream about her; it was always the same dream: he would go up to her, but just when he was about to clasp her to him, she would rot away in his arms.

For a week he was seen entering the church every evening. Monsieur Bournisien even paid him two or three visits, then gave up on him. In any case, the priest was disposed to be intolerant, and fanatical, said Homais; he would fulminate against the spirit of the times, and every other week, without fail, he would include in his sermon an account of the last agony of Voltaire, who died eating his own excrement, as everyone knows.

Despite the frugality in which Bovary was living, he was nowhere near paying off his old debts. Lheureux refused to renew any of the notes.

Seizure became imminent. At that point he turned to his mother, who agreed to let him take out a mortgage on her property but at the same time sent him a flood of recriminations against Emma; and she demanded, in return for her sacrifice, a shawl that had escaped Félicité's ravages. Charles refused it. They quarreled.

She made the first overtures toward a reconciliation by proposing to take the little girl to live with her; she would be a help to her in the house. Charles agreed. But when the time came for her to leave, all his courage abandoned him. This time the break was complete and irrevocable.

As his feelings of affection for others weakened, he clung more tightly to his love of his child. She worried him, however; for she would cough sometimes and had patches of red on her cheekbones.

In constant view, across from him, thriving and merry, was the family of the pharmacist, who had every reason in the world to be content. Napoléon helped him in the laboratory, Athalie was embroidering a fez for him, Irma cut out little paper circles to cover the jams, and Franklin could recite the multiplication table all in one breath. He was the happiest of fathers, the most fortunate of men.

Not so! A secret ambition consumed him: Homais wanted the cross of the Legion of Honor. He had no lack of qualifications:

"One, that I distinguished myself, at the time of the cholera epidemic, by my limitless devotion to duty; two, that I published, at my own expense, various works of use to the public, such as . . ." (and here he cited his treatise entitled *On Cider, Its Manufacture and Effects;* also, his observations on the woolly aphis, sent to the Academy; his volume of statistics; and even his pharmaceutical thesis) "not to mention the fact that I am a member of several learned societies" (he was a member of only one).

"Lastly," he exclaimed, with a pirouette, "if only because I acquit myself with distinction as a fireman!"

Then Homais was drawn to those in Power. He secretly performed considerable services for Monsieur the Prefect at election time. In short, he sold himself; he prostituted himself. He even addressed a petition to the sovereign in which he begged him to *do him justice;* he called him "our good king" and compared him to Henri IV.

And every morning, the apothecary would pounce on the newspaper looking for his nomination; it was never there. At last, unable to stand it any longer, he had a star-shaped section of lawn designed within his garden to represent the decoration, with two clumps of grass growing out at the top to imitate the ribbon. He would walk around it, his arms folded, meditating on the ineptness of the government and the ingratitude of men.

Out of respect, or out of a sort of sensuality that made him proceed slowly in his investigations, Charles had not yet opened the secret compartment of the rosewood desk that Emma had been in the habit of using. At last, one day, he sat down in front of it, turned the key, and pressed the spring. All Léon's letters were there. No possible doubt, this time! He devoured every one, down to the last, then searched every corner, every piece of furniture, every drawer, behind the walls, sobbing, howling, wild, out of his mind. He discovered a box and staved it in with one stamp of his foot. Rodolphe's portrait leaped to his eyes, surrounded by overturned love letters.

People were surprised at his despondency. He no longer went out, received no one, refused even to call on his patients. Then they claimed he *was shutting himself up to drink.*

Now and then, however, some curious person would hoist himself above the garden hedge and stare with amazement at this savage man with his long beard, his filthy clothes, weeping aloud as he walked.

In the evenings, in summer, he would take his little girl out with him and go to the cemetery. They would return home after dark, when the only light in the Square was in Binet's attic window.

Nevertheless, he could not savor his grief to the full, for he had no one close to him who could share it; and he visited Mère Lefrançois from time to time so that he could talk about *her.* But the innkeeper listened to him with only one ear, having, like him, her own troubles, for Monsieur Lheureux had at last started his transportation service, Les Favorites du Commerce, and Hivert, who had a great reputation for running errands, was demanding an increase in wages and threatening to go work for "the Competition."

One day when he had gone to the market in Argueil to sell his horse— his last resource—he met Rodolphe.

They turned pale when they saw each other. Rodolphe, who had merely sent his card, first stammered some excuses, then grew bolder and even had the nerve (it was very warm, this was in August) to invite him for a bottle of beer at the tavern.

Leaning on his elbows opposite him, he chewed on his cigar as he chatted, and Charles was lost in reveries in the presence of this face that she had loved. He felt he was seeing something of her once again. It was amazing. He would have liked to be this man.

The other went on talking about plowing, livestock, manure, uttering banal phrases to fill all the gaps into which some allusion might have slipped. Charles was not listening to him; Rodolphe noticed this, and in the mobility of Charles's face, he could follow the progress of his memories. It was turning crimson little by little, his nostrils were contracting and widening rapidly, his lips were quivering; there was even a moment when Charles, filled with a somber fury, fastened his eyes on Rodolphe, who, in a kind of terror, stopped speaking. But soon the same dismal lassitude reappeared on his face.

"I don't hold it against you," he said.

Rodolphe had remained silent. And Charles, his head in his hands, went on in a dull voice, with the resigned tone of endless suffering:

"No, I don't hold it against you anymore!"

He even added a grand phrase, the only one he had ever spoken:

"Fate is to blame!"

Rodolphe, who had determined the course of that fate, found him very compliant for a man in his situation, comical even, and rather low.

The next day, Charles went to sit on the bench in the arbor. Rays of light passed through the trellis; grape leaves traced their shadows on the sand, jasmine perfumed the air, the sky was blue, cantharis beetles buzzed around the flowering lilies, and Charles was suffocating like an adolescent under the vague outpourings of love that swelled his grieving heart.

At seven o'clock, little Berthe, who had not seen him all afternoon, came to call him for dinner.

His head was leaning back against the wall, his eyes were closed, his mouth was open, and he was holding in his hands a long lock of black hair.

"Papa, come!" she said.

And thinking that he wanted to play, she pushed him gently. He fell to the ground. He was dead.

Thirty-six hours later, at the apothecary's request, Monsieur Canivet came. He opened him and found nothing.

When everything was sold, there remained twelve francs seventy-five centimes, which was used to pay Mademoiselle Bovary's fare to her grand-mother's house. The old woman died the same year; Père Rouault being paralyzed, it was an aunt who took charge of her. She is poor and sends her to work for her living in a cotton mill.

Since Bovary's death, three doctors have followed one another in Yonville without success, so promptly and thoroughly has Monsieur Homais routed them. He himself has an infernally good clientele; the authorities treat him kindly and public opinion protects him.

He has just been awarded the cross of the Legion of Honor.

NOTES

EPIGRAPHS

xxxiii **To Marie-Antoine-Jules Sénard:** Sénard was the lawyer who successfully represented Flaubert when he was tried, following the first, serial publication of *Madame Bovary* in *La Revue de Paris,* on charges of posing a threat to morality and religion. This dedication, thanking the lawyer, was added when the novel appeared in book form.

xxxv **To Louis Bouilhet:** Bouilhet, a poet, a native of Rouen, an early friend of Flaubert's and his closest from the age of about twenty-five on, spent nearly every Sunday with Flaubert during much of the time Flaubert was working on the novel, often giving him valuable critical responses to his work. This dedication was the only one in the first, serial form of the novel.

PART I

3 **busby:** A cylindrical military headdress made of fur with a bag hanging from the top down one side.

5 **the *Quos ego:*** A threat of punishment; in Virgil's *Aeneid,* I, 135, these are the words spoken by the angry god Neptune as he is about to chastise the disobedient winds in order to help Aeneas in his journey.

5 **toque:** A flat-topped, brimless cap.

5 ***ridiculus sum:*** Latin for "I am ridiculous."

6 **an enlightened thinker:** The French term is *philosophe,* which means, literally, "philosopher" but refers in this context to the group of Enlightenment thinkers, scientists, and men of letters that dominated the intellectual climate of the eighteenth century and contributed directly to the Revolution; it included Voltaire (see note to p. 68), Diderot (see note to p. 294), and Rousseau, whose novel *Émile* proposed progressive theories of early childhood education.

7 **Angelus:** The bell announcing the time for the Angelus, a Roman Catholic devotion said morning, noon, and evening.

8 **first communion:** Communion is a Christian sacrament in which bread and wine are partaken of as a commemoration of the death of Christ. In the Catholic Church, children usually aged about seven are intensively prepared

313

for their First Communion with instruction in church doctrine in the form of the catechism; the day of their First Communion is then celebrated with great ceremony.

8 **Saint-Romain fair:** A fair held every November in Rouen.

8 *Anacharsis:* Perhaps this was Jean Jacques Barthelemy's *The Travels of Anacharsis the Younger in Greece,* a learned imaginary travel journal and one of the first historical novels.

8 **baccalaureate:** In the French educational system, the degree conferred following the examinations that conclude secondary, or high school, studies.

8 **the Eau de Robec:** A tributary of the Seine that ran through the poorest neighborhoods in Rouen; the waterside dyeworks emptied their wastewater into it, hence its sordid, multicolored appearance. In present-day Rouen, the rue Eau de Robec is lined by restored half-timbered houses; the tributary itself has been mostly paved over and remains as a narrow, contained stream crossed by footbridges and flowery decorative arches in the cobbled pedestrian street—a picturesque tourist attraction.

9 **materia medica:** The branch of medical science covering the substances used in the treatment of diseases.

9 **stamping his feet against the wall:** That is, standing as he ate and stamping his feet against the wall to warm them—as Flaubert makes clear in earlier drafts.

10 **Béranger:** Pierre Jean de Béranger (1780–1857) was a popular French lyric poet whose first collection of songs was published in 1815. Flaubert did not have a high opinion of him, as he remarks in a letter: "There are some things that allow me to judge a man immediately: first, an admiration for Béranger . . ."

10 **public health officer:** A public health officer, as opposed to a licensed physician, was allowed to practice medicine only within a certain *département* and could not perform important surgery without a doctor present. This certification was eliminated in 1892.

10 **livres:** The livre was a monetary unit whose value fluctuated over time, but which was here equivalent to a franc.

10 **Mère Bovary:** *Mère* and *Père* ("Mother" and "Father"), when used with the last name, are terms of address replacing "Madame" and "Monsieur" when speaking to or of a woman or a man of a certain (advanced) age. They are less formal terms and may—but do not necessarily—imply affection or condescension (see, e.g., Balzac's novel *Le Père Goriot*).

11 **leagues:** The league is a unit of distance that varied according to time and place but for Flaubert at this time was equivalent to about 2.5 miles.

12 *celebrating Twelfth Night:* The French is *faire les Rois* ("to act or play the Kings"). In this Catholic tradition, dating from the sixteenth century, people celebrate Twelfth Night, or Epiphany, by dining or supping with friends or family and sharing a cake in which a bean has been hidden—the one who finds the bean will enact the part of one of the Three Kings.

12 **his *young lady:*** In French, *sa demoiselle*—that is, his daughter.

13 **cotton nightcap:** A man, in those days, generally wore a cotton nightcap to bed, and a cotton nightshirt. Instead of the nightcap, he might wrap a scarf around his head, as Charles does later. A woman also wore a cotton nightcap, one that tied under the chin, along with a nightgown. There was more fear of the night air then, and not only was one's head covered but the bed was usually hung with curtains to keep out the drafts, and it generally stood against a wall, perhaps in an alcove, as does Charles and Emma's bed later in the book.

13 **eau-de-vie:** Literally "water of life." This is a clear fruit brandy with a very light fruit flavor and a high alcohol content, made typically from pears, apples, plums, cherries, raspberries, or peaches and produced by fermentation and distillation. It is usually not aged but bottled right away, and drunk fresh, often after dinner as a digestif. Similar drinks are German schnapps and Czech slivovitz.

14 **Dieppe ivories:** The seaport of Dieppe, in Normandy, was the center of French ivory carving from the sixteenth through the nineteenth centuries, ivory and spices being two major imports during that time. Thomas Jefferson, for one, owned a set of chess pieces carved from Dieppe ivory in the late eighteenth century.

14 **calico:** A plain cotton fabric.

14 **orrisroot:** A preparation derived from the roots of several varieties of irises; it is cleaned, dried (to concentrate its aromatic essential oils), and reduced to a powder; it smells like violets and gives a nice scent to linens.

14 **saltpeter:** The common name for the chemical compound potassium nitrate. Forming naturally in white efflorescences or "brushes" on a wall, often of a stable or a cellar, it looks like a tuft of soft fiber.

14 **Minerva:** In Roman religion, the goddess of wisdom, medicine, the arts, commerce, handicrafts, and war, commonly identified with the Greek goddess Athena.

14 **lorgnette:** A pair eyeglass lenses equipped with a short handle on one side for holding them in front of the eyes. They were not only of practical use but also carried or worn by women as a fashion accessory.

15 **farmyard:** Flaubert uses the word *masure,* italicizing it—it is the Norman term.

15 **the leather of her ankle boots:** On a farm particularly, it was the centuries-old custom, persisting even today among some populations, to wear wooden shoes or clogs (*sabots*) over one's slippers or shoes when going outside, or in the kitchen, in order to protect them. Clogs could be carved at home, or they could be bought at a market. (See the mention of the sabot makers' hut on p. 142.) The modern-day equivalents, made of molded hard plastic, are still sold in French markets. Emma's clogs would have had thick heels and soles. Her boots, fitting inside the clogs, were of a thin, delicate leather, with, probably, low heels.

16 **Madame Bovary the younger:** Confusingly, there are in fact three "Madame Bovarys" in the novel: Charles's mother, sometimes referred to as "the elder Madame Bovary" or "Madame Bovary senior" or "Mère Bovary"; Charles's first wife, sometimes called, as here, "Madame Bovary the younger"; and Charles's second wife, Emma Bovary, after whom the novel is titled, who at this point in the story is still "Mademoiselle Rouault" but who, later on, will also be referred to as "Madame Bovary the younger." (Likewise, "the elder Monsieur Bovary" is Charles's father.)

16 **tapestry work:** Embroidery on canvas resembling woven tapestry. Embroidery of one sort or another, along with drawing and music, was part of the traditional education of a middle- to upper-class young lady, and she would usually continue, throughout her life, to occupy some of her leisure hours doing embroidery.

17 **scarifying:** That is, lacerating him or flaying him: here, Flaubert, son of a doctor, is deliberately employing a medical term that, in surgery, means to make scratches or small cuts (as in the skin).

17 **pilings:** In a seaside region such as Dieppe, a house built on unstable or wet land would have pilings sunk first, on which its foundations would then be laid.

17 **ecus:** An ecu was an old silver coin originally depicting the shield (*écu*) of France on one face and was worth about three francs at this time.

18 **sou:** An old coin made of nickel and worth one-twentieth of a franc.

21 *glorias:* A *gloria* is a warm alcoholic drink composed of coffee, sugar, and eau-de-vie or rum.

21 **Around Michaelmas:** In this predominantly Catholic country, different times of the year were often designated by saints' days rather than calendar dates. Michaelmas, Saint Michael's Day, or the feast of Saint Michael the Archangel falls on September 29.

22 **Maître:** Literally, "master," a term of respect customarily employed when addressing teachers, lawyers, and also, as in this case, big landowners.

23 **jaunting-cars ... charabancs ... gigs ... spring-carts:** A *jaunting-car* was a light, low-set, open, two-wheeled carriage in which passengers sat sideways, either back-to-back or face-to-face; a *charabanc* was a long, four-wheeled, open carriage with several rows of transverse benches or seats facing forward; a *gig* was a light, open, two-wheeled, one-horse carriage with one seat; a *spring-cart* was a light, two-wheeled cart open on all sides, with road springs, used mainly for moving furniture or other goods or for carrying passengers on occasion.

23 **tippets:** A tippet is a scarf for covering the neck or the neck and shoulders, with ends that usually hang down loose.

23 **fichus:** A fichu is a lightweight, triangular scarf worn on the head or over the shoulders, when it is tied or fastened in front, sometimes tucked into a low neckline.

23 **dress smocks:** The smock was a loose, shirtlike overgarment reaching to just below the waist or down to the hips; it was worn over other clothes to protect them; it had typically been worn by farmers and working-class men in France for several

hundred years by the time it disappeared in the twentieth century. The dress smock, or *blouse de cérémonie,* would be worn by a farmer or peasant on a Sunday or another special occasion: it might have little starched pleats at the collar and sleeves or be embroidered with white lace on the shoulders and front; it was usually belted at the waist. The farmer might have inherited it from his father or even his grandfather. (He might also own a redingote, or frock coat, but take it from the back of the cupboard only once or twice a year—say, on Easter.)

25 **nonpareils:** Tiny sugared almonds, narrow confectioner's ribbon, or tiny sugar pellets.

25 **cork-penny:** A game in which one puts coins on a cork and attempts to knock the cork over with a quoit or puck.

25 **"under my thumb":** Most likely the game in which one player grips the other by the fingers and attempts to trap and pin down the opponent's thumb.

26 **addressed her as *tu:*** In French, *tu* is the informal, affectionate, or intimate form of the word "you," as opposed to the formal *vous.* The distinction is disappearing, but even thirty years ago it was carefully preserved and complicated. Husband and wife might continue to address each other by the formal *vous.* An important stage in a friendship or love affair was marked by the change from *vous* to *tu.* Certain individuals, of a particular age and class, would never abandon the formal *vous,* except when addressing a child.

26 **bodice:** The upper part of a woman's dress, covering the body from the neck to the waistline or just below.

27 **Cauchois headdress:** At the time of this story, the Caux region, like every other region of France, had its own typical costumes, including women's headdresses, and the latter were particular to each individual town and even village.

28 ***Dictionary of Medical Science:*** This is the *Dictionnaire des sciences médicales,* edited by Charles-Louis-Fleury Panckoucke and published in Paris in twenty-five volumes (1812–22).

28 **whose pages were uncut:** Until fairly recently, books in France were customarily sold with their pages uncut (i.e., the printed sheets making up the book were folded, sewn together, and bound, but their edges were not cut). Slicing through the edges of the pages with a knife—as one sat in a café, for instance—used to be a happy ritual to perform before one could begin reading the book. Here, of course, the implication is that none of the books' many owners had ever read them.

28 **espaliered apricots:** That is, apricot trees trained to grow flat against a wall.

28 ***boc . . . tilbury:*** The word *boc* is from the Norman patois, or dialect, and refers to a little open cabriolet, or light, two-wheeled, one-horse carriage. The *tilbury,* another type of light, two-wheeled carriage, had recently been introduced from England and was considered very fashionable. In those days one's fortune and elegance were easily measured by the luxury of one's carriage and horse or pair of horses.

29 **scarf he wore around his head:** See note to p. 13.

29 **guard stone:** A stone set close to a wall, at the corner of a building or next to a gate or door, to protect it from being damaged by a passing carriage. In French it is called a *borne,* which is also the word for "milestone," from its resemblance to the latter.

29 **highway:** This word is used along with "big road" or "main road" throughout the novel to mean the road that connected the surrounding villages and towns and the city of Rouen.

29 **like a man . . . after dinner:** The French for this curious comparison is *comme ceux qui mâchent encore, après dîner, le goût des truffes qu'ils digèrent.* Comparing Charles's blissful "ruminations" (the word "ruminate" also means, with respect to a cow, chewing its cud—that is, something already swallowed) with the aftertaste of a truffle is certainly an antiromantic gesture on Flaubert's part. Not to everyone's taste, and yet highly esteemed by some and very expensive, truffles are strongly flavored blackish fungi that grow on the roots of oak trees and are sniffed out by specially trained dogs and pigs. They have many culinary uses, being shaved over pastas or salads, combined with roast meats or cheeses, or, where a working farmer hunts them for himself, simply mixed into an omelet.

29 **muffs:** In cold weather, in addition to wearing gloves or mittens, a woman might carry a muff—that is, a warm, tubular covering, often made of fur— either to keep her hands warm or merely as a fashion accessory.

30 ***Paul and Virginia:*** A love story by Jacques-Henri Bernardin de Saint-Pierre published in 1788. The story is set on the Isle of France (now Mauritius) in the Indian Ocean, depicted as a paradise far from corrupt civilization. The two young lovers are doomed: Virginia dies in a shipwreck, and Paul then dies of grief. The story, highly romantic and very popular, became enduringly famous.

30 **Mademoiselle de La Vallière:** Louise Françoise de La Baume Le Blanc de La Vallière (1644–1710), mistress of Louis XIV from the age of seventeen, bore him four children. She was eventually replaced in his affections and retired to a Carmelite convent, becoming celebrated for her piety.

30 **catechism:** A manual of religious instruction in Christian doctrine consisting of questions and answers to be memorized.

31 **Abbé Frayssinous's *Lectures:*** Abbé Denis de Frayssinous (1765–1841) is famous chiefly for the lectures he gave at Notre-Dame and other churches in Paris and for his instrumental part in the religious revival during the Restoration (1814–30).

31 ***The Genius of Christianity:*** A defense of Christianity by François-René de Chateaubriand against attacks by French Enlightenment philosophers and revolutionary politicians. Its publication in 1802 made Chateaubriand one of the most important writers in France. His writings, full of melancholy, exotic description of nature, and evocative language, were highly influential on nineteenth-century French culture generally; specifically, he is considered

a founder or forerunner of romanticism in French literature, which flourished under the Restoration.

32 **postilions killed at every stage:** In the period during which *Madame Bovary* takes place, one form of long-distance travel was by stagecoach: a fare was paid for a seat in the coach; the coach was pulled by one or more pairs of horses; the tired horses were exchanged for fresh horses at relay stages, where there would be an inn with stables; postilions were men who rode one of the front horses to guide the team.

32 **Walter Scott:** Sir Walter Scott (1771–1832), a Scottish poet and novelist of the Romantic period, was an important influence on the development of the historical novel.

32 **ogives:** An ogive is a diagonal arch or rib across a Gothic vault; it is one of the characteristic features of Gothic architecture.

32 **Mary Stuart . . . Joan of Arc, Héloïse, Agnès Sorel, La Belle Ferronnière, and Clémence Isaure:** Mary Stuart was better known as Mary Queen of Scots (1542–87), the only child of James V of Scotland; because of her strong claim to the throne of England, she was a threat to her half sister Elizabeth I, who eventually had her put to death. Joan of Arc, a heroine of French history, led her army to victory against the English in Orléans in 1429 while still a girl and was subsequently burned by the English as a witch. Héloïse (1101–64), a beautiful and learned woman, became known for the love letters she wrote to her husband and former tutor, the philosopher Pierre Abélard, after they were forcibly separated; she had entered a nunnery and he a monastery. Agnès Sorel (c. 1422–50), the politically powerful mistress of Charles VII of France, was said to have been poisoned by the dauphin, Louis XI. La Belle Ferronnière was the nickname of one of the mistresses of François I; he was devastated by her sudden death. Clémence Isaure, a wealthy fifteenth-century patroness of poetry in the Languedoc region of France, though she has statues in Toulouse and Paris, appears to have been purely legendary.

32 **Saint-Louis . . . Bayard dying . . . Louis XI's ferocities . . . Saint Bartholomew, the Béarnais's plume . . . Louis XIV:** Saint Louis, or Louis IX (1214–70), was a pious, ascetic, and diplomatic king of France, 1226–70; he was said to have held court and delivered judgments sitting under a large oak in the forest of Vincennes. Pierre du Terrail de Bayard (1474–1524) was a French military hero who died in battle. Louis XI (1423–83) became king of France (1461–83) after many years of rebellion and intrigue as dauphin (see Agnès Sorel above). Saint Bartholomew was one of the Twelve Apostles of Jesus; the reference here is probably to the famous Saint Bartholomew's Day Massacre (August 24, 1572), in which large numbers of Huguenots, or French Protestants, were killed and which resulted in the resumption of civil war in France. The popular Henri IV, first of the Bourbon kings, nicknamed "the Béarnais," led his troops into battle (most notably at the victorious Battle of Ivry in 1590) with a snow-white plume on his helmet. Louis XIV, the "Sun King," was a lavish patron of the

arts and literature; his long reign (1643–1715) saw a great flowering of French civilization; see also note to p. 30 on Mademoiselle de La Vallière.

32 **keepsake:** In English in the original.

32 **New Year's gifts:** The custom, in France, of giving gifts on New Year's Day began as early as the thirteenth century and did not die out until late in the nineteenth, when it was supplanted by gift giving on Christmas Day.

33 *ladies:* In English in the original.

33 **Turkish slippers:** Boots or shoes with a very long, pointed toe.

33 **Giaours:** From the Turkish *giaur,* "unbeliever," a scornful term once applied by Turks to infidels—that is, usually, Christians.

33 **Argand lamp:** A lamp invented in the late eighteenth century that burned whale oil and gave a brighter light than earlier oil lamps. It was the lamp of choice until it was replaced by the cheaper kerosene lamp c. 1850.

33 **hackney cab:** The equivalent of today's taxi.

33 **Lamartinean meanderings:** That is, reveries in the style of Alphonse Marie Louis de Prat de Lamartine (1790–1869), a poet, writer, and statesman regarded as the first truly romantic poet in French literature. His subjects were nature, religion, and love, all subjectively presented. Flaubert scorned him: in one letter to Louise Colet, he remarked, "We must look to *wellsprings*—Lamartine is no more than a faucet." In another he referred to Lamartine's verses as "garbage."

34 **post chaise:** A four-wheeled traveling carriage with, usually, a closed body seating two to four persons. It was either hired from stage to stage or drawn by horses hired from stage to stage, and the driver or postilion rode on one of the horses. For those who could afford them, they were speedy and convenient.

35 **cottage:** In English in the original.

35 **pellets of bread crumbs:** These pellets were used to erase charcoal drawings.

36 **mouth-rinsing bowls:** Bowls containing warm, flavored water presented at the end of the meal for rinsing the mouth and the fingers. They were considered a refinement reserved for high society.

38 **barrier ditch:** This is *saut-de-loup* in the original; also called a "ha-ha," it is a fence placed in a deep ditch so that from a distance there is no apparent break in the meadow. This passage is one of those in which Flaubert abruptly switches tense from past to present, as though to imply that his landscape is real and still exists today. Proust saw these sudden irruptions of the present tense as signaling a more enduring reality.

38 **prunella-cloth shoes:** Prunella is a heavy woolen fabric used for the uppers of boots and shoes. Prunella shoes were softer than leather but good only for summer wear.

38 **barouches:** A barouche was a fashionable four-wheeled carriage with a driver's seat high in front, two double seats inside facing each other, and a top that folded accordion-style over the backseat.

39 **Djali:** Emma's dog is evidently named after a pet goat that figures in Victor Hugo's novel *Notre-Dame de Paris* (1831; *The Hunchback of Notre-Dame*).

39 **lancet:** A small, sharp, flat-bladed surgical instrument used for bloodletting, vaccinations, and small incisions.

40 **in front of the apron:** The apron of a carriage was a piece of waterproof cloth attached in front of the driver's seat as a protection from rain or mud.

40 **park:** The private grounds attached to a château or prosperous country house, usually including lawns, woodland, and pasture. Access to the house would be along what the French would call an *avenue,* which Henry James would also have called an avenue, and which we would describe as a drive or road. Within the park would be *allées,* or alleys—walks bordered by trees or bushes.

40 **decorated:** That is, having medals or ribbons denoting various honors either in their buttonholes or pinned to their jackets.

40–41 **"Jean-Antoine . . . 1693":** Although the names are fictitious, the battles did actually take place.

41 **jabot:** A decoration of lace or a thin fabric such as muslin attached to the base of the shirt collar or the front of a neckband and spreading down over the chest.

42 **gloves in their glasses:** This would have indicated that they did not wish to be served wine.

42 **Comte d'Artois . . . Marquis de Conflans . . . Marie Antoinette . . . Monsieur de Coigny . . . Monsieur de Lauzun:** The Comte d'Artois (1757–1836), brother of Louis XIV, was later Charles X, king of France (1824–30), and a friend of Marie Antoinette; he was deposed in favor of Louis-Philippe. Louis Gabriel d'Armentière, Marquis de Conflans (1772–1849), was a peer of France and a field marshal. Marie Antoinette (1755–93), married at age fifteen to the timid Louis XVI of France, had numerous love affairs in the early years of her marriage; she was guillotined at the time of the Revolution. Marie François Henri de Franquetot, Duc de Coigny (1737–1821), was part of Marie Antoinette's intimate circle. Armand Louis de Gontant-Biron, Duc de Lauzun (1744–93), was rumored to be one of Marie Antoinette's lovers.

42 **prepared herself:** In French, *faire sa toilette,* which we would once, in English, have called "performing her toilet," consisted of everything involved in preparing herself to go into company: dressing, applying makeup, arranging her hair. It could also be a time of sociability, during which one would entertain friends.

42 **barege:** Named after its place of origin, Barèges, a town in the Pyrenees; a gauzy fabric usually made of wool and silk or cotton.

42 **foot straps:** Straps that extended down from the bottoms of the pant legs and passed under the foot; these were quite common at the time.

43 **ritornello:** A short instrumental motif, repeated before each couplet of a song or each repetition of a dance.

43 **quadrilles:** The quadrille is an intricate four- or five-part dance for four couples in square formation, fashionable in the late eighteenth and nineteenth centuries.

43 **little gold-stoppered bottles:** Although several previous translations have inserted the word "perfume" or "fragrance" into the description, the French original does not specify what is meant to be in the bottles. In fact, it is clear from earlier drafts of the passage that what Flaubert had in mind was not perfume but vinegar—presumably to revive a woman suffering a dizzy spell brought on by the heat, the close air, her exertion, and perhaps her tight corset. Later in the novel, vinegar is produced for this purpose, first in the bloodletting scene, when young Justin faints at the sight of the blood (see p. 112) and then when Emma herself faints over dinner (see p. 182).

43 **Lace trimmings . . . clinked on bare arms:** At least three times in the novel, Flaubert employs a peculiar syntax, grouping first a series of three subjects, then a matching series of three verbs, each verb corresponding to only one subject. The second and third instances occur during the scene of the agricultural fair (see pp. 115 and 131).

43 **louis:** A louis was worth twenty francs.

44 **Saint Peter's . . . the Colosseum:** Saint Peter's Cathedral is in Rome. Tivoli is an ancient city near Rome celebrated for its beautiful setting, its waterfalls, and its ruins. Castellammare di Stabia, a resort town and spa in southern Italy, lies on the site of a Roman resort buried by an eruption of Mount Vesuvius, the only active volcano on the European mainland. The Cascine was a very large park in Florence on the banks of the Arno; it was a popular tourist attraction in the nineteenth century particularly, and always figured in the list of "must-sees." Genoa, a city on the Riviera, is the chief seaport of Italy; the steep and narrow streets of its old section are very picturesque. The Colosseum, an amphitheater in Rome near the Forum, is the most imposing of the Roman antiquities; seating about forty-five thousand spectators, it was the site of gladiatorial combats until A.D. 404. With his usual cynicism, Flaubert is having his characters admire only the most typical of the tourist attractions.

44 **jumping a ditch:** A reference to steeplechasing. Racecourses had only recently been introduced into France—the Jockey Club was started in 1833—so racing vocabulary might well be unfamiliar to Emma.

45 **After supper:** The schedule according to which refreshments were served at a ball was fairly rigid in those days. The maraschino ice that Emma consumed might have been served at about 11:00 P.M., the ample supper at 2:00 A.M.

45 **Trafalgar puddings:** Also known as jam roly-poly, shirtsleeve pudding, dead man's leg, and dead man's arm, this was a traditional English dessert invented probably in the early nineteenth century and consisting of a suet pudding rolled out flat, spread with jam, and then rolled up. While not necessarily tastier than a traditional French dessert, it had the attraction, at that time, of being English.

45 **cotillion:** Apparently, some versions of the cotillion were rowdier than this one, incorporating pranks and challenges, but at the least it was the dance that ended the evening and involved frequent changes of partner.

45 **Emma did not know how to waltz:** The waltz, introduced into France from Germany around the turn of the nineteenth century, was still regarded as somewhat risqué, since it involved a great deal more body contact and turbulent motion than the sedate traditional quadrille, for example, with its facing lines and fingertip contacts. Mothers feared for their daughters as they were whirled away in the confusion of the cotillion.

46 **whist:** A card game popular at the time, enjoyed by King Louis-Philippe himself.

46 **brioche:** A roll baked from light yeast dough enriched with eggs and butter.

47 **breeching:** The part of the harness that passes around a horse's rump under the tail.

49 **Pompadour clocks:** The Marquise de Pompadour (1721–64) was a mistress of Louis XV and a Voltairean; she employed artists to decorate her residences and encouraged the manufacture of Sèvres pottery.

49 **"Marjolaine":** A familiar abbreviated reference to "Les Compagnons de la Marjolaine," a well-known, anonymous, centuries-old popular song with many verses, about a company of night watchmen seeking brides.

49 *Corbeille . . . Le Sylphe des Salons:* *Corbeille* (1836–78) was a fashion magazine. *Le Sylphe des Salons* (1829–82, under various names) covered, at various times and in various combinations, literature, the fine arts, the theater, and fashion.

49 **the Bois:** The Bois de Boulogne, a forest at the edge of Paris containing the racetracks of Auteuil and Longchamps and many avenues and bridle paths; a favorite recreation spot starting in the seventeenth century.

49–50 **Eugène Sue . . . Balzac . . . George Sand:** Eugène Sue (1804–57) was the author of popular and sensational novels about the Parisian underworld and slum life; they were serialized in the newspapers during the 1830s. Honoré de Balzac (1799–1850) was one of the foremost novelists of France, author of the vast *Human Comedy.* George Sand was the pseudonym of Amandine-Aurore-Lucie Dupin, author of some eighty novels and widely popular in her day.

50 **petits bourgeois:** The French term for members of the "petite bourgeoisie," or lower middle class, which includes minor businesspeople, clerical staff, craftworkers, and tradespeople such as shopkeepers. Unlike the "haute bourgeoisie," or upper middle class, members of the lower middle class may work alongside their employees. This class is also distinguished from the working class, which relies solely on selling its own labor to survive. Emma, of course, is here agreeing with Flaubert himself, in deriding what she (or he) sees as the mentality of the class—narrow, prejudiced, conservative, culturally unenlightened.

51 **bloodlettings:** "Bloodletting," or "bleeding," in which some blood was drawn from a patient's artery or vein, was widely practiced in Western medicine

from antiquity through the eighteenth century as a treatment for any number of complaints, including congestion following acute heart failure (for which it actually is effective). (See bloodletting scene, p. 111.) Leeches were applied to draw blood from smaller blood vessels.

52 **catarrhs:** A catarrh is a chronic inflammation of the mucous membranes in the nose and air passages.

52 **emetic:** A substance that induces vomiting.

52 *La Ruche Médicale:* "The Medical Beehive"; this is Flaubert's adaptation of the name of a medical journal published in Paris from 1844 to 1899 called *L'Abeille Médicale* (The Medical Bee), which was accompanied by a supplement called *La Ruche Scientifique* (The Scientific Beehive).

54 **Érard piano:** Sébastien Érard was a French instrument maker who specialized in the production of pianos and harps, greatly developing the capacities of both and pioneering the modern piano; Louis XVI and Marie Antoinette commissioned pianos from him, and other prominent owners of his pianos included Beethoven, Chopin, Fauré, Haydn, and Liszt.

PART II

61 **Yonville-l'Abbaye:** A fictitious place but based in part on the real towns of Ry and Forge-les-Eaux, in the latter of which Flaubert had spent time with his family. It is meant to be about twenty miles from Rouen.

61 **small river:** Flaubert says in one letter that he has in mind a river the size of the Eau de Robec, by which Charles lived when a student—evidently narrow enough so that a plank bridge can be extended across it for cattle and removed when necessary.

62 **farrier:** A specialist in the shoeing of horses and other work animals such as oxen and mules, and in the care of hooves.

62 **in the last years of the reign of Charles X:** That is, in the late 1820s. The reactionary and repressive Charles X was forced to abdicate after the bloody three-day July Revolution in 1830.

62 **piece of straw matting:** That is, as protection against the cold.

63 **a Gallic cock, resting one foot on the Charter:** The cock, or rooster, was the symbol of France. The Charter was a document first drawn up and conferred in 1814 under Louis XVIII, binding the monarchy to a constitution that guaranteed to the French citizenry certain rights, such as freedom of conscience; it was revised following the deposition of Charles X in 1830 but continued to form the basis of France's constitution until 1848.

63 **Bengal lights:** Blue lights used for signaling and illumination at sea; also, lights or flares of various colors. They derive their name from the fact that the main source of saltpeter, one of their ingredients, is India.

63 **"Vichy, Seltzer, and Barèges Waters, Depurative Syrups, Raspail's Medicine, Arabian Racahout, Darcet's Pastilles, Regnault's Ointment, Bandages, Baths, Medicinal Chocolates, etc.":** All common remedies of the time, some of them

patented; racahout, a gruel whose main ingredient was acorn flour, was commonly used by the Turks and Arabs and introduced into France and America in the early nineteenth century as a food for convalescents, consumptives, and those with "debilitated" stomachs. Chocolate was at this time more usually regarded as medicinal than as an ingredient to be enjoyed in desserts and drinks.

63 **the cholera outbreak:** The cholera pandemic reached the Rouen area in April 1832 and remained until October.

64 **white punk:** A dry, light, spongy substance derived from bracket fungi, known as "horsehoof" or "tinder" fungi, which grow on certain deciduous trees such as birch, beech, and oak. It is highly flammable and is used to ignite fuses.

65 *Hirondelle:* Literally, "Swallow"—often used as a name for a boat or land vehicle, and connoting swiftness; in this case, of course, Flaubert's choice of name is ironic.

65 **for Poland . . . the flood victims of Lyon:** The Warsaw Uprising took place November 29, 1830; benefits for the Polish victims of repression were organized throughout Louis-Philippe's reign. The flooding of Lyon took place in 1840.

65 **we've got hay in our boots:** The French expression "to put some hay in one's boots" is equivalent to the English "to feather one's nest." There are numerous French expressions involving hay: in an agricultural society, a good store of hay symbolized economic security.

66 **frock coat:** A man's coat, usually double-breasted, with knee-length skirts front and back. Flaubert paid particular attention to the clothing of a character because of what it revealed about his personality and way of life.

66 **the egotism of a bourgeois:** One of Flaubert's main animosities was against what he considered the bourgeoisie and bourgeois ways of thinking—that is, narrow-mindedness, complacency, pride, preoccupation with material gain and material possessions, and lack of deep culture.

66 **like a dead fish:** This is "like a shad" in the original, shad being an important food fish, hence more familiar in Europe than in the United States.

67 **tithe:** A contribution to the church of approximately one-tenth of one's yearly income in money or goods that was at first voluntary and later became established as a legal tax. It was outlawed at the time of the French Revolution.

68 **Socrates, Franklin, Voltaire, and Béranger:** Socrates (469–399 B.C.), Greek philosopher famous for his view of philosophy as a pursuit proper and necessary to all intelligent men; he lived by his principles even though they ultimately cost him his life. Benjamin Franklin (1706–90), the independent-minded American statesman, inventor, scientist, and writer, was popular in France, where he was sent on a diplomatic mission following the American Revolution. François-Marie Arouet de Voltaire (1694–1778), a skeptical, rationalist, commonsense philosopher, writer, amateur scientist, and prime representative of the French Enlightenment, was much admired by Flaubert. The poems of Béranger (see note to p. 10) expressed republican and Bonapartist ideas, for which the poet was twice imprisoned.

68 *The Profession of Faith of a Savoyard Vicar:* Book 4 of *Émile,* a novel by Jean-Jacques Rousseau (1712–78), in which Émile's moral and religious education is summarized; Rousseau, Swiss-French philosopher, author, and political theorist, advocated a natural religion that offended ecclesiastical authorities.

68 **the immortal principles of '89:** The principles of the French Revolution, as expressed specifically in the "Declaration of the Rights of Man and Citizen" (1789).

68 **milliner:** Maker and seller of women's hats—an important item of dress at the time in which the novel is set.

69 **wet nurse:** A woman who cares for and, specifically, suckles babies who are not her own—this was done for pay, and women of the bourgeoisie and the upper classes would usually give their children into the care of a wet nurse for the period of their infancy or even for the several years of early childhood. In the novel, Emma Bovary will employ one for her own child.

70 **coryza:** Common head cold. The pharmacist, Homais, tends to favor a specialized scientific vocabulary.

70 **scrofula:** Tuberculosis of the lymph glands, especially in the neck, most common in children; or the swellings or abscesses that are symptoms of it.

70 **novenas:** A series of prayers extending over nine days and made in honor of a saint to ask for his or her intercession.

70 **Réaumur:** A temperature scale in which 0 is set at the freezing point of water, while the boiling point of water is 80. Réaumur was once in wide use but was gradually replaced by other scales during the nineteenth century.

72 **"L'Ange Gardien":** This may be either a poem by Marceline Desbordes-Valmore (1786–1859)—a highly regarded poet much admired by her contemporaries, and whose reputation has endured—set to music by composer and singer Pauline Duchambge (1786–1859), or a song by Béranger (see note to p. 10).

73 **Delille . . . *L'Écho des Feuilletons:*** Jacques, Abbé Delille (1738–1813), was a French poet and translator and member of the Académie Française who specialized in descriptive nature poems. *L'Écho des Feuilletons* (The Echo of the Literary Supplements) was a collection of stories, anecdotes, et cetera, compiled from contemporary newspapers and magazines.

73 *Le Fanal de Rouen:* "The Rouen Beacon"—a fictitious Rouen newspaper. Flaubert was at first going to have Homais write for the real *Journal de Rouen,* which he despised, but was persuaded to change the name of the newspaper.

73 **Buchy, Forges, Neufchâtel, Yonville, and vicinity:** Of these places, only Yonville is fictitious.

73 **list slippers:** Slippers, often homemade, woven or braided from "lists," or strips of coarse, usually woolen cloth.

75 **treble clef:** Flaubert is referring to a system of notation of the higher pitches in music, used, for instance, to write a tenor part. He may be insinuating that Léon has only a partial or superficial knowledge of how to read music.

75 **sacristan:** An officer of a church in charge of the sacristy and ceremonial equipment.

75 **law of 19 Ventôse, Year XI, Article 1:** A law passed (on March 10, 1803) when France was still using the Revolutionary calendar, established in 1793 and lasting until 1805. Ventôse was the sixth month of that calendar, and ran from February 19 or 21 to March 19 or 21.

76 **ermine:** The prosecutor's ceremonial robe would have been ornamented with a traditional band of ermine, the white winter pelt of the weasel.

78 **this sinner's name:** The name Madeleine is derived from the name of the biblical Magdalena, who was, until recently, mistakenly believed to have been a prostitute.

78 **Napoléon . . . Franklin . . . Irma . . . Athalie:** Napoléon Bonaparte (Napoléon I, 1769–1821) was emperor of France (1804–15). For Benjamin Franklin, see note to p. 68. Irma is perhaps named after the character in *Irma, ou les malheurs d'une jeune orpheline* (Irma, or the Misfortunes of a Young Orphan), an Indian story by Elisabeth Guénard de Méré (1751–1829). Athalie is the heroine of a tragedy of the same name by Jean Racine (1639–99), France's foremost classical playwright.

78 **six boxes of jujubes:** The jujube, or Chinese date, is the fruit of the jujube tree. It can be made into a paste that is used as a remedy for cough, bronchitis, and pneumonia.

78 **"The God of Good Folks":** An anticlerical poem (1817) by Béranger (see note to p. 10).

78 **barcarolle:** A Venetian boat song.

78 **the Empire:** The rule of Napoléon I, 1804–15.

79 **"The War of the Gods":** A poem in the style of Voltaire's "Pucelle" by Evariste Désiré de Forges, Vicomte de Parny (1753–1814), published in 1799. A mock-epic poem directed against the church, it was banned by the government in 1827.

79 **the six weeks of the Virgin:** The six weeks between Christmas and the Purification (February 2); it was believed that a new mother should abstain from physical exercise during a period of the same length of time.

80 **cows in their wooden collars . . . horns:** In the original, *vaches embricolées;* in Normandy at that time, cows would be fitted with a sort of wooden collar that prevented them from browsing on trees and particularly from eating the apples from the apple trees in their pastures. Also, they were not usually dehorned, as they almost always are nowadays in the United States.

80 *Mathieu Laensberg:* A famous almanac originating in Liège and first appearing in the seventeenth century, distributed by peddlers throughout the nineteenth century.

81 **nankeen:** A sturdy, yellowish cloth originally loomed by hand in Nanking, China, from a naturally yellow-brown variety of cotton.

85 **osmazome:** Once believed to be the main flavoring component of certain meats and mature poultry, obtainable in making stock or broth.

85 **calefactors:** Homais's abstruse scientific term for "stoves."

85 *écarté:* A card game for two people using thirty-two cards, in which ten cards are dealt, five to each player, the eleventh being the trump.

86 *L'Illustration:* A long-lived (1843–1944) popular journal covering politics, manners, art, and fashion.

86 **full double six:** The game of dominoes continues until one player has earned three hundred points; the double six is the tile with the highest number of points.

86 **Pierrots:** The Pierrot was the stock comic character of French pantomime, played with whitened face and loose, sometimes very ample blouse and pants. The character, broadly or subtly interpreted, is traditionally naïve and sentimentally romantic.

86 **name day:** The calendar day honoring the saint after which one was named; in France at that time, this was a more important day than one's birthday.

86 **phrenological head:** A model of the human head marked with the different areas believed to govern different aspects of the personality; phrenology, or the study of the shape of the skull, was a serious science with many devotees at that time.

89 **Born a Gascon:** Gascony is a region in the southwest of France that includes the Pyrenees Mountains, which form the border with Spain, as well as the swampy and sandy Landes along the Atlantic coast.

90 **Trois Frères . . . Grand Sauvage:** Fictional stores in Rouen.

92 **La Sachette in *Notre-Dame de Paris*:** A character in Victor Hugo's 1831 novel—a "pathetic creature," according to Vladimir Nabokov—who, a single mother, loves her daughter with an intense passion.

95 **Le Pollet:** An outlying district of Dieppe where fishermen lived.

96 **cowls:** A cowl is the hood or hooded cloak worn by a monk or a nun.

96 **prie-dieux:** A prie-dieu (literally, "pray to God") is a small wooden prayer desk with a cushioned kneeling bench and a sloping shelf on which to rest a book.

98 **Mont-Riboudet:** A play on words—*mon Riboudet,* "my Riboudet," is a homophone of *Mont-Riboudet,* "Mount Riboudet."

100 **Ascension:** In the Christian faith, Ascension Day occurs on the Thursday forty days after Easter and commemorates Christ's ascension into heaven.

100 **genuflecting:** An observant Catholic, upon entering a church or, inside a church, when passing in front of the altar, faces the altar and bends one knee as a sign of worship, simultaneously making the sign of the cross.

101 **diachylon:** An ointment originally composed of vegetable juices, later containing lead; used as a plaster to be applied to abrasions and wounds to reduce swelling.

102 **Caribs or Botocudos:** The Caribs are the Amerindian people of the Lesser Antilles Islands after whom the Caribbean Sea was named; the Botocudos were

a tribe of South American Indians of eastern Brazil who wore large wooden plugs in their earlobes and lower lips.

103 **grisettes:** Young working-class women who dated students and were known to be rather loose in their morals.

106 **Jesuit:** A member of the Society of Jesus, a religious order founded by Ignatius Loyola in 1534; in this case, however, Homais simply means that Léon will seem sanctimonious, or "holier than thou."

106 **Latin Quarter:** The district of Paris situated on the Left Bank of the Seine River where the old university was located—its teaching delivered in Latin—and where many institutions of higher learning are still located; it is still the student quarter, with a lively artistic, intellectual, and night life.

106 **the Faubourg Saint-Germain:** Once an outlying district (*faubourg*) of Paris, the Faubourg Saint-Germain, situated on the Left Bank of the Seine, borders the Latin Quarter on the east and was at the time of the novel one of wealthiest and most fashionable of Paris neighborhoods. It takes its name from its sixth-century abbey church, Saint-Germain-des-Prés.

110 **vapors:** According to beliefs at that time, a nervous or mental disturbance caused by exhalations rising from the blood, "humors," or bodily organs into the brain.

111 **yellow gloves . . . gaiters:** Flaubert is contrasting the disparate elements of Rodolphe's outfit. At that time yellow gloves were affected by dandies (see the scene at the opera, p. 195); a gaiter, on the other hand—a cloth or leather garment covering the upper part of the shoe and sometimes the lower part of the leg—would have been more common.

111 **syncope:** Medical term for a fainting fit.

112 **phlebotomy:** Homais's more technical term for bloodletting. See note to p. 51.

115 **the starched headdresses . . . and relieved with their scattered hues:** This is the second instance of Flaubert's eccentric choice of syntax, in which three subjects are presented serially, followed by their three matching verbs (see note to p. 43). Thus, it was the starched headdresses that gleamed whiter than snow, and so on.

116 **the old man's rat in his cheese:** The reference is to a fable by Jean de La Fontaine (1621–95) called "The Rat Retired from the World" in which a hermit rat lives in seclusion inside a cheese and refuses help to a delegation of fellow rats in need. It is a satirical gibe aimed at religious hermits and monks in general.

117 **Agronomic Society of Rouen:** This organization is fictitious, but there did exist a Seine-Inférieure Agricultural Society.

118 **promissory notes:** A promissory note is a promise, in writing, to pay at first presentation or at a predetermined future time a sum of money to another person or to his or her account.

120 **cambric:** A very delicate linen fabric.

120 **twill:** A linen or cotton fabric closely woven in such a way as to appear to be crossed by diagonal lines.

120 **vamped:** The vamp is the part of the shoe or boot that covers the front of the foot—the instep and toes.

122 **landau:** A heavy, four-wheeled carriage with a hood divided into two sections that could be folded back.

124 **Chariot of State:** *Le char de l'État* is as common a poetical or literary expression for the government of a nation as the English "ship of state," and could have been translated that way; in Monsieur Lieuvain's speech, however, this mixed metaphor—the chariot tossing in the waves—not only is Flaubert's deliberate gibe at the art of speechifying but also foreshadows an important later episode in the novel.

124 **undermining the foundations:** Toward the end of the book, it is Homais who is, for a short time, undermining the foundations.

130 *ex aequo:* The beginning of the Latin phrase *ex aequo et bono,* a legal formulation meaning "according to what is equitable (or just) and good (or fair)." It is used in decisions made according to principles of what is fair and just under the circumstances, overriding the strict rule of law. Here, of course, it is put in the mouth of an official awarding a prize for the best pig, in order to show up his pomposity.

131 **Barn dust . . . hardened them:** This is the third instance of Flaubert's use of an eccentric syntax that matches a series of three subjects to their three respective verbs.

132 **shakos:** A type of tall, cylindrical military cap with a peak or a visor, sometimes decorated with a plume, chain, or ribbon, and with usually, on the front, a metal badge bearing an emblem or sometimes a regiment number.

133 **fiacre:** Generally, a carriage available for hire; in this case, the landau in which the Councilor is traveling.

134 **dithyrambic lines:** A dithyramb is a tribute written in an exalted or grandiloquent style.

134 *A Thousand and One Nights:* Also known as *The Arabian Nights' Entertainments,* this is a collection of ancient Persian-Indian-Arabian tales, originally in Arabic, arranged in its present form in about 1450 and translated into French and published in France by Antoine Galland from 1707 to 1717. The tales, each self-contained, are linked by their supposed teller, Scheherazade, who, condemned to death by her husband, tells one story each night, postponing the climax of each story until the following night and thereby indefinitely postponing her execution. (She is eventually pardoned.)

135 **vestries:** The vestry, or sacristy, is the room in the church where the sacred vessels and sacerdotal robes are kept; the word is also used symbolically, as here, to represent religion or clericalism.

135 **apostles of Loyola:** The Jesuits (see note to p. 106).

138 **tricot:** A close-knit, sturdy twilled fabric of wool or wool and cotton.

139 **blowing:** Panting, recovering their breath.

144 **pipe:** Flaubert himself kept a pipe and a glass of water on his bedside table.

146 **oxalic acid ... rosin ... bone black:** *Oxalic acid* is a strong acid used for bleaching and cleaning, especially for removing rust; *rosin* is a solid form of resin obtained from pine trees and other plants and is used to make varnish, among other things; *bone black* is a substance obtained by charring animal bones and is used especially as a pigment or adsorbent.

149 **picots:** Norman dialect for "turkeys."

150 *poor Emma:* For Flaubert himself, "poor" was often a term of affection.

151 **furze:** A spiny evergreen shrub.

152 **strephopodia:** The medical term for clubfoot. Terms for different varieties of clubfoot will be employed in this chapter, usually with an accompanying explanation in the text itself.

152 **the volume by Doctor Duval:** Vincent Duval's *Traité Pratique du Pied-Bot* (A Practical Treatise on the Clubfoot, 1839—available online) was Flaubert's main source for the medical information in this chapter. The book contains the pertinent information that Flaubert's father, Achille-Cléophas Flaubert, attempted, unsuccessfully, to cure a woman of clubfoot by keeping her leg locked in an iron brace for nine months. In this case Doctor Duval himself subsequently operated successfully on the patient.

153 **claudication:** Lameness, limping.

154 **Ambroise Paré ... Celsus ... Dupuytren ... Gensoul:** Ambroise Paré (c. 1510–90), surgeon to four kings of France, introduced more humane medical treatments and promoted the use of artificial limbs. Aulus Cornelius Celsus (fl. A.D. 14) wrote an eight-volume work on medicine, *De re medicina,* that became very influential when it was rediscovered and published during the Renaissance. Guillaume Dupuytren (1777–1835), prominent French surgeon, lecturer, and author, described a contraction of the hand that bears his name. Joseph Gensoul (1797–1858), French surgeon specializing in the eyes, nose, mouth, ears, performed the first removal of the upper jaw.

154 **encephalon ... ablation ... superior maxilla ... *tenotomy knife* ... lint:** *Encephalon,* brain; *ablation,* surgical removal; *superior maxilla,* upper jaw; *tenotomy knife,* a surgeon's slender knife with a blunt curved tip, for the subcutaneous cutting of tendons; *lint,* a soft, fluffy material for dressing wounds, prepared by scraping or fraying linen or cotton cloth.

155 *de visu:* Legal phrase, in Latin, meaning "having seen it ourselves."

156 **entrechats:** In ballet an entrechat is a jump into the air during which the dancer repeatedly and rapidly crosses the legs back and forth alternately.

156 **ecchymoses ... edema ... tumefaction ... phlyctenae:** Again, Flaubert is offering a succession of specialized medical terms: *ecchymoses,* bruises; *edema,* an abnormal accumulation of fluid in connective tissue; *tumefaction,* swelling; *phlyctenae,* small blisters containing transparent fluid.

157 **poultices:** A poultice is a soft mass of bran, bread, or another substance, spread on cloth and usually heated, and applied to bruises or infected areas of the body; it was another favorite remedy for a wide range of ailments.

158 **Bon-Secours:** Notre-Dame du Bon Secours in Blosseville, a richly decorated pilgrimage church in the vicinity of Rouen to the southeast, on an elevation overlooking the Seine.

158 **holy water:** Water that has been blessed by a priest used as a purifying agent in Christian ritual.

159 **strabismus, chloroform, lithotrity:** *Strabismus* is the abnormal alignment of the eyes because of a muscle imbalance—perhaps the doctor is referring to an operation to correct this; *chloroform,* a colorless, sweet-smelling toxic liquid once popular as a general anesthetic; *lithotrity,* a surgical operation to crush stones in the bladder or urethra so that they can be passed out of the body.

160 **apoplexy:** The older term for a stroke—a rupture or obstruction of an artery in the brain.

164 *cold cream:* In English in the original.

164 **dimity:** A lightweight, sheer cotton fabric with fine cords.

165 **centimes:** A centime was one-hundredth of a franc.

165 **Saint Peter's Day:** June 29.

166 **fifteen napoleons:** A napoleon was a twenty-franc gold coin.

166 *Amor nel cor:* Italian for "Love in the heart." Flaubert's mistress, Louise Colet, had given him a cigar case (or holder) with the same motto on it. By the time the novel was published, their affair had ended. She was hurt by his inclusion of this detail, and in revenge she wrote and published a poem called "Amor Nel Cor" in which she referred to a certain novel as the work of a "traveling salesman."

168 **Duke of Clarence in his butt of malmsey:** George Plantagenet, Duke of Clarence (1449–78), a troublesome royal relative, was rumored to have been "privately executed" in the Tower of London by being drowned in a vat of malmsey wine. Shakespeare included him as a character in *Richard III.*

175 **Hôtel de Provence:** A fictitious Rouen hotel on the banks of the Seine. Emma will later stay there with Léon on their "honeymoon."

178 *manchineel tree:* An evergreen tree native to tropical regions. It produces a small, applelike poisonous fruit, and standing under it is dangerous because of the toxic effect of contact with its blistering, milky sap.

178 *A Dieu!:* Literally, "to God"; the preceding *adieu,* "goodbye" or "farewell," is a one-word form of the original *à Dieu,* just as the English "goodbye" is a contraction of the original "God be with ye."

183 **snuffbox:** Snuff is pulverized tobacco to be inhaled through the nostrils.

183 **Bois-Guillaume:** A town just outside Rouen.

183 **sternutative:** Homais's fancy word for a substance that causes one to sneeze—for example, snuff.

183 **emollients, dulcifiers:** An *emollient* is a substance that softens or soothes inflamed tissues; a *dulcifier* is a form of tranquilizer.

183 *That is the question!:* A rather irrelevant, but popular, quotation from Hamlet's soliloquy in Shakespeare's *Hamlet,* act 3, scene 1.

184 **mustard plasters:** A mustard plaster was a pharmaceutical preparation, one of whose ingredients was powdered mustard, stiffer than ointment and usually applied to the body spread on a piece of cloth; it was a counterirritant and was used to bring the blood to the surface of the skin.

186 **tisanes:** A tisane is a drink containing a small amount of a medicinal plant substance.

187 **host . . . ciborium:** The *host* is the eucharistic bread (made of unleavened wheat and natural water) symbolizing the body of Christ in the Christian sacrament of Communion. The *ciborium* is a goblet-shaped vessel used to hold the host.

187 **reliquary:** A container for a religious relic—that is, for an object venerated because of its association with a saint or martyr.

188 **Monseigneur:** The archbishop of Rouen.

188 **Monsieur de Maistre:** Joseph de Maistre (c. 1754–1821), writer, was a passionate Roman Catholic, fine stylist, and literary enemy of eighteenth-century rationalism; he believed the world should be ruled absolutely by the pope as spiritual leader. Flaubert's contempt for this thinker is indicated by his referring to him with an ironic "Monsieur" instead of giving his whole name.

188 **troubadour seminarists or repentant bluestockings:** Seminary students striving to be poets; "bluestocking" was a derisive term originally applied to certain eighteenth-century women who held, or attended, evening salons devoted to intellectual discussions.

188 *Think On It Well . . . Intended for the Young:* The first title is *Pensez-y, ou refléxions sur les quatre fins dernières* by the Jesuit Paul de Barry (1587–1661); the second, *Homme du monde aux pieds de Marie* (1836) by Victor d'Anglars; and the third, an adaptation of the anti-Voltairean *Des Erreurs de Voltaire* (1762) by the Jesuit Claude-Adrien Nonnotte (1711–93).

189 **Good Friday . . . sausage:** In Christian ritual, Good Friday, the Friday before Easter, is the anniversary of Christ's death on the cross and is observed as a day of mourning. Meat is not eaten on that day (or on any Friday, in Catholic practice); the elder Bovary's behavior would therefore be very offensive to his pious wife.

190 **catechism class:** A class of instruction in Christian doctrine, using the catechism.

191 **the famous tenor Lagardy:** A fictional character.

191 *Castigat ridendo mores:* "It corrects our morals with laughter"—eventually to become the motto of classical comedy, it was composed by the poet (and champion of "living Latin") Jean de Santeuil (1630–97) for the Italian harlequin Dominique to use in his theater.

191 **Voltaire's tragedies:** See note to p. 68.

191 *The Urchin of Paris:* A vaudeville play (1836) in two acts by Jean-François-Alfred Bayard (1796–1853) and Émile Vanderbruch (1794–1862).

191 **Galileo:** Galileo Galilei (1564–1642), Italian astronomer, mathematician, and physicist who upheld the Copernican theory that the earth revolved around the sun—a theory denounced as dangerous to the faith—and was tried by the Inquisition in 1633. Threatened with torture, he was forced to recant the theory of the Copernican solar system and sent into exile in Siena under house arrest.

191 **the Fathers:** The Church Fathers: early Christian writers from the first century A.D. to Saint Gregory I (c. 540–604); they formulated doctrines and codified religious observances, and their scholarly works were subsequently used as precedent.

193 **Sieur Lheureux:** The word *sieur* (literally, "lord") is a formal title equivalent to *monsieur* (literally, "my lord"), now either obsolete or restricted to legal use. It could also be used ironically. In one of his letters to Louise Colet, Flaubert referred irritably to their friend Maxime as "sieur Du Camp"; Du Camp had suggested he needed to live in Paris in order to succeed as a writer. Du Camp caused further irritation by suggesting that Flaubert wear a "small wig" to disguise his premature baldness.

194 **parterre . . . loges:** The *parterre* is the part of the floor of a theater behind the orchestra; the *loges* are the boxes or small compartments in various sections of a theater, containing a few seats.

194 ***Lucie de Lammermoor:*** The French version of *Lucia di Lammermoor* (1836), an opera by the popular Italian composer Gaetano Donizetti (1797–1848), was first performed in Paris in 1839. It was based on Sir Walter Scott's *The Bride of Lammermoor* (1819).

195 **cavatina:** In opera, a short aria.

196 **doublet . . . dirk:** A *doublet* is a man's close-fitting jacket; *dirk* is the Scots word for "dagger."

198 **barley water:** Also called orgeat, a drink based on a syrup originally made using barley, later with an emulsion of sweet and bitter almonds; during these years it was customarily served at evening dancing parties as well as at the theater.

201 ***O bel ange, ma Lucie!:*** The last words sung by Edgar, Lucie's lover, after he stabs himself (in act 3, scene 2, in the French version).

201 **Tamburini, Rubini, Persiani, Grisi:** Respectively, Antonio Tamburini, an Italian baritone; Giovanni Battista Rubini, an Italian tenor; Fanny Tacchinardi-Persiani, an Italian soprano; and Giulia Grisi, an Italian soprano, all famous opera singers of the early nineteenth century.

PART III

205 **La Chaumière:** La Grande Chaumière was a dance hall on the boulevard Montparnasse near the boulevard Raspail (then known as the boulevard d'Enfer [Hell]). It was started as a combination amusement park and beer garden by an Englishman, Tickson, in 1783, the name coming from the fact that it was then a collection of thatched cottages (*chaumières*). After a change of ownership in 1837, it eventually became so popular that the boulevard Montparnasse

was called "the boulevard that leads to La Grande Chaumière." Its customers were mostly students, and the polka and the cancan were danced there for the first time.

205 **Luxembourg:** The Luxembourg Garden, a large park in Paris bordering the Latin Quarter.

205 **Code:** This is the Napoleonic, or Civil, Code, promulgated by Napoléon I in 1804 and embodying the private law (i.e., regulating relations between individuals) of France. A version of it is still in force.

205 **grand apartment . . . garret:** The original French text contrasts *entresol* (entresol or mezzanine) with *quatrième étage* (fourth floor). The entresol apartment was one located on a mezzanine floor, usually between the ground floor and the second floor. In the sort of tenancy arrangement that existed in Paris at that time, the wealthier families occupied the lower floors of a building, with tenants becoming progressively poorer as one ascended, since the upper floors, being less attractive—colder and with lower ceilings, besides being harder to reach in the days before elevators—were cheaper to rent.

208 **clematis:** A vine with three leaflets and usually white or purple flowers.

209 **four scenes from *The Tower of Nesle*:** *La Tour de Nesle* was an immensely popular historical drama (1832) by Frédéric Gaillardet (1808–82), rewritten by the elder Alexandre Dumas (1802–70); set in the early fourteenth century, it was based on a legend concerning torrid love affairs that took place there involving the daughters-in-law of Philip IV. The tower itself was an early-thirteenth-century guard tower on the Left Bank of the Seine opposite the old castle of the Louvre, on the present site of the Institut de France.

212 **parvis:** From the word for "paradise," a court, a square, or an enclosed space in front of a church.

212 **trefoiled:** Ornamented with a stylized leaf having three rounded leaflets.

212 **verger:** A church official in charge of looking after the church, keeping order during services, or serving as an usher or a sacristan (see note to p. 75).

212 *Marianne Dancing:* The folk name for the thirteenth-century stone carving, on the left-hand portal, of Salome dancing before her father, King Herod of Palestine, who ordered the execution of John the Baptist. The descriptions of the cathedral in this chapter are entirely faithful, except concerning the holy-water basins that reflect the nave; these are to be found in another Rouen church, Saint-Ouen.

213 **holy-water basins:** Small basins attached to a pillar or wall inside the entrance to a church containing water blessed by the priest; the devout, upon entering the church and, often, before leaving it (see p. 216), may dip three fingers (symbolizing the Trinity) or five (symbolizing Jesus's wounds) or any other number or combination of fingers in the water and cross themselves.

213 **blue window that shows boatmen:** As pointed out in the note to p. 38, every now and then Flaubert's narration shifts into the present tense, when he is describing something that still exists at the time of his writing, or that he

wishes to portray as though it still existed. In this instance the present tense reflects reality: the cathedral still exists, as does this window.

214 **Amboise bell:** Cast in 1501, it actually weighed over thirty-six thousand pounds and lasted nearly three hundred years, when it cracked and was melted down for cannon. A fragment of it could still be seen in a Rouen museum in 1847, according to a memoir written in that year by a visiting Englishman.

214 **Pierre de Brézé:** A soldier and politician (c. 1410–65) in the service of Charles VII, for a time very powerful in court, who died seneschal of Normandy.

215 **Louis de Brézé:** Grandson (1463–1531) of Pierre de Brézé, Louis was also a grandson of Charles VII and Agnès Sorel.

215 **Diane de Poitiers:** A noblewoman (1499–1566), widow of the much older Louis de Brézé, and subsequently mistress of Henri II, having a strong influence over him till his death in 1559.

215 **the Amboises:** Uncle and nephew, both cardinals. The uncle, Georges d'Amboise (1460–1510), minister to Louis XII, was also a patron of the arts and contributed to the promotion of the Renaissance in France. The nephew, Georges II d'Amboise (1488–1550), was elected archbishop of Rouen in 1511 and cardinal in 1545.

215 **Richard the Lionhearted:** Richard I of England (1157–99), who was rarely in England and had an event-filled reign scarred by conflict. He appears in Sir Walter Scott's novels *Ivanhoe* and *The Talisman.*

215 **Calvinists:** Adherents of the movement started by French Protestant theologian John Calvin (1509–64).

215 **The steeple:** Still being constructed at this time, it was made of iron and replaced several earlier wooden ones destroyed by fire; it incorporated open spaces so as to be less vulnerable to strong winds.

216 **the north door . . . flames of hell:** The reference is to the Portail des Libraires, one of the side entrances to the cathedral, with its thirteenth- and fourteenth-century carvings.

216 **And the heavy vehicle started off:** The itinerary followed by the carriage is more fantastical than reasonable, though the places mentioned along its route are real.

216 **Pierre Corneille:** Playwright (1606–84) and native of Rouen.

219 **capharnaum:** The name is that of a town in northeastern Palestine associated with Jesus of Nazareth's ministry, but the word, meaning a place containing many objects in disorder, was probably associated with *cafourniau,* meaning "lumber room" or "box room."

220 **court of assizes:** Superior court for the trial of civil and criminal cases.

220 **sword of Damocles:** An ever-present danger; from the story in classical mythology wherein Syracusan tyrant Dionysius I (c. 430–367 B.C.) demonstrated to one of his courtiers, Damocles, the precariousness of rank and power by suspending a sword over his head by a single hair, during a banquet.

220 **Fabricando fit faber, age quod agis:** "Practice makes perfect" or, more literally, "It is by making that you become a maker, whatever it is that you do."

221 *"Conjugal . . . Love!":* This is the *Tableau de l'amour conjugal* by Nicolas Venette (1632–98), a professor of anatomy and surgery at La Rochelle. Published in 1686, it was considered the first study of human sexuality in the West and was reprinted numerous times, though Flaubert, in a letter to Louise Colet, called it "an inept production."

226 **power of attorney:** A legal document authorizing one to act as the attorney or agent of the one granting it—that is, if Charles gives Emma the power of attorney, she will be able to act for him, legally and financially.

228 *"One evening—dost thou recall?—we were sailing . . .":* The opening of the fourth verse of a poem called "Le Lac" by Lamartine (see note to p. 33) published in his *Méditations poétiques* in 1820. The poem is addressed to the lake and evokes the poet's absent love.

229 **the briefs:** A brief is a concise statement of a client's case made out for the instruction of counsel in a trial at law.

230 **Mère Rolet came:** The lovers were corresponding by way of Mère Rolet—thus her frequent appearances at the house.

230 **staves:** A staff in music is a set of five horizontal lines and the four spaces between them on which the notes to be played are marked; there are two staves in a piece of piano music—generally, the right hand plays the higher notes (on the upper staff) and the left hand the lower.

231 **the Miséricorde:** A convent school in Rouen.

235 *bathing odalisque:* The reference is to a series of paintings by Jean Auguste Dominique Ingres (1780–1867). The odalisque, a female slave or concubine in a harem, was a popular subject of paintings at this time and earlier.

235 **the** *pale beauty of Barcelona:* The reference is most likely to a poem by Alfred de Musset (1810–57) titled "L'Andalouse," which appeared in his first collection, *Contes d'Espagne et d'Italie* (Tales of Spain and Italy, 1829).

236 **Some of them would get out:** In other words, they would walk up the hill in order to lighten the load for the horse.

236 **beaver hat:** A hat made of beaver skin or a fabric imitation.

237 *Oft in the warmth . . . :* Flaubert evidently noted on his manuscript page that he had taken the blind man's song from Nicholas Edmé Restif de la Bretonne (1734–1806), a novelist and dramatist who wrote prolifically about Paris low-life, including particularly its women, as well as a number of tracts on social reform.

241 **hectares:** Metric units for measuring area, each equal to about two and a half acres.

247 *monacos:* Slang for money, cash (literally, the coin of Monaco).

247 **dazzle . . . the bourgeoisie:** With the ellipsis in his phrase, *éblouir . . . les bourgeois,* Flaubert may be alluding to the common expression *épater les bourgeois* ("shock the conventionally minded").

247 **footmuff:** An open box or bag lined with fur, for keeping the feet warm.

248 **Pommard:** A Côte de Beaune wine from Burgundy in eastern France.

249 **garus:** An elixir composed of cinnamon, saffron, nutmeg, et cetera, used as an aid to digestion.

249 **Cujas and Bartole:** Jacques Cujas was a sixteenth-century French lawyer; Bartolo da Sassoferrato was a fourteenth-century Italian jurist.

252 **protest of nonpayment:** A sworn statement in writing that payment of a promissory note or a bill has not been received.

254 **ells:** An ell was a unit of length, mainly for cloth, equal to about forty-five inches.

254 **antimacassars:** An antimacassar (from "anti-" plus "Macassar," a brand of hair oil) was a cover to protect the back or arms of a piece of furniture.

256 **nanny:** Flaubert describes Félicité variously as "servant," "maid," "cook," "nanny"—she functioned as all of these.

258 **Mid-Lent Day:** A day halfway through Lent, the period of fasting and penitence in the Roman Catholic religion; in some places and at some times, it was marked by festivities.

265 ***cheminots:*** Usually spelled *chemineaux,* the name, in Rouen, for little unleavened loaves that were eaten during Lent. Originally Flaubert planned to make a love of this bread Homais's "one human weakness," then transferred the weakness to his wife.

265 **century of the Crusades:** The Crusades were a series of wars, most of them in the twelfth and thirteenth centuries, undertaken by European Christians to recover the Holy Land (historic Palestine) from the Muslims.

265 **hippocras:** A sweet wine infused with cinnamon and cloves or other spices, popular in medieval Europe.

266 **"cornea"... "sclerotic," "facies":** The *cornea* is the transparent part of the eyeball that covers the iris and pupil and allows light into the interior; *sclerotic* means affected with sclerosis, or hardening of certain tissues of the body; a *facies* is a facial appearance and expression characteristic of a specific medical condition.

266 **liards:** A liard was a coin made of copper and worth one-fourth of a sou.

266 **antiphlogistic salve:** An ointment that counteracts inflammation.

268 **Steuben's *Esmeralda* and Schopin's *Potiphar*:** Reproductions of popular paintings of the day. The German painter Charles Auguste Guillaume Steuben, or Karl August von Steuben (1788–1856), did more than one painting in which the Gypsy Esmeralda appears, at least one of them including her pet goat Djali; she was a character in Victor Hugo's novel *Notre-Dame de Paris* (1831; *The Hunchback of Notre-Dame*). Henri-Frédéric Schopin (1804–80) was a German-born, naturalized French painter of historical and biblical subjects; it is not clear which painting of his this is.

272 **at Bautzen and at Lützen:** Victories of Napoléon I in 1813 over the Russians and the Prussians.

272 **the French campaign:** Lasting from January to April 1814, this was Napoléon I's doomed attempt to resist the invasions of France by allied forces and to keep his throne.

272 *Legion of Honor:* A national hierarchical order created by Napoléon I in 1802 as recompense for civil and military service.

277 **damascened:** Ornamented with inlaid work using precious metals.

277 **display of arms:** A wall ornament consisting of weapons arranged in a pattern.

277 **Boulle clock:** A clock featuring inlaid decoration of tortoiseshell, yellow metal, and white metal, named after André Charles Boulle, a cabinetmaker who died in 1732.

283 **my little shoe:** The custom was for a child to set out one of her shoes the night before New Year's Day or Mid-Lent Day; it would contain one or more small gifts or coins in the morning.

284 **theriaca:** A mixture of many animal, plant, and mineral ingredients and honey once thought to be an antidote to poison.

284 **berlin:** A fast, light, fashionable covered carriage with two interior seats, four wheels, and a separate hooded rear seat.

284 **Bichat:** Marie François Xavier Bichat (1771–1802), French anatomist and physiologist. He studied and classified tissues and wrote several books on anatomy. His work was the basis for modern histology, the branch of anatomy that deals with the microscopic structure of plant and animal tissues.

286 **siccity . . . pharynx . . . epigastrium . . . superpurgation:** Again, Homais is using some specialized medical vocabulary; *siccity* is dryness; the *pharynx* is the part of the alimentary canal between the cavity of the mouth and the esophagus; the *epigastrium* is the part of the abdomen above and in front of the stomach; *superpurgation* is extreme purging—as would result from the use of an emetic.

286 **Amphitryon:** The name is that of a king in Greek mythology in whose absence a banquet was provided by the god Zeus, assuming his form and deceiving the guests as well as Amphitryon's wife, Alcmene. The story has been retold in many different dramatic works. In the version offered by Molière in his play of the same name, when Amphitryon returns home in the midst of the banquet and challenges the assembled banqueters to decide which of them, he or Zeus, is the true host, their answer is "Le véritable Amphitryon est l'Amphitryon où l'on dine" ("The true Amphitryon is the one who provides the feast"). "Amphitryon" has since come to be synonymous with "generous host."

287 **cantharides, the upas tree, the manchineel, the viper:** *Cantharides* was a preparation of dried beetles (such as Spanish flies) used as a counterirritant; *the upas tree* is an Asiatic and East Indian tree with a latex that contains poisonous substances used as arrow poison; for *manchineel*, see note to p. 178; a *viper* is a venomous snake.

287 **Cadet de Gassicourt:** Charles-Louis Cadet de Gassicourt (1769–1821), an illegitimate son of Louis XV and eventually chief pharmacist to Napoléon I (1809), published numerous works on the sciences and other subjects.

287 **torrefied it himself, triturated it himself, and compounded it himself:** Again, Homais is using technical vocabulary, in this case pharmaceutical—he has roasted, ground, and mixed the coffee.

287 *Saccharum:* Latin for "sugar"—Homais is once again parading his (superficial) learning.

287 **holy oil:** Olive oil blessed by a bishop for use in a Roman Catholic sacrament, in this case extreme unction, a ritual in which the priest anoints a critically ill person and prays for his or her recovery and salvation.

287 **soutane:** An ankle-length robe with close-fitting sleeves and buttons down the front worn by Roman Catholic secular clergy.

288 **stole:** A long, narrow band worn around the neck by bishops and priests.

288 *Misereatur . . . Indulgentiam:* Two short prayers normally following confession and preceding extreme unction, in the Roman Catholic rite. The *Misereatur* consists of the following: "May the Almighty God have mercy on you, forgive you all your sins, and bring you to everlasting life." The *Indulgentiam* consists of the following: "May the Almighty and Merciful Lord grant us pardon, absolution, and remission of our sins."

288 **began the unctions:** During the anointing, the priest traditionally says the following as he anoints certain specified parts of the body: "Through this Holy Unction, and through the great goodness of His mercy, may God pardon thee whatever sins thou hast committed by evil use of (sight, hearing, smell, taste and speech, touch, and ability to walk)." Traditionally the priest anoints six places; in this scene Flaubert specifies five, for some reason omitting the ears (and with them the sense of hearing).

289 **passing bell:** The church bell that is tolled to announce a death.

292 *Cover her entirely with a large piece of green velvet:* Although the original could mean that the cloth should cover the outermost coffin, Flaubert's earlier drafts make it clear that the cloth was to be placed directly over her body inside the oak coffin.

292 **rationalist:** The French term is *philosophe.* The *philosophes* held that human reason ought to be the supreme guide in human affairs, and they were therefore skeptical of religious and political authority. As usual, Flaubert is not entirely sincere in dubbing Homais a *philosophe:* it is Homais who styles himself a rationalist, not Flaubert who respects him as such.

294 **Voltaire . . . d'Holbach . . . the *Encyclopedia*:** For Voltaire, see note to p. 68. Paul Henri Thiry, Baron d'Holbach (1723–89), a French philosopher, was a proponent of naturalistic and materialistic views and vigorously opposed Christianity. The twenty-eight-volume *Encyclopedia,* or *Methodical Dictionary of the Sciences, Arts, and Trades,* published between 1751 and 1789, was mainly the work of Denis Diderot, the French philosopher, novelist, and dramatist. It was one of the great literary works of the eighteenth century, with articles contributed by a group known as the Encyclopedists, or *philo-*

sophes (which included Voltaire); its spirit of rational inquiry led it to oppose religious authority, superstition, and the like.

294 *Letters of Some Portuguese Jews . . . Proof of Christianity,* by the former magistrate Nicholas: The first is the truncated title of *Letters of Some Portuguese, German, and Polish Jews to Monsieur Voltaire* (1772), a rebuttal to Voltaire's skepticism by the prominent Christian apologist Abbé Antoine Guénée (1717–1803). The second is apparently not by Nicholas but actually by one M. de Genoude (1792–1849).

294 **catalepsy:** A condition characterized by the persistence of postures or facial expressions and the lack of response to external stimuli.

294 **magnetism:** Perhaps a reference to the German physician Franz Anton Mesmer's (1734–1815) theories concerning the curative powers of magnetic force fields, especially popular for a time in Paris in the late eighteenth century.

295 **camphor, benzoin:** *Camphor* is a fragrant compound obtained from the camphor tree; *benzoin* is a fragrant balsamic resin, one of whose uses is as an incense.

295 **miasmas:** Noxious atmospheres, or vaporous exhalations formerly thought to cause disease.

297 **fill the gaps with wool:** Although the original is ambiguous, Flaubert's earlier drafts make it clear that the gaps he had in mind were between her body and the oak coffin, not between the two outer coffins.

297 **she was placed on display:** The French is *on l'exposa*—she "lay in state."

298 **chasubles:** A chasuble is the long, sleeveless outer vestment worn by the priest celebrating mass.

299 **serpent:** A bass cornet made of wood and shaped like a snake, no longer in common use.

300 **the *De profundis*:** This is Psalm 130, a penitential psalm—that is, one especially expressive of sorrow for sin; it is used in liturgical prayers for the faithful departed and takes its name from its opening line, "Out of the depths have I cried unto thee, O Lord."

301 **aspergillum:** A perforated vessel containing a wet sponge and used for sprinkling holy water.

304 **Pentecost:** Again, a date is identified by the religious observance associated with it. Pentecost occurs on the seventh Sunday after Easter and commemorates the descent of the Holy Spirit on the apostles.

306 **leprosy:** A chronic, infectious bacterial disease mainly affecting the skin and the peripheral nervous system and resulting in rashes, numbness, weakening of muscles, and often deformity.

306 **primary schools . . . Ignorantine friars:** Primary schools were created in France in 1833 by François Guizot, minister of education under Louis-Philippe; the Ignorantines (*frères ignorantins*) were brethren of the Christian Schools, a religious fraternity founded in 1680 that offered a free education especially to

children of the poor. Rouen was their headquarters from 1705 to 1770. They continue to thrive as an international institution.

306 **Saint Bartholomew's Day:** The reference is to the Saint Bartholomew's Day Massacre; see note to p. 32.

306 *cho-ca* **and** *revalentia:* Health foods, the first made from chocolate, which became very popular and widespread by the end of the nineteenth century.

307 **Pulvermacher hydroelectric belts:** These first appeared in England in 1850 or before; they consisted of linked metal plates that were supposed to improve the health through the application of mild electric shocks to the body, but they were eventually dismissed by the medical establishment as quackery.

307 **Scythian:** The Scythians, a nomadic people who flourished between the fourth and eighth centuries B.C., inhabited mainly the area between the Danube and the Don rivers. They wore belted tunics often adorned with gold plaques.

307 **a Magian priest:** A member of the priestly class among the ancient Medes and Persians.

307 **Temple of Vesta:** Vesta was the Roman goddess of the hearth; her public cult maintained a temple in which her priestesses, the vestal virgins, tended a fire that was never allowed to go out.

307 ***Sta viator . . . amabilem conjugem calcas:*** The Latin text reads, "Stay, traveler . . . you tread on a lovable [or lovely] spouse." Homais evidently remembered the first words of an epitaph he may have come across in his reading of Voltaire, who discusses it: "Sta, viator, heroem calcas"—"Stay, traveler, you tread on a hero's dust."

310 **cantharis beetles:** See note to p. 287 on cantharides. This golden-green beetle is also known as a Spanish fly.